LIFE FORCE PRESERVE

LIFE FORCE PRESERVE

Book 2

WEST END WILLIAM

by

COURTNEY LEIGH PAHLKE

Published in the United States
by eBooks2go, Inc.
1827 Walden Office Square, Suite 260, Schaumburg, IL 60173

ISBN: 978-1-5457-5442-9

Library of Congress Cataloging in Publication

DEDICATION

I'd like to dedicate this book to my mom for being the most supportive and hard-working woman I know and look up to...

I'd also like to dedicate book two to the women of the Windy City Pi Phi Book Club, you ladies rock and made my very first author event special and a moment I'll hold in my heart—xoxo

CONTENTS

PROLOGUE

"Anna?"

There's a nagging pressure burning the back of my eye sockets. Even with my eyes closed, I feel the burn. It's what I imagine swimming in salt water with my eyelids taped open feels like. I rub my eyes and readjust my head against the wadded-up jacket on Jack's lap. His fingers are intertwined with my hair, nestled against my scalp.

"Anna?" Donavan repeats.

"Huh?" I crack open an eye, feeling the sting amplify.

Jack shifts himself upright in his seat, yawns, and massages my head. His hand movement stops as he dozes off.

"I've received confirmation. Your family, along with Jessica and her family, are all safe," Donavan says.

"Oh, good. Thank God," I whisper, trying not to wake Jack.

"They're bringing them all together to explain the situation at large—"

"That's good news," Jack interrupts Donavan. "How long was I out?"

"Three and a half hours," Donavan says.

I roll to my other side so I can look up at Jack. I feel Jack's hand grip my back in support as I twist my spine. Heat permeates through his hand. The whites of Jack's eyes are streaked with ruby-red speckles.

"You feeling okay?" I stare at Jack and touch his face. "You're really warm."

"Just tired," Jack says.

"Catch a cold during your reckless dash around the city, eh?" Donavan looks at Jack through the rearview mirror.

"You heard about that?" Jack asks.

"Oh yes—lucky you didn't get everyone killed," Donavan says.

"What about Sam and Leslie? Am I responsible?" Jack asks.

"We have reason to believe our operations may've been tapped into, prior to your attempt at the Chicago Marathon."

"Can't believe they're gone." Jack looks out the window.

"You heard him. It's not your fault. Try to get some sleep." I grab ahold of Jack's hand and squeeze it.

"Get some rest, kid. You need it."

"You think my family and Jessica's family will be okay?" I ask.

"All I can say is, they're safe now and should be out of harm's way once they're brought together—squad's working on that now. Once they're assembled, they'll be stripped of their phones and other GPS-enabled devices; then they'll be informed of the severity of the situation."

"Has anyone refused to listen or opted out?" I ask.

"This is our first time implementing the strategies we'd put in place for Interhybrid evacuation." Donavan looks over his shoulder toward me and turns back to the road. "Anna, you're in the first wave of Interhybrid disclosures and evacuations. Our projections were wrong. We've declared a state of emergency ten years earlier than we'd originally planned."

"I hope they don't freak out. If there was a way I could talk to them, it might help get them out sooner." I squeeze Jack's hand again.

"You can't. I'm sorry, but you'll be with them soon. They're in the respected hands of the CIA. We plan carefully and tactfully through each division. So trust me when I say they'll want to go to the bunker once we reveal our footage, documents, and the incubation period for the virus that will soon be responsible for wiping out Bangkok. I'm sure they've been following it on the news."

What about the rest of the world? What's the plan?"

"It's critical we get Interhybrids to safety first and not cause more of an uproar. Without you, we can't combat this. We'll be wiped out in a matter of weeks."

"How long will it take to get us out?"

"We project forty-eight to seventy-two hours—that's on the high end."

"What if you can't get us out in such little time?" I ask.

"We have no other choice but to get you all out."

Glancing out the window, I see a Welcome to Nebraska sign. I unlock my hand from Jack's and sit up in my seat. There's nothing to see but flatland and frozen grass for miles. Snow flurries stick to the windows and melt. I turn and look at Cindy. Her eyes are shifting side to side underneath her eyelids as she sleeps. Can't even imagine what she's dreaming about right now. I'll never forget the fear I saw blazing in her eyes. I unbuckle my seat belt and lean over to pull up her blanket. Cindy punches the air.

"Oh my," I blurt out as I fall backward. I hit the back of Donavan's seat.

Jack wakes up as I bounce off the driver's seat back. He flings forward and lifts me back to my seat.

"You okay?" Donavan asks.

"What happened?" Jack asks.

"She scared the shit out of me." I hold my chest. "I was pulling the blanket up, and she—I don't really know what that was."

"What's she doing?" Donavan asks.

"Not sure I can answer that. She's sleeping, but it looks like she's about to scream at the top of her lungs at any second," I say. "Threw a punch in the air, but it wasn't a real punch."

"She waking up? She should be good for another two hours," Donavan says.

Jack buckles me in and turns to Cindy. "I think she's having a nightmare."

"You kids ever see *Carrie?*"

"Uh, we're adults, so—"

"You're both millennials, and millennials act like kids," Donavan interrupts Jack.

"Not this again." Jack buckles his seat belt, crosses his arms, and closes his eyes.

"Anna, seen *Carrie?*"

"Yeah, of course."

"You know the part at the end? The very last scene—the grave?"

"I know where you're going with this. Cindy made me jump more than the ending of *Carrie.*"

Donavan laughs. His pitch resembles Count Dracula—the one from *Sesame Street.* "She'll be fine. Trauma affects people differently. We'll keep her resting and let the professionals take over once we're safe."

"It's awful seeing her like this."

"We can get her back to full strength, but that's not the challenge. It's the time constraint," Donavan says.

"She's strong-willed." I turn and look at Cindy.

"We'll know once we assess the impact from the event."

"What happens after you get everyone like me out?" I ask.

"Once we get to phase three of Interhybrid evacuation, our military, police, and anyone working in fields we've established as operation add-ons inside our database will be addressed and called to duty, including retirees and veterans who're capable of operating firearms. Our worldwide directory has been monitored closely by partnering divisions within the CIA."

"Will all the people in Bangkok die?"

"Military officials and field agents are in evacuation mode in Thailand and surrounding countries. Protocol is Interhybrids, then doctors and hospital patients. Government officials will have their own evacuation routes and access points. Once we get everyone in position, everyone will be directed by officials to their individual access points. But Thailand and its surrounding countries are in a different boat than the rest of the world. They've got less than twelve hours to get their subjects to—"

"She doesn't like that word—*subject*," Jack interrupts Donavan.

I pinch Jack. "Sorry—think he's talking in his sleep. Please continue."

"It's complex, but each country has designated headquarters. They're given options depending on the country's situation. Our new drone and sea-level carrier technology will allow us to transport serum globally through a grid-like pipeline."

Jack opens his eyes and wads the jacket in his lap like a pillow. He points for me to lie back down. I look at Donavon in his rearview mirror and see his eyes glued to the road. I slide over to Jack and snuggle the back of my head against his stomach. I feel Jack's thumb caress the side of my face. He makes me feel safe.

A high-pitched siren fires off from the front of the car. Jack and I sit up.

"Right now? We're in the middle of nowhere," Jack utters.

The siren blares a second time.

"What's that sound?" I look at Jack.

"An emergency—almost highest level," Jack says.

"Where's it coming from?" I glance around the front seats.

"It's a small device that works like one of those things—you know, it looks sort of like a garage-door opener."

"He means pager," Donavan interrupts. "Can one of you millennials reach over your seat and grab a burner phone from the duffel bag? Bag's on the ground. Hurry, please."

Jack and I unbuckle our seat belts and turn around.

"Here, hold the blanket up while I search the bag," Jack says, handing me one of the blankets draped over Cindy. "Careful of your back." Jack grabs my other hand and cups it over my side handle.

I feel smitten as he holds his hand over mine and leans over the seat.

The siren blares again. Blankets burst in the air as Cindy pops upright. "Get them—grab them. Where's my gun?" Cindy screams.

Jack headbutts the ceiling, cracking one of the dome lights, and falls backward. I grasp at his arm but feel my weight shift. We smack against the back of the driver's seat. Donavan jerks the wheel.

"What the hell's going on back there?" Donavan scoffs.

"She—she's awake. Pull over before she's alert," Jack says, lifting me off him and back on the seat. "Crawl to the front seat if she acts crazy."

"Okay," I say.

"She's not an animal with rabies, for fuck's sake. She's having a nightmare. It's the shit we gave her." Donavan steers to the side of the road.

"Bryan!" Cindy shouts, leaning over the seat. Her eyes roll to the back of her head as she looks at Jack.

Jack and I slam our bodies against the driver and passenger seats. The unexpected blast to Donovan's seat causes him to whip forward. He grips the steering wheel and maintains control of the vehicle.

"Hey, you?" Cindy grumbles.

"Should I crawl to the front seat? She's scaring me." I clench Jack's arm.

Cindy exhales and sucks in air. She gasps as she flails over the back of our seat. She uses her hand to open an eye and stares at Jack. "Bryan? Where are they?"

"She's scaring me too," Jack says.

"Hang on." Donavan steers to the side of the road and slams on the brakes. We come to a screeching halt. He shifts the gear to park and kicks open the door.

"What're we out to go and be? Today is fine," Cindy mutters.

"Cindy?" I ask.

"Maybe she's talking in her sleep," Jack says.

"Stay in the car," Donavan says, darting to the back of the vehicle. He grabs a duffel bag from the trunk and opens my door. "Scoot over a sec." He rips the zipper open and grabs a kit from the bag.

Cindy falls backward in her seat and sways her body upright.

"Just half a dose for now. You're doing okay. Bryan's meeting you at headquarters, but you've gotta rest for now." He injects her with a needle. "Lie her down and tuck her in—lots of blankets."

"On it." Jack leans to the back row. "Oh, here's the burner."

"Can I do anything to help?" I ask.

"Keep your spine straight and buckle up," Donavan says. He slams the door and hops back in the driver's seat. Without hesitation, he straps himself in and slams his foot on the gas pedal. Using his mouth, he tears off the activation strip on the burner and powers it on. He dials a number and enters a long code.

"She's resting peacefully again," Jack says, twisting back in his seat.

I stare at him. I'm at a loss for words.

"Not sure if this was your generation, but you guys ever see *Tommy Boy*?" Donavan asks, using his shoulder to hold the phone to his ear.

"Huh?" Jack asks.

"*Tommy Boy*. There's a scene—you know, with the deer in the car?" Donavan looks at us through the rearview mirror. "The way Cindy woke up, and you two—never mind. Hello?" He clutches the phone and looks down at the screen. "Been a good day with my oldest niece and her kids. Was going to take them out for ice cream once they're back from shopping. It's almost beach weather today."

Huh? I look out the window and see miles of dried-up, patchy farmland. The dreary skies add an ashy filter over the bare trees and ice-filled cornfields. The snow flurries are thicker than they were ten miles back, as barn roofs are now speckled with patches of white from the snow accumulation.

"Could use a four-hour nap," Donavan says.

Jack and I observe the phone conversation. I'm hearing gibberish, but Jack's sitting tall in his seat. He bites at his lip and squints when Donavan talks. He understands the language.

"Windows are dirty, but a car wash would clean it right up." Donavan rubs his chin as he listens to the person on the other line. He sucks in air and holds it in his chest. "Now?" He exhales. "Could use some gas and maybe a nap. I've got about seventy miles until the gas light comes on."

I study Jack's face while he listens to Donavan's conversation.

"Yeah, I'm too tired—going to find a spot to take that nap. Any recommendations?" Donavan searches out the rearview mirror. "You got it." Donavan hangs up the phone and drops it in his coffee.

"What's going on?" Jack asks.

"They're rerouting some of the first-wave squads," Donavan says.

"In fourteen minutes?" Jack asks.

"How on earth did you get fourteen minutes from that conversation?" I ask.

"Seventy miles. Omit the zero and double the number in front of the zero," Jack says. "So we're picking people up?"

"No. We're pulling over at the next gas station so I can finish the conversation—"

"In fourteen minutes," Jack interrupts and looks at me. "Thirteen now."

Donavan points at a sign for the next gas station. "I'll run in and grab a bunch of shit for you guys to eat, so tell me what you want. Looks like we're driving straight through, then stopping at headquarters in Boulder, Colorado."

"They say anything else? They say why?" Jack asks.

"Said it's urgent. Think we're meeting another squad in Boulder, possibly picking up another vehicle—military vehicle. Also mentioned something about an emergency landing site and asked for me to call them back from a highway exit."

"How far until Boulder?" Jack asks.

"Enough time for you to eat a bunch of gas station food and take a nap so I can focus on the road," Donavan says.

"I get the hint," I say.

"You must sleep," Donavan says.

"I know—get it. It'd be easier to sleep if I knew what I was resting for." Jack leans his seat back.

"I'm being transparent when I say that aside from us meeting another squad, I've got no clue what the emergency landing's about. I'll know in twelve miles. Since you can't leave the vehicle, what kind of meal would you like—gas station hot dog or a packaged sandwich?"

I point at Jack for a response, wad up a jacket, and toss it onto his lap.

"Surprise us with the first thing you see," Jack says.

"You may regret that." Donavan smirks through the mirror.

"I wonder who they'll be bringing with them." I smile at Jack as I lean on my side and close my eyes. Jack pinches my cheek.

I am William.

The eyes—those eyes—are everywhere I go,
no matter where I may be.
Those eyes. The eyes—they're red with fire.
They're with me. I cannot plea.
So I drink and I drink, and they won't go away.
I've numbed myself to the core.
I'm lost without you.
Can't think without you.
My heart and my mind are sore.
And I will drink. I drink.
Those red eyes.
I can't think without
you. Here.
Anymore.

—Glasgow, Scotland, January 2019

My nose tingles, and snot's freezing around my nostrils. The temperature's plunging quickly. I feel like I dipped a paintbrush in Tacky Glue and smeared it into the lining of my nasal cavity before skydiving over Antarctica. Brain matter may spew from my nostrils if I blow my nose hard enough—ultimate brain freeze.

I cup my hands over my mouth and huff as hard as I can. That did nothing. Absolutely nothing. Winter is hell this year, and I wish I could intervene.

Dear Winter,

I'm sorry I forgot to write you last year. You weren't around, so I forgot. I'm writing you now because I remember how ruthless you were when you'd pay a visit and linger around a while. The serene snowflakes last month were a nice gesture, but I don't recall the people of Glasgow following that up with a welcome party. You remind me of my college girlfriend, who'd show up topless at my door after every breakup. "I'm sorry, Will," she'd say, and I'd forgive her. I'm opting out of this vicious cycle. So, dear Winter, kiss my ass.

I tuck my hands inside my sleeves and stare ahead. Balding trees perfectly align the dirt road leading toward the woods. I've never been on-site this close to dark. It takes twenty minutes round trip to walk to the construction site and back to where I'm standing. The sun will be down in eight minutes. I don't like the dark. *Hurry up, idiot.*

I tug at the collar of my jacket, which is barely covering my neck. The material won't stretch upright unless I tear a hole at the seam. I didn't want to pay full price for a new jacket, so this is what 50 percent off feels like when factoring in quality with lower than average temperatures.

Trees rattle in the distance, synchronizing with my clattering teeth. I cross my eyes as I try to watch my breath swirl in front of my nose and into the air. I'm still hammered off the whiskey and lager at the pub. I'd never be out here doing this right now if I wasn't experiencing the doubles—quadruples, I guess—when I cross my eyes. Tonight I'm brave. Like Robin fucking Wood. Wood? Wait. Aye, Robin Hood. Maybe a jalky Robin Hood.

"Go now, get in there," I mutter into my jacket collar. I feel a hint of warmth from my whiskey breath against my neck.

I pull out my flask and take a swig. The burn warms my core. I turn around and look down the hill toward the employee parking lot. My cab's waiting. I said I'd be quick. Better be quick. Wind blows at the exhaust, forcing gray whirls of pollution to zigzag into the air. Lights from the back of the cab beam red on the gravel surface. The vehicle rolls backward. *Wait. No. Where the hell you going?*

"Stop," I choke. I jump up and wave my hands in the air. *Can't leave me.* I run down the hill, flailing my arms. *You can't leave.* The icy ground boosts my speed. *You can't leave me out here, lady.* She didn't seem like the bailing type when she picked me up from the bar—or did she?

I hear a thud behind me and pat my pockets. My flask. *No, not my flask.* I dig my heels into the ground to slow my speed. My shoes scrape against the ice as I force a halt. I'm moving too fast. Need to stop. Need to stop now. My right foot lodges into a pothole, causing my body to whip back. I flail my arms around to catch my balance, but it's not working. My stomach drops. I toss an arm out and punch the ground. I grip at the dead grass beneath the snow and stop my body from rolling a second time down the hill.

I turn toward the cab. The brake lights turn off, and the vehicle stops. A bungee screech echoes through the trees from a forceful tug at the shifter. *Good for you, cab lady, showing your aggravation from a football field away. The way you handle the shifter on that car is like watching a water-balloon launcher after releasing a dud.* The interior lights blink on. A black boot wedges into the crease of the driver's door. The driver kicks the door open and steps out of the cab.

I straighten up and cup my hands around both eyes to gauge the activity. She stretches her arms above her head and walks to the other side of her vehicle. I scoot along the side of the hill and stare. She squats next to a bush to pee and holds her middle fingers in the air.

"Sorry." I cover my eyes, turn around, and look for my flask. The gunmetal flask is easy to spot in the snow. I scurry up the hill and snatch up my guilty pleasure. My hands shake as I twist off the top. The whiskey burns, but it feels good. It's warming the inside of my torso. I've got five minutes until dark. I take another swig of bravery serum. The long-legged cabbie with an attitude won't get paid for the long ride if she bails.

At least one person knows I'm here: a woman who thinks I'm a creep who just gave me the double middle finger midpee. I tuck my flask in my back pocket and jog into the woods.

Two Hours Earlier

"One more?" the bartender asks.

"Make it a double," I say.

"No doubles. I'll serve you one more Clan MacGregor, then yer switching to lager," he says.

"Don't tell me what to do, old man," I grumble.

"What'd you jist say?" The bartender rolls up his sleeves.

"Give me one more Clan MacGregor and a Carling—two of them, please," I say.

"One Carling."

"Two. And one Clan MacGregor."

"You want two lagers and whiskey, but yer only getting one."

I stare at the bartender. "Fine, the whiskey."

The bartender has excess hair growing out of his ears. I can't look at anything but the salt-and-pepper hair protruding from his saggy earlobes.

"Want a menu? Maybe it's time to eat something—soak up the booze." The bartender reaches for a menu.

"Nah, I'm good.

"All right. Anything else?" he asks.

Actually, I'd like some tweezers. I feel my eyeballs straining in opposite directions as he steps backward.

"Is that a no?"

I shake my head. "But keep the tab running."

I look around the bar. The walls are filled with colorful Sharpie scribble. Years of signatures from pissed visitors fill every crevasse of the little bar. It looks like shit. Peanut shells cover the ground, and I'm picking up hints of something stale. If I were to transform this odor into a cologne, the potion would require three equal parts: skunk, plywood, and armpit sweat. If I weren't already tipsy, I'd probably puke. Wait a second—I still might.

I stare at the bartender. He's probably used to the pungent concoction. The bartender scratches at his receding hairline as he slops a wet rag over the mess behind the bar. He tosses a second rag on the ground and marches over the stained piece of fabric, causing the juices to bleed through the fibers. *Good for you. You must be the human responsible for single-handedly turning this townie bar into the dump that it is.* There's at least a decade of damage on the wood from the old man aggressively stomping towels drenched in twenty-five-cent beers into the finish.

I sip my drink and glance below my stool. Yes, I'm certain now: The chocolate-covered stains are layers of Guinness spillage from the local drunks dropping their drinks and walking them into the crappy wooden floor—an alcoholic epoxy. I wipe the rim of my glass with a napkin.

I prefer whiskey on the rocks. It provides an efficient buzz, and I can get to bed at a reasonable hour. Beer takes too long. I take a sip and shake the glass. The ice cubes clatter against my teeth as I use my tongue to sift for traces of liquid. The ice feels like someone rubbed a wad of snow against my gums. My drink's empty. *Come on now. What's taking him so long?*

I shake my glass—he'll listen to my empty glass. Ice cubes spill over my glass and glide across the bar.

The bartender steps off the rag and stares at me. "I tink it's time to order some food, Mister—"

"Norwick. William Norwick." I grab some of the ice cubes and toss them back into my glass.

"Hang on. I've heard yer name before. You go by Will?" The bartender kicks the rag into a corner behind the bar.

I nod. "Aye, sometimes."

"How old are you?"

"Thirty-two."

"You live here, Will? Near the West End?" he asks.

"Aye, whole life." I flick the rest of the spilled ice on the ground.

"Don't throw yer ice on the ground. I have a towe—wait." The bartender straightens his stance and crosses his arms. "I heard about you."

The bartender stares at me. He's scratching his head and clenching his teeth. I can't make out the expression he's wearing, because I'm back to staring at his eardo.

"Yer West End Willie. Yer banned from every bar within a mile of here."

"Don't know the name." I shake my empty glass once more.

"You sure about that? You fit the profile. Early thirties, sloppy, poor manners, lonely stoater—"

"Pretty sure," I say, spilling another cube over the rim of my glass.

"One more, Willie, then yer cut off." The bartender grabs my drink and dumps out the ice.

"Fine. One more, then—in a fresh glass."

"So the drunkard answered to his name. Huh, Willie?" he asks.

I tip my head up at him. "I don't like that name."

"You started a fire in my cousin's bar two blocks over—nearly burned the place down. I should call 'em right now while you drink yourself stupid. He can settle the mess up with you in person." The bartender reaches for his phone.

"I'm not causing any trouble. Was an accident."

"He's coming out of pocket fer a lot of the damages, prick. You wouldn't return any of his calls."

"It was an accide—"

"Yeah, tell him that."

"I gotta new number. Ex-wife cut me from the phone plan. An honest mistake and shit timing."

"You passed out in the corner of his bar and knocked over a row of candles." The bartender pats his pockets for his phone. "Yer banned from all the bars on yer side of town. West End Willie: the local drunkard."

"I told him I'd make it right."

"You said that months ago and won't return his calls. He wants to ring yer neck."

"Go ahead. Call yer cousin. I got a new number. I'll prove it." I swat at my pockets.

"You stay right here until I get ahold of him." The bartender slides a glass of whiskey across the bar.

"You used the same glass."

"I'm not going waste my time cleaning an extra glass, not for West End Willie." He holds his phone against his ear and glares at me.

"I'm a paying customer and I'd like a fresh glass."

"Ran out of clean ones—"

"I see clean ones. They're right behind you, damn it. I'll go back there myself and get one if I have to." I stand up and wobble to my feet.

"You step foot behind my bar, you won't be getting that last drink. Sit down and have that drink before I take it away."

The bartender watches me sit down and brushes through the kitchen door. I look at the dirty glass, pick it up, and throw it over the bar. Glass shatters and whiskey sails in the air. I lick a drop of Clan MacGregor from my lip.

"What the hell's going on out there?" the bartender yells from the kitchen.

I feel a chill against the back of my neck. I take a whiff of air. There's a foul breeze, like someone's blowing their musty breath into the pores of my neck. Goose bumps form.

A cowbell jingles as I hear the door creak shut behind me. *That was fast.* I'm not sure I remember what his cousin even looked like. Maybe I was a little tipsy. I guzzle my whiskey and twist around on the barstool. I feel my stomach jolt as I catch my balance. There's a man with a buzz cut, dressed in all black, standing in the entranceway. I squint and drop a foot from the stool.

"Look, man, jist met yer cousin here at his bar—got a new phone number. Was going through a divorce. I'm gonna make it right." I slide off the stool and hit the floor. My cheek sticks to the man-made epoxy. I peel my face off the floor.

"Excuse me?" The man with the buzz cut walks toward the bar.

"That's not my cousin, dummy. I can't get ahold of 'em," the bartender scoffs.

"Stopped in for a drink. Everything okay?" buzz cut asks.

"This drunkard threw his full glass behind the bar." The bartender balls his hands into fists.

"Yer American," I say to buzz cut.

"Yes." Buzz cut crosses his arms. "Why? You don't serve Americans?"

"We serve everyone. Come in and have a drink. He's annihilated, and I'm calling the police," the bartender says.

"Nah, I'm not," I say, using the barstool to pry myself from the ground. I walk to my seat.

"Don't sit back on that stool," the bartender snaps. His phone rings. "There's my cousin ringing me back. I gotta take this call."

"Go ahead. I'll call the authorities," buzz cut says.

"Aye, thanks. First drink's on me, and feel free to kick the shit out of 'em. I never saw it." The bartender points a finger at me, then walks around the bar. He answers the phone. "Yer never gonna believe who's at my ba—" The bartender storms through a door marked Employees.

I sneak to edge of the bar and grab the bottle of Clan MacGregor. I pull a flask from my back pocket and give buzz cut the evil eye as I pour the whiskey in my flask. "You put one hand on me, and I'll beat you to death."

"Watch your pour," buzz cut says.

"Whatcha say to me, eh, Mister American?"

"Your pour—you know, your aim," he says.

"You come in here and boss me around, eh? Mister Arnie Swarztenegartor," I snarl.

"You're spilling all over your pants. You're missing the flask completely," he says, taking out his phone.

I step back and stretch the flask so it's away from me. "Oh, tanks." I squint my eyes and put the bottle back in its place.

"It's Arnold Schwarzenegger," he says.

"What?" I swig the last of the whiskey.

"You said the name wrong. It's Arnold Schwarzenegger." Buzz cut taps at his phone.

"Is that right?" I twist the top back on the flask and tuck it back in my pocket. "Don't listen to the man behind the bar. He's an asshole and got me wrong."

The bartender storms back out. "Yer talkin pish out here, aren't ya?"

"Nonsense," I shout.

"Cousin's tucking in the children and says he'll see you at the station. He's got some friends on duty tonight," he says.

"You gonna beat a payment outta me? How's that gonna bring yer cousin's bar back? I'll make it right."

"I may close early to come watch." The bartender looks at his watch.

"Here, jist take my phone. Call anyone in my phone, and they'll tell you I'm good for the money." I feel around for my phone. "Where the hell's my phone?"

The bartender looks at buzz cut. "Charlie, my cousin, he's got a hell of a right hook." He turns to me and throws a hook shot into the air.

"I already told you told you: I changed numbers. Didn't know. Yer makin' a mistake."

"I called the police while you're back there. They're on their way." Buzz cut nods at the bartender.

"Shit, man, my phone's gone?" I look at the floor and up at buzz cut. "You steal my phone?"

"I don't have your damn phone," buzz cut says.

"Suppose you lost yer wallet too?" The bartender takes the stool I was sitting on and kicks it away from me as he walks behind his bar. He snaps open a beer and guzzles it down.

"No, I've got my wallet. See?" I grab my wallet and hold a wad of money in the air. "Here." I lean over the bar and force the money into the bartender's hand. "It's more than the bill—for yer troubles. I'll make it right with yer cousin too."

The bartender drops the money on the bar and counts it.

I pat down my pockets again. "Must've left my phone at work. Shit," I mutter.

"Think I believe yer lies, Willie?" The bartender grabs the wad of money and stuffs it in his back pocket. He turns to buzz cut. "Thanks for yer help. What's yer name?"

"Julian. Name's Julian," buzz cut says.

"Thanks for yer help, Julian." The bartender sets a glass down in front of Julian and shakes his hand. "I like to keep my bar clean of people like hi—"

"He's—he *is* Ernie Schnatztegator." I point at Julian.

"Cut it out," Julian mutters at me and stands up.

"Yer name's not Julie," I say.

Julian kicks me hard in the shin.

"Ow, why'd you do that for?" I shout.

"Be quiet," Julian says.

"You kicked me," I growl.

"Don't you ever shut the hell up? I see why you want this idiot arrested," Julian says.

The bartender adds ice to the empty glass in front of Julian. "What's yer poison?" the bartender asks.

"Clan MacGregor on the rocks." Julian says, grinning at me as the bartender turns to grab the bottle.

"You in Glasgow for work?" the bartender asks, pouring the whiskey in the glass.

"Visiting one of my vendors. My hotels close by." Julian sips his drink. "Good whiskey—goes down smooth."

I salivate from hearing the ice cubes knock against the sides of the glass. "Prick," I mumble to myself as I shuffle away from the bar. I back into the stool the bartender shoved and feel my foot hook into the leg of the stool. My stomach drops as I plummet to the ground like a life-sized dummy being tossed from a moving vehicle. *Shit.* I lay still and listen. They're still talking. *Lay still, and they won't notice.* I wait a few seconds and use my arms to toggle my body toward the door.

"Look at tis stoater." The bartender points. "I'm pressin' charges if I see 'em again."

The cowbell jingles, and two men walk inside the bar. They look down and stop in the entranceway.

"I'm open. Jist step over the drunken idiot. He's on his way out." The bartender gestures for the men to come in as he wipes down the bar.

"I'll get him out. They'll be here any minute." Julian finishes his drink and hands the bartender a tip. "Thanks for the whiskey."

"Stop in for a drink before you leave town," the bartender says.

"Okay, will do," I shout at the bartender.

"Not you, dummy." Julian walks toward me. "You know what? Been a stressful day. I'm taking a few swings while I still can."

"What? No," I plead. I roll on my back and hold my arms out in defense. I lower them as the two new customers step over my body. They ignore me and walk to the bar.

The bartender nods at Julian and steers his attention to the two men. "Extended happy hour tonight, gentlemen."

I lift my head and watch the men sit at the bar. A large figure blocks my view. I hear a stomp and feel the vibration next to my head. I turn to one side and spank my head against a black leather boot. I skim my eyes from the top of the boot and up a dark pair of jeans until I see Julian's face. He bends over and grabs ahold of my jacket. He whips me upright. "Stand up."

I close my eyes and crouch up to both feet.

"Let's go. Move it." He launches me against the wooden door and body slams me until the door swings open.

I hear the cowbell as I tumble onto the sidewalk. "Please, Gilligan," I plead.

"Stand up, you sloppy mess," Julian demands.

I pull myself on my forearms.

Engine growls echo from down the street as a vehicle peels around the corner. The sounds get louder as it gains speed. I look up and see a vehicle heading full speed in my direction. The driver flashes the brights from halfway down the block and slams on the brakes in front of the bar. The squealing from the brakes are loud enough to shatter a window.

Julian opens the door and points for me to get in. "Get up and get in."

I look up at him.

"Now," he demands.

I jump to my feet. "What's tis?" I ask.

"Get in the car." Julian leans over me.

"Wait, Ernald."

"It's Arnold. And again—not my name." He crosses his arms.

"The Exterminator."

"Wrong again. Get in the damn vehicle, you drunk idiot, before you give me no choice."

"Juliette, I'm not troublemanic."

"Jesus. I don't have time for this shit." Julian leans over and looks at the driver, then back at me. "You're being problematic." He pulls back an arm and forms a fist.

"Wai—" I hear a pop and feel pain in the back of my head. Everything is gone.

CHAPTER 3

Thirty-Nine Minutes Ago

I hear tapping. It's consistent. Persistent. *Ignore it. Sleep a little longer and rest. Try to relax. There's nothing to worry about in this place—there's no pain, only peace. There's nothing to worry about here. It was all just a nightmare—brother is home. He's home.*

I hear the tapping. It remains consistent. Its persistence is alarming. Leave me alone—I'd like to stay here. The muffled snapping echoes inside my head. The snaps are paced like a beat to a song, but soft. They were part of a song. There's a breeze on my face as though I'm lying underneath a high-powered ceiling fan. The beat stops.

"Hey, get up. Wake up." I hear a man's voice.

"Stop doing that." I shake my head.

There's silence, followed by slapping sounds and a burning sensation on my cheeks. "Hello?" The man's voice echoes.

I open my eyes. "No. You. American." I sit up and hit my head against a window. I turn to see the entrance of the shitty bar where I overpaid. I press my forehead against the glass and watch my body heat fog up the window.

"Oh my God, what'd you do?" I hear a woman's voice.

"He's fine. Aren't you?" Julian pokes me.

"Are you takin' me in?"

"You're in a cab, you idiot. Please focus, unless you want to get your ass kicked by the Glasgow Police, that bartender, and his crazy cousin."

"Why're you helping me?" I ask.

"Seem like a guy who's had some bad luck. Didn't mean to knock you out that bad." Julian slides out of the cab. "Meant to knock you out, just not like that."

"Tanks?"

"Cut that shit out—your drinking. It's the worst it's ever—"

"Where am I taking him?" the driver interrupts.

"Wait, you're a woman." I stare at the female cab driver.

"Watch yer mouth," she says.

"He's out of it. Ignore him." Julian leans in the cab and looks at the driver through the rearview mirror.

"Fine. Shut the door," she says.

"Just keep a lid on it, buddy," Julian says.

"What's that mean?" I ask.

"Put a lid on it? It means to—"

"It means shut the hell up," the driver interrupts as she slams on the gas, then brakes to force the door shut.

"Yer bitter, woman."

She locks the doors. "Which is it? Police station or you tell me where to take you, and you keep yer mouth shut?"

"Sorry, it's not you. My wife left me, and I'm the one who's bitter."

"Spare me the sob story. Where to?"

"Take me away. Take me to work. Not work, er, Cuningar Loop. The construction site jist a couple miles south of the park. I can tell you the roads as we get closer," I say.

"The middle of the woods jist before dark? You up to no good?" she asks.

"Left my phone at work and need to grab it." I scoot to the middle of the back seat and wrap my arms around the driver and passenger headrests. I lean forward and stare at the woman driver. "Know how to get there?"

She steps on the gas and hits the brakes, tossing me into my seat. "Put yer seat belt on, and don't bother me while I'm driving."

"I'll put a zit on it."

"Nope, yer wrong. That's not what the American man said." She turns down a street.

"How'd he say it, then?" I ask.

"It's a common phrase. He said to lid the top."

"What's that mean? What you said?"

"Yer not supposed to say anything. Shut ye geggy." She turns up the radio and accelerates. "We need gas. I'm stopping first," she yells over the music.

She turns down a main road and whips a quick right to pull into a gas station. I roll down my window for fresh air. She opens door and looks back at me. "Be right back," she says, shoving a wad of gum in her mouth.

The interior lights beam on her while she talks, and her ruby-stone earrings distract me. I didn't hear what she said. I stare at her earrings.

"Hey." She whistles at me. "You gonna puke or something?"

"Fine. I'm fine." I stare at the red stones in her ears as she slides out of the front seat. The interior lights turn off as she slams the door. I hate her earrings. The way the light reflected off the bloodred stones on both ears felt like I was staring into the eyes of the devil. I close my eyes and see them—the bright red fiery eyes of the devil.

"Not tonight." I slap myself in the face and reach for my flask. *Keep your mind out of the shitter, William.* I take a long swig and wait for the driver to return.

CHAPTER 4

Present

Five minutes left until sunset. I guzzle the last of the whiskey as I tread deeper into the woods. Everything around me is dull and lifeless. The trees look like nutrient-deprived skeletons compared to their summer bodies, when they're well nourished and full of color.

I normally like this walk every morning. It's my ten minutes of nature and fresh air to get my mind right before a long day at work. The uphill stride gets my heart going just enough to sweat out the booze from the night before. The sun looks nice when it shines between the treetops, and it feels like I'm looking through a kaleidoscope if I stare up high enough and turn in a circle. I like to drink my coffee straight from my thermos and listen to the guys talk about their marriage problems as I trail behind them. I keep to myself, even though they all know Shelly left me. They gossip like teenage girls.

The moon is clocking in for the night shift. The time left until dark has dwindled to a minute or so. I need to be efficient. Grab the phone and go. Grab and go. *Hurry up, drunk ass.* I leap over a pile of wood and snap a stick in half. I miss my landing strip and feel a fire ignite from the bottom of my shoe and through the arch of my foot—a firework.

I lean over and pat my frozen fingers along the bottom of my shoe. The wood pierced through my shoe. *My favorite shoes.* I jam my foot into a pile of snow. "Shit." The snow's frozen. *Drunk idiot.* Only an idiot would catapult their foot into a frozen surface. *Have another drink.*

Focus. Keep moving. Deep breaths. I see my breath circling in front of the moon. The unreachable light fixture makes my breath look like clouds in the sky. I use my sleeve to wipe the frozen snot from my nose. The air stings.

I lurk deeper into the woods. The ground crackles like pop rocks as I hobble across the frozen ground. It's quiet between the wind gusts. I'm the only thing contributing to the racket in the woods. I see one of the trenchers and the new dump truck we brought on-site Monday. I'm not too far now. *Watch for holes.* I dug one right around here—I think.

The sun's almost set. I barely see the lingering hues of orange and fuchsia as they vanish into the ground. Today's sunset mimics a match going out in an ashtray overloaded with cigarette butts. Today will be over soon. I had another shitty day. What a shitty day.

Wind coils, causing a branch to snap in the distance. The loud split ricochets between the rustling trees. *Stay focused. You're almost there.* Darkness strikes my corneas. It's happened. Nightfall. I can't see a thing. I look up. The moon is useless—only a pinprick of light covered by a cloud. *Thanks for your help, you stupid moon.*

I shuffle deeper into the woods, pausing to tap my toe in front of me. Steady steps. Frozen particles slide in and out of the hole in my shoe. I can't decide if this is soothing my fresh wound. It's like gargling saltwater for a nasty case of strep throat—it hurts like hell but may aid the wound.

I walk over a frozen shrub and brush against a bush. The branches produce a pop as they pierce through my jacket. One of the branches rips into my skin as it glides across my forehead. *Damn it.* Felt like my ex-wife's cat. I always let the thing bite me—hated that cat. I slide away from the obstacle and stop.

I see a spark of light in the distance. *There.* Not sure who the hell would be messaging me this time of night, but I owe you—whoever you are—even if it's a scam call. *Thank you, phone-call con artist, but I'll still never answer your calls.* I suck in the winter air. It feels soothing as it enters my lungs. The air's sharp enough to tickle the inside of my chest cavity, just enough to relax me. *Keep going. You made it this far, stupid.*

I stride toward the little light from the ground and plow my foot through a sheet of ice. Water trickles through my shoe as my foot sinks through a pothole. *My favorite shoes.* I'd like to rip them off and beat them against the nearest tree until I shred them to pieces. I spent a lot of money on these shoes. I *will* tear them off my feet once I get out of these woods and piss in them before I throw them in the middle of the road.

Wind cuts through the fibers of my jeans, causing the water in the material to rise. My pant leg is freezing, adding weight to the one leg as it hardens—an ice-covered cast. The sudden burning mimics shin splints.

I haven't felt pain in this region of my leg since my attempt at uni football. The pain was due to field sprints—not my shin hairs freezing to my jeans, then tearing from my skin with a single step.

I hear a crunch in the distance. The noise has two syllables—six if I count the echoes through the trees. I rub my eyes and a second round of snot from my nose. I hear the sound again. This time it's louder. "Hello?" I stand and stare into the darkness. The sound stops.

I see my phone light up. *Almost there. Grab and go, William.* Grab and go. I hold my hands out in front of me and feel around. The cold completed its route through my lower limbs and began its course through my upper extremities. It feels like someone chopped off my fingers at the knuckle. They're raw, but the throb feels as though the slice was done quickly.

I grab the nearest tree and use the trunk to heave my weight forward. I collapse to my knees. I roll my kneecaps over a pile of frozen twigs. Ignoring the sting, I lunge forward and plop my hands to the ground, surprised my hands didn't snap off my wrists as they contacted the ground. The wind rustles through the trees and stops. It's quiet.

I pat the ground. It feels rough, like I'm caressing a Christmas tree. A pine needle wedges underneath my fingernail. I pluck it out using my teeth and spit it on the ground. Leaning forward, I swipe my hand against a sleek surface. My phone.

I pry myself up and tap the screen. Three missed calls from unknown numbers and a text from my boss asking me to call him. Phone's nearly dead. Time to get the hell out of here. *Go home, William.* I tap on the flashlight and point the light at my shoes. They look like shit, and I'll be mad about this for weeks. I could tell myself otherwise, but I know I'll make a thing out of this.

I shuffle a few steps and shine my light on the canopy of one of our dump trucks. The light beams, and a figure ducks inside the cab. A hand peels from the window. The door clicks shut.

I crouch. "Who's there?"

I rub my eyes with the backs of my hands. I've been drinking, fell off a stool a couple of times, thrown into a door, and knocked out cold within a couple of hours. I couldn't be thinking clearly. *It's all in your head.* Skimming the light from the front to the back of the machine, I squint my eyes and watch for movement. Nothing. The cab looks empty.

"Yer on private property and should bolt before I call the police. I'm holding my phone. See? All it takes is one push of a button."

I squat and shine the light below the machine. The light is bright enough to see in between the front and rear wheels, even the large tree trunk between the two. The tree trunk is hefty enough to nearly fill the space between the front and rear tires. I hear a crunch in the snow and see a shadow duck behind the front tire.

"Saw you in the dump truck. You're on private property. And a construction site." I shine the light toward the front wheel and take a step toward the machine. "MPLX plant partners and landowners will press charges—seen it happen before with trespassers."

I take a step and shine the light from another angle at the front wheel of the dump truck. I loosen my jacket collar. Could be the alcohol wearing off. The echo of the frozen tree branches clinging together feels comforting now.

I slide my feet through the snow and jerk the light back to the center of the truck, revealing the tip of a black rubber boot. Someone's here. *How long has he been watching me from inside the dump truck?* I feel him waiting for me to move, but I can't. I'm stuck. I'm sober.

I bite down on my lip and wait. I lower myself, keeping the flashlight in place, and feel around for a large stick. He's hiding for a reason. I yank at a frozen stick.

"Know what? I'm not going to say a thing, man. Just came back to the site for my phone. Never saw you, so we're good." I crack the stick in half. "Heading home. Again, won't say shit—believe me. About to lose my job anyways."

I shift and point the stick at the machine, slowly backing away. The rubber boots slither around the tire as I stride backward. I keep the flashlight in front of me and use the stick to tap for objects behind me.

I stumble backward away from the stranger and stop. My heart skips a beat as I watch the shadow freeze. He's looking at me; I can feel it. I hold the light in front of me. The glow flares over a ghostly pale face and devil-red eyes. It widens its eyes at me and opens its mouth.

Run, William. Get the hell out of here. I turn around and see another shadow. The size of the shadow grows larger as it runs at me. It grabs my neck and throws me in a choke hold. I fall to the ground, and the lights go out.

CHAPTER 5

*C*lick-clack. *Click-clack*—two sticks beating together. *Click-clack. Click. Clack. Click. Thump. Thump. Thump.*

The sound is close, I think.

Thump. Thump. Thump.

Just leave me be.

Thump.

"Will? Think yer doorbell's broken," a voice trails off. "Will?"

"Ugh." I try to swallow, but my mouth's too dry. "Hang—hang on."

"You hear me in there?" The voice trails through the crack of the door.

"Stop pounding on my door. Hang on a sec." I muscle out as I force myself up.

My head is pulsating, and I can't make it stop. The throbbing punches are consistent and feel like someone's beating a piece of plywood against the top of my brain. The aches and pains resemble symptoms of a nasty virus. I groan as I roll to one side.

"Will?"

"I said hang on," I choke out as I roll from my couch onto the floor. "Shit." I stand up and lunge toward the door, but my blanket is wrapped around my ankles. I tumble to the ground. Kicking the blankets off my legs, I crawl and use the door handle to pull myself up. I thrust at the lock and yank open the door to see Ethan.

"What time is it?" I ask, staggering toward the couch.

"I'm early," Ethan says, pressing the door open.

"I need more sleep." I flop back on the couch.

"I know I usually wait for you in the car, but I'm glad I came up to yer place." Ethan looks around and scratches his head. "Yer place is boggin'. When was the last time you cleaned the hou—"

"Hadn't had time to clean lately. Why're you here so early?"

"I know today's gonna be rough on you. Thought I'd stop by an hour early and take you out for coffee."

I search the floor for my pants. "Don't remember falling asleep on the couch."

"Jesus, Will. Was going to give you the day off, but you'd drink yerself stupid before the day's over."

"Don't need the day off." I look at Ethan. He looks like he's getting younger. His face barely shows wrinkles, and he's not losing his hair, even with two kids and a wife.

"Where'd you go after work yesterday? Thought you said you're going home to write yer speech?" Ethan walks into the living room and turns on the light. "The event's tonight. Let's see yer speech."

"Had a bad night." I scratch my head and feel a lump. "I don't remember going home, and it wasn't from alco—"

"Should be living to honor yer brother." Ethan walks around and collects some of the empty bottles from around my place.

I look around the room for a bottle that isn't empty. There's a bottle of Clan MacGregor with a shot left at the bottom sitting on a bookshelf. Ethan dumps a handful of bottles and food containers into a box on the ground and makes his way toward the bottle on the bookshelf.

"Sarah and I knew today would be like this. She wants to come over and help you get ready before the event tonight."

Don't touch the bottle on the bookshelf. "Don't send yer wife here. I'm fine."

"Since when did you start referring to Sarah as 'my wife?' She's *your* good friend too. What's the matter with you, eh?" Ethan walks to a window and cracks open the blinds. "It's going to be a sunny day." He sets the garbage box in the middle of the room and walks toward the bookshelf.

"Yer right. Can you grab me a glass of water and give me a minute? I'm a little out of it. Didn't mean that about Sarah—she's my friend."

"Yeah. Fine."

I wait for Ethan to leave the room and jump to my feet. He's right: this place looks like a shithole. The light reveals the dishes scattered around the room and piles of dirty laundry. I walk toward the bookshelf, stomping over my clothes from the night before. *There're my pants.* I grab the bottle and shriek as I feel a needle pierce through the bottom of my foot. I keel over, cradling the bottle of whiskey like catching a ball before it hits the ground. "Ah, shit."

"What the hell you doing?" Ethan turns off the kitchen faucet.

I ignore the pain in my foot and rip open the bottle of whiskey, chugging it as fast as possible. "I stepped on something," I say, tucking the bottle under a pile of clothes on the ground. My heart races. *Please don't catch me.*

Ethan walks into the room. "It's probably broken glass from all the bottles you got laying around. I'd like it if we can sit down and have a talk."

I lift my foot and feel around the bottom. "What the hell's in my foot?"

"Hang on." Ethan squats down and hands me a glass of water. "Drink this." He grabs my foot and looks at my heel. "You've got a new woman?"

"No."

"Aye, right." Ethan picks at my heel. He stands up and tosses a piece of something shiny at me.

"What tis it?" I ask, patting around for the culprit.

Ethan snaps his fingers and points next to me.

"I don't have time for games; I'm tired." I stare at Ethan. "How're yer clothes like that all the time?"

"Like what?"

"Pressed. No wrinkles. Always looking like new clothes."

"Sarah found a steamer at—"

"Nah. No more—it's too early." I look down at a pile of dirty clothes. I'm envious. Shelly always kept up with the laundry and liked doing it. I never understood why. I'd make us a dessert and pick out a movie to watch by the time she was done. It always worked out. "Trying not to think about Shelly right now—her and Sarah are always together."

"I get it. It's none of my business."

"I'm not seeing anyone," I growl, brushing my hand against a sharp edge. I flick the small object into my palm and hold it in the daylight. It's an earring. A round diamond ruby. I drop the earring and jolt back.

"It wasn't electrical when I touched it." Ethan laughs and grabs the earring from the ground. "You know you'll step on it again within minutes—attention span of a goldfish. Hurry up and get changed. We're running out of time."

I stand up and limp toward the stairs. "Cab driver."

"Cute. I don't have to go out of my way to pick yer drunk ass up every morning. At least I could drive a cab. You may never get your license back."

"Thanks. I wasn't being ungrateful. The earring was my cab driver's from last night."

"Pulled yer cab driver?"

"No, I was drunk, but I remember the freaky earrings. Where's my wallet?" I shuffle back to the pile of clothes and shake through them. The whiskey bottle rolls out from the pile and stops at Ethan's feet. I find my wallet. "She didn't rob me."

"Good for you."

"I must've passed on in her cab."

"Classy."

"And she helped me get in my home."

"Solved." Ethan tosses the bottle with the rest of the empties. "Hurry up and get changed. I'll be in the truck waiting." Ethan walks out with the garbage.

I stagger upstairs. The wood feels soothing against the earring wound. I get to the top of the staircase and flip on a light. My shins and feet are covered in scratches and bruises under a brighter light. I ran into something.

I walk in my room and look around. Where to begin? It's a disaster. Mismatched socks drape over a half-open dresser drawer. The drawer below contains clean underwear with holes. *Who'd want to sleep with a holy underwear man?* I grab a pair of underwear and pick at the clothes on the floor. I toss a bottle off my bed and take a seat.

How did I get here? I'm an orderly person. *Try again today.* I used to get up every morning and run before work. I wanted to run a marathon. I'd slip back in just as Shelly was waking up, and I'd have breakfast ready before she came downstairs. Why can't I wake up feeling good about myself anymore? I know it's possible. I used to wake up happy most mornings, though right now I feel most comfortable hiding under a shell. Ethan chucked a rock through my shell by coming over here without a warning. He should've told me he'd be an hour early.

I stare at the corner of my room. It's the only clean spot to channel my eyes and not feel ashamed for the life I've succumbed to—my filth. The bedroom wall is a boring shade of gray and draws no emotion. I feel misplaced. Even though I've done my best to fit in with society, I'm still empty inside.

Come on. Don't give in today. You don't need a drink. No drink after work—tonight's a big night. I pull the dirty pants and sweatshirt from my floor up to my face and take a whiff. *Okay, they'll do.*

I stagger into my bathroom and toss my clothes over the shower-curtain rod. A speedy shower while steaming the clothes I wore over a week ago must work for now. I turn on the faucet, twisting the nozzle as hot as it will go. I can be out the door in ten minutes, feeling like a new man.

I shut the bathroom door and lay a towel along the large crack between the bathroom floor and base of the old door. The bathroom is the coldest room in the house. Whoever installed the windows in this place was an amateur and may very well be responsible for some of the high electric costs in the neighborhood, or at least become an immediate suspect for any household hypothermia cases. When I come home from work today, I'm going to get to the bottom of who did this and make it known. *You say this every day, dummy.* Today is different. I'm going to be different today.

I plant my hands on both sides of the bathroom sink and force myself to look in the mirror. The person staring back at me looks aged and unhealthy—couldn't be me. I smile as large as I can and see a ghostly imposter of my old self with a hungover face that resembles a gross combination of Beetlejuice and the Grinch.

"Whoa." I jump away from the mirror. I close my eyes, slap my face, and take another look at myself. Now I only see Beetlejuice. At least I narrowed it down to one look. *Good for you.* My green eyes look hideous with the bloodshot red in place of the white. My eyeballs look like Christmas ornaments. I pull a gray from my head and jump in the shower.

I lock the door and stride toward Ethan's truck. The fresh air feels good this morning. I notice Ethan in his truck. He's staring out the window and scratching the side of his head with his back turned to me. I reach for the door handle on the passenger side and stop. A woman's voice echoes through the speakers of his truck. I step backward and listen.

"I don't think he'll pick up my call. He's very angry with me," a woman's voice quivers through the Bluetooth.

"You kidding me?" I rip open the passenger door. "Hang up now, Shelly."

"Whoa, hang on a minute," Ethan raises his voice. "Shelly, Will just walked up. Nearly gave me a heart attack."

"What the hell are you doing, man? Shelly, hang up the phon—"

"Shelly. No, don't hang up," Ethan interrupts.

"I'm not getting in." I slam the door and walk up my driveway.

Ethan hops out of the vehicle. "She's really worried about you." He runs in front of me.

"I'm taking a sick day. Move out of my way."

"Will, don't do this. Let's grab that cup of coffee and talk this through."

"Nah, I'm good."

"Shelly's worried about you, man. Today's the year anniversary of—well, she was checking in to see how yer holding up."

"She left me when I needed her most."

"You pushed her to leave you," Ethan yells. "You gave her no choice. It's unbelievable that you still can't see that. Yer worse than ever."

"I'd like to be left alone."

"You'll have to move soon if you keep up like this—low-income housing will be the only way you can keep up with yer expensive habits. Shelly said you've been burning through your savings—almost all of it."

"I want to move back home."

"Not like this you won't. Shelly still loves you. Yer being a selfish piece of shit."

I storm forward, knocking my shoulder into him. He steps back and puts his arms in the air.

"I've got a business to run and don't have time for this. You can take a cab to work if you calm down. I won't ding yer pay if you take the day off. Just work on yer speech and have some respect for yer brother."

"Aye, prick." I fumble the keys. I don't want to turn around, because I feel him staring at me. He won't turn to his car until I'm inside my home. I unlock the door and slide inside.

"You gotta be there by seven—don't forget."

"Aye, right." I slam the door behind me.

I press my back against the door and slide to the ground. I feel the outside air leaking in from under the door. Winter sucks. *What did I just do?*

CHAPTER 6

I beat the back of my head against the door and stare at my filthy home. I've only been living here five months, and I've accumulated a couple years' worth of mess. Prior to this place, I was poked at for being overly attentive to every speckle of dust. The term *obsessive-compulsive* was thrown at me over and over. *So, what do you want from me now, eh? Ethan stops in and declares me a slob?*

I tilt my head upright and survey the room. This bachelor pad doesn't look pleasant from this angle. I follow the light from the blinds Ethan cracked open. I'm not ready to confirm his statement, but it looks like I've had beer goggles on for just a bit longer than a drunken weekend in college. My tables are covered with months of unopened mail and empty beer cans. I haven't dusted the place yet, but I know I own a vacuum. I found a receipt for the vacuum recently and believe it's in a closet. I'll take the new vacuum for a spin next week.

"Ethan, I appreciate you making it over today—so glad you got my invitation. Sorry for the mess. My butler's on vacation this week." I roll my eyes and clap my hands. A round of applause for self. *What was that, Ethan? You said you didn't get a formal invite, but you came over here anyway and extended the invite to Shelly, and I bet you told her what my place looks like.*

I kick my shoes off and slide them in front of the bench next to my front door. I lean over and toss them underneath the bench. There's a jingle as my shoes collide with the wall. *I know that sound.* Twisting my torso to the floor, I plop my weight onto one side and shimmy to see what's stuck under the bench. I shake my shoes and hear it again. Harley. Harley man's collar. I grab his collar and tuck it against my chest. I'd do anything to add more years. Should've called Shelly before taking him in—that I regret.

I squint at the collar and see a couple of his hairs still attached. *I miss you more than you'll know, Harley man.*

Seems like yesterday when my brother and I brought Harley home for Shelly. She always wanted a dog, but her family wouldn't allow it. She'd always stop to pet every dog, no matter where we walked, so I decided to surprise her with one of her own. I remember watching Harley take off through the house, and I remember her smile when she first saw him. The bubbly blonde jumped out of her chair and tossed her book over her shoulder to greet the German shorthaired pointer on the floor.

"Hello, puppy," she said, cradling the baby in her arms. "Jason?" Shelly turned to my brother. "Jase, where'd you find him?"

"What? Me?" Jason turned his head to me and opened his eyes as wide as they could go.

"Did you get a puppy?" She released the pup and watched him run to Jason.

"What puppy?" Jason signaled for me to step in.

"Jase, go ahead, tell her the story." It was always fun watching my twin brother bail himself out of a situation, especially when I got to put him on the spot. It was like sitting back and watching myself on camera. We were terrible liars; we couldn't surprise someone if you paid us.

"My puppy?" Jason buckled.

"The puppy eating yer shoe right now." Shelly laughed. "Well, now he's peeing on yer shoe."

"Shit." Jason kicked the pee off his foot. "Don't know how the little guy got in here." Jason stared at the ground and stopped talking. An awkward shutdown.

I walked up and kicked Jason in the back of his shin. "It's a friend's puppy. Why? Do you want a puppy?" I asked like an idiot. I realized I was just as bad as my brother at the lying thing. We both looked stupid. Jase and I grew up with Shelly and shared the same friends. Why would someone believe I had some new friend who lent me their puppy?

"You bought us a puppy?" she asked. The friend comment gave it away.

Jason broke the awkward silence by giving me a shove. "Did we surprise you at all?"

"I was surprised the moment a puppy ran in. You two should've let the puppy in and waited outside. Yer both bad liars—it's the only time you try to act like someone else, and you still end up acting like the same person, crazies." Shelly laughed as she crawled on her hands and knees toward the puppy.

"He looks like a Harley or a Harry," Jason said, stepping out of his wet shoes. "You love yer uncle Jason, right?" He clapped his hands and the puppy.

"Jase should've taken home his puppy brother." Shelly released the dog and watched him scamper to Jason.

"Nah, need to find a woman first. I'll borrow him to use as bait. Look at the way Shelly melted when she saw him." Jason held out his arms to embrace the puppy. He dropped his arms as the puppy slid to a stop, grabbed his shoe, and ran out of the room.

"Not sure he liked hearing that his uncle wants to dangle him as bait." I got up and followed the puppy.

"He was the calmest of the litter, but now—"

"He *does* look like a Harley, doesn't he?" Shelly smiled at Jason. "Good name."

I walked in the room carrying the puppy struggling to jump from my arms. "Harley it is." I leaned down and handed Harley to Shelly.

Shelly cradled him in her arms. "Hey, Harley, meet yer mum."

"Like yer gift?" I asked Shelly as she pulled Harley to her face and rubbed her cheek and against his.

"It's the best present I ever had. Love you." She kissed me while the puppy tore away at my shoe. It felt so good to give her something she always wanted but was too afraid to ask for.

Six months later, Ethan, Jason, and I ran a practice marathon with the full-grown version of Harley. We thought we worked out a solid plan with a logical amount enough of distraction, where Jason and I wouldn't ruin the proposal by acting weird. We tied a bow with my life savings of a ring to his collar and waited in our places for Shelly to come home. She said she would be home in five minutes.

What were the odds of a pizza delivery guy showing up at the wrong house within the five-minute countdown to one of the biggest moments of a man's life? A loud doorbell and a delivery guy holding fresh pizzas was the gun sounding off for the out of shape men's beer-buzzed marathon. Harley hit the delivery guy in the nuts as he took off between the surprise guest's legs.

"Get the dog," I yelled back at Jason and Ethan as I plowed over the delivery guy.

"The ring! The dog has the ring!" Jason shouted from behind me.

"Oh shit. The ring." Ethan took off in a full sprint. "Help us, pizza man," Ethan's voice trailed in the distance.

We chased Harley halfway through the neighborhood, when we saw Shelly's car rolling up to the stop sign ahead of us. I wish I could see her face the moment her full-grown puppy and three tipsy guys with a slow-rolling pizza delivery guy tailgating behind us. We swept past her like tumbleweeds and could barely catch our breath.

"Think she saw us?" Jason choked out.

"Shut up, Jase," Ethan snarled and sprinted past us like he was getting close to crossing the finish line.

"I feel"—I gasped for air—"I feel that last beer coming up." I said, coughing up phlegm. I sucked in as hard as I could, tilted my head so I still had view of the dog, and spit.

"What the shit, man? You just spit on my face, asshole." Jason slowed his pace.

"Sorry. Sorry, Jase." I tugged my shirt over my head and looked back at Jason. "Catch." I threw my shirt at Jason. "Shit, I see Shelly coming."

The three of us turned to glance at Shelly. She kicked off her high heels into a neighbor's yard and started jogging. "Harleeeey. Harley dog." We heard Shelly's voice trailing behind us. "Harley maaan."

"She's. Gonna. Catch. Up. Shelly. Was. Track. Star." I turned forward to see Harley crossing between the neighbor's lawn.

Beeeep. "Mailbox!" the pizza delivery guy shouts from the window.

Ethan turned forward and reamed his arm into the top of a mailbox. The mailbox ripped off the top of the wooden post and crashed onto the street.

"Ow, shit, that hurt."

"I'll get it." The delivery guy stopped in the middle of the road and got out from his car. He picked up the mailbox and propped it back on the post. A car turned on the street and stopped. He flashed his brights and honked at the delivery guy.

"Way to block the road," a man shouted from the window of the other car. "Almost hit you, dummy."

We heard squealing breaks behind us and saw the pizza guy appear at the end of the next driveway.

"Harrrrlleeeyyy," Shelly screamed from behind us.

"Damn, s—she's fast. Catching. Up. *Quick.*" Ethan held his arm and picked up his pace.

"Shit. Okay. Maybe he'll know Shelly's voice and run the other direction." Jason said, wiping sweat from his forehead.

"May—maybe. He'll—he may turn around from voice." I gasped for air as we chased Harley up a driveway and toward an open garage.

"But. But—she'll see ring." Jason blew his nose in my shirt.

"Hey," I yelled.

"Already has yer spit. Yer. Spit's. On. It," Jason growled.

Jason and I hopped over a bush at the bottom of the driveway that led up to the open garage. The owner of the house appeared in the doorway and watched us. He looked through the large glass door, holding his dog on a leash. The handle bent, and he stuck one leg on his porch. He saw Harley heading for his garage, realized there was a live chase going on in his yard, and slid his foot back inside his house. He pulled his dog away from the window in order to prevent further doggy drama.

"Can you see bow?" I shouted.

"Yes. Bow's there," Ethan confirmed.

"Ring on bow?" I gasped for air.

"Can't tell," Ethan forced out.

"Please, ring. Please stay on the bow, ring." I felt cramps on both sides of my abdomen.

"Bow looks loose," Ethan updated, following Harley back down the driveway.

"Who tied bow?" I yelled as I signaled Jason to spread out. "Circle dog."

"I tied bow." Jason wheezed.

"Shit. Okay—start—watch—ing for bow fall off. Jason—bad at bows." I coughed.

"The beer's not settl—settling." Ethan pulled his arms up and tucked them behind his head to help him breathe.

"Harley, Mommy's home." We heard Shelly's voice growing closer.

Harley stopped. His ears pointed up, and he looked around. Jason and Ethan glanced at Shelly.

"Circle him. Now." Ethan barely got the words out before he collided with Jason. "Damn it—my arm again."

The pizza guy threw his car in park and hopped out. "Look," the fourth member of our newly formed crew, belted out. "Look, yer dog's wearing out." He approached the circle.

"Uh, yeah. Thanks—"

"Steve. Name's Steve."

"Have my own dog at home. Trick is, stay calm," Steve said.

"Harley, come here. Come here, now," I demanded.

"I meant yer voice. Keep a calm voice with the dog." Steve used both hands and signaled for me to turn it down a few octaves.

"You're a good boy." I lowered myself to the ground.

Harley wagged his tail.

"Once he's trained, you'll learn. Yer giving him dominance right now, and—"

"He's in training. Thanks, Steve," I interrupted.

"Good boy, Harley. Come to Uncle Jase." Jason lowered himself.

"Him too. Yer both praising him." Steve shook his head.

Ethan slowly walked in place, side to side, like he was waiting for the whistle blow to begin a football drill. He looked ready to lunge at the dog like a goalie diving for a ball.

Jason and I crouched back up and followed Ethan's lead.

"Harley, sit," I gently commanded.

"Yes, Harley, sit," Ethan repeated.

Harley sat on his hind legs in the middle of the driveway and licked at the bottom of his paw.

"Look at that. Training classes are paying off," I whispered. "Come here, Harley."

"Don't ask 'em. Tell 'em to come," Ethan said.

"Yeah, you gotta be firm," the pizza guy agreed.

"Aye, fine." I put a hand up in the air. "Harley, come."

Harley bent his front legs and lowered himself to lay on the driveway.

"Good boy. Is the ring on the bow?" I looked at Ethan, who was closest to Harley.

"Can't tell. He's bending his neck too much."

"Think you can lean in and grab his collar." I studied Ethan's sweaty face and the gash on his arm. I held my breath, awaiting a quick response. Any blinking caused sweat from my forehead to trickle in my eyes and make them burn. It hurt like hell to blink.

Ethan nodded and reached his arms out in front of him, ready to pounce.

"Haarleeey, come to Mommy," Shelly screamed and clapped her hands in the distance.

Harley straightened up on all fours and took off through the yard toward Shelly's voice. Shelly jumped up and down a few times and took off running toward our house. Harley gained speed and followed his mum.

"Gotta be kidding me," Jason scorned. "Runt of the litter, eh, Will?"

"Don't you remember? You picked 'em." I shook my head at Jase and laughed. I chased after the dog.

Ethan took a deep breath and followed behind me.

Jason looked at Steve. "Hey, man, can I have a ride back?" Jason jogged with the pizza guy to his car.

We watched Harley's speed increase as he recognized Shelly up ahead. His gallop turned into a full canter.

"She'll see bow and ring," Ethan choked out.

"I know." I tried to gain speed and hold on to my side cramp, but Harley was too far gone. Growling sounds echoed through the neighborhood as a car gained speed behind me. The pizza guy passed me in his Toyota Prius, with my brother hanging out the passenger window.

"Shelly. Shee—ll—lyyy." His voice trailed off like a kid being whipped around on a roller coaster.

Ethan and I ran to the middle of my front yard, but it was too late. Harley was sitting in front of Shelly, wagging his tail. She smothered him with kisses. Ethan and I looked at Jason. Jason jumped out of the Prius and was running in a full sprint toward Shelly and Harley. Halfway across the lawn, he pulled a U-turn back to the driveway. He held the hood of the pizza delivery vehicle as he vomited his beer onto the driveway.

"She sees it. Ring's still on bow," Ethan said, shoving me. "It's happening. Go. Ask her. We'll laugh at this years from now," Ethan said, forcing his hands behind his head. I wiped sweat from my face and walked toward Shelly. I got down on one knee in front of Shelly as she untied the bow off her baby.

I wipe my eyes and pet the hairs left on Harley's collar. "You were a good boy." I clench his collar and stand up. My stomach feels nauseous, and I feel my heart beating rapidly. *Wish you were here, Jase.* I grab an empty bottle and hold it over my mouth. The leftover drops tap my tongue. I need more.

I walk over to my desk and slide out the chair. My desk is the only thing in this house still immaculate. I run my hands across the desktop. It feels rough and uneven, just the way I envisioned the rustic piece to turn out. I squat down toward the seat of the chair. My tailbone cracks the edge of the seat and the chair slides out from underneath me. I grasp the bottle tight as I bounce against the ground.

Flipping over, I roll my eyes at the chair, then stare at the bottle "See that, Greg? Chair wanted to off us, but I saved the day." I pull it toward the desk, climb in the seat, and set Mr. MacGregor in front of me. *I love you, desk.* The mismatching shades of wood give it personality, as I hoped for when building it. This was the last piece of furniture I made before I moved out of Shelly's and my house, and it was the only piece of furniture I brought with me. When I lean forward, I still smell the sweetness of the oak even though the wood has long since dried out.

I open the drawer and find the program for tonight's event. The program looks so real. I skim the flyer. *Harnessing Life: Strengthening Safety Gear Regulations for Those Building the Future. In Loving Memory of Jason B. Norwick.* I crumple up the flyer and swat the bottle off the desk. It shatters to the floor.

"Sorry, Greg."

I can't talk in front of an audience. I'm not ready to talk in front of anyone. I close my eyes. *It's been a year since you died. I can't do this. You see me at all, Jase? I see you. I replay what I saw over and over—it won't stop. Make it stop. Jase? You weren't supposed to leave me like this. Damn it. I know you didn't want to leave. Every time I close my eyes, I see the way you looked at me—those last few seconds. One two three. I want to drop the memory like I just dropped Greg. I'll find another Greg—easily. I'm meeting him shortly. Greg's going to be okay, but you? Why can't you be more like him? You'd like Greg—you two would get along great. He stops me from replaying yer terrified face from the moment I wake up to the moment he forces my mind to close it out. It won't stop playing. Over and over.*

Yer eyes were wide open like you'd seen something. What'd you see, Jase? Greg can't even help me with that one. It looked like you were trying to shout something, then you ran out of time. Answer me, Jase.

I shake my head and feel a burn inside my nostril. Tears drop down my cheeks and stand up. This is too much right now—way too much for me. I fold the paper in half and tuck it in my back pocket. I grab an empty flask. I'll change shirts and find a bar by the event to sit and write this thing out, because I can't write this thing sober.

CHAPTER 7

I tuck my hands in my pockets and step into the big blue bus. The bus is packed with people bundled from head to toe from the freakish winter temperatures. I sit down and look at my coat. I haven't dressed up since Jason's funeral. I pick at lint on the sleeves. Not sure why I thought wearing the most expensive jacket I owned would ever make me feel okay about the situation. I hate this situation and would spit on it if I could. I look up to make sure I'm on the right bus.

My flask slides out from my pocket and whacks the ground. Two women sitting across from me turn their heads and watch me grab my flask from the aisle. I look out the window and ignore their judgy stares. My mouth's dry, and I'm hungry—must be sobering up.

The bars by Central Station are farther away than I'd like them to be, but they're a safe zone for me. No one will bother me over there. The bar and restaurant scene by the station experiences high volume of visitors coming and going throughout the day, so I'll blend in well. I'll find a nice bar, order a meal, and write my speech. The day is young.

I see Central Station. The sun shines on the multicolor stone and accentuates the forest-green hue that serves as the contrasting color of the building frame. The name Central Station spreads across the building inside the grassy color that drapes across the frame of the overpass for people to see as they drive underneath the station. The windows aligning the overpass are tall and symmetrical, with white bars flowing across the windows, mimicking an antique birdcage.

We approach the Central Station sign and turn left, driving parallel with the station. Bars and restaurants align both sides of the street. My heart races as I consider the potential fun. I stand up and get ready to jump out at the next stop.

I feel the wind rift up my sleeves as I step off the bus. There're people passing by in both directions. Why would someone feel lonely in a beautiful city like Glasgow? I stick my hands in my pockets and strut down the road. It's eleven in the morning, and I've got the entire day ahead of me. I tip my nose in the air and suck in as much life at once.

Walking along the busy street, I notice the bars haven't unlocked their doors yet. The key will be to find a restaurant, any restaurant, that serves food and alcohol. I see an aqua awning that reads "Good Drinks and Good Food." Opens at eleven. I'm sold.

I walk inside the empty establishment and look around. The wooden walls are packed with years of photos from visitors forced to take pictures in order to legitimize this place, which only means that they care to stay around a while. I guess bragging rights can only help. I look down. My shoes don't stick to the floors. I've been in the bar scene for a year now, and for the first time it smells like an orange-based cleaner and not the sticky beer and bleach combination.

I grab a menu from the hostess stand. There's a gluten-free menu sitting in front of the regular menu—no need to see more. I'm convinced, whenever a restaurant has a gluten-free section, it usually means they've perfected the dishes listed on their regular menu. There's a "Seat Yourself" sign standing next to the menus. I look for a comfortable booth and sit down.

"Sit wherever you'd like," I hear a screechy voice.

"Just sat down—no rush," I call out.

The place is chilly. The booths are made of wood. The wood curls at the top and has custom carvings throughout. They look nice but hurt like hell to plop down on. The waitress storms in, tying an apron as she approaches my booth.

"How are you today?" Her voice is high-pitched and piercing.

I slide back in my booth. Why is she talking so loudly? It's just me here—no need to shout. "I'm good."

"I see you have a menu already." Her voice grows louder.

"Any drink specials?"

"Of course." The pitch nearly brings tears to my eyes. "We have a long list today. If you want beer, we have a few specials runnin—"

"I'll take a whiskey on the rocks. Yer favorite whiskey." I can't listen to her any longer.

"I've got several I like."

"Surprise me with a Scotch." Please stop talking.

"Sounds good. I normally work the night shift, so let me see what we have left from last night's event. We should have another shipment this afternoon."

"Yeah, fine." I watch her strut toward the bar. She's a tiny little brunette. I'd never think a sound so hoarse could come out of something so cute and petite. I can see why she's placed on the night shift. She'd hopefully blend in better with loud music and crowds.

I pull out the program and slap it on the table in front of me. The waitress strides back to my table and lays down a glass of whiskey.

"Hope you like it."

"Yep." I use a hand to plug an ear. "I'll try yer bannocks, and keep the drinks coming." I watch her nod and walk off. "Oh, can I borrow a pen?"

"Of course." She raises her voice and pulls one from her apron. "Anything else?"

"Nah, thanks."

I open a napkin and doodle circles to get the pen working. Not sure I'm ready to open this door. I've spent a year holding it shut because the pain was too much to handle. I press my lips against the glass and inhale the whiskey in a single gulp. I stare at the napkin.

Thank you for being here today. I know Jason would be amazed by the number of supporters standing in this room. I'd like to think he's here with us now, watching from above.

I look up and flag the waitress for another round. *Please don't talk when approaching the table.* She flips a glass on the bar and gives a healthy pour. I look down at the napkin and stare intently so she gets the hint that I'm trying to focus. Her heels click against the floor as she walks toward me. There's silence as she swaps glasses. She gets the hint.

"Welcome."

I jump and crack my head against the wooden seat back. Her voice raised several octaves. How's that even possible? She's so petite.

"Sit wherever you'd like." She greets a group walking into the bar. "I'll grab some menus."

I squint my eyes at the group walking in. *Please don't sit over here— please don't.* I'm sure I look like a creep glaring at the newcomers. One guy points to a television on the other side of the bar, and the group follows his lead. I look at the napkin.

I don't know a lot of people in this world with an identical twin. There's a special bond that's shared, which is different than just having a close sibling.

It's surreal to live life with someone you take your first breaths with. Jason could look at me during any moment of the day and know what I was thinking just based off the way my head was angled or which fingernail I picked at. He knew I met my wife the moment he saw us together at this bar in our hometown our first visit back from uni (remove this part if Shelly comes to event). He never admitted it, but I'm sure he was pissed he was the one in the bathroom when she tripped and spilled her drink on me.

Jason and I were inseparable, to the point we worked side by side, even in our adult careers, and we were both passionate about change and developing a better community for the residents of Glasgow. We couldn't be prouder or more supportive of our best friend, Ethan, and to be a part of such a talented team (point at Ethan).

It's difficult for me to stand up here today without him next to me. I'm still trying to come to terms with why this happened, as I know it wasn't his time, because I'm still here. A year ago today we were in the midst of building the new high-rise, and I was several floors below Jason when I heard his line snap and the buckle pop. I looked up after the snap echoed between buildings and saw him dangling over me. He looked at me and looked scared. I'd never seen him look like that before. Seconds later he flashed by me and went headfirst into the pavement.

I toss back the whiskey and flag the waitress for another round. Tears roll down my cheeks, and I taste snot that dripped down from my nose and into my mouth. I pick up the napkin and use the corners to dab my nose and eyes. I try every day to erase the image of his head. The blood. I finish the drink.

We had the equipment tested and found the tear in the line among other malfunctions were due to poor quality from materials that were substituted in order to keep costs down at an overseas plant. Stricter safety standards must be set to ensure the equipment we use will do its job. Jason had his entire life ahead of him. I miss him every second I breathe, and it's been hard breathing without him here.

Thank you for having me here tonight to share my story (drink a lot).

The waitress walks up with a drink. "How's it going?" she shrieks.

"I'll take the check please."

"Yer foods on its way out," she squeals.

"I'm not feeling well. You enjoy it or give it away." I slam the drink and watch the waitress hustle to grab the check. It's time for a new place with a new vibe. I fold the napkin, tuck it in my pants, and grab a wad of cash for the bill.

I shove the door open and storm out into the cold. A stroll around the neighborhood to find another bar without an ear-wrenching server is on the top of my list. I pull the napkin from my pocket and neatly fold it as I walk into the street. I reach in my pocket for my wallet and lay the napkin inside.

Beep. Bleeeeeeep. A car slides to a halt, tapping my leg. I turn and stare through the windshield at the driver. The driver rolls down his window and throws his hand in the air.

"Ye trying to get yerself killed? Get out of the road, stoater," the driver screams.

"Er, sorry." I look at the man.

"Move it." The driver honks at me.

I shimmy back onto the sidewalk and go inside the bar next door to the place I walked out of. The place has a few customers—more than the last joint. I walk toward the corner of the bar, the side without customers, and grab a stool. All the stools are made of black leather and have tears so large the foam spews out from the center.

The bartender acknowledges me with a nod as he pours a customer's drink. Guns N' Roses blares through the speakers, intensifying my first impression of the decor. Black chandeliers align the cherrywood bar. I look at the mirror behind the bar and the black-and-red candle wax that's splattered from the uneven candles, forming a frame around the mirror. I glance in the mirror and see a lonely drunk with a messy beard. The music cuts to a guitar solo that feels like its singling me out as I stare in the mirror. I don't recognize this person.

"Whatcha drinkin'?" The bartender stands in front of me.

"Aye, whiskey on the rocks. House whiskey," I say, snapping out of it.

My phone rings. Ethan's calling me.

"What's up?" I answer.

"You all right?" Ethan asks. "Sorry for earlier, mate. I'm not doing well myself, so you must be struggling."

"I'm good. Wrote speech." I nod at the bartender as he lays a napkin down with my drink.

"Whe're you?"

"I'm at a bar by Central Station."

"Which one? I'm gonna join you. Casey said he'll move his work in my office so I can leave."

I slide my drink over and read the napkin. "Uh, I'm at Black Chandelier." I laugh. "Oh, I get it. There're black chandeliers above my head—nice. Clever."

"How many deep?"

"Not many. Just got here."

"Order me a double. I'm leaving now."

I watch the bartender flip through stations on one of the television monitors above the bar. I stare at the screen and sip my drink. A commercial for a local dental studio appears on the screen. I hate the dentist. The scraping against my teeth makes me want to puke. The commercial makes a visit to the dentist look glamorous, as though the patients are walking out of a relaxing massage during holiday. It shows a close-up of photoshopped smiles, then cuts to an excited man walking out of the uppity building after his heart-stirring visit to the dentist. The happy man smiles at his wife as she picks him up in her luxury vehicle. *What the hell was that?* If Shelly picked me up in a sports car after my appointments, I may've thought twice about going to the dentist.

I chuckle to myself and take another sip. The stupid commercial reminds me of Jason and the last time I saw him before watching him free fall from the top of a building. Rubbing my face, I look around the bar to see if anyone was watching me laugh alone on a barstool. That felt good. Laughing felt good. It's been a while. First time I've been able to shed the disgusting replay of his death and laugh at something funny. I forgot what it feels like—uncontrollable laughter.

It was almost a year ago to the day—one of my last memories of Jase. I had a dentist appointment scheduled in the afternoon and had to be home after to help Shelly make dinner. Shelly and I spent hours in the kitchen, as we had Jase, Ethan, and Sarah coming over for dinner. We'd been getting together twice a month for "family dinners," where we'd switch off hosting, cook a nice dinner with copious amounts of wine, and end the night with card games. No one ever bailed on family dinner night, as it was too much fun. Six of us came together nearly every other week for years, until Jase caught his girlfriend of two years cheating on him with her trainer at the gym.

We withered down to a dinner party of five, and the leisure cooking ended because Jason was getting fed up of thinking about his horrible, cheating ex-girlfriend. He turned the bimonthly dinner ritual into one of those cooking contest shows, pitting Shelly and I against Sarah and Ethan. Jason nominated himself as the judge and decided which couple won at the end of each month. We went along with it—whatever helped him move on from the breakup.

It was our turn to compete in the *Amateur Couples Cook-Off Challenge: Month Four*. We were determined to beat Shelly and Ethan. We were prepared to go overboard with "gourmet," after Jase stated, "Ethan's and Sarah's cooking is superior to Shelly's and Will's," at the end of month three. We only had one win and needed to tie it up. We strongly disagreed with Jason's judging and blamed it on our desire to be sitting with our guests, spending quality time with the little time we get, rather than yelling at them from the kitchen, unable to retain conversation. Jason poked further by insisting, "Natural chefs like Sarah and Ethan can host and cook at the same time."

We were in the kitchen, preparing to tie the cook-off, when the doorbell rang. Jase came over early to sit at the island and taunt me while I peeled potatoes. He was wearing too much cologne and was dressed in new clothes. I couldn't get him to unglue his eyes from his phone, as he was in the middle of an intense text convo.

"Yer not going to screw us up. We've been prepping since we left Ethan's and Sarah's two weeks back." I grinned.

"Actually, I came over early because I gotta leave after dinner," he said.

"What? You can't leave. Yer the judge." Shelly walked in front of Jason and crossed her arms.

"I'm staying for dinner, just leaving right after."

"No games?" Shelly looked disappointed. "We bought something new to play tonight."

"I'm meeting someone for drinks and—"

"Who?" I interrupt.

"This girl I've seen a couple times and—"

"The one from the wedding?" Shelly asked.

"Aye."

"You like her. You've been seeing her over a month or so now," Shelly said.

"Aye."

"Call her and invite her for dinner. She'll have fun with us." Shelly pointed at his phone.

"Too soon." Jason unlocked his phone and opened a text.

"But you like her. Yer waiting for her messages and haven't taken yer eyes off yer phone since you got here." Shelly looked at Jason, smiled at me, and walked out of the room with an armful of table settings.

"She's great, but leaving for six months to take on a project in Spain," Jason said as he walked to the liquor cabinet.

"When?" I signaled for Jase to pour me a glass too.

"Little more than a week."

"You should still invite her over," I insisted.

"Haven't told her about you yet. Told her I've got an older brother—left out the identical part," Jason explained.

"Yer telling her lies?" Shelly's voice echoed from the next room over.

"Technically, he's not lying," I said.

"Jist tell her you have a twin. It's not a big deal," Shelly said.

"It's a big deal. You guys haven't been out in the dating world—er, ever."

"Could've made the first move on Shelly, but you didn't."

"I liked her best friend—"

"That you ignored all through high school and uni," Shelly interrupted.

"I was shy." Jason sipped a glass of whiskey on the rocks. "You guys have so many nice bottles of whiskey, and you've never opened them." Jason handed me a glass.

"Not really my thing." I clicked glasses with him and sipped the whiskey.

"To my older brother." Jason held his drink up and sipped it.

"You think the sixty seconds earlier you came out from yer mum's crotch counts as having an older brother?" Shelly asked.

"Well, technically—"

"It was a long sixty seconds," I talked over Jason.

"Aye, right." Shelly grabbed Jason's phone from his hands and waited for him to look her in the eyes. "Jase, yer in yer own head about the twin shit, and I think it's bizarre that you lie to women about having a twin. Men lie about a lot of bull when they're impressing women, but a twin? Will, you find it odd?"

"Uh, I like having a twin," I said.

"Wasn't the answer I was looking for. But, if I were to guess, I think Amy scarred you." Shelly grabbed the glass of whiskey from my hand and took a sip. "Gross, I prefer my wine."

"Amy?" Jason asked.

"How the hell did you guys forget about Heartbreak Amy?" Shelly asked. "Remember? Uni? Bathroom night—she scarred me for life."

"Oh shit. Almost forgot about that." I grabbed the glass of whiskey back and took a swig.

Heartbreak Amy had long brown hair that nearly touched her butt. Jase met her at a bar one night at uni while he was out with our flatmates. She wrote on a napkin and had her girlfriend slap it down in front of him as she walked to the bathroom. He approached her at the bar, and they talked all night, even made plans to hang out the following day. Our flatmates said Jason was smitten around her. Jase and Amy spent a lot of time together for about two and a half weeks, until the night she took off running from our flat. It was the first and last time Shelly and I would ever meet Amy.

Shelly and I came back to campus after spending two weeks taking care of her sick mother. We hadn't slept much in the duration we were gone and decided to crash at my flat after walking in and hearing silence. My flatmates were gone, and we didn't care where they were. We needed to pass out. I almost fell asleep driving, and Shelly had period cramps so bad we had to pull over almost every hour so she could change her tampon. We locked ourselves in my room, turned the sound machine on, and fell asleep with our clothes on.

When I woke up to use the bathroom in the middle of the night, I realized we had slept through an after-hours party. The flat smelled like cigarettes and spilled beer as I strolled past the living room. The lights were dim, but I could see my flatmates had stacked all our living-room furniture together. My feet stuck to the old wooden floor as I tiptoed through a messy trail of empty beer cans. I stopped to admire the impressive fort my flatmates built with the furniture. They stacked everything up like Legos and used one of my flatmate's mattresses as the tabletop.

Instead of flipping on the bright bathroom lights, I used the living-room light to guide me to the toilet. When I looked through the mirror, I saw one of my flatmates sleeping sideways on a beanbag in the entranceway of his room. *Missed a good time tonight*, I thought. I stood over the toilet to pee and saw a shadow cross under the light from the bathroom mirror. I tried to flush the toilet, but the handle was flimsy from someone clogging it. I squatted below the sink and felt around for an unopened toothbrush, when I felt two warm hands grope my shoulders. I stood up and felt Shelly's arms wrap tightly around my waist from behind. She kissed my back and pulled my shirt over my head.

"Guess we only needed a little sleep," I said.

Shelly whipped me around and hopped up on top of the sink. She squeezed my cheeks and pulled me in for a kiss. I heard a clunk and a crunch of a beer can against the wood floor. I pulled my head back and listened. Shelly kissed around my neck, distracting me from the noise, but I couldn't help but think the fumbling around in the living room was someone making their way to the bathroom in order to puke up the hours of shots mixed with late-night beer pong.

"Someone's walking around the living room," I said, stretching my neck in the air to listen. "It got crazy in here when we were sle—"

"Tonight was amazing—loved meeting your flatmates," a woman's voice—not Shelly's voice—said.

"Will? You in the bathroom?" Shelly's voice trailed. "Looks like the guys got drunk and played *Tetris* with the furniture again." Shelly laughed.

"Shelly?" I cupped my hands over my face to block fake Shelly. *Who the hell are you?*

"Who is Shelly?" fake Shelly asked.

"Uh, my girlfriend," I scoffed, feeling my blood pressure rise. "Who the *hell* are you?" I flipped on the light and slammed my back in the wall. "Ah, shit," I jolted away from the wall after slamming the back of my head into a towel hook. It felt like an electric shock, which caused me to whip my body toward the stranger. I was able to hoist to one side and avoid her completely as I plowed through the shower curtain. I grabbed for the shower curtain, but it was too late. The curtain rod whipped full speed onto the top of my head.

"Shell?" I asked, pressing my palms on the ground. I folded my neck against the side of the shower, shifted my weight into my palms, locked my legs against the side of the bathtub, and slowly pulled my weight to my feet.

Shelly stepped in the bathroom, but the stranger stepped in front of the entranceway. The stranger spread across the entrance like a parking garage boom gate barrier. She cut Shelly off quick, causing her to almost trip backward, which could've resulted in Shelly cracking her head against the hallway wall. From my bathtub view, I felt my stomach drop when Shelly's heels tipped backward. It was like watching someone flip a car in reverse and roll over the spikes during a rental car return.

"Who're you?" The girl slurred her words and stretched her arms out between the doorway. She was gripping both sides of the door like a human roadblock.

"I'm Shelly. What's going on in here?"

"You should leave. We don't know you." She glared at Shelly.

"What? We? Is this a joke?" Shelly lowered herself to make eye contact with me.

"I got up to pee, was too tired to turn the light on, and thought she was you," I said.

"Bullshit," the girl said as she stepped under the light. She had mascara smeared under her eyes and was standing in a tank top and men's shorts. "You said you wanted us to be in a relationship just a couple hours ago. Yer a liar." The brunette stranger slapped me hard in the face and stumbled back to the doorway.

"Don't you hit him like that." Shelly stepped through the doorway and glared at her. "Yer clearly wasted—can't even stand on two feet. Then you slapped my boyfriend of six years." Shelly clenched her teeth. "William, what's going on? Who is she? Should I call the polic—"

"Girlfriend? Yer a liar." The girl turned and slapped me again. "You said you wanted me to be yer girlfriend—said you've *never* met anyone like me." She grabbed a wad of toilet paper and burst into tears. "Almost had me fooled, *Jason*." The girl brushed past Shelly, stomping across the empty beer cans as she staggered toward the door.

"No, no, no. Wait, that's *not* Jase," Shelly chased after the girl. "That's his twin brother." Shelly ran into the side of the misplaced couch and tumbled to the ground. "This is Jason's brother, Will. We've been out of town, taking care of my sick mum." Shelly peeled herself from a layer of beer on the ground. "Please don't go. Jase and Will—they're identical twins, an easy mistake. Known them since we were kids."

I stood up and wobbled out of the bathroom entrance. "She's right, and I can prove it. Give me a minu—"

"What's going on?" Jason said, staggering down the hallway. He scratched his head. "Yer back. Thought you'd be at Shell's till tomorrow. This is Amy." Jason's expression dropped as soon as he saw Amy's hand on the doorknob.

"Oh my God. Is this some sick joke?" Amy released the doorknob and turned to face Jase and me.

"No, this is my brother—"

"It's like you've been cloned," Amy interrupted Jason.

"This is my brother, William. I said my brother was out of town with his girl—"

"I just groped your brother and kissed him."

"What?" Jason glared at me.

"Not the way yer thinking," I said, looking at Shelly.

"Shell?" Jase turned to Shelly.

"What?" Shelly yawned.

"Wasn't prepared for this. *Not* prepared for this. Identical twins—I can't even tell you two apart. It's freaky," Amy blurted.

"They're easy to tell apart, trust me. It's five in the morning. Let's sleep a few hours, and you can meet us after the booze wears off and we're not standing in a dark room." Shelly gestured for Amy to come in and stay. "Judging by the way you guys decorated the living room earlier—which is nice, fine by me—I think you guys should try to sober up."

Amy released the doorknob and walked toward Jase.

"We can all laugh at this tomorro—"

"Goodbye, whichever one of you is Jason."

"Uh, that's easy. I haven't moved from the spot I've been standing in," I said dryly.

"William," Shelly snapped.

Amy grabbed her purse and phone. "Can't find where I put my shoes."

"Please stay," Jason pleaded.

"Fine. Just find my shoes," Amy said.

Jase walked down the hallway toward his room. Amy rolled her eyes at Shelly and me, then took off shoeless out the door.

"Where's Amy." Jason stopped behind us, holding a pile of Amy's belongings. From our silence, he knew she took off.

The three of us stared at each other for a minute and didn't say a word, because we all knew exactly what had happened. We watched Jason fumble around the flat for his shoes and jacket. He threw her stuff in a shopping bag he peeled off the sticky ground and took off after her. That was the last time he ever saw Amy.

I finished my whiskey and set the glass in the sink. "Ethan and Sarah will be over soon."

"Please don't bring up the Amy stuff to Ethan and Sarah." Jason held his hand out for his phone.

"We won't, but Shelly has a point. The Amy thing maybe gave you a complex. You took what she said in a drunken state to heart."

"No, I didn't."

"You didn't date anyone the rest of uni after that," I said.

"Aye, right. Can we move on to something else now?" Jason's phone lit up. "She's calling. Be right back." Jason grabbed the phone from Shelly and took off out the front door.

Jason came back in a half hour later. Ethan and Sarah were on their second glass of wine, waiting for us at the table. Shelly, Jase, and I sat down, and I passed around a tray filled with vegetables and stuffed mushrooms.

"These are the small bites before we begin wine pairings and the appetizer course," I said.

"Oh, yer getting fancy on us. Trying to pull some magic?" Sarah reached for a stuffed mushroom.

"Five-course-dinner fancy," I said.

"And wine pairings. I'll be walking around with yer menus shortly." Shelly stood up and poured a round of wine, then pranced out of the kitchen.

"They're hoping to tie us by getting us drunk off wine and going over the top." Sarah turned to Ethan.

"Aye, but Jase won't be fooled by the menus and distractions. He knows to focus on the taste of the food. Right, Jaso—"

"No mind games," I interrupted Ethan. "We're tying the cook-off tonight because our cooking's that good." I leaned over the table and squinted my eyes at Sarah, Ethan, and Jase. I displayed my best game face. The intimidating yet charming gourmet chef face.

"Doesn't he look like a pirate when he makes that face?' Sarah laughed.

"A constipated one," Jase agreed.

"Vey constipated." Ethan sipped his wine.

I opened my eyes as wide as I could and tilted my head to one side. I flashed my backup game face—the "I'm going to win this challenge" face.

"Whoa. Weird." Sarah turned to Jase and Ethan.

"Doesn't it look like he—"

"Shit his pants?" Ethan interrupted Jase.

"Was about to say that." Sarah chuckled.

"Hopefully whatever he ate isn't in our five-course meal." Ethan chuckled.

Shelly walked in the room with a new bottle of wine and menus. Harley pranced into the room behind her. She took one look at me and took a few steps back, almost tripping backward over the dog. "If yer gonna puke, aim for the floor. That's my grandma's good tablecloth, William."

"You serious right now." I relaxed my face and glared at Shelly.

"Oh, good, thought the whiskey made you sick. I'm buzzed from it," Shelly said as she laid the next bottle of wine on the table.

"Yer all a bunch of asses." I grabbed the bottle and poured myself the first glass. Harley curled up at my feet. "See? Harley knows yer all picking on me."

"Cheers, everyone." She held her glass up and smiled.

We held our glasses in the air. Everyone took a sip of their drink but me. I watched my beautiful wife sip her glass of wine. She was so excited about cooking the five-course meal and couldn't drop her smile as she drank her wine. Her red lipstick stained the rim of her glass, and her blond curls bounced as she sat back in her seat.

Shelly grabbed the bottle of wine and started pouring everyone a sample. She was wearing a devilish grin, different from her cute little toast, as she carefully poured each glass. I looked around the table to see if anyone else noticed her sneer. An innocent bystander would think she was either passing around winning scratch-off tickets or getting ready to jump up and scare one of us. She normally slouched a little at the table, but her torso was stretched upright, several inches higher than usual. The only other time she'd perk upright like that at the table was when she's about to win in cards. That's how I always knew when to fold in blackjack.

I adjusted my posture on the chair and noticed Shelly biting her lip as she set the bottle of wine on the table. She grabbed her glass of wine and held it between two hands, cupping the top like she was reading a magic eight ball. I knew how to read this face, as I'd seen it many times before. Shelly was getting ready to pounce, hiding her intentions behind that mischievous grin. She held back by biting her lip. She had something to say but was biting her tongue, and she was very good at that. By the constant wine and peppy little toast, I knew my wife was schmoozing and guiding us to our comfort zones in order to nonchalantly throw one of us on the hot seat. I'd been her sous chef since noon, so it couldn't possibly be me.

"So, ah, Jason." Shelly stared at Jase.

Oh, good, it's not me. I thought I'd test her next move to make sure I was completely out of the hot seat, so I stood up to use the bathroom. Harley jumped on all fours, ready to follow.

"Sit, William," Shelly demanded.

Harley and I sat down at the same time.

"Good boy, Harley," Jason said.

"And there's it is." Ethan extended his arm out toward Shelly. "We've finally pinpointed Harley's alpha."

"And Will's," Jason snarled.

"Let me start again." Shelly gulped her wine. "Jase, didn't you say today you were driving two hours to pick up your new washer?"

"Aye." Jason chomped on a carrot stick.

"How's it working?" she asked.

"What?" Jason grabbed the two appetizer plates and started picking at them.

"Yer new washer. How's it working?" Shelly sipped her wine.

"Good." Jason focused his attention on the food.

I raised an eyebrow at Ethan and Sarah from across the table. I stared at the two of them as they chomped away at celery sticks and watched Shelly's randomness. I twitched my arm, grabbing Ethan and Sarah's attention. They slowed down their chewing.

"So the washer's good?" Shelly asked.

"Aye, good," Jason said.

"That's good." Shelly placed her wineglass in front of her, then pressed her elbows against the table and leaned forward.

"You sure it's good?" Ethan asked dryly. He jumped from Sarah kicking him under the table.

"It's good," Jason confirmed.

"Good." Shelly sipped her wine. "I've also noticed yer teeth—so white. Smile really quick."

Jason lowered his carrot and grinned for a second.

"Great smile," Shelly said.

"*Good* smile." Ethan leaned back in his chair and crossed his arms. "This is about to get interesting," he whispered to Sarah.

"Thanks?" Jason turned to me.

"Now, William, you smile," Shelly insisted.

Oh no, she called me William. I feared I knew where the conversation was leading. I smiled and made eye contact with Jase.

"Wouldn't you guys say Jason's teeth are much whiter than Will's teeth?" Shelly looked at me, then followed Jason's eyes back to his plate.

"Jase's teeth are pretty white," Ethan agreed.

"Pretty white," Sarah echoed Ethan.

"Should I buy some whitening strips?" I asked.

"So today I thought I'd surprise William—"

"William? Shelly's full-named you more in the last five minutes than the time you got drunk at uni and puked on her flatmate's cat," Ethan said.

"Let her talk." Sarah swatted at Ethan's arm.

"So, earlier today, I ran some errands. Bought groceries for tonight and thought I'd surprise my lovely husband with the watch he's been gawking at for years." Shelly sipped her wine. "I bought the watch used for half the price, and since I was down the street from his dentist appointment—"

"Shit." I stared at my brother.

"Not sure where this is going, but they're both slumping in their seats." Ethan clapped his hands.

"Ethan, muzzle," Sarah scolded.

"Muzzle it," Shelly reiterated.

"I had the watch gift wrapped and waited for him to walk out of his appointment so I could surprise him." Shelly looked over at me. "I make him go to the dentist and know how much he hates it, so I wanted to do something nice."

"He's not wearing a watch, so what did these two idiots do?" Ethan asked.

"Jase? Will? Got *anything* to say?" Shelly asked.

I looked at Jase and read him within seconds. *We're not getting out of this one. Shit.*

Jase looked back at shelly and shrugged.

That's right; just keep quiet.

"So I pulled up to the dentist's office and saw Jason strutting down the sidewalk carrying a bag overflowing with toothbrushes and other dentist swag." Shelly stared at me, waiting for a reaction. "Have anything to say about this?"

"Me? I, er, uh."

"Did you go to yer dentist appointment?" Shelly asked.

I tried to skim passed Shelly's eyes, but it was too late. She lured me in with her intimidating gaze. I didn't know how to answer. There was no point in lying. My palms felt sweaty as I sat in silence. I froze.

"Will always hated the dentist." Ethan broke the awkward silence.

"Will, say something." Shelly got up and walked to one of the dining-room cabinet's and grabbed a small box with a bow. She laid the box in the middle of the table.

"You really found that watch?" I changed the subject.

Shelly ignored me and looked at Jason. "Jase?"

"Huh?"

"Did you go to your brother's dentist appointment?" Shelly pried.

I noticed Ethan's face was turning bright red. He bit down on his lips and tipped his head at an angle so he could release laughter into his sleeve. He looked once at me and Jase and stopped eye contact altogether. Sarah pulled her sweater over her face and stopped watching. I could hear her giggling from inside her sweater.

"How far away were you?" I asked.

"William, I know the difference between you and yer brother, even from afar. I thought maybe you were still inside, so I called you. You said you were done early and were with Jase unloading the new washer at his place."

I was busted.

"This brings me to my next question: How long has Jason been going to your dentist appointments?" Shelly looked in my eyes without blinking once.

I turned to my brother.

"No, don't look at Jason. You keep yer eyes right here."

I stared at Shelly's smirk.

"This is awesome." Ethan poured himself more wine.

I understood why she was so eager to sit us down at the table.

"How long has he been going to yer dentist appointments?" Shelly asked.

"Yer teeth do look better than Wil—"

"Ethan, cut it," Sarah intervened.

"Five years or so—maybe six," I admitted.

"I like the dentist." Jason smiled.

Ethan chuckled and spit the end of a carrot on the table. We watched the carrot roll to the middle of the table and broke into laughter. He turned to Sarah. "I'm thinking about how my breath would be without seeing the dentist for six years."

Sarah was midsip with her wine and snorted so hard that red wine came back up and spewed from her nostrils.

Shelly took one look at Sarah and burst into laughter. Jason and I watched the three of them crack up, and Ethan fell off his chair, causing us to join the contagious laughter.

"I'm gonna pee my pants. You guys are so weird." Sarah threw her napkin in the air and took off running to the bathroom.

We watched Sarah scamper to the bathroom and noticed her pants were darker in some areas. Sarah peed her pants.

CHAPTER 8

I laugh and sip my drink. I look around the Black Chandelier to make sure I don't look like the crazy man at the other end of the bar, unable to control his emotions. I make eye contact with the bartender.

"Another round?" the bartender asks.

"Yeah, but make it two doubles on the rocks. I have a friend joining me."

"Sure thing."

A woman walks in. She's wearing all black and a hat that's covering her face. She struts past me and toward the back of the establishment. Her gait is full of purpose as she moves quickly. The bartender grabs a menu and walks around the bar as she slides into a booth with her back toward me. Antisocial. Totally fine. I don't consider myself much of a conversationalist.

A truck pulls up in front of the bar and backs into a parking spot. It's Ethan's truck. I bet he already left the work site and was halfway home when he called me. He hops out of the truck and whips the door shut.

I see his face through the dirty bar windows. The well-dressed, clean-cut look he had going for him earlier has changed. His hair looks like someone threw him in a headlock and ruffled his head. His shirt's untucked, and his jacket is inside out. *What the hell happened to this guy?* He looks like he got on a roller coaster and rode it backward eight times in a row, then spent another fifteen minutes riding the spinning teacup.

Ethan leans over and stares at himself through the passenger-side mirror. He uses his fingers to comb through his mangled head of hair. His dark hair looks like distorted crow feathers, and combing it is only making him look more like a crow that's been chewed up and spit out by a predator.

He storms into the bar. I point at his drink and slide out the barstool next to me. His dark complexion cannot hide the redness underneath his eyes. He's been crying.

"You okay? Sit down and have a drink with me." I watch him pull off his jacket. He carelessly tugs his arms from both sleeves, causing his jacket to switch back to right side in. I guess his ride from my house earlier stirred up some emotions about Jase. Must've kept himself composed for me, then lost it on his way in.

Ethan plops on the stool and grabs his glass. "Thanks."

"I was watching a commercial before you got here—a dental commercial." I sip my drink.

"Aye?" Ethan takes the straw from his glass and lays it on the napkin.

"It made me think of last year. The last dinner we had with Jase. Remember?"

"The dinner my wife peed her pants laughing so hard?"

"Aye."

"She made it halfway to the bathroom and collapsed on the ground. I would've made her sit on newspaper the drive home had she not squeezed in Shelly's pants."

"Was that last time we're all together, before he—"

"No shit." Ethan sips his drink. "Can't imagine the shit you two pulled off."

"Got you a few times."

"Me?"

"We got Carmen. At work. You went on vacation."

"Tell."

"Jase and I switched hats a few times. I wanted to try the new machines."

"Jist stop there. Don't need to know the stuff that could've cost me my business."

"Yer right."

"Since you can no longer pull that crap, what happened?"

"Was easy. Carmen didn't notice one of us had stubble on his face, and the other didn't. Simple. The machine ran great. Good edition."

"Took me almost a lifetime to tell you two apart."

"How'd you tell?"

"Jase thought before he spoke, and you'd speak without thinking."

"That so?"

"You two could have the same haircut and look head-to-toe identical, but as soon I'd ask you both a question, I'd know immediately. Being an only child would've been hard if I didn't have the two of you as brothers."

"Here's my speech." I slap it in front of him and stand up. "Gonna pee." I flag the bartender for another round and see Ethan decline from the corner of my eyes.

"Jist a water. I'm driving." Ethan's voice trails off as he reads my speech.

I walk behind the woman in black as I stroll to the bathroom. She's drinking water and staring at a paint-splattered canvas nailed in front of her. I slow my stride behind her and give the painting a look. It's an ugly painting. No wonder she's sitting in a dark corner contemplating the disaster she considers art.

The woman tilts her head my direction. *Did I say all that out loud?* She's staring at me from the corner of her eye. I pick up the pace and jam my back into the men's bathroom door. When I walk out of the bathroom, she's gone. She must've heard all that.

"I'll have one more." I make eye contact with the bartender and sit down next to Ethan.

"Yer speech—"

"See that weird woman?" I interrupt.

"Nah, but yer speech was well written." Ethan sips his water. "Should slow down on the whiskey so yer able to say it right."

"There's something I've been wanting to tell you from that day, when Jase died."

"What's that?"

"Someone was standing next to him." I grab the drink from the bartender's hand and inhale it.

"What?"

"I saw someone standing next to him—Jase—when he died."

"What're you saying?" Ethan turns on his stool so he's facing me.

"Nah, never mind." I take another long sip.

"Slow down. What'd you say just now?"

"Nah, nothing. You won't believe me."

"You told the police—"

"Aye, saw the line snap."

"The hell ye rambling on about, eh?"

"There was a man"

"Man?"

"Standing next to him. He was dressed in black, wearing a hood over his head."

Ethan slides his water in front of me.

"I couldn't see his face." I push the water away.

"Yer not making sense."

"I couldn't make sense of it. The guy was a lot taller than him—we're taller than the average man too." I sip my whiskey. "He was standing behind him in the background and took off. He was there, then he was gone."

"We have security clearance when we're working on those projects. You know that. There's cameras—"

"I know. I think I made it up in my mind."

"They tested the line. He wasn't the first case with a wire snap. Yer drunk and want something to blame."

"I've seen these figures since. They wear black and have red eyes. I see 'em in the dark."

"William, you sound insane."

"I know how it sounds. Wanted to let you know, in case."

"In case what?"

"Something happens to me."

"Nothing's going to happen to you. You're yer own worst enemy. You know that, right?"

"Aye."

"Yer a bad drunk, Will. Sometimes I feel I've lost you both." Ethan waves at the bartender and hands him his card. "It's on me."

"Thanks."

"Let me drive you home."

"Nah, going to grab a bite and practice my speech some more. I'll see you there."

"Fine. Big night tonight, so make sure you honor Jase by staying sober." Ethan signs the bill and lays money with the receipt. "I know it was hard for you to write that out, but it was well written. Just read it off the napkin like that."

"I will." I stand up and hug Ethan. "See you in a few hours."

"Call me if you need anything." Ethan zips up his jacket and turns toward the door.

I watch Ethan leave the bar and slide back in his truck. I lean over and see him peel out of his parking space and down the street. The bartender takes Ethan's empty glass.

"I'll take a Carling."

CHAPTER 9

I look at my phone. Three hours until the event. I'm not ready to give a speech, and I'm uncertain whether I'd ever be ready to talk about my dead brother. My phone shows I have eight messages from Ethan and one from Shelly. *Get off my back, you two.* I open Shelly's text. It's been a month since I've heard from her.

> *Shelly: Good luck tonight and stay strong. Ye got this ... Yer stronger than ye think!*
> *Me: K Thanks.*
> *Me: Going tonight?*
> *Shelly: ... typing ...*

I stare at the screen. *What's that woman going to say next?* What more could she possibly say to me. This is the longest Shelly and I have gone without seeing or speaking to each other since we were kids. I really wanted to look nice the next time I saw her. Maybe if I had a nice haircut, groomed my beard, and worked out some, she'd look at me and wish she didn't leave. My phone lights up.

> *Shelly: Of course I'll be there.*

I grab my phone and search through train times from Central Station to Edinburgh. "One more, and I'll pay for the last two drinks," I call out to the bartender, laying a wad of cash on the bar.

The bartender swaps my empty glass with a new one. I wait for him to step out from behind the bar and pour the drink in my flask, ignoring the stares from people sitting at the other end of the bar. If one of those guys says something, I'll knock them out.

The cold air wafts up my coat sleeves as I thrust open the door of the bar. I turn around to thank the bartender one last time and stop. The whiskey went right to my head as the black chandeliers hanging over the bar now look like a jagged blur. The black candlesticks of each fixture now look like oval racks of spray-painted antlers dangling from the ceiling.

I stroll to the end of the sidewalk and turn a corner. People are bundled in their winter's warmest as they scurry in and out of the little stores on Gordon Street. Parts of the charcoal-colored sidewalk look glossy from ice patches. I walk to an intersection and wait for the light to change. The cars are moving too fast for me to dart across the street. I feel as though I'm walking 30 percent slower than my normal stride, while everything else that crosses my periphery is moving in overdrive. Eating something should've been a priority before I drowned my liver in whiskey.

The light changes, and I try not to look down at the marbled-colored bricks while I cross the street. The colorful brick that make up the street between the two sidewalks are aligned perfectly and run parallel with the direction I'm walking. I'm trying to walk in a straight line across the brick as though I'm crossing a balance beam, but I can't. The whiskey has ahold of me. People pass me in both directions, and they stride with purpose. They look powerful, energetic, and happy. Each person looks well rested as they strut across the street. I'm envious.

Looking up, I devour the structure of each building, valuing the integrity within each design. The nineteenth-century Victorian architecture permeates throughout the city, and so does the preservation of the red-and-blond sandstone. To go back in time and construct without the enhanced technology I've got available with the touch of a button would be incredible.

Each of the buildings lining Gordon Street are close in height, varying between five to seven floors. The large windows in each building are symmetrical and utilize the space well. Their earthy tones of apple-cider blond and macadamia contrast well with the smoggy gray of the afternoon sky. I veer down an alley and make sure I'm alone. The buildings block the chilly breeze that's spilling into the narrow alley. I untwist the top of my flask and take a huge swig—needed a break.

I pop my head out from the alley, look around, and slide back on the sidewalk. I look down at my feet. My feet are too tight for my shoes. They're overly snug inside each black pleather boot, and one foot feels as though it developed its own pulse along the bottom arch. I should've dedicated a few extra minutes to locating my favorite shoes.

A woman in a licorice-red peacoat, texting on her phone, clips me on the shoulder as she scurries by. She turns and shakes her head at me as though I should've made way for her grand appearance. *I'm so sorry, Your Highness. Next time I see you coming from afar, I'll be sure to roll out that fancy red carpet to match your ugly coat.* She turns to put her phone in her purse, and I see a sparkle from her matching red earrings.

Ruby red like the cab lady. My heart beats faster, and I feel myself driving over bumps as I look out the dark window of her cab. I see flashes of trees, a hooded figure, and red eyes. The red eyes are locked in with mine. I'm looking up because the owner of the devilish eyes is abnormally tall. I can't run, because it's too late. My heart beats faster, and I hear a thud, like a piece of plywood snapping in half as it's cracked at high speed against cement. My head burns, and everything goes dark. I shake my head, trying to rid the horrific glimpse, and feel a throb. I rub around the back of my head and feel the lump. It's fresh; it's sensitive to touch. No, that didn't happen—was a drunken nightmare from an awful night's sleep. I search around for a bench.

Controlling the dizzy spell with deep breaths, I see a bench by a bus stop on the other side of the street. I massage my head and jog across the one-way multicolored lane. The colorful bricks amplify the dizziness as I pace over them diagonally. A bus driver lays on the horn and slams on his brakes as I cut him off. People turn and stare at me from the sidewalk. I slide onto the bench as a police officer walks out from an alley. He stares at the bus and looks around. I wait for the police officer to vanish back into the alleyway, then take a quick swig from my flask. The wind soothes me as I cross my arms and lean back against the bench. I close my eyes and think of something positive. I see Shelly's uplifting smile. Her perfect teeth and bright lipstick. Her contagious smile and inviting eyes could flip the frown of the Grinch himself.

"Look—buuus, Mum."

I hear a child's voice.

"Sit on Mum's lap. Bus is coming soon," says the boy's mother.

I keep my eyes closed and pretend I'm sleeping. Too buzzed for side conversations. Shelly and I were trying to have a baby this time last year. I really wanted a baby. I would've been a great dad.

"*Beee. U. Sssss.* Bus," the little boy says.

"That's right, mate."

"I gotta go potty, Mum. Can I potty on the bus?"

"Right this second?" the woman asks her son. "We have a very short bus ride. Can you hold it?"

"Aye. *Beee. U. Sssss.* Ride," the child confirms. "Mum?"

"What?"

"What's wrong with that man?"

"Charlie, whisper. Don't point—it's rude," the woman says softly. Her phone rings. "Hey, we're almost on the bus. What? Yeah, let me get that from my purse." I hear the woman fumbling around in her purse. "Hang on. Charlie, sit and be patient." I hear the woman stand up and shuffle through her bag.

I feel a poke on my shoulder. "You dead, mister?" the child whispers at me.

I ignore him and keep my eyes closed.

He pokes me harder. "Wake up."

I peel open my eyes, sit up, and smile at the little boy. I adjust my jacket and see my flask fall in front of the bench. The little boy slips to the ground and picks up my flask. He waves it at me. The boy's act of kindness grabs his mother's attention, causing her to yank the flask from his hand.

She slams the flask down next to me on the bench. "Come on, Charlie."

"Bus. What about bus?" the boy groans.

"We're finding that bathroom, and yer gonna wash yer hands," she says, hanging up the phone to pick up her child. She walks away with him in her arms. "That man's drunk. That's what unhappy people do to numb themselves and not face reality, like yer uncle Peter." Her voice trails off.

I want to follow her down the sidewalk and tell her that I'm not a drunk, and she shouldn't judge people. I'm just a man who got tired and was taking a nap at the bus stop. But I must convince myself first. The truth is, I'm miserable, and I don't like the reality I'm living in. I just want to drink. I open my flask and take a long guzzle. This is what makes me happy right now.

The cold is numbing my face. It's hard to wiggle my nose. Opening my mouth feels like I'm stretching a rubber band, which means it's due to the cold and not a whiskey infliction. I stretch myself upright from the bench and see Central Station across the street and one block over. Spotting the same police officer walking down the sidewalk, I stroll to the end of the street and cross at the light like everyone else.

The sun gleams through the cracks of the wavy clouds. The clouds look like fluffy mashed potatoes pulling away like curtains on a stage. I love how the sun reflects off the gold accents as I walk up to the train station entrance. The hunter-green pillars naturally guide the onlookers view up, so they'll notice the matching green glass-walled overpass with the massive white-trimmed windows that bridge across the green. I watch the cars drive down Argyle Street and vanish as they drive under the golden Central Station sign draped across the green overpass.

I walk in place and try to loosen the death grip on both of my feet. I'm early enough to ensure a roomy seat to kick my feet up. I wait for a group of women to pass and stroll in the station behind them.

It's bright inside the station. The sun sliver lingers through the glass of the longitudinal ridge and furrowed roof, intensifying the natural lighting as it highlights bits of the blond sandstone structure of Central Station. Each rafter crisscrosses underneath the glass-paneled roof, adding a unique touch to this location.

I teeter to one side of the entrance and lean against an acorn-brown wooden wall bordering the entranceway. No one's looking, so I grab my flask and swig. The beginning of a piano tune vibrates throughout the busy building as people hustle in and out of Central Station. The first wave of workers—the lucky people who get to leave their jobs hours earlier than the rest of us—are calling it a day.

A bright echo from the piano evolves into a mellow tune. I shuffle through the crowd toward the pianist. He jolts side to side as he expresses himself through the sounds of the keys. I scuttle onto an electric-green mat with enlarged letters spelling "Piano Garden" spread along the bottom. The pianist leans forward and closes his eyes, moving to the pace of his song. I inch in closer to get a better look—best view can only be over his shoulder. Standing on the tips of my toes, I line my feet up to the back of the stool and lean over the musician's shoulder. He makes it look simple. I hold my hand out in front of me and pretend to follow along. The pianist leans in and thrusts himself backward, plowing into my belly. He jumps up from the stool and backs into the piano. The music abruptly stops, followed by random key pounds. Everyone walking by the piano in the station slows down and stares.

"Sorry. Sorry 'bout that." I see two police officers walking toward the piano. "Yer very good." I grab his hand and shake it as though he were an acquaintance I hadn't seen in a while. "Nice seeing you again." I wave nonchalantly at the pianist and nod to the officers as I walk over to tickets.

My phone rings. It's Ethan. I send him to voicemail. I'm still pissed that Ethan's talking to Shelly—my Shelly.

Ethan: Where r u?
Me: At central.
Me: Talking rain.
Me: *Taking train to Ethiopia.
Ethan: ???
Me: El Salvador.
Ethan: Yer drunk. I can pick u up.
Me: *Edinburgh.
Me: Buying train ticket now.
Me: I'm fine.
Ethan: K.
Ethan: See u there.

I buy a ticket and make my way toward the train. I'm early but see others already boarding the train to Edinburgh from up ahead. I pat at my flask to make sure it's hidden from any police patrolling around the train boarding and speed walk toward a train door. There are people everywhere moving around at differing paces, and trying to watch them all is making me feel dizzy. I slow my stroll as I realize the whiskey's making me walk at a diagonal. A woman stands in front of me and the entrance to the train. She's looking down at her phone and won't move out of my way. I attempt to squeeze around her, but she starts coughing without covering her mouth. Holding my arm over my face, I back away from the distracted woman and follow behind her selfish strides.

I plop down on a seat. I'm not too close to the exit of the train where I won't have to deal with people leaning into me, and I'm just past the bathroom in case someone decides to selfishly take a shit and smell up the small communal space—it's flu season after all. I'd squeeze my butt cheeks together the entire time, no matter how bad my stomach hurt, and save a train car filled with people from having to express their feelings directly on social media through pictures and videos.

The only person sharing the cart with me is a man facing the other direction with his head tipped down. His hair looks like someone took a comb and swiped it up as they held a blow-dryer to the ends of his hair. They then completed the look by using a hair spray bottle filled with superglue to dowse the top half. I turn and look at my reflection in the train window. I'm not sure why I'm judging a man I don't know—look at me. The face I see looking back at me in the window looks like a burly slob of a man he once was.

The man ahead of me looks to be falling asleep in his seat, so I pull my jacket up as a shield and down the rest of the whiskey in my flask. I feel that last gulp infecting my mind. My face feels feverish, and there's a sucking feeling behind my eye sockets.

A woman boards the train and sits down in the middle of our car. Her blond curls bounce off her shoulders as she sits down with her back facing me. *Shell?*

I lay my ticket out and close my eyes. My head feels heavy, like someone duct taped a brick to one side of my head. I nestle my head against the window. My body needs rest.

"Will, you awake?" Shelly knocked on the bedroom door.

"Huh? What? Come in," I said.

"You did it again—last night." Shelly walked in the room.

"What'd I do?" I reached for Shelly's arm, and she pulled it away from me.

"Drank to much and backed my car through the garage door."

"Shell, I wouldn't do th—"

"But you did." Shelly sat on the bed next to me. Harley rolled onto his back so she'd pet him. "You did—right after you screamed about the red eyes you said were watching you through the window—blamed the red-eyed people for Jase's death."

"Don't remember any of this. I'd never do that."

"If yer too drunk to remember anything, then I guess it never happened, right?" Shelly hugged Harley.

"I honestly don't know what yer talking about."

"You'll see the garage door and my car—my car may need a tow truck. Called Ethan—he's on his way over to help you."

"Help me with what? What? Lemme wake up a minute." I sat up in bed.

"You had yer license taken away last month for drunk driving. Why would you fight with me for my car?"

"I dunno."

"Ethan should be here soon. My mum's waiting outside."

"Tell Mum to come in. Why's Una waiting outside?" I asked.

"Yer not healthy to be around right now. I'm going to go home for a while—"

"What's going on? Why're you talking pish?" I jumped out of bed.

"William."

"What? Why'd you call me William?" I searched around the room for my pants.

"This is hard for me," Shelly said.

"What's hard? Why're you talking like this, Shell?"

Shelly looked numb. The whites of her eyes were red, and her mascara looked as though she stepped under a shower and then rubbed her eyes. "When I come home in a few weeks—months, however long it takes you—I don't want you to be here."

"You being serious?" I felt like throwing up.

"Yer so much worse since the family meeting, and you'll never understand why unless you get sober." Shelly wouldn't look me in the eyes. "Ethan and I were the only two who didn't follow through with the plan the day of the intervention. I regret that now, and I understand it now."

"They were making something out of nothing." I rolled my eyes.

"Yer family was showing tough love, and now I am too." Shelly took a deep breath.

"Shell? Tell Mum to come in. Let's make a cup of coffee and talk this thing through," I pleaded.

"I had a miscarriage." Shelly teared up.

"What?" I walked toward Shelly.

"Three weeks ago."

"Why didn't you tell me?"

"You haven't been sober." Shelly looked at the ground. "Had a late miscarriage. Doctor said it's rare, but it happens."

I watched Shelly wrap her arms around her stomach and wanted to hold her so bad, but she backed away.

"I'm leaving. It's time I take care of myself for a bit—you should too. I feel the pain of loss, and I'm not going to go running to alcohol for a solution."

"Wait." I follow Shelly out of the bedroom. "You can't leave—I'll stop drinking." I wanted to grab her and hold her back.

Shelly walked down the staircase without looking back. "When yer sober, we'll talk. I can't stand to see you like this anymore—I'm too stressed."

"Please don't do this."

Shelly's phone rang. She looked at her phone and continued down the stairs. "Ethan's pulling up."

"Shelly, wait. Please tell yer mum to come in." Still drunk from the night before, I almost tripped to the bottom of the stairs. My heart dropped in my stomach, watching her open the door. "Don't you love me?"

"I do. But Ethan and I should've listened to yer parents." Shelly walked out the door. "Goodbye, Will."

"Don't you have to pack a bag?" I searched for any reason for her to come back.

"No, packed my bags two weeks ago. Mum and Dad picked everything up while you were at work. I'm letting Harley stay with you, but if Ethan says he needs to go with me—well, then, he's coming with me."

A loud bang causes me to jolt in my seat. I open my eyes to a train full of strangers. When the hell did we start moving?

CHAPTER 10

It's warm inside the train. My hands are clammy, and I feel sweat bursting through the pores above my upper lip. If my facial hair didn't soak up the moisture permeating through my skin, I'd have to keep wiping my face. The beard's been great—a continuous sweat rag for times such as these. I lift my head from the window. There's a kink in my neck that feels like someone tied a leash to my throat and yanked at it while the whiskey waterboarded me with nightmares.

I rub my head and try to rid the awful memory of Shelly giving up on me. Mr. Whiskey, which I consider a dear friend of mine, rebelled today—tried to blister my mind by implanting painful memories of Shelly. *Yer supposed to be helping me, not turning on me like Ethan.*

Anxious. I'm feeling anxious. I turn my head and look at the person sitting next to me. I pull back as I lock eyes with an older woman wearing a red shawl over her face. I almost smacked my nose into her face. *How long has this woman been watching me sleep?* I smile and look forward. I force my eyes in her direction. She's still giving me the stare down. *Keep staring, weirdo.*

The man in front of me is picking at his nose, and the woman sitting next to him is asleep. She leans on his shoulder for pillow support, but he props his arm up to keep her on the side of the bench she paid for. He turns and scoots against the window so she'll fall onto his lap the next time she drops her head for a stranger's support.

Sitting in front of the nosepicker is a man reading the newspaper. The woman beside him is holding up a mirror and tweezing her eyebrows. Between yanking at hairs, she looks around the train to make sure no one's watching and plucks whiskers from her chin. *I saw that. You didn't think I was watching, but I saw you.*

Just in front of the bearded woman is a man dressed in a suit. He's expressionless but widens his eyes every time the two high-pitched teenage girls sitting across from him receive a text. The man is biting down on his lip and sits up as though he's going to tell them to shut the hell up.

Avoiding another awkward stare from my neighbor, I look out the window. The snow's growing denser the farther we migrate away from Glasgow. The sun's almost down, but I'm able to see lines of evergreen trees covered in untouched snow as we breeze by. We turn under a bridge, and I feel the train accelerate from the pit of my stomach. I see snow flurries swiping against the window as the sun dissolves into the ground. The darkness from outside causes the windows of the train to resemble mirrors. I lean back in my seat and notice the woman next to me is staring at me through the window reflection. If there were such thing as a hair magnet, she'd be the inventor. Her stare alone causes every hair to rise on the back of my neck. *Good for you. Keep staring—unleash the hidden talent.*

I hear a monotone voice listing off destinations from over the loudspeaker. *It's my stop.* "Excuse me." I wait for the women to stand up so I can get off the train. She looks up at me. I stretch a leg over her lap, feeling a sharp pain in my groin. I lift the other leg, praying she doesn't interfere with my manhood while I'm vulnerable.

I stagger out from the train and feel the force of two hands clamping firm on my shoulders, forcing me to turn around.

"Wrong stop. Next one." I hear a man's voice.

"Huh?" I try to turn and look at the man, but he guides me by force.

"Waverly's the next stop. This is Haymarket"

I look up and see a sign for Haymarket. "Aye, uh, okay?" I walk back on the train, releasing my shoulders from his death grip, and turn around. The doors close behind me, and everything goes gray—can't see a thing. Pressing my face against the glass I glare out from the window. *Who the hell was that?* I strain my eyes toward the front of the train. Wind coils and brushes a layer of snow under a light post. The snow sparkles like confetti as it spreads across the ground. The man's nowhere in sight. The passengers who've exited the train have already scurried out of the cold.

The train jolts as we depart from Haymarket Station. I stick my face against the window and skim the vicinity as we pull away. *Smack.* Two hands crack against the window and move with the speed of the train. The large pale hands fog up the glass. I stumble onto my back and see two devil-red eyes squinting at me through the window. The red vanishes when it blinks. I have the same feeling, like dropping during a roller-coaster ride. It feels like someone's brushing their finger up my spine with a vacuum, forcing my hairs to rise through each follicle. My stomach barely caught my heart.

I slap a hand over my mouth and throw my body against the opposite door. The impact to my back makes me cough into my hand. I look up and see another set of windows above my head. *No.* My chest is tight from forgetting to breathe. I'm nauseous and feel like I might puke at any second. Rolling on the ground to the center of the two doors, I force my weight to my knees and cup my hands behind my head. *Breathe. Just breathe.* I stand up and slip back inside the train cart.

"Did anyone else see that? Out the window—the glowing eyes?" I choke out.

The passengers turn and stare at me. No one speaks. One woman shakes her head. I can't tell if she's saying no or shaming me. It takes three seconds for everyone else to go back to what they were doing before my bizarre interruption.

I lean against one of the metal poles and turn my back to my audience. Through the window reflection of the train door, I notice one of the passengers—the man in the suit—was gone.

CHAPTER 11

I step off the train and look around. The frigid air burns my skin as it slaps me in the face. I wish I could slap it back and tell it to leave me the hell alone. Backing into the nearest light post, I search for the red eyes and anyone I can point fingers at as the culprit. Everyone passing is bundled in layers and keeps to themselves. Slipping into a crowd of people, I begin the slanted uphill climb.

The lights in front of each bar, restaurant, and shop are welcoming as I walk up the curving road. Each business looks new and remodeled on the inside, even though they're all located inside each of the historical buildings that outline both side of the winding uphill street. Brightly colored awnings, such as tangerine and jungle green, pop as I make my way around the first wind in the road. The slanted walk up Edinburgh's roads helps a person keep warm during this time of year.

When the weather is nice, the sidewalks are filled with outdoor seating for many of the restaurants. Shelly and I use to sit at some of these spots and people watch. Tourists come flocking on and off the busses from the station down the street, and we liked watching visitors' reactions when they walked around the first wind in the road, exposing them to a twisting S curve of old Scotland mixed with the pizazz of nightlife and jaw-dropping views. We loved watching all their faces as they took in the beauty.

Halfway up the next big street curve, I see people laughing while enjoying cocktails at a bar. The bar has a giant fireplace, and a group of people dance and laugh as they hold their drinks in front of the cozy perk in the middle of the establishment. I look at my watch. One drink. I'll still make it in time for the charity opener.

The inside of the bar is toasty, and the low hanging stream of lights draping from the ceiling add to the coziness. Rock music blares in the background as two women awkwardly sway to the sound of a guitar. I sit at the bar and pull my notes from my pocket. I can wing this thing if I must. It's my brother after all.

"What can I get you to drink?" the bartender asks.

"Two shots of yer house whiskey, and I'll be on my way," I say.

I turn and stare at the fireplace. The red eyes—what's happening inside my head? A ghost? The devil?

"Here you go." The bartender lays down the tab.

"The Ibis Hotel—is it close to here?" I ask.

"Two-minute walk."

I look out the window and see Sarah and Shelly scurrying up the hill. They're dressed in layers with their arms locked as they walk by the bar.

"Actually, one more shot. Just saw my ex and her friend pass by." I catch my balance on the stool just as the bartender turns away.

I take the shot, throw money on the bar, and stagger toward the door. The pain in my foot is finally gone. The whiskey did the trick. I make my way to an intersection and spot the hotel to my right. The words on the hotel front are blurry, but if I cover a hand over an eye, I can make out the spelling.

"Watch out," a man yells as I accidentally clip him on the shoulder.

"Whoopsie. You should watch where yer going," I scoff.

"Yer not worth it," the man's voice trails off with the wind.

The hotel is nestled between two buildings, which compliment the almond, mud-brown, and cork-brown colors of the two neighboring buildings. The bright red lights that sit below the main hotel signage have blurry rings that look to be vibrating. The trippy circles appear to be moving away from the lights and up into the air.

I cover my eyes and shake my head, ready to readjust my focus. I look at the building once more and—*eyes?* The lights of the hotel taunt me like the red eyes of my living nightmare. I feel my heart beat faster and look over both shoulders. *Get inside, idiot—they never show up inside lighted places.* I race toward the door and see the sign for the event directing attendees to the main floor restaurant and bar.

I hear the echo of Ethan's voice from over the microphone. It's happening. It's almost my turn. Stepping into the crowd, I see people everywhere. They're all staring intently at the stage. No chatter or side noise, everyone is listening to Ethan talk about—

"Jason was one of my best friends, who fell to his death a year ago today," Ethan says.

No. I cover my ears and look down. *Shut up. Stop it, Ethan.* The room begins to spin, and I feel my heart fluttering too fast for comfort.

"Jason was one of my best friends. He fell to his death a year ago today," Ethan says.

No. I cover my ears and look down. *Shut up. Stop it, Ethan.* The room begins to spin, and I feel my heart fluttering too fast for comfort. Ethan's voice sounds muffled. He sounds like he's humming in a cave.

"William?" I hear a woman's voice swirl with the racket of Ethan's.

"Huh?" I release a hand from an ear.

"You okay?" Shelly looks at me.

"Fine. I'm fine." I let go of my other ear and tune out Ethan's words.

"Hey, Will, how you holding up?" Sarah walks up and stands next to Shelly.

"Fine."

"We know this is a hard night for you," Sarah says, stretching her arms out at me for a hug.

I lean in and let her squeeze me. *Good job, Sarah—just squeeze out any lingering feelings I have left for you and Shelly.*

"Yer gonna do great up there," Shelly says.

"Okay."

Great, so now my ex's poking at me while the other devil woman hugs out my soul. I pull back so Sarah will let go of me.

I avoid making eye contact with Shelly and look over at Ethan. Not sure what's better at this point. If I turn around and talk to these two, I'll regret it. If I listen to Ethan talk about my brother another minute, I might snap. I'd rather scratch my fingers on a chalkboard in freezing temperatures while watching paint dry. I turn and walk away.

"William, where you going?" Shelly asks.

"Bathroom."

I walk toward the main entrance of the hotel and see a man smoking a cigarette. Been a while, but I could use one. I brush open the door and ask him for a cigarette.

The snap of the lighter and the flash of the flame are soothing. I inhale, hoping it will taste as relaxing as it looks. The first drag feels like thumbtacks sliding down my esophagus. I cough into the cold air and watch my breath penetrate upward with the smoke.

"I'll smoke it. Ye shouldn't be smoking if you don't do it already." The man holds out his hand for the cigarette.

I hand the cigarette back to its original owner and walk back inside. I'm going to do what I came here for and get the hell out.

"Ethan just called yer name." Shelly walks behind me.

"Thanks." I brush past her.

"Did you start smoking? You smell like smoke?" Shelly says.

"I love cigarettes, and they love me back." I don't know why I just said that.

"Fine. Good luck, then." Shelly's voice trails off from behind me.

I slither through the crowd and make my way toward the temp stage I had helped Ethan build last week. Ethan looks at me and hisses out air. I know that look. The "where the hell have you been" look. I can't look at him. It's time everyone learned the truth.

Ethan holds the microphone out for me to accept and greets me as I step onto the stage. I lean forward to allow the obvious hug for the audience. He pats my back in comfort. The lights are blinding, and I feel I may have a fever. Everything's moving slow. The claps from the audience sound like a dump truck dropping tennis balls into an empty in-ground pool. The applause is out of sync and annoying, like listening to a crowd of tone-deaf sleepwalkers clapping to a sound only they can hear. Some of the sleepwalkers are listening to EDM as they clap, while the others clap like they're sitting in a room full of kids singing nursery rhymes. It's ear-wrenching. *Stop clapping. That won't bring Jason back.*

I grip the microphone and look around at the people staring at me. The light's blocking my view of the audience. I step in front of the spotlight and stare at the people in the front row. The light shifts and beams over me once more.

"Feel like I'm in a microwave up here." I step away from the blinding light. It follows me again. "Fine, you win."

I hear chuckles. *Go ahead. Drink those fancy drinks and laugh at the loser being forced to talk about his dead brother. This charity's a scam.*

Everyone stops their squawking as I glare around the audience. I've never seen most of these people. Jason didn't know these people.

"My twin brother, Jason—"

I look around and can't find Ethan. Gripping the microphone tightly, I stare at some stranger in the audience and fumble around in my pockets for my speech. The spotlight flickers, obstructing my view of all the other audience members. I whip my arm up and block the harsh glow from above. *Stop the damn light.* I feel alone. *These people don't get what your*

death's done to me. You've ruined me, Jase, but it wasn't your fault. I know.
I know because I saw.

"My brother, Jase—" I feel sweat dripping from my forehead. "Jason's death wasn't an accident. My brother's line was cut. Jason was murdered." I see Ethan sprint toward the DJ and two other men pushing through the audience. "There was a man—tall, dressed in all black. I watched this man slice my brother's—"

Ethan rips the microphone from my hand. He flags for security. *You're flagging security on me?*

"Sorry for the disruption. We're hoping after tonight he finally goes to a rehabilitation center." Ethan ignores me.

"You saw something on the cameras. Huh, Ethan?" Security grabbed my arms. "Why'd the footage fail, Ethan?"

"Sorry, this man's been drinking heavily." Ethan glares at me, signaling for security to remove me from the event.

"Quick break before the next speaker," Ethan says, allowing the music to take over.

"Let go of my arms," I demand.

"Wait. I'll get him out of here," Shelly insists. "You've got the entire evening. I'll get 'em out of here now."

"Don't want to go with her. I'd rather get my ass kicked by you guys." I flail my arms around.

"Come on, William—ouch, stop." Shelly backs away and holds her forehead. "You hit me in the head."

"Didn't mean to." I look up at the security guard. "She's evil. Will rip yer heart right out of yer chest and leave it out to rot."

"I know you didn't mean to. Now let's go," Shelly says.

"Awright! Stoap!" a woman shouts. She drops her bag and storms toward Shelly. "Yer safe now. You awright?" The woman walks in front of Shelly and stops. She turns to me and whips her skinny, noodle-like arms into the air like a hawk.

Shelly ducks and lunges underneath one of the woman's arms. "I'm fine. Was a misunderstanding."

"I saw that violent man hit you. I'm calling for help. I'm calling the police!"

"It was an accident. He's drunk but wouldn't hurt anyone. Please calm down."

I turn and point to Shelly. "She runs over hearts with her car for fun. She does *that* for fun. Yer a mean woman. A werewolf. A light-haired werewolf she-devil."

"Yer gonna let him talk to you like that?" the woman asks. She pats at her pockets and grabs her phone. "I'm calling for help."

"No, this man's not violent," Shelly says to the woman, signaling her to go back inside the event.

"Yer emotionally violent," I blurt out to Shelly.

"You done yet?" Shelly asks.

"Nope." I look into Shelly's eyes. She's pissed. "I'm done."

"I'll get him out of here. Thank you." Shelly smiles at security.

I feel a release from both arms and pound my head against the wall. There's a dull pain followed by numbness behind my ears. A second grip tugs at my arms. It's a lighter grip.

"William, walk now. Walk right now." Shelly's voice sounds far away.

"Uh?"

"Walk, William," Shelly demands, forcing one of my arms around her neck. "People are watching you make a scene."

"No." I cough.

"No?" She asks.

"Yer the—yer devil woman—"

"Jist shut up before the police come," Shelly says.

"Yer the police? Since when?"

"Stop," Shelly scoffs.

"Proud of you. They give you a gun?"

"You smell like weed. Did you smoke something?"

"I'm a Marlboro man."

"More like pothead. Yer high. Never mind. Please walk. Please. One foot. Next foot. Walk." Shelly slips my arm over her shoulder.

"I smoked *one* cigarette. Lay off me."

"You've never smoked anything in yer life. How'd you know the difference between a cigarette and a joint? Yer wasted."

"What?"

"Forget it."

"How about shoot me? Use yer police gun—"

"I'm still in accounting. You made that up."

"I'm ready to see Jase—"

"Stop talking like that. I'm taking you home."

"You? Ha! I'd rather kiss a door's ass."

"Doesn't make sense—at all." Shelly pulls me away from the hotel entrance.

"I don't like you."

"Don't like you very much right now either."

"I don't love you."

"Stop talking." Shelly tugs hard at my arm.

"Ow."

"Didn't pull you that hard," Shelly says.

"My head."

"You were tossed into a wall headfirst."

"Why'd you do that to me, devil lady?"

"Please stop calling me that."

"Okay." I close my eyes.

"Okay?" Shelly slaps me. "Wake up. What would yer parents say if they saw you like this? Huh?"

"Don't hit me, lady."

"Yer going home. You gotta work with me down the hills."

"Can you walk Harley?"

"What? Harley? Just so you know, I've known about Harley. Sarah and Ethan told me—"

"About what?" I trip over a curb.

"Really? Yeah, I'll take the dog out. Just keep walking, please."

I strain to keep my eyes open. There's a release in pressure from the inside of my calves as we turn off the sloping, downward road. I see a railing leading to a stairwell under a flickering light. *What the hell's going on?* The wind coils through the narrow wynd, heaving between the surrounding buildings.

"Shell?" I force the other eye open.

"Hold on," she says.

"Where're we goin'?"

"I know a shortcut."

We stop under a light post. The burnt orange light stains the scenery around us. The buildings look filtered, as though I'm wearing pumpkin-colored goggles. I look down a long, narrow flight of stairs.

"Stairs might be quicker." Shelly grabs my arm and holds on to the railing.

I tighten my grip on her arm and grab on to the other side of the railing. I accept any body heat penetrating through Shelly's sleeve—it's a cold night. The fresh air driving up the stairway is sobering as we tackle each step one by one. My ears burn from the wind treating my lobes like escape tunnels. I feel the vibration from each crunch against the bottom of my shoe as I step down each ice-treated stair.

"Hang on, Shell," I say, stopping halfway down the stairway. "Need. Second."

"Maybe the stairs were a bad idea."

"What's that?" I close an eye and point at the bottom of the steps.

A hooded figure steps underneath one of the calypso-orange lamps. There's a tall man standing in the middle of the path. A second individual wearing all black brushes past the man, blocking the bottom of the staircase. The second man climbs the staircase.

"We should turn around," Shelly says.

"Aye." I feel my heart beat faster.

"Step backward slowly." Shelly yanks at my sleeve.

We step back and clench the sides of the staircase.

"I'm drunk," I whisper.

"I know. Just keep moving, please."

We slide over the next step. The person climbing the stairs flips up a furry black hood as he crosses under one of the light poles. I can't see his face, but it looks to be a tall, slender man—taller than me. The man climbs the stairs, skipping a step in between. He speeds up.

"Faster, William. Go faster."

"Trying." I feel Shelly lifting my weight up two more steps.

"We're going to turn and run on the count of three. Just get to the top, and we'll see people back on the main road."

"Okay."

"One." Shelly jerks me up another step. "Two—"

The man gains speed as he darts toward us. Another person dressed in black appears under the light and stands behind the man at the bottom of the stairs. The figure is holding something in his hand. It looks like a rifle as it brushes under the light. My heart skips a beat, and I feel a tingle in the back of my head.

"One has a gun—"

"Three. Go!" Shelly tugs me around, and we turn. "Help!" Shelly lets out an ear-piercing scream. "Help us!"

We turn to lunge at the next step and run into a man dressed in all black. I bounce off the padding of his jacket and slip backward. I feel my stomach drop and stop as the man flying up the stairs catches me midfall. I feel my feet plant back onto the step. Shelly flails her arms at the man.

"It's a trap!" Shelly screams. "Help!"

CHAPTER 12

"Stop screaming. Please stop screaming. You're drawing attention for no reason," the man with the padded jacket says.

"Help us!" Shelly screams, trying to break free.

"We're not going to hurt you," the man who caught my fall says as he constricts Shelly's arms.

"Let her go!" I yell.

"Stop yelling—not here to cause trouble." The man releases Shelly. He has a deep, calming voice. His black beard is so thick it could be mistaken for a ski mask.

"Shell, stop." My racing heart slows down a few beats. The tingling in the back of my head vanishes.

I turn and look down the stairs. The two hooded figures at the bottom of the staircase are no longer anywhere to be seen.

"What do you want from us? Take my purse." Shelly yanks her purse strap over her head and hands it to the man with the deep voice. "There's money and a brand-new phone and a nice wallet—take it. We won't say anything."

"Take my wallet—phone. My phone too." I reach toward my pocket, and the man with the deep voice knocks my arm.

"Take your purse. We don't want your purse. Just calm down," the man in the padding says.

The man wearing the padded jacket has salt-and-pepper stubble on his face. He bears an expressionless face and looks to have a shaved head, judging from the receding hairline his hood barely covers.

"What do you want, then?" Shelly pleads.

"You must go back to the main road. There's been an incident down below," the man with the deep voice says.

"Why didn't you just say that?" Shelly asks.

"Trying not to draw attention. It just happen—"

"Are you officers of police?" I interrupt the deep-voiced man.

"What'd you just say?" deep voice asks.

"Who? You walking to me? Talk. You talking to me?" I ask.

"Jesus. Look at his eyes," deep-voiced man scorns.

"Stop." The man in the padded jacket holds his arm out in front of deep voice.

"I'm exhausted," deep voice mutters. "Look at his eyes under the light. I'm telling you he's stoned." He steps toward me. "You've moved to pot, you little shi—"

"Shipment of drugs gone wrong. There's been cases trickling in—weed laced with rat poisoning, and he's being precautious." Padded jacket nods his head.

"I see." Shelly looks around.

"If you don't mind, we're resolving an unrelated incident from earlier. If we could kindly ask you folks to head back to the main roa—"

"Folks?" Shelly asks.

"American man." I poke at the man's padding. "Yer the American. I know you, Arnlad Shitzoo."

The man with the deep voice laughs. "What the hell he call you?"

"Stop," the man in the padding says. "We've never met."

"You hit me—hard," I say.

"What're you talking about?" Shelly asks.

"This American man. He was at the bar, and he hit me."

"You're right—he's drunk and stoned as shit. He needs to go home," the man in the padding says.

"That's where I was taking the stoater," Shelly says.

"You hit me." I poke the man's padding. "You. Hit. Me."

"William, stop doing that," Shelly scolds.

"We can detain him for a few hours and hose him down. We'll give him back sober," deep voice says.

"No, we're leaving. Thank you." Shelly smiles.

"Just go back to the main road and make sure you stay in the light—"

"Walk in public places until you get to yer vehicle," the man in padding interrupts deep voice. "And use the sidewalk directly in front of the train station. There's been a lot of calls tonight, so police are posted up."

The two men step out of our way.

"Okay. Aye, thanks." Shelly pulls at my jacket. "Come on, Will. Let's go."

"I know you—"

"Shut up, William," Shelly snaps. "Have a good night."

I grip the railing and climb. "I'm cold."

"Me too," Shelly says as she guides me back up the staircase. "Wait." Shelly stops and looks back at the two men. "Hey, how'd you know I was parked past the train station?"

The two men walk down the stairs and don't turn back.

CHAPTER 13

I feel pressure on my shoulder. The tension stops. I'm cozy again. At peace. Comfortable. There's no pain—can't feel pain. There's nothing to see but a dark sky above me and a single star shining down. *Jason?*

A force on one of my shoulders makes the star flicker above me. *Stop it.* I adjust myself and look for the star. I feel a sting on my shoulder. A mosquito bite. I slap my shoulder.

"William." Shelly's voice startles the star, and it vanishes into the sky like a fading firework.

I grab my arm.

"Will, wake up. We're home," Shelly says.

I open an eye and see Shelly staring at me. The interior lights of her car illuminate her fluffy blond hair. With her warm stare, she looks like an angel.

"Home?" I ask.

"Come on. Get up. Let's get you to bed."

I nod and stare out the windshield.

The headlights beam on the front of our house—the home Shelly and I saved every bit of our hard-earned money to buy together. We really wanted a detached home and waited until we had enough saved to afford one of our own. The bright red door pops from the rest of the white exterior of the house. It worked. The bright door works. I haven't seen it in a while. I felt like a stranger visiting the home I had helped restore—red door looks great. The large black lantern next to the door looks like a piece of art. The headlights beam off.

"You need me to help you get out? Slept the entire drive home," Shelly says.

"Home?"

"Yes. You coming?"

"In there? You sure?"

"I can take you back to yer place in the morning. I'm worried about you." Shelly slides out of the driver's seat.

"Why the hell are you worried about me? You don't have to pity me." I wait in the car.

"That came out wrong—sorry. Just come in and get some rest. I'll make some tea."

"I'll be gone first thing in the morning." I get out of the car and follow Shelly inside the house.

I walk in the house and close my eyes. It smells like home—I miss this smell. Aromatic scents of apple cinnamon and coffee mix with the earthy smells from the old hardwood floors. There's a hint of leather intertwined with the mix coming from the mocha-brown reupholstered couch in the next room over. It feels like any minute Harley will come running up to greet me. *Get out of your head. He's dead. Wake up. Shelly doesn't want you anymore. Stoater.* I open my eyes and close the door.

Shelly races to the kitchen and lays a pot on the stove. I can't help but follow her. It feels as though I'm not here and am watching her through a television. I want to look away, but I feel like I'm seeing her for the very first time. She has a smirk on her face as though she's never made tea before and wants to make it right. Can't really screw up tea, but you'd think it's possible by watching her bite her lip. She's a beautiful woman. The type who wears makeup because she was taught she needed to—she's beautiful without it.

Shelly bends over to throw away a wrapper. I watch. *No, look away. Look. Away.* She stands up and turns around, catching my wandering eye. I look down at the ground.

"Going to get some rest. No tea for me," I say.

"Really? I'll grab you some ice, then."

"For what?"

"Yer head. You hit yer head. Don't you remember?"

"I'm tired." I turn and walk toward my leather couch. "Wake me up in the morning."

"At least sleep upstairs."

"Our bed?"

"No, I turned the nursery into a guest room."

"Guest roo—"

"For now. There's a bed in there."

"Couch is fine." I walk to the couch and run my fingers against the leather. "Love this couch."

"Fine. I'll bring down a pillow and blanket."

"Don't need one."

"Fine."

"Good night, Shell." I plop down on the couch and sink in. The leather has stretched over time. It stretched perfectly.

"I'll lay some—"

"Jesus, Shelly, you scared the shit out of me. Don't do that again." I hold my hands above my head.

"Sorry. Was going to say I'll lay yer tea down if you decide you want some later."

"Aye, fine. Good night." I turn on my side and close my eyes.

"Will?"

"What?" I open my eyes and see Shelly squatting in front of the couch.

"Should we call the police?"

"Why would *we* do that?"

"Those men from earlier. Was thinking about it while I was driving home. Something's not adding up. There wasn't a single officer on duty in front of the train station."

"Too tired to think right now. Tell me about it in the morning." I close my eyes.

"Sure."

I open an eye and watch Shelly turn off the lights in the living room. She grabs a blanket off another couch and lays it over me. She closes the blinds and locks the front door.

The teapot screeches.

"Gonna turn off the teapot, and I'll run up for a pillow."

I hear her feet tap across the wooden floor as she scurries into the kitchen to turn down the pot. There's clinking from the dishes in the cupboard.

"Ouch," she yelps from the other room.

I'd like to ask if she's okay, but a water burn compared to a broken heart—well, she can handle it. There are fumbling sounds in the kitchen. Familiar clinks and clanks of dishes from the cabinets. She leaves the kitchen. I hear foot pattering from behind the couch as she strolls from the kitchen to the stairwell. I close my eyes and try to fall asleep. The living room dissolves, and I feel my eyeballs relax inside their sockets.

CHAPTER 14

Shelly walks to the top of the stairs and veers inside the guest bedroom. Grabbing a basket from the closet, she slides the comforter from the bed and plops it inside. The wind taps at the window, and a breeze whistles through the cracks. Shelly drops a pillow from the bed on top of the comforter and walks over to the window.

The crow-black sky owns the night. Consistent clatter from the bare trees sounds like children sword fighting on the front lawn. Shelly pulls the blinds shut and struts out from the room. She grabs a sweater from her bedroom and peeks in the mirror.

The clattering from the guest bedroom grows louder. Shelly sticks her head out the master bedroom door and sees a shadow in front of the guest bedroom. The shadow mimics the waves of a sailboat sail. The bedroom lights flicker.

"Will?" Shelly whispers. "You awake?"

The breeze from the guest bedroom strengthens, causing the curtains to flap loosely in the shadows. Grinding sounds of rubbing metal replace the tapping racket. The lights flicker on and off as the wind forces the door to slowly close.

Shelly places her hands on the back of the door to stop the wind from closing it all the way. The door creaks as she slides it open. With both hands trembling, she moves with the door. Peeking inside the bedroom, she searches around. The window is open. The latch on one of the bifold doors snapped off. She grabs her phone and taps the signal button for emergency, sharing her location.

Holding her hands out in front of her, she uses her foot to kick the door to the wall stopper. She lunges backward and listens for noise. The room is empty.

"Damn it." Shelly walks in the room and scoops the window latch from the ground. The latch is bent and rusted at the base. "Piece of crap." She shuts the window. Searching around the room, she looks at her desk next to the bed and dashes to the drawers.

Rummaging around the desk drawers, she grabs a pen. The bedroom lights flare off and on. The door creaks open. Shelly jumps and swivels toward the door. The door stops. Wind whistles through the fractured window. The windows blow open. She uses her hip to slam the drawer shut and darts to the window. Forcing the windows shut, she jams the pen in place of the broken latch. The lights flicker off.

"Will? You hear me?" Shelly shouts. "Will? The power went out."

"Huh?" Will rolls to his other side on the couch.

Shelly looks out the window. The neighbor's lights are on. Pressing her forehead against the window, she forces her eyes down the street. "Will?"

A figure springs in the window. Bloodred eyes align with Shelly's, blocking her view of the street. The red eyes are large and hungry as they glare into Shelly's—a devilish fire surrounding two enlarged black pupils. The whites of its eyes look sunken as the color of hell bleeds out. The figure blinks. Its breath fogs the window. The lights come back on.

"Will, up here now!" Shelly screams. "Will—"

A hand shatters through the window and grabs Shelly by the throat, lifting her off the ground. Glass from the window sinks deeper into her eyes as she struggles inside the tightening grip. She chokes as she frantically kicks. The figure pulls Shelly to its face, squeezing tighter. Shelly gasps for air. "Hel—help m—" Shelly chokes for air.

Shelly tears as she stares into its demonic eyes. She stops kicking as the figure lets out a shrieking gasp for air. The red eyes open and close as its body jolts forward, releasing Shelly from its grip. The figure vanishes as Shelly falls backward, hitting her head on the back of the desk chair.

CHAPTER 15

"Shelly?" I shout from downstairs. "Shell? What's that pounding? I'm coming up there. Shell?"

"Shelly?" I make my way to the top of the stairs and search her bedroom. Sounds of sirens echo through the guest bedroom. I see emergency lights beaming on and off against the hallway walls from the front of the house. There's a breeze coming from the guest room. As I walk toward the room, I see glass scattered on the ground and the curtains flapping—Shelly's legs.

"Shelly?" I walk in the room and see Shelly bleeding on the floor. "Oh my God, Shelly."

I plunge to the ground and grab her. Her feathery blond hair is soaked in blood from the broken glass. Her face is almost as red as the blood in her hair.

"Shell?" I turn her head toward me, and my stomach drops. There's a piece of glass wedged in her eye. I cover my mouth and choke down a mouthful of spit.

"It hurts," Shelly cries.

"Hold still. *Don't* move." I jump up and grab a pillow from the bed and cower over Shelly. "I'm lifting yer head up and laying it on a pillow. Stay calm, Shell. I'm here."

Shelly moans.

"I'm getting my phone and calling an ambulance. Yer okay. You have a cut in yer eye, and we need to get you to a hospital. You must lay still." I grab Shelly's hand, lean over, and kiss her cheek.

Shelly groans.

"Deep breaths." I run to the door but run into the door. My heart's racing, and I want to puke. I force out air and slap myself in the face. *Sober up, stupid.* Running full force toward the staircase, I use my heels to break and hook my arm on the railing to slow down. *The bedroom phone. Landline.* I push off the railing and dart into our bedroom. Shelly's moaning echoes down the hallway.

"Lay still, Shell," I shout as I throw myself at the nightstand and dive for the phone. I snatch the phone from the charging dock and hit the emergency dial as I storm into the bathroom. The phone dials and rings as I rip through the bathroom cabinets. *Come on, Shell, where'd you move the damn first aid kit?*

I hear a woman's voice on the line but interrupt her. "My wife had an accident. There's glass in her eye—window shattered. Hurry."

"Calm d—"

"No time to calm down. Send an ambulance—*now.*"

"Is your location three four three—"

"Aye." I hang up and tear the first aid kit from the cabinet.

I rush across the hall. The top of the kit bursts open and bandages scatter everywhere like confetti spiraling to the floor.

"Shelly? Can you hear me?" I fall to the ground and toss various bottles back into the kit.

Shelly moans.

"I'm here, Shell," I say, heaving the kit with me into the room. I drop to the floor next to Shelly and grab ahold of her hand. Ripping the cap off a bottle of peroxide, I soak a gauze pad and dab it against the open wounds around her face.

Shelly shrieks.

"I'm sorry, babe." I drop the gauze and cup her hand. "An ambulance is on the way. Hold still." I look at her face and choke back tears. There's a piece of glass jammed in the center of her eye—an angel with a wound. She doesn't deserve pain.

The doorbell rings, and there's pounding at the front door.

CHAPTER 16

I squeeze Shelly as the banging racket amplifies from the front door. Her hands feel like there's ice cube condensation squeezing through the pores of her beautiful hands. I look down at her frozen fingers as I cup my palms over hers in order to heat them up. She's wearing her wedding ring. My ring?

The beating noise grows louder from the entranceway. It sounds like people taking turns heaving logs against the door. If they continue, they'll bust in.

"Hang on!" I shout out to the hallway. "Shell?"

"Wha?" Shelly asks faintly.

"Help's here. They're going to take you to the hospital, okay? Shell?"

"Huh?"

"Stay awake, babe." I brush her hair back with one hand and squeeze her other hand tightly. "Going to let go for a second to let the medics in." I feel her squeeze my hand and let go.

I jump to my feet and sprint toward the hallway. The high-pitched *blings* from the doorbell are relentless between each thud against the door. Grabbing ahold of the railing, I launch myself down the staircase. My stomach drops as I fall backward halfway down the steps, head bobbling like I was being double-bounced on a mini trampoline. I slide to the bottom. *Shit, that hurts.* I want to stop right here, lay for a while, and take a break, possibly a nap—but I can't. Shelly's hurt.

I crawl to the door and unlock it. I grip the handle and try to pull myself up, but the door plows open. Strangers in uniform flood inside. The wind whistles behind them.

"We received an emergency call," an officer blurts.

"She's upstairs," I say.

The floor vibrates as two officers stomp over me and trod up the staircase.

"She needs help—now. Right now. Needs to go to the hospital." I kneel and look at the other officers.

"Hang tight," an officer says.

I hear a scratchy noise and a beep from the officer's radios. "Paramedics already contacted and en route. Hand marks around her throat—possible strangulation. Domestic violence."

"Ran 'em through the system. They're married."

"What's going on?" I try to stand, but one of the officers holds their hand out for me to stay put.

The radio crumbles with static, and another officer's voice blares over the speaker. "He's living under a different address. Has arrest records for public intox—no license—"

"Who? Me?" I ask.

"She's incoherent. Let's get her to a hospital—take him in." The officer demands over the speaker.

"Wait. No." I watch two officers as they step toward me. "Yer wrong. I was here—she—she was upstairs, and I was on the couch. I was asleep and heard her screaming."

"Before or after you strangled her," a female officer says.

"Huh? Strangled? No—"

"Stay where you are," the female officer says.

I hear an ambulance.

"Yer wrong. You've got yer story wrong," I plead.

"She's unable to confirm any story at this time." The female officer pulls out a pair of handcuffs. "Take 'em in?"

"Cuff 'em," an officer confirms over the radio.

"No. No, I didn't do this. I didn't do anything." I try to stand, and an officer forces me to the ground.

"Don't move," the female officer says.

"Is she okay? Shelly? I must see my wife—right now," I demand. "You know you can't do this. You can't do this to an innocent man. *Can't* do this to me."

"Sit still," one of the officers says.

"I must see her!" I yell.

"William Norwick, yer under arrest for domestic battery—"

"Me? No." I roll my eyes and chomp down at my lip. "Can I please get up? I need to make sure she's okay—now. I'm getting up right now." I press my weight on a forearm.

"Get down," an officer shouts, kicking my arm out in front of me.

"Stop that right now," I grunt as my chin ricochets off the ground. "I'm losing my patience. You've got no reason to knock me down. We're on the same team."

"We need you to answer some questions about what happened in yer home before she was knocked out."

"I don't live with her. We're separated," I interrupt the officer, feeling my lips through the cracks in the floor. "Get out of my way and let me see her." I swivel to my side and kick one of the officers out of my way. I thrust my arms from side to side and strike my legs as hard as I can.

"If yer separated, divorced, or whatever, why the hell are you here while she's laying on the ground nearly strangled to death one floor above?" one of the officers scorns.

"I wasn't up there when it happened. I heard her yelling for me and saw the window—"

"And?"

"Officer McHenry, I was asleep on the couch down here. Don't you peg this on me, asshole." I feel the alcohol wearing thin.

"So yer saying she strangled herself?" the female officer asks.

"She wouldn't do that. You've got it all wrong. She has glass in her eye from a shattered window—"

"She was strangled, and the marks on her neck are too large to be from her own hands," a deep voice carries down the stairs. "The hand marks on her neck are too large for her petite hands. Imagine a Venus flytrap the size of an almond clenching around a sewing needle."

"Huh?" I'm confused.

"We're taking you down to the station for questioning," an officer shouts as they pin me facedown on the ground.

"Need to get an ambulance. Shelly's got glass in her eye. She's injured bad. Get an ambulance now." I feel pressure around my wrists.

"Sir, the ambulance will be here any minute," says a female officer.

"She's got glass in her eye," I repeat.

"Is yer name William Norwick? Can you explain what you saw?" the female officer asks as she cuffs me.

"What?"

"Can you confirm yer name please? You two have an argument?" another officer asks.

"Huh?"

"He's heavily intoxicated. I can smell it permeating through his pores," the woman officer says. "You have the right to see a solicitor."

"What about Shelly? Can't leave her here!" I scream.

"We're taking you in—get up." An officer tugs at my handcuffs.

"I'm arresting you under section one of the Criminal Justice Act 2016 for potential domestic—"

"Yer not listening to me," I interrupt the officer.

"Domestic abuse." The officer ignores me.

"Abuse? What? I didn't do anything to her!" I shout against the floor.

"The reason for your arrest is that I suspect you have committed an offense, and I believe that keeping you in custody is necessary and proportionate for the purposes of bringing you before a court or otherwise dealing with you in accordance with the law. Do you understand?"

I wriggle around in attempt to loosen my limbs from the uncomfortable death grip of the Glasgow police force. "I'd never hurt that woman. Said my vows, and I meant them. She hurt me."

"And because the pain was so bad, you decided to hurt her in return—"

"I'd never lay a hand on her."

"Strangle marks on her neck show otherwise," an officer's voice trails from the top of the staircase.

"Still love her. Mad at her, but I still love her. When she wakes up, she'll tell you it wasn't me."

I suck in air and hold my breath. How the hell do I weasel my way out of police restraints and get upstairs to Shelly? I must see Shelly. *What do I have to do to get you to release me from your reckless and biased sneer trap? Hello? I didn't do it.*

What's the quickest way to get me to Shell? If I keep my mouth shut for a minute, at least thirty seconds, one of them will feel a relaxed briefly and loosen their grip just enough for me to take control and dominate. I'll break away, then take them all out. Address the problem at hand like a Jedi. I must be slick and athletic in order to break away and take over the situation. It'll be too late for them to react because I'll have already kicked the shit out of them all—well, not the woman. Don't hurt the woman.

I wait for the uninvited guests to march upstairs and zigzag around on my stomach. My forehead presses against the floor, and it's beginning to hurt my neck. Nope. I'm stuck. Zigzagging won't work, because I'm pinned down at the end of my limbs like a night crawler predissection in science class. *Wait for a distraction, dummy. Use your brain.*

I wait for one of the officers to talk to another and jolt and jerk my body side to side. *That's it—wiggle loose.* I thrash my elbow back and swing my limbs in every direction possible. I lift my head and pry my shoulders from the ground.

"Sit still, asshole." One of the officers uses his foot to pin my head against the ground.

"Please let me. See. Her." I can barely move my mouth from the officer's foot digging into the back of my skull. My mouth's nearly suction cupped to the floor as I choke out words. *Way to go, Jedi. You really showed them.*

"You can't see her." The female officer assured. The reason for your arrest is that I suspect you have committed an offense, and I believe keeping you in custody is necessary and proportionate for the purposes of bringing you before a court or otherwise dealing with you in accordance with the law. Do you understand?" the female officer asks, grabbing me by my shoulders.

The front door busts open. Footsteps accompany an array of voices as more people join the depressing Norwick house party. A breeze wafts up both of my pant legs. Goosebumps form. The foot clatter sounds like a cattle of storm troopers blowing by as I lay helplessly on the ground. Their heavy boots clunking against the ground causes fluttery vibrations against my chest. I try to look up but feel a boot plunge against the back of my head, forcing me to remain in place. When I look up, I see blasts of laser-blue flares from the ambulance lights striking against the cream-colored walls. The swirly blinks resemble a distorted kaleidoscope through my crooked view from the floor.

The female officer squeezes my shoulder and tugs. There's another forceful grip against the opposite side. The second clench is rougher—intentional. I fidget around. Can't—I'm stuck. The dull pain lodging into one of my shoulder blades feels like Edward Scissorhands peeling me off the floor while wearing oven mittens. *Please just leave me be.*

"Lifting you on yer feet. One. Two—"

"Wait," I interrupt. "Only if we can go upstairs and see Shelly—"

"Three." The female officer ignores me.

Guess I have no choice—cold-blooded lady. Pressure seeps to my forehead as the two officers heave me from the floor and stand me upright. I feel like a puppet—a shackled police puppet. I've got no control. They're in control now.

"Shelly? Shell, can you hear me?" I scream.

"Shut up!" an officer blurts from the stairs.

"You can speak with her after we get her to a hospital, and yer cleared," the female officer says. "Station's under construction, so yer going to the station across the river."

"Cleared?" I ask.

"You'll be let go temporarily once we're able to determine that you're not the prime suspect," Officer Scissorhands declares. "Doesn't mean yer innocent, though. If we find you guilty, and you lie—"

"We should take 'em in before they bring her down." The woman officer points her head toward the door.

"I must see her," I plead.

"Come on, get 'em out of here," she says, releasing me to the hands of the other officer.

I twist and shove him as hard as I can. The male officer loosens his grip enough for me to kick at him. I sway one of my legs back and punt at him.

"Nope," he says, wailing my body against the front door—my front door.

I strain my eyes at the staircase. I'm less than three strides from the first step. "Shelly, yell if you can hear me—scream something if you're awake. I need to know—"

"Enough," the woman officer interjects, glaring at the officer holding me in handcuffs. "Move him away from the door so we can get the hell out of here. He's giving me a headache."

My wrists sting from the yank to my handcuffs. I feel like a horse in reins. Obediently, I back away from the front door—the one I installed with my bare hands. I look toward the staircase.

"Don't even think about it." The male officer looks at me and jerks my body so I'm facing the front door. "Please keep calm. You can yell all you want at the station—just stop screaming in our ears. We gotta take you in."

"No, you don't. I didn't do anything," I scoff.

"We've got to rule out as much as we can—standard protocol," the male officer says, thrusting the front door open. "I'm Officer McHenry.

She's my partner, Officer Casey." Officer McHenry points at his female counterpart.

"You two really think I'd do something like this to the one I love?" I shake my head.

"Nothing you say now will have any impact. Yer going to the station no matter what," Officer McHenry says.

"Can't we talk here? I'd like to talk here."

"Let's go." Officer Casey forces me out the door.

"Not yet. I said hang on." I try to plant my feet in a wide stance to prevent the officers from lugging me out the door. One of the officers shoves me, and I lose my balance. Fail. I catch myself and widen the position of my feet, feeling another force against my back. My stomach flutters as I lose my balance and tumble to the ground face-first, like a street sign flopping over. Failed again. I lay limp like a rag doll as the two officers pull my dead weight from the floor.

The wind slaps me hard in the face as I step outside with the two officers. The cold air feels refreshing against my face. It's sparing me additional time from a massive hangover. One of the officers tightens my cuffs, strangling my wrists. With the number of government officials on the property, one would think I'm a politician, a serial killer, or maybe both. Neighbors from across the street wander toward the bottom of the driveway, watching the action take place.

The driveway's lined with law enforcement vehicles from the garage door to the street. The marbled lights blare on and off from the ambulance and police vehicles. The blinking lights look as though they're synchronized for an EDM concert. When the lights blink off from the ambulance, the other lights flash on the police cars. Crystal-blue fluorescent lights crisscross with blazing streaks of cream-colored accents. As the lights blaze on, they illuminate the neon yellow and blue checkers that stripe across the sides of the police vehicles. The dizzying light show cancels out the aiding effect the wind has on my hangover. The whiskey aftereffect is present now and is here to stay.

"Can we move faster?" I ask, pulling at my handcuffs like a horse in reins "The sooner you realize I'm innocent, the quicker I can get back to Shelly."

"Now you can't wait to come down to the station?" Officer McHenry asks.

"Don't think it's us slowing you down. It's probably the booze. You look like a penguin that's trying to walk sideways," Officer Casey says.

I turn and glare at Officer Casey. Her lips are chapped, and loose strands of hair from her ponytail stick to one of her eyes. My eyes water at the sight. *Don't you feel that?* It'd be like walking around with a Q-tip stuck to your cornea.

"How much you drink tonight?" Officer McHenry asks.

"Maybe you blacked out and don't remember what happened in the house, huh?" Casey says.

"I'm fine. Yer lady friend's trying to peg the blame on me—"

"She's doing her job," Officer McHenry interrupts.

"She's labeling me the bad guy so she can take me in, end her shift, and get drunk with her feminist friends." I tug at my cuffs.

"Go ahead and run yer mouth. Yer helping me form an opinion." Casey yanks hard at my cuffs.

More neighbors walk across the lawn and join the driveway party. I look away and pull the cuff against my back.

"How's yer relationship with the neighbors?" Officer McHenry asks.

"Fine. Would be nice if you'd unlock the cuffs so I can give them a neighborly wave."

"Bet yer wave's some kind of hand gesture for piss off," Officer Casey scoffs.

"Nope. They all like me. Yer making me look like a criminal, forcing me to walk out in handcuffs."

"You wouldn't listen," Officer McHenry says.

"Like we said, yer an innocent man until we—"

"You think I look innocent? Look at me?" I interrupt Officer Casey. "You painted the perfect gossip story for the neighborhood."

"We're taking you in for questioning and never said yer guilty. You'll get to see yer wife—"

"Ex-wife—er, separated," I interrupt Officer McHenry.

"Whatever the relationship, since she's unable to answer questions, and it's protocol to get as much information as we can, we'll be questioning others," McHenry says.

"We'll know real soon how much yer neighbors like you," Casey says.

CHAPTER 17

I'd like to meet the asshole—the inventor responsible for the metal bindings compromising my manhood as I bobble around the back seat of a police car. Handcuff styles should vary by the degree of the crime. I'm an innocent man, and I can't wait to embarrass them in front of the entire police force.

"Can I make a phone call?" I ask.

"When we get to the station." Officer McHenry glances at me from over his shoulder. His neck is too wide for his police uniform.

"Cuffs are cutting off my circulation. She put 'em on too tight."

"Relax, we'll be there soon." Officer Casey drives over a speed bump.

The back tires bounce over the bump. I spring into the air like I was riding on the back of a galloping horse leaping over a hurdle without warning. My stomach drops, and I land on my wrists. "Ah, shit. That was intentional."

Gaping out the window, I search for distractions. Anything to keep me distracted from Officer Casey's torturous driving. The heat isn't circulating properly to the back of the car. Could be another form of punishment before interrogations begin at the station. Bending my fingers at the brims of my knuckles without them snapping in half feels like an accomplishment. How the hell did I go from napping on the couch at my ex's warm house to a squad car icebox? *What the hell happened tonight?*

Streetlights gleam through the windshield of the police car. A low-lit glow shines through the steel mesh divider protecting the officers from back-seat aggressors. The light strikes at the mesh, casting a plaid-like shadow that looks like a spider web dangling over a wired fence. I look down and watch the kaleidoscopic pattern swirl against my chest. The whirly sight makes me dizzy, so I lean forward and stare through a single mesh opening.

We drive until the road dead-ends and turn onto one of the main streets leading to popular bars and restaurants. The first layer of decorative lights highlights the downtown night scene from afar. Strands of multicolored lights blink simultaneously, offering a warm welcome to a potential customer.

There's not much action around town tonight. Most bars are closed for the evening, and the cold weather prevents people from congregating outside the entrance after close. We coast down a street decorated with exuberant awnings and coordinated fixtures. I scout for new whiskey bars—latest spots under new ownership where I'd be welcomed. There's potential, but they're closed for the evening.

I close my eyes. I'm okay. I'm coming down from a nasty booze buzz. The mind can play tricks on someone under the influence. I had a lot of whiskey—too much earlier. A lonely party. I suck in air, hold it in, and exhale through my nose. I'm in a cab heading out for a nightcap. In a cab. I'm in a cab.

"Hold on. Speed bump—two in a row," Officer Casey says.

I pop up and down. Bounce up again, feeling my hair brush against the headliner, and drop at a sideways angle onto my forearm. *Damn it.* The damn cuffs. I must say something before she breaks my wrists. In fact, I'm being hauled to the station in a police car. Reality check: I'm in a car with people who would shun back-seat drivers.

Structurally, this vehicle probably exceeds most safety ratings when compared to the other vehicles in its class. I'd buy it, but without the aftermarket performance add-on—the Officer Casey feature. The jerky movements and braking malfunctions are enough for me to believe there's a loose nut behind the wheel. I know aftermarket accessories can't legally void a vehicle's warranty, and a human can't be an aftermarket accessory, but metaphorically speaking, the Casey performance package will teach you why you should do your research before buying a used car. This car will look good in photos, but anything under the hood with the way that woman drives—forget it.

We approach a changing light. Officer Casey taps the brakes and pumps the gas. She hesitates and stomps hard on the brake. I body check the back of the driver's seat. This time my kneecaps braced the impact. I bite my lip and wiggle my arms. The cuffs slide lower, relieving my circulation a smidge. I squeeze my hands into fists to get the blood flowing.

We turn on Dixon Street and slow down. A man wobbles out from Hootenanny's Bar and walks into a garbage can. Finally, some action. Looking backward, he pats at his pockets and trips over the curb. The man catches his balance by groping the hood of the nearest car parallel parked on the street. He slides his fingers around the outline of the vehicle and stops at the side mirror. Sloping at a downward angle too low for his height, he drapes his lanky arm over the mirror. What the—is he posing for a picture or trying to prevent the spins? He holds his position.

"Slow down. What's his deal?" Officer McHenry points.

The man doesn't move a hair.

"Strange. Could barely walk and now he looks like a mannequin in a side plank," Casey mutters as she lets her foot off the gas.

"Doesn't he look like that pirate from that one beer commercial?" McHenry turns and looks out the back window at the man.

"The pirate part, aye. Like that Caribbean pirate movie," Casey says.

"A disgruntled Jack Sparrow. Circle the block once," McHenry says.

"Jack Sparrow was drunk the whole movie. So yeah, the description matches." Casey turns and circles the block.

I want to see the man rip a mirror off a stranger's car and topple over. It will make me feel better about myself. We approach the street.

"He's standing now," I say.

"Let's see if he plans on driving like that," Casey says.

The man grabs his phone from his pocket and begins typing as he stammers in the middle of the street. Eyes glued to his phone, he struts toward the other side of the street. He uses one hand to pull the phone closer to his face and the other hand to pick at the inside of his ear. The phone casts a light on his face. He squints with one eye, squeezing his other eye shut.

"See? Told you—just missing his eye patch." McHenry chuckles.

"Hopefully he's finding a ride," Casey says, passing alongside the man. "He didn't even notice us. I'll circle again."

The man staggers between two parked cars and slips. He catapults his phone, landing on his butt.

"Hang on." Officer Casey stomps the brakes. "He okay?" She shifts the car in reverse.

I nosedive into the mesh barricade. Her words registered seconds after my nose wedged through one of the mesh holes. My body bullwhips in the other direction, and the momentum heaves my body against my seat back.

"Hey!" I bellow.

"Sorry—said to hold on," Officer Casey says.

"To what?" I ask. "Can't use my arms for obvious reasons. And you need to say hold on before you react, not while doing it. Almost broke my nose." I wiggle my nose, seeing double as I cross my eyes. The skin burns above my nostrils like someone cut it with a three-blade razor.

"Let's get 'em off the ground." Officer Casey ignores my plea and backs up.

The man stares at us. He rubs his eyes and drops his jaw.

"Why's he looking at us like that?"

"He looks scared," I say.

"He's annihilated or high—both much of the time."

"You sure he's looking at us?" I ask, watching the man cup his mouth.

"Should see the way drugs affect some people," McHenry says. "Some look like zombie Muppets trolling around town."

"He's shaken from the fall—was a pretty nasty spill," Casey says.

"Probably a good thing he's intoxicated and couldn't stiffen up," McHenry says.

"Let's get him up and check him out before someone runs him over." Officer Casey steers to one side of the road, throws on the police lights, and makes a U-turn.

"I'll get 'em up," Officer McHenry says, hopping out of the vehicle. He taps the Airwave transmit button on his uniform as he shuts the door.

"What's he doing now?" I ask.

"Hell if I know." Casey unbuckles her seat belt.

The man thrusts his arms up in front of him, signaling for McHenry to stop. He cups his face and shakes. The wind blows back his hair as he releases one hand from his mouth and points at us.

"Not sure he likes you two," I say.

"This guy's an oddball," Casey says, opening the door. "Why's he afraid of us? We're just the police. We're not *that* scary."

"Ha!" I shake my head.

Officer Casey opens her door and stops. The man pops his palm out in front of him and shakes his hand for us to leave him alone. "He's on something." Casey grabs her flashlight and shines it at the man. "Look at his face."

The man flips over to one side and screams at the top of his lungs, "Run!" He pries himself off the ground, kicks off his shoes, and takes off.

Casey clicks off her flashlight, slides into the vehicle, and slams the door. "Why the shoes?"

Officer McHenry hops back in the car. He buckles his seat belt and watches the man run in a crooked diagonal. "Bath salts or Tide PODS—you pick."

"He's pretty bad. Must've tried them both at the same time."

"Where's he going?" Casey asks.

"No, no, no, turn around, pirate. Come back this way," McHenry scorns. "I'm gonna run after him. Pull forward."

"He won't get to Clyde Street. The cars are flying down there," I say. "Right?"

"He'll stop. He's too messed up to follow the construction signs," Casey says, maneuvering around parked cars.

"Stop the car. I'm going after him," McHenry orders.

"Stopping car. Is that okay with you back there?" Casey asks.

"It's fi—"

Still too late. This time I lick the mesh. She pumps the brakes too soon.

The shoeless man stops at the temporary construction fence marking the dead end. He kicks over the cones and grips the fence.

"What's he doing?" McHenry thrusts open the door and runs toward the man.

"He's climbing the fence," I say.

"McHenry will catch up. That man's climbing without shoes in freezing temperatures. Fences like that are hard to hold on to without something sturdy to boost momentum."

The man pulls himself up and lodges his feet through two fence holes.

"Watch. He'll weaken and let go," Casey says.

The man stretches upright and climbs another foot. He swings one of his legs out and plants it against the "Dead End: Do Not Enter" sign.

"Crap, found his momentum," Casey says.

McHenry turns and runs at us. He gasps for air as he pumps his elbows up and down at a forty-five-degree angle like a track star approaching the last straightaway of a race. He hurls himself inside the vehicle. "Bad. Cramp. Bad side cramp. He'll get over that fence. He's getting over that fence."

"A persistent pirate." Casey looks at McHenry. "He wear you out?"

"Head toward Clyde Street, and we'll scoop him up before he reaches the road." McHenry ignores his partner.

"Fox Street to Maxwell, and I'll pull to the side of Clyde. Should be an easy scoop as long as he makes it over to the other side." Casey flips on the emergency lights and peels away.

"Wait. Scoop up? Yer gonna put him in the back with me?" I ask.

"We're not sticking to our gym plan. We went once," Officer Casey says, ignoring me.

"Aye, right. It's cold out—only reason I'm out of breath."

"You run like you have your pants dropped around yer ankles, and I'm sure I'm worse. Bring yer gym clothes tomorrow."

"Talk about this later," McHenry growls. "Let's get this guy before he causes a pileup on Clyde."

"Fine, I'll text Ellie to remind you." Casey turns down Clyde.

"Stop getting my wife involved in everything all the time. Pull over here—piano store back lot. I know a shortcut."

I brace myself for facial impact, beating Casey to the braking system.

Officer Casey jerks the wheel, steering us into a back parking lot. "Yer wife told me you're snoring again and blood sugar's spiking, so she's already involved—"

"Great, you chirpy birds are back to flocking around the nest," McHenry interrupts.

"Because we care. You and I—we're not the same people we were in our thirties. You're Snory McSnorson, and I'm going gray."

"Nice chat. Very encouraging, right before I jump out of a car to chase down a free-climbing crackhead without shoes." McHenry kicks open the door.

"If I pull down Clyde and see and you and Jack Sparrow dodging cars—"

"I won't miss 'em. I'm calling this in." McHenry slams the door and presses his Airwave transmit button on his uniform. "Officer McHe—" his voice trails off in the wind.

Casey rolls down the window. "Careful. Love you." She watches McHenry take off through the parking lot.

Uh, that's weird. Can't unwind that one—wish I didn't hear that.

"Doesn't he look like he's running with his pants around his ankles?" Casey shakes her head.

I wake a few seconds. More awkward seconds pass, and I change the subject. "Please don't put that man in the back of the car with me. He's insane," I plead.

"I agree. There's something wrong with that man, and I wouldn't want to sit next to him either," she says.

"Thank you for understanding." I exhale. "What's your plan, then?"

"Very simple. We'll have the man on bath salts steer the ship, and I'll sit in the back seat with the man we're questioning for strangle marks around a woman's throat. Sound like a plan?"

Maybe we should invite McHenry's wife? I look out the window and bite my tongue.

"Bad joke. Sorry." Officer Casey looks at me through the rearview mirror.

Now she's being nice because I'm a witness to their little secret.

"He'll be cuffed. He won't bother you. We'll hold him with us until backup arrives." She shifts the car in reverse and backs up. "Hopefully I won't have to run and—"

A dull thud hinders Officer Casey's voice as the back wheels of the police vehicle plow over a sturdy land barrier. The thump was large enough I felt the vibration from the bottom of the car against the bottom of my feet.

"What was that?" I lift my feet from the ground.

"Was high enough to feel like I rolled over a curb of one of those damn cement dividers," Casey says.

"No, can't be. We didn't drive over it when we pulled into the lot," I say.

"I hit it hard too. My TPMS sensor came on."

"Think about it: You would've hit the curb when you pulled in. You drove straight back—reversed the way you drove in. There was no curb. Please listen. I'm no longer drunk, I think."

"Aye, great. Here we go."

"Listen to me. Yer not the best driver, too aggressive, and you scare the shit out of me, so I've been paying attention. You drove in, parked, and reversed the same way you came in. We didn't drive over a curb. Trust me: my face would know."

"If I ran over an animal—"

The windshield shatters. An earsplitting rupture of crinkling debris vibrates inside my head like I'm sitting underneath a chandelier during the heat of a 7.0 magnitude earthquake. Chards of glass whip at every crevasse of the police car like they're catapulting out of a turbo-spinning pinwheel. The loose particles striking against the driver and passenger windows sound like someone pitching a wad full of sand and rock salt against mirrors.

"What's happening?" I shout. I hear quick breaths from the front seat.

"Hang on. Don't yell," Casey whispers. She shakes her uniform and glass crinkles down the sides of her seat. "This is Officer Casey. Need backup now half a block from Hootenanny's Bar at Fox Street and the back lot of the piano place—Mac-something. Vehicle's been struck."

Static hisses through Casey's radio. Choppy bits and pieces of a man's voice fades in and out of the radio. "Ca—y whe—n—ing."

The radio dies. The silence is replaced by a howl in the wind, duplicating the pitch of a man's voice.

Casey presses her radio "McHenry, can you hear me? I've been hit." Casey utters. "You okay?"

"Me?"

"Aye. You okay?"

I jiggle glass from my face and head like a dog shaking water from its fur after a bath. Shards of glass trickle inside my clothes. They feel like ice cubes tapping against my bare skin. "I'm okay."

"Hang on. Don't move. See that? Over there? Movement along the buildings. Get down slowly. Try to roll down to the floor so yer not hit by stay a stray bullet. Hear me?"

"Aye." I lower myself onto the seat. Speckles of glass rub against my flesh as I lean forward.

"Slow movements," she whispers. "The blow came from the front of the car, not below." Casey holds down her radio. "McHenry, can you hear me? Adam? Shit, radio's dead."

"Yer boyfriend's with the pirate, and he'll come back when he sees we're not on Clyde," I whisper.

"Boyfriend? Adam McHenry's my brother. Casey's my married name," she whispers.

"Oh, sorry."

"Please let me think. I need you to duck all the way down to the floor if you can." Officer Casey unholsters her gun.

"I'm cuffed. Uncuff me."

"Just get down on the ground in case they fire again. I'll crawl around and pull you out." Casey ducks, turns on the brights, and holds down the horn. Shadows dive away from the light. "Over there—I see them."

"Them?"

"There's three of them. Dressed in all black, and they're making a run for it." Casey cracks open her door and slips out from the driver's seat. "I'll pull you out once we're clear. Be prepared to run."

"Wait."

"Drop to the ground. It's for your own safety." She clinks the door shut and holds her gun in front of her. "Adam?" Officer Casey's voice trails off.

I lean sideways and smack the side of my head against my window. Twisting my head, I plant my forehead against the window so my forehead bears the weight of my body as I shimmy my legs onto the floor. Like a worm, I wiggle my body to the floor, stuffing as much of my lower limbs under one of the front seats. Glass digs into my chest. I'm stuck. My body's too long. I'm the worm trying to burrow through cement. My chin hooks over the door panel as try once more to jam my body on the floor. *How the hell will she get me out of this position?*

Digging my chin into the door panel, I press my face and look out with window for Casey. She jogs alongside two vehicles parked inside the lot. Movement from inside one of parked vehicles catches my eye. I freeze and hold my breath. Red eyes appear in one of the windows the parked cars. *No—it can't be.*

Officer Casey walks backward and squats to the ground. She shines her flashlight underneath the vehicles and holds the gun in her other hand. "Get up. Look up." I pull my wrists hard in the cuffs and wiggle my feet. Pieces of windshield roll under the rims of the handcuffs and plant inside my already raw-rubbed wrists.

"Officer Casey, come back. They're behind you." I bang my forehead against the window and scream at the top of my lungs. "Turn around. Look in the car." I gasp for air. "Somebody help. Turn around, damn it. Help!" I arch my back and stretch my legs as hard as I can underneath the seat. "Help, Officer Casey!" I bite at the door handle. My teeth clamp against the metal as I slide my tongue around for the handle. Dull pain infects my gums as I hold the handle with my teeth and rip it way from the door. Police car. It's a police car, and I'm in the back seat. I'm locked in. I suck up my saliva and spit at the ground. Mouthful of germs for nothing.

The high-pitched scream of a helpless woman ripples off the parking lot buildings and disintegrates into the air as the wind carries her cry for help to the dismissive night skies. I tip my ear toward the open windshield and listen for Officer Casey. It's quiet. I only hear the swooshes of wind funneling through the broken windshield, pinging scraps of glass around its interior like a low-powered sprinkling system.

A loud clank echoes in between the windshield gusts mimicking the sound of a door slamming shut. I hold my breath and listen. What do I do? I close my eyes and see the demonic bloodred pupils. *Shit. Shit. Shit.*

A bang from a gunshot rumbles into the sky. I bite my lip and close my eyes. *Please protect me, Jase. I'm not ready to go yet.* Squealing brakes and engine purrs follow the single gunshot. I smell exhaust as it seeps inside the car.

There's a plunk on the door coming from the opposite side of the vehicle. The door handle jingles. I hoist my chest in the air—my final attempt to break free. Nothing. My eyes water, and I bite down on the sides of my cheeks as pain radiates through my core. That stupid twitch did nothing but invite more glass to my skin party. This time my chest is playing host.

The passenger door creaks open from behind, creating a second wind tunnel. I feel a draft on my neck as the wind rifles through my hair. The hairs on my neck rise as I feel the presence of someone watching me. Someone's standing behind my lifeless body. I've got nothing—no plan of attack. *Play dead. Play. Dead.* I *do* look dead. I close my eyes and slow my breathing. *Please don't hurt me.*

"What the—look," a raspy-voiced woman says, poking at my shin.

"How the hell? Looks like he's a part of the seat frame," a man says with an accent so thick, his *r*'s roll.

"Police heading toward bridge. Five blocks," a high-pitched woman shouts from afar.

"Push or pull?" the raspy-voice woman asks.

What? No, just leave me.

A second vehicle screeches to a halt. I can feel the engine grumbles vibrating against my body. The vehicle is stopped behind me. "Got to get 'em out of here!" a man shouts from the second vehicle.

"Just drag him out!" the high-pitched woman yells.

Don't touch me.

"You should see this. He's wedged under the seat, and his backs arched up. Looks like a merman—"

"Don't have time. Rip the front seat forward and get 'em out," the man in the second car interrupts the woman with the raspy voice.

"About to cross the river. Less than two minutes—three minutes if pushing our limit," the high-pitched woman announces from the other car.

"Push his legs from under the front seat, and I'll drag 'em out at an angle," the man with the accent says. "Hey—hey, remove the cuffs. Get the cuffs off. Don't want to pull an arm out of socket."

Yes, take the cuffs off.

"Don't have time. Pull 'em out, and we'll pop his arm back in the socket later!" the man shouts from the second vehicle.

No, don't do that.

"Take the damn cuffs off. I'll drive," a man with a deep voice says.

There are five of them.

"Too damn picky—every single time," the man from the second vehicle growls as he slams the door. "Move out of the way. Damn adrenaline junkies."

"You've got just above a minute—a minute thirty's pushing it," high-pitched woman says.

"Stay calm. You got this. But hurry up."

The glass around my wrists pierce through another layer of skin as the man squeezes his hand around one of my cuffs. Another stranger stretches my arms back as the man holds my wrists tight. I feel like the teddy bear I had growing up when I'd play cops and robbers and tie his arms behind his back. I would drop kick him into the jail I made in the basement. *I'm sorry I did that to you, Teddy.* The tighter the man squeezes my wrists, the more he lodges the chips of glass. Choking down pain without jolting in reaction would be easier if I hadn't sobered up. I fight back tears.

"Hold his body still." The man holding my wrists grunts, sticking his knee in my back. He breaks open the first handcuff. "I hate these gloves," he growls as he applies force.

I grind my teeth, forcing an overbite in order to hold back screaming at the top of my lungs as the stranger wedges glass through my skin from wedging his hand into my back. I'd like to wail him of my back, rip free from the handcuffs, and pluck the glass from my skin. The windshield debris feels like a fiery infestation. My wrists feel tight, and I hear a snap.

"And we're good." The man clamps the second handcuff. "Jose, help her while I grab him from the other door."

The release of tension in my shoulders, neck, and spine as my hands drop to my sides feel as though I've been revived from almost choking to death.

"Forty seconds," high-pitched voice says.

"On phone confirming backup," deep voice says.

"Ask to add a minute of power outage," raspy voice adds.

"Call down to the front desk in a minute. The heat's not working in my room," the man with the deep voice says.

What the hell? Am I in the middle of a sick prank?

"One, two—we push, you pull. One, two," the raspy woman says, forcing her body weight against my legs. My legs slide out from underneath the seat.

"One more push. We'll get 'em this time—he's really wedged in there," the man with the accent says.

"Twenty-five seconds."

"Last chance," raspy-voiced woman says. "One, two, three—"

"Jose, take off yer gloves. Come here—yer in backup," deep voice man says.

My torso feels like it's being ripped in half at my waistline. I suck in air and hold my breath as my body glides against the back seat. The man pulls me out with his arms wrapped around me like a bear hug. I feel my feet brush the concrete and punch my arms into the air. I break free from the man's grip and plant my feet on the ground.

"Shit—scared the crap out of me. You're coming with me," the man says, standing up straight.

I lean forward and punch the man in the eye. "Get out of my way!" I scream and take off running down the street.

"Ah, shit." The man folds over and holds his eye. He rips the cuffs and tools from the seat "He popped me in the eye."

"Just go—get the hell out of here before they arrest your drunk ass," the man with the deep voice yells. "Jose, take the cuffs and tools."

"We gotta move—must move now," the high-pitched woman yells from the other car. "Get in your vehicle."

I feel glass trickling inside my shoes as I run back toward the bar scene. Their voices echo from the parking lot as they hop inside their vehicles.

"This won't end well. He's going to jail," raspy voice woman says, slamming the door.

"Separate. Plans B's already intact."

I run to the end of the side street and see two unmarked cars blow past me. It's pitch black. Taillights blare red as the two vehicles approach one of streets off in the distance. The cars spilt in two directions and vanish into the night. I plop on the ground and pull off my shoes. Glass clinks around inside my shoes. I shake them out and pluck pieces of windshield from the bottom of my feet. Brushing a hand inside my shoe, I feel glass stuck to the lining. I rip at the lining. Slivers of glass particles prick my fingers.

High-pitched sirens bounce off the river. Reflections from police lights flicker off the frozen body of water. Streetlights beam over me like spotlights as the power turns on. I stand up.

CHAPTER 18

My heart's racing as I search for the nearest exit. I slide my shoes on and run toward the edge of the road. A razor-sharp pain permeates through my body from the ball of my foot. I collapse to the ground like a statute tipping over. The sirens grow louder.

I rip my shoes off. The glass rips through my thumb and pointer finger as I dig it out from the bottom of my foot. I jump to my feet and whip one shoe between a parked car and a curb. Holding the other shoe in my hand like a track baton, I sprint barefoot to the temporary construction fence aligning the dead end in the road.

I kick the cone and hoist my shoe like a shot put to the other end of the construction site. I grip the fence and lodge my feet through two fence holes. Stretching upright, I climb another foot. The cold air whistles through the fence. I swing one of my legs out and plant it against the "Dead End: Do Not Enter" sign. Found my momentum.

Scaling frozen fence wires feels like you're climbing a jungle gym made of icicles. Slick and numbing. I lunge up, wrap my hands over the top of the fence, and peek down below. Three police cars speed down Clyde Street. Their lights glisten as they pass the other vehicles driving parallel to the river. The cars swerve onto a side street. Storefronts of local business align Clyde Street and wrap around to the street closest to me, forming a large backward L shape. The corner storefront is long enough. It blocks the back parking lot where the crime scene continues.

I wrap the first leg over the top of the fence, planting my foot inside the next first hole my frozen foot locks into. An explosion of shouts vibrates off the buildings surrounding the back-parking lot. The outbursts intensify. I lift my other leg over the top of the fence and drop to the other side. If the temperature were any colder, my feet may have snapped off my body upon ground impact. I run to the edge of Clyborn Street and dart into four lanes of traffic. Running with frozen feet feels like I'm running through puddles of slow-drying glue. I know my feet are guiding my strides, but the numbness forces me to look down and check if my feet are still there.

A car roars in front of me. Another car follows close behind. I sway backward and jump onto the tips of my toes, sucking my stomach in hard enough to maintain balance while avoiding vehicle annihilation. One of horn until and screeches to a halt behind me. Tucking my butt in, I squeeze through the next lane of traffic. I spot the ice-covered river ahead. I stumble over the curb and fold my body forward to prop my hands over my legs.

High-pitched wails from the sirens amplify as the police cars zoom through the halfway point of the bridge. The frozen river boosts the kaleidoscopic flashes of the emergency lights as more police cars pour behind the other vehicles. *Think quick. Think. Quick.*

I storm to the edge of the sidewalk and grab ahold of a frozen pearly-white metal railing. There's nowhere to run and look discrete in front of the traffic on busy Clyde Street. There's no one else roaming around this close to the water at this time of night. I let go of the icy railing and see that it lines a sidewalk that leads down a spiraling walkway to the riverfront path. The bottom of the walkway is roped off for slick conditions. The streetlights along the riverfront path are out. Gripping ahold of the railing, I run down the winding sidewalk.

I stop halfway down and duck behind the concrete wall to peek up at the crime scene. The high beam flares from emergency vehicles fill both ends of Clyde Street. I duck as the vehicles blow past me, pouring on to every road leading to the reported crime scene location. Door slams reflect off the frozen river as officers surround the scene. I glace up and see the glowing dots from flashlights panning the scene. The spheres of light grow in circumference as the officers migrate closer to my direction. Dogs bark from across the street. *Bloody hell, they've got police dogs with 'em.*

I peel my frozen hands from the metal railing and push off down the slanted sidewalk. The wind hisses in my ears. I'm not sure where I'm going or who can help me. I rip the rope bearing the Do Not Enter sign over my head and knock against the cones marked Watch for Ice. The bottom of one of my feet throbs as though there's rocks glued to the bottom of my shoe. I charge down the sidewalk. My front foot glides across the slick surface too fast for the other foot to keep up. My body hurls forward, and my stomach drops as I plummet to the ground.

I use my arms to scrape my body across a rock salt and the chunks of ice that were missed. Planting my palms on the ground I push myself onto my feet. Fragments of rock pierce into my skin as sting as though I was doing a handstand over shattered beer bottles. I stand up and look around. Ethan's home is a fifteen-minute drive from this point and I won't last that that long on foot. *Where's my damn phone? It's at Shelly's—maybe at Shelly's. They probably took if for evidence. Can't go to my place.*

A dog barks. Clinks and clanks vibrate off the metal railing as officers trickle down the ramp. There're gaining on me. I suck in air and thrust my chest out for faster strides. The brisk air burns as it enters my lungs, forcing me to cough it back up.

"He's over there," a police officer announces.

The sidewalk turns a sharp corner revealing naked branches from a large tree that lies outside the sidewalk radius. The moon sheds enough light around the tree for me to notice an opening from the walkway—my last-ditch effort to break away from the police pack hunting me down. I'm out of breath, and my gasps for air are solely out of desperation now. One more cough or choke will lead them to me. I may as well turn myself in. My chest feels tight, like it's constricted by rubber bands.

I veer off the path and dart inside the open space. Scurrying to the tree I search for the exit. There must be an outlet leading back up to the main road. The open space resembles the size of a small basketball court. Dusky clouds cloak the moon depleting the nightlight glow. Shadows cast over a large mural filling the entirety of the back wall. A spark of moonlight from a brief opening in the clouds causes a flicker in the mural—a doorknob. I push off from the tree stump and race toward the door as the moon disappears.

The pitter-patters of shoes thumping against the cement catch up behind me. There's a rumble of voices and weight to the back of my shoulders. The force against my back causes my neck to snap backward as my center of gravity shifts from underneath me. My head lashes forward accompanying the direction of my body but with a half-second delay. I crumble to the ground.

My chin burns as the skin brushes against the pavement like trashed brake pads. I open my eyes. Everything flips to slow-motion. Police circling me. A police dog bowling. Flashlight streaks. The transient movement reminds me of pressing the fast-forward button on a remote to the slowest speed mixed with sketchy internet connection. The picture will move slowly, and the screen may freeze for a second or two.

More flashlights bob up and down as the people in uniforms multiply. An officer drops their flashlight in front of my face. I follow the light glow pointing to the middle of the graffiti art mural and see beady black eyes of a tiger staring back at me. The tiger's nose wrinkles inward as it growls at its intruder with blades of sharp teeth—ready to launch and annihilate its prey.

A blow to my back knocks the wind out of me. An officer plows a knee into my spine as he rips my arms behind my back to handcuff me. My hearts racing and I can't catch my breath. I stare up at the tiger mural. The black eyes transform to red. My hands and face tingle as I go to sleep.

An angel exists,
when you least expect,
they're watching you—
you'll see.

And they will persist,
they'll spring to effect,
they're watching you—
you'll see.

When these angels appear,
you shouldn't fear,
if masked from another kind.

You must stay awake,
lives are at stake,
your purpose, soon you will find.

"Jase?" I cough. Someone's stacking fifty-pound dumbbells, one at a time onto my chest. I fight through the pain and listen for his voice.

"Will?" a voice trails off.

"Jason? Where?" It hurts to speak—there's too much pressure riveting out from underneath my ribcage. "Where. Are you?" I muscle out.

"Hang on. Here we go, he's conscious," a man's voice trails off. "William Norwick?"

"Wha?" I ask.

"Can you open yer eyes?" the man asks.

I flitter an eyelid open to a blinding light. My eye stings. I squeeze it shut like a frightened oyster closing its shell.

"Yer under arrest for leaving a crime scene ..."

I close my eyes as an officer rambles off a laundry list of wrongful accusations.

CHAPTER 19

If I gathered my worst hangovers from the year and multiplied them by another fifty-two weeks of binge drinking and self-sabotage, it would equal to how badly my body aches right now. Ruby-red-and-burgundy stains cover my hands from blood spraying through the skin lacerations on my chin. Both hands look as though I splattered merlot and ketchup across the skin, then baked my arms in the sun for several hours. My head may as well of been beaten with a wine bottle as the throb alone is enough to force me to bed rest. My wrists are raw, and the numerous pops to my spine infect my limbs with electrical anguish.

"Yer arresting officers—where'd they go?" a policeman demands from the crowd of aggravated colleges forcing me to move faster up the winding sidewalk.

"Where's Casey and McHenry?" a woman shouts from the fleet of officers.

Brother and sister team gone missing, and they're pinning this on me.

"What'd you do to them?" another man scorns.

"The windshield exploded. They left me," I say.

"Doesn't add up. Casey called for backup," another officer sneers behind me.

"Was running from attackers, just like they were—"

"Bullshit," someone yells.

"Why doncha bolt ya rocket." I grit my teeth. "I'd like a solicitor—now!" I yell.

"We'll provide you with a solicitor," the officer holding my cuffs says.

I'd like to speak my mind. But I think of Shelly, bite my tongue, and look ahead. Steering away from further confrontation is the best thing for me right now.

We walk to the edge of Clyde Street. Traffic builds in both directions of the busy street as authorities' direct traffic. Vehicles from various news stations scatter to the sides of the road. The first reporters on the scene assume position, ready to jump at the story. I whip my head away from the crowd that's consuming one side of the street, only to see the population growing on the opposite side. People hold their phones, bracing for the right moment to capture a shot or video of a real live criminal. *I'm innocent, you assholes.*

"Wife's in the hospital. May lose an eye, and I can't be with her because of yer assumptions. You'll regret this—trust me."

"We're following procedure. She's unable to communicate, so we'll need you for further questioning in regard to yer initial arrest," the officer holding my handcuffs says.

"Why won't anyone listen to me when I say we were attacked—"

"You fled the scene of an accident—two officers missing. We're placing any suspects from the scene in custody. It'll be a long night for you." The officer releases my handcuffs and opens the door to his vehicle. He's in his early twenties and by far one of the youngest looking officers I've seen.

"Thanks for the talk—feeling relieved." I roll my eyes and slide across the back seat of his car.

"Yeah? That's good. Glad to help," he says.

I gape at the young officer as he slams the door in my face. He ignores me. Straightening his posture, he struts around his vehicle to converse with fellow policemen. His ignorance infuriates me. Why the hell can't the guy with no shoes run by and punch him in the back of his head? I'd be forever grateful.

Onlookers inch closer to the line of police officials guarding the front of the vehicle holding the "violent criminal." Security flags at them to move back and get out of the way. A news anchor and cameraman approach the rejected spectators with camera time. I can't bear to watch the live broadcast of a situation they know nothing about. Feels like I'm watching the news, except the windshield's my flat screen, and I'm watching strangers rip apart a man they know nothing about. I'll think twice the next time I watch the news.

Ignoring the live development of fake news, I stare out my window. The shoeless man scampers up the spiral walkway and onto the sidewalk. He brushes through the crowd and darts across Clyde Street, fazing no one. What's wrong with you people—man with no shoes runs past a crowd of officers and they don't even flinch.

An officer knocks on my window and dangles two large Ziploc bags containing both of my shoes. "Look familiar?" he shouts at the window.

The officer jumps inside the vehicle and flips on the siren, enhancing the full effect of the hero arresting the violent criminal. I'm mortified. He waves at some of his police buddies like a cocky, fraudulent hero as he peels his car away from the scene. He knows nothing about the situation.

He fidgets with the heat controls and floors the gas pedal, speeding close to double the speed limit because can—he's captured a violent criminal. I watch him through the mesh divider. The officer is younger than me by eight to ten years, as he can barely grow facial hair. He smirks to himself as he grips the wheel. *Great, must be this guy's first arrest.* If we have another windshield followed by a horrific encounter with the red-eye stalkers, this guy wouldn't know what to do. He'd piss and shit his pants—get us both killed. At least Casey and McHenry were reactive, whereas this baw bag clearly lacks street smarts. Where the hell did Casey and McHenry go?

The young officer turns down Gorbals Street, passing drivers on the Victoria Bridge. The way he's running drivers to the edge of the road, one would think I'm being driven to detonate a bomb. Sirens from police cars trailing close behind grow shriller as they catch up to our vehicle.

The police parade follows our car to the entranceway of the station. The vanilla and blue two-story structured building mimics the colors beaming from the top of the police cars. The parking lot's congested with double-parked cars. There's a banner draping across the building welcoming another Glasgow Police Department during their rebuild. This can only mean double the staff, double the arrests under one roof, and double the time it'll take for me to get to Shelly. *Damn it.*

The young officer helps slide me from his vehicle and walks me toward the side of the building. Officers from the trailing vehicle help him escort me through the side door of the station. We enter behind an officer guiding a disgruntled woman wearing cat ears, kicking her legs against the wall.

"Stop doin' that," the officer says to the woman.

The woman kicks the wall harder.

We slow down behind the cat woman and lion tamer. I stand on my toes and look through the line. Looks like I'm the fourth arrest in line for check-in.

"Stop. Freeze right now," the officer says, grabbing at the cat woman's cuffs.

The woman rips free from his grip and backs against the wall so she's facing the officer. She cackles.

"Need some help?" young officer asks, releasing my shoulder.

The woman launches at him. She spits in his face and hisses as loud as a deep puncture to a high-pressure hose.

"Sick—yer a sick woman," young officer shouts and dry heaves at the floor.

"Go ahead. We'll take 'em in." One of the assisting officers grabs my shoulder.

The young officer cups his mouth. "She spit in my mouth—I felt it. I'll get sick." The young officer knocks into cat woman and darts down the hallway.

I stand on my toes and sift through the others ahead of me in line. One man rolls his eyes in the back of his head and is praising the concrete wall. An officer with a red mustache brushes past the freak show and points at me.

"Bring 'em this way!" the officer with the red mustache shouts as he scoots the line to the wall. "Wait. Stop." He slides on a pair of rubber gloves and grabs a pair of booties from his back pocket. "You can't be walking around with blood on yer feet." He slides the booties over my feet and peels off the rubber gloves, tossing them in a toxic waste can.

We pass the line of lawbreakers and wrong doers. People shoot dirty looks at me for skipping the line. Not sure why this is—the quicker they move up the line the sooner they face time behind bars. Idiots.

"Right this way. Let's have a chat in the room." The officer with the red mustache pats my back. "Been chaos at this station with two police units sharing one roof. We've got double the criminals pouring in with double the amount of police officers I've never seen in my life." He opens a door and points for me to sit down.

"Can you please take off the cuffs?" I ask.

"Now that you can longer escape, we won't need them." Larkin grabs for the keys.

The officer runs his fingers across his red mustache and stares at me intently. He waits a few seconds, then nods in approval. There's a release of tension in my wrists as the cuffs click open. A part of me wants to sway around and punch the officers in face. I could take two of them down, slip out of the room, and into the crowd.

I pat at my wrists and look around the room. The room's empty except for a table and three chairs. This room's familiar, as I've seen it on crime shows. I'm standing in the middle of an interrogation room.

CHAPTER 20

The room is small enough to trigger claustrophobia even in the strongest of minds. The thermostat feels as though it's been bumped to the highest setting as there's beads of sweat forming above my lip and cheeks. I've been in the room less than three minutes. The officers can step in and out of the fiery room and give their bodies a break, while I'll just have to stick this one out. Enough time in here would cause the spins.

"Go ahead, take a seat. I'm Officer Larkin, and I'd like to talk with you a bit." The officer with the red mustache walks toward the door with the other officer.

I nod.

"Good, then," Officer Larkin says.

Knowing the drill from movies and TV shows, I walk to the chair that's pushed in at the table.

"I'm going be asking you a few questions about two incidents you were involved in. I'd like to get your version of the story and ask some questions, if that's all right with you," Officer Larkin says.

I nod.

"Would you like a water?"

"Please." I watch Officer Larkin follow the other officer out of the room.

I collapse onto the navy-blue chair and slide underneath the table. The chair is made of wood and is wobbly. One of the legs may give out if I slide back too quickly. There's an awkward dip inside the center of the chair quite possibly making this one of the most uncomfortable chairs I've ever sat in. There's a large window made up of reflective glass. I recognize this from the movies—an observation mirror. How many people are lined up in front of the window, watching my every move as I adjust to the room temperature?

I avoid looking at myself in the mirror and look at the ground instead. There are dents in the manila wall next to the door. The gashes are of various shades of grayish blues. The wall art must be from angry maniacs hurling their chair against the wall—explains why my chair wobbles. There are droplets of blood smeared into the raggedy carpet fibers. The blood is on my side of the table. Makes me wonder if they beat the answers they want out of each criminal.

The knob rattles and the bottom of the door scuffs the carpet as it opens. Officer Larkin steps in alone. He walks over to me and stares at me for a second before handing me a bottle of water. He rolls up his sleeves and walks around me. I turn my head and watch him until he stops behind me. Chills stagger up my spine. *What's he going to do to me?*

Officer Larkin circles round the rest of the table, pulls over a chair, and sits down in front of me. He scratches at his mustache and crosses his arms. "You've requested to have a solicitor?"

"Yes."

"Why?" He leans forward and studies my face.

"I've done nothing wrong and need to get out of here to check on my wife—"

"You're separated."

"Yes." I adjust my posture in the chair.

"You two working things out?"

"I'd like to."

"Report indicates you've got nothing at the house—no clothes, only one toothbrush, no shoes—"

"She was taking care of me. Got too drunk at an event earlier in the evening."

"Alcohol leads to aggression in a lot of individuals. We see it all the time."

"I'd never lay a hand on Shelly—or anyone."

"We've scooped you up a dozen times in recent months and threw you in the drunk tank. We've got phone records from employees of local bars and restaurants—customer phone calls and complaints to prevent you from violence. One report says you fell off a barstool and caused a fire. The week before you had an altercation with a bouncer at the door—"

"I'd like a solicitor now," I interrupt.

"Let me finish." Officer Larkin leans back in his seat and crosses his legs. "We also know yer records clean prior to yer brother's death. It was tragic. I know—I was one of the responding officers."

I open the water and guzzle it down. Someone must've turned up the heat again.

"I also showed up late to the event for yer brother tonight and heard you gave quite the show—a drunken mess. Shelly's in the hospital undergoing surgery. If you cooperate—answer some investigative questions—we'll be able to assign officers to yer case and start connecting the dots."

I stare at the officer. Can't decide whether he'll believe me or twist my words and use them against me. "When will Shelly be ready to answer questions?" I ask.

"We should know more in the afternoon."

"What time is it?" I ask.

"Five in the morning."

"I'd like a solicitor and will wait here if I have to for Shelly to wake. You'll see for yerself that I'm innocent. I'll accept yer apology for keeping me from consoling Shell."

"Fine, then. I'll stop there and get officers out for questioning based on the facts we've got based on yer known locations leading up to the incident in Shelly's home."

"I've done nothing wrong, you'll see."

"How 'bout we move on to the missing officers from my unit, Officers Casey and McHenry."

I plop my elbows on the table and run my hands through my hair. "Ask yer officers when they get back to the office."

"We would if we knew where they were, which is why we're going to need you to answer some investigative questions. You have a solicitor in mind?"

"No, I've never been involved in a mess like this before."

"Lucky for you, yer buddy gave us a name for one."

I release my head and drop my arms to the table. *Thank you, Ethan.* "Is he at the station?"

"He's talking to officers in the other room."

"Am I on the news?"

"Aye, yes."

"I'm sure he's embarrassed. Is he pissed about earlier?" I ask.

"All I care about right now is getting you that solicitor and finding my missing officers."

"Think about it: When would I've had time to break a windshield? I was sitting in the back of a police car with my hands cuffed to my back. How could I escape from the police car and still have time to hide two officers loaded with guns? Please tell me how you think it's possible. How is that possible, huh?"

"Yer getting smart now?" He exits the room and walks back in holding a bag. "Yer cuffs and the tools used to cut them—found them both."

"It's my right to have a solicitor present."

Officer Larkin grabs a document off the table and slams it in front of me. "Sign this document." Larkin tosses a pen on over the document. The pen rolls off the table and hits the ground.

I lean over to pick up my pen. "Yer agreeing to having—one second, it's a long name—" Officer Larkin pauses to grab a document from his pocket. "Kyle Arthur Stagenth ... werld as yer solicitor, then?"

"Yes."

"Due to the seriousness of the crimes we've brought you in questioning for—and because we've got a year's worth of paperwork, phone records, and written reports linking to you with destructive behavior—we have reason to believe yer a danger to the public. We have the right to hold you."

"What? For how long?"

"As a senior police officer, I'm approving this unit to hold you for the next twenty-four hours. If we have enough evidence to charge you, we will do so within the twenty-four-hour period. Anything you'd like add, you'll let us know?"

"Aye."

"Excuse me for a moment while I contact your solicitor." Officer Larkin stands up and walks out of the room.

My skin burns as though I was leaning inside an oven. I'd like to take my chair and throw it as hard as I can against the door. Funny how fast I'm swayed to side with anyone who's sat in this hot seat. I understand the frustration and why you threw your chair at the door. I remove a layer of clothing from over my head and use it to fan my face.

Officer Larkin enters the room. "Won't use this against you—sending more officers out for my missing two. Any information you may have is appreciated."

I want to help, but they'll never believe me. "I want to speak to my solicitor."

"How'd you get out of the vehicle, *damn it?*" Officer Larkin demands.

"Get ahold of the solicitor." I ask.

"Yer solicitor won't be here for another hour or two, so I'll need to move you to a temporary holding area, as we're at capacity and need to use the room." He signals for me to stand up. "They'll move you to a custody suite from there."

Larkin chaperons me out of the room and leads me down a narrow hallway. He stops. "See he's still in there answering questions." Officer Larkin points through the observation window in another room.

"Who?"

"Yer friend." Officer Larkin flails his hand toward the observation window gesturing at the man in the hot seat.

I see a man with messy, dark brown, slicked-back hair. He's face is clean-shaven, and his teeth look like they've had several whitening treatments. "Wait—no, I've never seen the man in my life."

"Come on, let's go. You can nap in yer custody suite—"

"Stop a second. Yer not listening to me. I've never seen that man before in my life. I thought you were saying my friend Ethan was here—"

"You'll straighten out yer problems with yer solicitor." Officer Larkin spins me around and locks me in cuffs.

"Ready? We're leaving," an undercover officer says, strapping on a vest.

"Wait, there's been a misunderstanding." I pull away from the officer.

"Don't start with me." Officer Larkin nods his head at two officers in front of us. "This one's 'bout to get out of control—watch 'em." He hands me over to the two officers and walks away.

"They had red eyes," I shout. "The attackers had red eyes."

"No." Larkin turns around. "Yer gonna have red eyes after detoxing with kleptomaniacs and junkies."

I swivel my head side to side in attempt to make eye contact with my escorting officers, but either of them makes eye contact with me. They stare ahead without expression, following procedure. I pull back and limp in between a step—last ditch effort to slow down and think. Both officers withhold any cue leading to a possible caring gesture per my situation. My feet leave the ground as the officers compensate for my lousy attempt in stalling the situation. Desensitization.

"Please listen. There's man in that room claiming he's my friend. He's lying." I point down the hall. Desensitization.

They ignore me. Desensitization.

CHAPTER 21

"**G**ive me yer finger," a man says.

"Piss off," I say.

"Look at my fingers," the same man says, lunging to one knee while fluttering his fingers in the air as though he's making birdcalls.

I back against the wall and look around for a place to sit. There's an open seat next to a man who's picking his nose and wiping it on the person passed out in front of him. This is different than the drunk tank. In the drunk tank, everyone's passed out and nonconfrontational, like the man unwillingly accepting boogers. It's a quieter scene. But during any moment at random, a person will pop out of their boozy coma. Usually they'll sit up and look around. Security will assess their level of intoxication, but they'll pass out for another couple hours or so. I've been there.

Eventually, we're able to stand up on two feet and walk around like zombies, which must be a sign of sobriety, as the officer on duty will shout something to see if we follow. I've seen a few guys stand up, walk to a corner of the holding cell, and pee against the wall. One time I saw a man get up and piss on another man passed out in the corner. The man shot up in a drunken rage and tackled the man to the ground—broke his nose. I've avoided the scene ever since.

This is far different than what I've experienced before. Everyone's coherent and angry. There are three holding zones. Two of them run parallel and are spaced far enough to fit a small office in between. The two are also small enough for someone to toss a pencil successfully from one cell through the bars of another. The third holding cell looks like the temporary add-in while the two police units function under one roof. The temporary prison pop-in turns the space into a *U* shape. The elongated desk for officers to post up almost complete the *U* shape, making it a complete square. Police align the desk and each holding cell has their own officer on guard.

There's a man with a bloody shirt forming his hands into fists pacing back and forth in the cell closest to me. "Ye looking at me, son?" he screams at me and rams his body against the bars.

I look away. I don't belong here.

"Sit down and shut up," the officer guarding his cell says. "Yer next to be booked."

"You stabbed that man. I saw it. Yer going down for murder," a man in the cell parallel to me shouts at the man.

"Yarreehh die too." The man with the bloody shirt slams his body against the bars closest to him. The others sharing his cell cower down and keep to themselves—except one man lying in the middle of the floor, laughing to himself. He walks over the man and taps against the bars on the opposite site before bolting toward his target guy.

"He confessed. Hear that, Officer?" He points at the man. "I did nothing—only defended the dead guy. You'll see." He glares at the man "Ye belong in hell, piece of shit."

The man in the bloody shirt beats his head repeatedly against the bars closest to the man.

"Stop yelling," one of the men in my cell turns and runs his head into the corner farthest from the confrontation.

I look down and pray the three aggressors are next in line to be booked and away from this scene. They're scaring the shit out of me. It takes the snap of a finger for one of them to switch. One of the officers at the desk gets an alert from their walkie and stands up. I couldn't make out the words from the man in my cell continuously thrashing his forehead against the metal bars. I'd like to scream at him to stop and shut the hell up. I'd regret that immediately, as I sense the others around me are on edge waiting for a reason to punish someone. A man sitting across from me in my cell rocks back and forth gritting his teeth as he grows impatient with the headbanger. He'll snap any second and stop the—he jumps to his feet and struts to the man.

"Yer giving me a headache. Please stop," he says.

Wow—okay, the man's asking politely. Didn't expect that.

"Wha?" the man stops beating his head and fluffs his chest out at the guy.

I search for the officers to make sure they're ready for a beatdown. I adjust weight on my feet and prepare to dodge out of the way.

"Yer gonna give yerself a headache, and this'll take longer. Don't let 'em do that to ya," the man reasons.

"Watcha say, eh?" The man in blood looks over his shoulder.

Good. I feel more at ease. At least I'm placed with the reasoning criminal. Not sure if this at all plays into the wolf in sheep's clothing concept. He could be the wolf or the sheep. He's probably both, because he's in here. But I'm in here. *You're innocent, dummy—don't get caught up.* I've done so much bad this year to my wife. My relationships with my family and friends. Maybe I'm one drink away from making this my reality. *Jason would flip if he saw me like this.* I don't belong here—would be a disappointment if I saw Jason pull this type of shit.

The officer at the desk continues the conversation on his walkie and signals for the officer guarding the bloody man's cell. He stands up, puts on a pair of gloves, and escorts my so-called partner in crime toward the bloody man's cell. *Great, this ought to be good.* I'd like to see the liar get his ass kicked. The man looks at me and looks away. I want to yell at him and call him a bloody liar, but I'd look like the others. I can contain myself—he's a liar, my lawyer will prove this.

The officer stops him in front of the cell and grabs for the keys. The stranger glances over to me. I can't help but grin—what lies has he fed to the officers? I raise an eyebrow, eager for him to meet his outspoken cellmate. *Go on, quit looking at me psycho, but go on.* Two muscular police officers hustle inside the holding zone, blowing past the tables. They signal for the stranger and the officer to step aside.

"It's yer turn." One of the heavyweight champion–looking officers points at the mouthy murderer.

There's a round of applause from the self-proclaimed vigilante. "Yer goin' down for murder. I'll watch you on the TV from my home while my wife cooks me dinner, prick."

The deranged man ducks underneath the office and plows himself against the bars, knocking his head so hard he passes out of the floor.

"Morning jist got easier. I got 'em. Go and see who's next," the huskier of the duo says to his counterpart. He bends over and scoops the man from the ground.

The stranger steps inside his cell, walks to a bench, and sits down with his back facing me. He kicks his leg up and skims around the chaos.

His clothes are wrinkle-free and his calm demeanor is off-putting. I find myself glaring at him, watching his every move. I'm unsure as to how I'd respond the next time he dares to shoot me a look.

"Yer turn. Let's go." Keys jingle against the metal.

I turn around and see an officer pointing at me. The officer looks in his late twenties with wavy blond hair. "Me?" I jab my finger against my chest.

"Aye," wavy blond officer says.

It's my turn. *Good, get me the hell out of this mess.* I jump to my feet and stride toward the exit of the holding cell. I slow my stroll behind the stranger. "You'll never get away with yer lies," I mutter at him under my breath.

"Taking you to booking."

CHAPTER 22

The door clanks shut. A loud screech follows as the metal components from the door latch together. I lower myself onto a floating wall-to-wall concrete bench. There's a bright blue pillow and a matching rectangular pad folded in half stacked next to me. Can't decide if the sleeping accommodations resemble a wrestling mat and enlarged ice pack inside a pillowcase cover or beat-up lawn chair covers—maybe a combination of the two? I raise my leg and catapult the folded mat. This is bullshit. I stand up and drop kick the flimsy pillow.

Being locked inside a custody suite is what I'd imagine it'd be like to be trapped alone inside a utility elevator without power. At least the elevator situation would exclude a full-body strip search and handing over my personal belongings. I glance at the door. There's a narrow cutout for a window measuring close to the size of a brick. It feels like I'm guilty, even though I've been inside for less than ten minutes. If this isn't prison, the real deal, I can't imagine how much worse this could get. I've been drinking, but I'm no criminal. I've had a bad year—been drinking a little much. Don't remember the last time I was sober. *How did I get here? How. Did. I. Get. Here? I'm sorry, Shelly.*

I lift my legs up on the bench and flip to one side. I bend my arm and use it as a pillow underneath my head. Not sure I've ever been this tired. It's as though someone stuck wads of lint in both eyes and rubbed the fibers around with their thumbs so they stick to the moisture like a lint roller. I'd like a shower and an ice water.

"Get up!" a voice shouts through my brick-crack door slit.

I force myself up and rub my eyes.

"Yer solicitor's here."

"Does he come here—er, do I go with you?"

"Yer coming with me." Keys jingle and clank inside the lock. The door opens, revealing an officer with beach-blond hair and a tall, slender build.

I plop to my feet and begin a slow shuffle toward him. Like a mopey fellow, I drag my feet and tuck my head down. I stare at the marks in the ground as I follow Blondie. There's banter from the holding cell as we steer down one of the hallways. One man's screaming about the boogie man through the slit in his door and another man's kicking his door and shouting for him to shut up from the door across from his.

Blondie opens a door and points for me to step in. A man in a suit is sitting at a table, back turned to me.

"Come on in, William, and take a seat," the man says.

"Fine. I'll sit," I say, walking toward the table. I turn and watch the officer exit the room and close the door.

"I need yer help." I scramble to the table and slide in another uncomfortable blue wooden chair.

"That's why I'm here." The man in the suit gathers papers and clunks them against the table.

"They've got the wrong. Wait—what are you?" I look at the man's soft complexion and notice his black eye. The black eye I gave him hours earlier. I jump up in my seat, knocking the chair to the ground.

"Sit down," the man demands.

"Why are you here? Why we're you there?" I ask.

"Please sit, Will." The man points at my chair. "I'm Arthur. Nice to meet you. I need you to read over some documents and sign a few thing—"

"Answer my question first."

"Sit down and shut the hell up for a minute," the man says softly. "Trust me."

I kick the chair up and slide back down. The man has dark brown curly hair and light brown eyes. The black-and-blue circle underneath one of his eyes highlights his eye color. The other eye is puffy from lack of sleep. Guess the two of us had the same kind of night, though only one of us is behind bars.

"I need you to read through these documents carefully before signing." He slides a stack of papers in front of me.

"Give me the pen. I'll sign." I hold my pen out and fumble through the documents looking for the signature line.

"I need you to carefully read these documents. It goes over my cost, among other policies, before you sign." He holds the pen in his hand.

"Aye, fine." I glance through the packet and flip through the pages. I turn to page four.

"Small font too."

I look up at him and watch him raise an eyebrow. His eyes widen at me as though he was saying, "Read that closely, dummy. Read. It. Closely. There's something hidden."

Sure enough, in the small font I see it:

Read this carefully, William. You're in grave danger. Shelly is going to be okay; we have other's watching over her in the hospital.

I look up.

"You may need to take out a loan to afford me. Read on. Officer Larkin will be in momentarily, once you've signed the documents."

No matter what. You must not look up. Keep reading these documents, as this is the only chance I'll have to explain what's going on. When you finish reading these documents, and if you have any questions, you must speak in code (ask questions about my cost). If you comprehend, you must initial first, then sign your name. Flip to the next page and see small font in the middle of the page. You're being watched through an observation window, so just take deep breaths and read.

I flip to the next page:

This is not how we wanted to explain everything to you, and we WILL go over everything thoroughly once we get you out of here. Shelly was attacked by the Astargarians—Stags, we call them. They have red eyes and you're not losing your mind. Shelly's awake and she's seen them too now too. She's been talking about it to Ethan and Sarah in the hospital, but they're blaming it on the drugs they have her on. Flip to the next page see refer to small font only.

I turn the page and feel my heart racing:

You must breathe and stay calm. *No matter what.* If you feel anxious think of how tired you are and if you must react, you must make it about you not being with Shelly. *Stay calm.* It's critical. If we're going to get you out of here. I'm an undercover agent with the LFP and so is your "friend." We are a division of the CIA. Your "friend" jumped inside the vehicle and was arrested in order to study your escape route.

It feels as though someone cranked up the heat again. I rub my head. It feels like I have a bouncy ball inside my stomach.

"You want some water?" he asks.

"Yes please. I'm feeling nauseous from the heat."

"Sure, I'll be right back. Can I have you sign your initials on that page for me first? Sign anywhere," he says, staring intently into my eyes.

I sign my initials and sign my name.

"Good. I'll be right back. Keep reading through and I'll let the officers know we'll be a few more minutes." He stands up and walks toward the door. An officer opens the door for him.

I turn to the next page:

> You have a rare blood type and due to your rare blood type, the Stags are hunting you down. We've been following you and Jason since birth. We've been protecting you and Jason since birth. There are others like you around the world who possess your blood type that are facing the same attacks. These attacks are meant to look like "accidents." The Stags are killing all of you in order to release a virus. The virus will dominate the human race. Why? Please turn to the next page.

I flip the page and jump from the sound of the door opening.

"Here's your water. You getting through the bank information okay?"

"Aye." I reach for the water and rub my forehead. "Just want to get out of here and see Shelly."

"That's what I'm here for. Think there's one more page, and I'll just need your initials and signature. They're ready to come in."

> Put simple, your blood proteins are the only way we can combat the virus. We understand this is difficult to process, but it's critical you remain calm. Do *not* speak to anyone regarding this letter. Do *not* speak to anyone without your lawyer/me present. It's urgent we get you out of here. They'll want to hold you for the night. At 21:00 hours an officer will toss a crumpled note the size of a pea into your cell with instructions. Read the note and swallow the paper. At 22:00 you'll be released. You must put your trust in us. We will answer all your questions tonight.

"Where should I sign?" I ask.

"Bottom."

I initial the document and sign my name.

"Good. I'll get Officer Larkin."

CHAPTER 23

Officer Larkin follows Arthur into the room. Both men are holding steaming cups of coffee. Seeing the steam makes me sweat even more. Right now, that looks as enjoyable as running a marathon in a snowsuit during the hottest day of the year. I'd do it, though, if it meant getting me the hell out of here. I'd make it a couple of blocks before the side cramps would kick in, push through another half a block, fall flat on my face. It's the thought that counts.

Larkin grabs a chair from the corner of the room and drags it next to Arthur. He grabs a pen from his back pocket and clicks it against the table.

"William Norwick?" Officer Larkin asks, squatting onto his chair. "Shit." The muddy brown liquid slops over the edge of his World's Best Dad mug, leaking across his hand and splatting against table. He sets the mug on the table and flicks the excess coffee from his hand.

"Ow." I flinch back in my chair and cup my eye. Feels like Officer Larkin shot me in the eye with a squirt gun filled with hot water.

Arthur grabs a tissue from his pocket and hands it to me. I dab at the coffee overspray on my eyelid and drop in on top of the table puddle.

"Let's start over. I'll be recording this conversation, all right?" Officer Larkin smears the tissue against the coffee, wads it into a ball, and wails it across the room. He slides a tape recorder to the middle of the table. "Okay?"

"Aye," I say.

Larkin turns the recorder on. "Mr. William Norwick, do you understand yer rights?"

"Yes."

"Mr. Norwick you've chosen to have a solicitor present during yer interview?"

I look at Arthur. He nods at me.

"Aye," I say as I use my finger to probe my eye. He must've used salt in his coffee instead of sugar.

"Why?" the officer asks.

"What?" I ask?

"You've chosen to have a solicitor present an—"

"Aye," I interrupt the officer.

"Let Officer Larkin finish talking before you answer," Arthur intervenes.

"Why'd you choo—"

"I'm sorry. Haven't slept," I stop Larkin.

Officer Larkin leans in his seat and folds his arms. He gapes at me.

I exchange glances with Arthur and skim to the other side of the table, catching the tail end of an eye roll from the irritated officer. It's too quiet. The elongated silence is making this worse.

"What?" I ask.

"How 'bout I sit back and enjoy my coffee while you interrogate yourself?"

"This is an interrogation? I'm being interrogated?" I ask.

"You must let 'em speak, Officer Larkin. It's only an interview. You've done nothing wrong—"

"Aye, right. You've done nothing wrong—" Larkin disrupts Arthur. "Yet." He points his finger in the air for silence. "William Norwick, why'd you request a solicitor?"

"Because I'm innocent."

"During this interview, please make sure yer answers are clear. Understand?" Larkin sips his coffee.

I nod.

"Can't record the sound of a nod."

"I understand," I want to reach over the table and slap the hot cup of coffee from his hand. Wonder how loud he'd scream if his mug toppled over his lap?

"For the recording, please state yer name."

"William Norwick."

"Age?"

"Thirty-two"

"Where're you from?"

"Glasgow. West End." I wipe a bead of sweat from my forehead.

The officer scribbles gibberish on his note pad. I look at Arthur.

"Question?" Arthur stops Larkin. "Were you on the scene?"

"I wasn't."

"I'd like to step in for a second if you don't mind. Where's William's arresting officer? I'd like to speak to the arresting officer." Arthur folds his hands on the table.

"Missing." Officer Larkin adjusts his back against the seat. "She's missing—her and the other arresting officer."

"I see." Arthur grabs a pen and scribbles notes. "And who informed my client of his rights?"

"Officer Casey—the missing officer. It's urgent we get as much information as we can right now so please let me ask my questions," Larkin scoffs.

"You're wasting your time with him. He's an innocent man," Arthur says.

"You know nothing about the case to make such quick judgments," Larkin says.

"Aye, right. Whatever you say." Arthur yawns.

"Think yer being funny?" Larkin leans over and plants his elbows on the table.

"Me? No." Arthur clicks the pen against the table and writes in his notes. "I'm just not sure why we're even having this conversation right now. You don't have a warrant, tackled one of my clients running for his life from an attack on your squad car, and accused another innocent man who was only passing by and heard—"

"You don't know—"

"Let me finish," Arthur says over the officer. "You accused and arrested a second innocent man who heard people screaming for help. The story he gave me over the phone—"

"We found his fingerprints on the hand cuffs and tools—enough to arrest him without a warrant," Larkin interrupts.

"My client picked them up when he was looking for the person screaming, and you tackled him down and arrested him." Arthur pounds the table. "Did you find his prints anywhere on or inside the vehicle itself?"

"He was seen fleeing the scene with the handcuffs and tools he used to let his friend free. My guys are still working the crime scene, and they'll check every crevasse of that police car for his prints."

"I don't know who that guy—"

"Hang on, William," Arthur interrupts me. "How could someone flee the scene when he didn't even know where it is? The damn cuffs were found outside the scene, and my client picked them up."

"I'm holding these men until we've got some answers. I'm looking for my missing officers."

"I understand, but you're looking at the wrong two men!" Arthur shouts.

"Not so sure."

Arthur sips his coffee.

"Let me continue—time's detrimental right now."

"Sure, just stop wasting my time with questions I'm going to need to see a warrant for."

The door brushes open, and Officer Blondie walks in. "Sorry to interrupt. We received a phone call—a detective on the phone. He mentioned Arthur and had an urgent message."

Arthur and Officer Larkin flip their chairs around and stare at Blondie. The silence in the room is uncomfortable.

"And?" Larkin asks.

"What?" Blondie asks.

"What the hell's wrong with everyone in this room? You all get whacked with a brick or something?"

I shake my head. "No."

"No sir," Blondie confirms.

"Pause the damn tape." Larkin points to Arthur. "Was asking what the urgent message was?"

"Now? Aloud?" Blondie says.

"Did I stutter? The detective say it was private—the information?"

"No."

"Waiting. Every second that passes interferes with us finding McHenry and Carey."

"The detective says Shelly's awake and should be ready to answer questions by tomorrow. I've got the detective's information. He says he'll be at the hospital in case she's able to respond sooner." He hands Larkin a note.

"I'll call him when we're done here. Thanks."

Larkin and Arthur rotate their chairs toward me.

Larkin reaches for the record button.

Arthur blocks Officer Larkin's hand. "It was still recording. I'd like to have a copy of this tape before I leave here. I believe the phone call could be considered evidence."

"You and I'll chat after the interview." Larkin sips his coffee. "William Norwick, would you like to give your statement?"

"Aye, I'm innocent."

"Yer being held at one of Glasgow's Primary Custody Centres with a temporary extension Ancillary Custody Centre. Due to the November 2018 Glasgow ARG. Station fire, yer being held under police custody at the Cumberland Street and Jane headquarters, temporarily accommodating two police unit headquarters. Do you understand why yer at this location?"

"Aye, the fire."

"Mr. Norwick, if we find yer statement's a load of pish, you'll be charged and sentenced. You understand?"

"Aye."

"What happened last night?" Larkin asks.

I look at Arthur.

"Go ahead. Shelly'll confirm your answers," Arthur says.

"I drank too much at my brother's charity event—event held for my dead brother, as you know. Made a fool out of myself in front of the audience. Shelly, whom I still love, drove me home—to her home—our old home. She offered to make me tea and said I could stay in the bed in the kid's roo—er, guest room. I didn't feel comfortable doing that, so I passed out on the couch. I woke up to her screaming. I'm not sure how long she was yelling for. I just heard screams, so I went upstairs. I saw she wasn't in her bedroom. She was lying on the floor in the other room."

"What'd you do next?"

"I got my phone, called the police, and kept he comfortable until you arrived. Yer officers said she had marks on her neck and accused me up strangling her. I'd never do that."

"Officer Larkin, quick question: Why was the glass from the second-story window busted from outside in? There are no trees. Maybe something or someone caused the marks from the roof. The roofline's even with the second-story window." Arthur sips his coffee. "If there was a confrontation, the glass would've been scattered out the other direction."

"How'd you get that information?" Larkin asks.

"It's a simple observation from seeing the outside of the house, mixed with common sense."

"Moving on." Larkin looks at me.

"Wait. I've got another problem—question." Arthur sits up in his seat.

"What's yer question?"

"We're you able to confirm the marks around Shelly's throat happened within the hour they were home from the event? Have you compared hand marks from photos with forensics with his hands? If not, I've got a guy. He can get that to you quick—"

"I'm gonna stop you right there."

"How far along was the bruising on her neck? Maybe this happened hours before she saw William Norwick. We're you able to confirm through images and footage. The marks were already there? You should think about releasing my client until you've got that warrant."

"Yer condescending nature is humorous, really. Forensics is already on it. They'd have it done sooner, but their magic wand is broken."

"Well, then, why—"

"No. You listen to me." Officer Larkin raises his voice. "Was going to announce the evidence once we had results from forensics, but hell, you got under my skin. We're working on multiple angles of footage from the altercation that took place in the lobby of the event. Officers are going through the guest list one by one and paying visits. We've already got one witness willing to give a statement about the abusive behavior they witnessed from William Norwick in the lobby. The witness said they even stepped in and tried to stop William from abusing a woman—Shelly. Should have our witnesses, footage, and forensic conclusion ready to go by tomorrow morning. I don't need that warrant to hold him here."

"I think we're done here for now." Arthur waves at the observation window for an officer to come in. "William, I'll be back in the morning to speak with you. I'd like to speak with my other client now."

Blondie walks in and walks behind my chair.

"You don't take orders from this shithead again. Hear me?" Officer Larkin snaps at the blond officer. "Now go ahead. Get him the hell out of here. This was useless."

"Not for me. I got what I needed. Bring in my other client, or I'll make some phone calls."

"You threatening me?"

"Not at all. More like testing you." Arthur props his elbows on the table, cups his hands, and stares Larkin in the eyes.

I straighten up in my crappy wooden chair and watch the CIA agent override Larkin by using the officer's own tactics on him. Officer Larkin's cheeks look like blobs of raspberry jam. Watching the two of them portray their best "No, I'm the one in control" game face is better than if they were to arm wrestle.

Arthur scoots his chair back at an angle so he's no long sitting alongside Officer Larkin. He hooks his arm around the back of his chair and leans forward without breaking eye contact. I look as though I'm judging the two men in a battle for dominance. Larkin's shoulders lock up as he bites the inside of one of his rosy cheeks. Arthur, on the other hand, leans forward just enough where Officer Larkin can't see his relaxed arm or his thumb drumming against the chair. I slump in my seat and peek under the table. Arthur's tapping his foot on the carpet like there's a kick drum—he's playing along with the officer because he was asked to, not because he wants to.

"Yer attitude's been intriguing, really. Go ahead and hang tight. Once I run a background check on you, I'll bring in yer next client."

"Perfect. Guess I could use a snooze, then. Your coffee's not that good."

"Get up. Let's go." Larkin grips his hands in fists alongside his body and nods at me to get up and follow him out.

"See you soon, Will, and stay strong for Jase and Shell—you'll be out soon. It's ten in the morning. They'll come by every hour and make sure you respond. Right, Larkin?"

"Testing my patience with protocol now?"

"See? Protocol. Take a nap and rest. They'll wake you *every* hour for a response."

I follow Officer Larkin out the door and look over my shoulder at Arthur. He rips the corner from his notes and wads it into a tiny ball. I walk past the observation window and watch him pitch the paper from the other side of the observation mirror. *What the hell just happened back there?*

CHAPTER 24

"**N**orwick?"

Hey. Hey, move it. Stop and listen. Turn around and back up. Look behind you. Look. Behind. You.

The voice—it's Mom. *Mom? Why're you waking me up? Thought it was the weekend. You said we can rest a little on weekends … Forgot about the list. I'm sorry. You sprung it on me and not Jase. Why? He's sitting right here and wants to help, and you don't want to talk to him. Why?*

Jason stands at the end of my bed staring at me with his arms dangling alongside his hips. *Jase?* "Jason—stop the act. Say something." His eyes sink deep in their sockets and a bluish stone-colored shadow drapes underneath his lower eyelids. Only a topnotch makeup artist could apply a color four times lighter than a person's normal skin shade and make it look as realistic as this.

"Should've called me. You know I'd go with you—they've been filming a lot around here." I stare at Jason. "You okay? You look borderline going to puke or eat my brains."

Jason's eyes widen.

"And … which one?" I ask.

Jason rests his eyes.

"Aye, nice chat." I lay back and roll over to one side. "Yer zombie look's one of the better I've seen. Next time take me with you. We can grab dinner somewhere after and invite the girls. Shelly would laugh."

The room is silent.

I peek over my shoulder. Jason doesn't move. "Aye, great. Stay in character, then, I guess. Just stand there and listen."

Jason doesn't move.

"So ... Mom's being weird. She's listed a chore for each letter of the alphabet and said the devil will chase me around until I finish zaccuming. That's not a thing. It's not even a word. She's adding letters to words. Weird right?" I peek over my shoulder again. "Jase—say something damn it."

He stares at me and blinks.

"Tell mom to relax."

"Yer next," Jason mutters.

"What? What does that mean?" I ask.

Jason turns around and walks toward the door. "You. Are. Nex—t."

Why're you talking like that?

"William?" A low-pitch voice interferes.

"What?" I jump. *Who's here? Who said that? Mom? Jase?* I shake my head. Aye, right—almost got me. Glad you two finally watched the prank show Shelly and I told you guys about. Good voice changer. Phone app or did you buy one—

"*Nor. Wick.* William Norwick, need a response."

"Huh?" I peel my eyes open and see a blizzard-white wall, so close to my face, my nose almost touches.

"Last time and I'm coming in. William Norwick, say aye." I hear the low-pitched voice again.

"Aye?" I ask, rubbing my eyes.

"Every hour, I need a response Norwick." The voice trails down the hallway.

"Aye," I repeat.

My heart's pelting against my chest cavity. A minute ago, I was dreaming though it's reality that is my nightmare. I rub sweat from my forehead and clear my throat. Have I been huffing pneumonia or did someone funnel grains of sand through my nostrils? My throat's raw but I'm too tired to figure out why.

I snort air through my nose and choke. I open my eyes and stare at the white wall. The dryness hasn't affected my nose picking up the pungent scent of a sweaty gym bag. Pulling my head back from the wall I see the remanence of food smear across the white with a fingerprint at the end of the marking. Gross. Where am I?

I'm in a boxy room. No. I'm in a holding cell. I look at the door. It's made of steel and looks like a giant freezer door with a horizontal slit for a window. I sit up and crack my head against the wall. "Shit that hurt."

Something sharp scrapes my finger as I massage the part of my head that greeted the germy wall. A piece of glass sticks to the top layer of my scalp. I flick it off my head and stand up. The thundering eruption and shrieks of shattering glass replay inside my head. The rooms spinning and I see officer Casey, windshield debris, and red running toward me. I sit down and cup the sides of my head. My heart beats faster as the room temperature cranks up. Deep breaths. Deep. Breaths. Calm yourself. I rub my temples and take in a long breath of air.

"Norwick."

"Huh?" I hear a woman's voice from outside the door and release the side of my head.

"Got yer meal. No food allergies or health conditions noted—correct?" she asks, holding out a tray bearing a compartmentalized plate of food.

"No restrictions, thanks." I remove the plate from the tray and a carton of milk. "Wait," I shout through the window slit. "What's the time?"

"Eleven," she shouts back.

I lay the tray on top of the stationary benchlike hunk of cement that's protruding from the wall and look around. Need to wait until twenty-one hours for the piece of paper. The toilet catches my eye. It reminds me of an airplane bathroom shitter. I feel like I'll get sick from touching anything around the room. How can I track the hours inside this box? Arthur mentioned officers doing hourly check-ins. I need something to notch or mark for hours passed.

There's a potent smell coming from the tray of food the woman delivered. I sit down next to the plate. The plates divided into three compartments: two for side dishes and a larger one for the main course. Mushy green beans and overcooked carrots were slopped together as one of the side dishes. There's a loaf of cornbread in the other. I poke my finger at the cornbread—stale as a rock. The main course is a sliced-up chicken breast mixed with rice and a thick custard-yellow sauce that could pass for some egg yolk and milk mixture. The pasty sauce looks thick. Enough of the concoction was used to hide the meat with the rice.

I bow my head down low enough to smell the food from a safe distance. The pungent smell burns my nose and causes my eyes to water. I turn over my shoulder and gag. Pulling my face inside my shirt I plug my nose and dab my eyes. There must be something that happens to a person's brain, like PTSD after experiencing a traumatic event, where an individual's able to subconsciously associate body senses even hours leading to the event that traumatized them. The smell reminds me of the rancid meat I ate in an airport coming home from South America. I didn't know there was anything wrong with the chicken I ate at the time, but after smelling this dish I remember a smell from twelve years ago I forgot about until now.

Shelly, Jase, Ethan, and I were eating at an airport restaurant during a layover from a two-week trip in South America. The airport was small and had limited restaurant resources. We sampled local foods the duration of our trip as we wanted the full experience. Rotten poultry would've been easy to detect if we weren't sampling dishes and labeling them as funky or interesting, for fourteen days straight.

The four of us split appetizers and two chicken entrees while jammed around a two-person table pushed in the corner of the little airport restaurant. The place was overcrowded, and our waiter had sweat dripping down the sides of his face. I made Shelly drink my water after watching our waiter lean over the table and seeing sweat drip in her glass. We waited a half hour to sit down and eat a meal at a place I've tried to delete from my memory until smelling the jail food before me.

We walked around the tiny airport another hour and decided to walk to our gate. That's when the cramping started.

"Slow down a little, backpacks getting heavy," I said.

"How? We through almost everything into carry-ons," Jase said.

"Yer back's hurting now? You've been walking around with thirty pounds on your back for two weeks," Shelly said.

"It's all catching up." I stopped in the middle of the airport to bend over and put my hands on my knees.

"You okay?" Ethan asked, removing my backpack. "It's pretty light. I'll take it on the plane with me"

"Thanks," I said as I forced my body upright. I trailed behind the group and stopped. "Now it's in my stomach."

"I'll buy a water." Shelly dropped her bag and took off for a convenient store.

"You look pale," Jase said. "Look at em."

"Go stand next to your twin so I can compare." Ethan said, watching Jase and I stand side-by-side. "Yer pale—sure you weren't drinking from the sweat glass."

"Don't talk about that right now, yer gonna make me sick," I said. "Now that's all I can think about—sweety ice w—"

"Water. Drink up," Shelly said as she removed the cap. She shook the bottle in front of me. "What?"

"Uh—" Jase glanced at me and widened his eyes. He moved Shelly over to one said, so wasn't standing in front of me.

I felt stomach acid come up to my throat.

"Yer such a sweetheart," Jase said grabbing the water bottle and cap from Shelly's possession.

"I agree." Ethan looked at me, saw I was fighting back the urge to vomit, and turned around.

"What's going on?" Shelly asked.

"No, nothing—"

"*Nothing.*" Jase echoed Ethan. "Yer timing's always great—

"*Great.* Timing … garbage by the wall and bathroom to yer right," Ethan said turning around and pointing to both.

I held my mouth and looked for the garbage can.

"No—not in public. Come on, follow me to the bathroom. Hold it in—keep yer hands cemented over yer mouth. If it happens, I'll worry about yer nose," Jase said handing Shelly back the water bottle. "Yer hands mouth my hands nose duty. Got it?" Jase's voice trailed off.

"He does realize that that holding Will's nostrils shut will suffocate him or drown him—right? Puke's a liquid. So … you getting excited about moving in together?"

"Ethan, please go check on them," Shelly said.

After thirty minutes jammed inside a men's airport bathroom, my stomach started to settle.

"Hello? Guys? Everything okay? We're boarding soon." Shelly's voice echoed through the men's bathroom.

"Hang on," Ethan shouted.

"Some guy was talking about finding security for the sick men in the bathroom," Shelly's voice grew louder.

"Aye," Ethan yelled back.

"Well, the guy said men—is there a sick man or are their sick men in the bathroom?"

"Men …" Ethan announced.

"Okay. Sorry for prying. So we talking two sick men or three sick men?"

"Two sick Norwicks," Ethan answered.

"I'm feeling better, Shell," I called out to Shelly. "Jase, on the other hand, needs some more time."

"Okay, babe—that's still fifty percent, which is how you and Jase walked in. Ethan?"

"Aye?"

"Should I change the flights? You think they're okay to fly another six hours?" Shelly asked.

"Will's coming out, and I think Jase is having sympathy pains. That twin thing that twins get."

"We'll be fine. I'll be right out," I said.

Shelly and I waited for Ethan and Jase in the back of the boarding line. Ethan came out of the bathroom first holding a handful of hand sanitizer. He cupped the substance in his hands, spreading it on his arms and around his neck. Jase staggered out behind him wearing one of his clothing layers like a towel wrapped around his head.

"I'm tired," Jase said as he approached us.

"I'm going to sleep the rest of the way home. Sorry guys, about that back there," I said.

"What the hell happened back there?" Ethan asked.

"You guys were fine one minute and the next—"

"Not sure I want to talk about it." I stop Shelly.

Five minutes after takeoff Ethan and Shelly's stomachs started to turn. Ten minutes after that and a full onset of food poisoning later began the flight from hell.

I pick up the plate and slide it by the door. Taking the plastic spoon from the plastic, I hold my breath, and scoop up a pile of green beans. I pull the napkin from the plastic wrapper and dump the veggies inside. Laying across the hard surface bench, I position myself, so my head is as far away from the rotting smell. There are still hints of the stinky meat, but it's manageable enough to fall asleep. I flip onto my side and grab a bean from the napkin. Puncturing my nail through the bean, I shred off a piece of the mushy vegetable. I lean over the opposite side of the bench, facing away from the door, and lay the piece of green bean on the ground. First marker is for eleven—made it through the first hour. I close my eyes, lift my head over my arm, and close my eyes.

Rest.

CHAPTER 25

The Weakest Link

Earlier That Morning

It was Otis's second week on the job. His occupation changed from managing call center night shifts to kitchen supervisor, after failing a drug test. With a family name embedded in the local community amid decades of politics, Otis was immediately placed in his new role at the police department. The written report stated *Otis left in order to diversify his experience within the law enforcement community and gain as much knowledge within each department hoping to one day make a positive impact for the future of our community.*

Otis was punctual his first week as kitchen supervisor, arriving approximately fifteen to twenty minutes early each morning. He expressed concern on nourishing those confined to a custody suite, acknowledging some being held are innocent until proven otherwise. His ability to lead the kitchen staff was apparent through his communication skills. Everything Otis did within each department of the justice system looked outstanding on his college-graduate resume. Though written reports turned in by fellow coworkers stated that Otis was arrogant, selfish, and a "spoiled little shit who hasn't worked a real day in his life." All reports were submitted to the head of the department and filed under a different name.

The morning started with freezing temperatures and cloudy skies. Traffic was lighter than usual. Otis hadn't gone to bed yet and was at a college friends house playing cards and opening a beer when his alarm went off for work. He disregarded his alarm, betting another round for his money back. The final hand went quicker than Otis could finish his beer. He slammed his beer can in front of him, slapped his chips across the table, and stormed out of the party.

Otis slid down an icy driveway catching himself as he locked arms on one side of his vehicle. He opened his trunk, grabbed a duffel bag, and tossed it on the passenger seat while his car warmed up. "Call Lara," he commanded his Bluetooth of his luxury sedan.

"*Calling Lara.*" The phone rings once and goes to voicemail.

"Call Lara," Otis said, lighting a joint.

"*Calling Lara.*" The phone rings twice and is sent to voicemail.

"Answer the damn phone, Lara!" Otis screamed, smacking the steering wheel. "Call Lara—Jesus, answer, you jealous, uppity princess wannabe. I can do better than you—"

"*I'm sorry. I don't have Lara Jesus answer you jealous up eprincess want to be I can do better than you stored in your contacts. Would you like to store as new contact?*"

"No! Text Lara."

"*What would you like to text Lara?*"

"Hey, babe. The boys and I were playing poker and lost track of time. Heading to work and won't be able to use my phone, so give me a shout."

"*Would you like me to repeat your message before sending to Lara—*"

"Send message," he said as he inhaled the joint while peeling out of the driveway.

Otis drove around the back lot of the police station, twenty minutes late for work. He was shifting his car into park when his phone rang. "Tried you twice and now I'm parking and going to work," Otis snapped.

"Um … nice to hear you too. It's early in the morning and you called me," Lara barked back. "Everything's always on yer terms—yer schedule."

"No, it's not. Yer in yer own head because yer probably reaching that time of the month."

"No, someone texted me saying you cheated on me last night at that party."

"I didn't, and I'd like to talk about this—really, I do, but I gotta go to work. It's my second week." He stretched up to fidget with his wavy brown hair in the mirror. "I've gotta walk through the police station and can't be on my phone—"

"*Really*? You being serious right now?" Lara asked.

"Yeah, why would I lie?"

"Funny. Because you told me you had keys to your own department, and you walked in through the back—that the kitchen was separate from the police station and because *you ran the department* I could sneak in yer office and have fun with you whenever I wanted. You forget telling yer girlfriend that? Or maybe you forgot you told me and not the other girl."

"I know I told you that. They're making us all check in through one entrance temporarily from the overcrowding of two stations." He paused and listened for a response. "Eventually, you can come by. I gotta go—minutes until the rest of the staff shows up." He took the last hit of the joint.

"Is there someone else?" she demanded.

"No. Go buy some tampons. Like I said, it's only my second week. Relax a little. Is this what I'll have to look forward to if I choose a future with you?" The phone went silent. "Lara?"

"What?"

"Let's have a chat later. I gotta start checking people in for their shift since some of them show up early. Unlike you, some people go to work." The phone went silent. "Lara?"

Muffled sounds vibrated through the vehicle's speaker system before Lara hung up on him.

"*Call ended.*"

"Psycho," Otis scoffed, bending the rearview mirror toward his face while he reached for eyedrops in the cupholder.

Otis stared at himself in the mirror. He tilted his head upright and forced eyedrops to his pupils. After a blurry face-off with his clock, he saw that he was thirty-five minutes late for his shift, which meant he had five minutes until employees arrived. "Shit." He grabbed his duffel bag and ran to the back door of the police department. The wind raged at the bits of his skin exposed to the hostile climate. His teeth clattered as he applied his thumb print and punched in the supervisor access code. Two vehicles pulled into the parking lot as Otis slammed the door.

With minutes to spare, he darted through the entrance and initiated the employee security system scan. He flipped on the master power switch for the kitchen and staggered toward the employee locker room. Otis forgot to grab his uniform from one of the girls at the party who wore it as she danced for him on the bar. He ripped his phone from his pocket.

Otis: *Great party.*
Otis: *You cleaned my wallet last hand dick.*
Otis: *When yer up see if my uniforms in other bedroom thnx.*
Otis: *and next holiday I'm taking you to Vegas.*

Rummaging around the locker room, Otis noticed an extra uniform folded over one of the benches. He shed his beer-splattered party clothes and slipped into the work apparel. Aside from the shorter sleeves, the getup fit perfectly. He rolled the sleeves up to his forearms, stuffed his clothes inside the duffel bag, and raced to the men's bathroom. Karate kicking the restroom door, Otis dipped his head underneath the faucet in a last-ditch effort to clean up for work. He pumped his hands with soap, cleaning his face, neck, and arms. The brief grooming session was completed after scraping his fingers against his teeth while using his fingernails as a toothbrush.

The buzzer bleated high-pitched echoes over the kitchen speaker system. The first wave of employees alerted they were at the back door for entry. The chime blared a second time.

"This is yer fault—making me late. *Good job Lara,*" Otis grumbled to himself.

Otis scurried around the kitchen, grabbing pots and pans and placing them on the burners. He pulled open cabinet doors and scattered mixing bowls across the island. His tardiness would be obvious to the staff if the kitchen was untouched. He ruffled up a pile of clean towels, using one from the pile to dry his hair before laying them together on the island next to the mixing bowls and a batch of seasonings. The buzzer sounded again causing him to jump and knock a jar of garlic power onto the ground. Otis hopped over the mess and jogged to the door.

"Morning." Otis opened the door and flipped on the internal security cameras.

"Freezing this morning—buzzer not working?" one of the employees asked as he cupped his hands to his mouth.

"Morning to you too, Pete," Otis greeted as he held the door open for Pete and the three employees trekking closely behind. "Sorry, was in the bathroom. You going to be in a bad mood all day?"

"Stand outside for five minutes and you'll understand." Pete brushed past Otis.

"I already did—probably longer trying to pick ice off the keypad." Otis folded his arms as he watched Pete and his posse scan their badges and walk through the metal detector. "I began prepping for meals but had to respond to some emails—that's when my stomach started acting up."

"Prepping's my job and has been for over fifteen years. Let me do my work," Pete said. Pete and the other early birds ignored Otis as they strolled toward the locker room.

"Of course. Since yer insistent on yer duties—go ahead and start breakfast. I'll be in my office answering emails." Otis turned away and stopped. "But I'll be walking around to make sure you're doing them correctly."

"Aye, right," one of the employees barked back at Otis, as he followed Pete in the locker room.

"That's exactly what I wanted to hear." Otis mouthed to himself as he rolled his eyes. "Going to be an easy day for me—because of *you*," Otis Laughed.

Otis's approached his office tucked conveniently in the back corner of the kitchen. The entrance of his office was steps from the back door. The positioning of the supervisor's office was convenient for management monitoring the staff entering and exiting the kitchen department and even more ideal for a pothead. The front of the office had a window large enough to view each station of the kitchen. Otis kept the blinds on the window cracked upright so he could see out and employees couldn't see in.

He ripped open his duffel bag and grabbed the keys to his office. The buzzer alerted the arrival of other staff members at the back door. The sound steered his head up and he noticed an envelope tapped to his door with the words *notice* stamped across the seal. Specs of wood from the door peeled off with the tape as Otis ripped off the envelope before anyone else could see it. He dropped the bag in and used his key to break the seal open. Another elongated ring from the backdoor made him jump.

"Can't get anything done without interruptions around here," Otis snarled.

"I'll get it," Pete shouted from the locker room doorway.

"Thanks." Otis unlocked his office, kicked his duffel bag across the doorway, and shut himself inside before Pete saw him standing next to the back door.

At first glance, Otis's office appeared organized. A large computer screen, a stack of papers, and a calendar was all he kept on his desk. Behind him was a bookshelf filled with literature. The ambiance of the office was that of an organized and knowledgeable being from an onlooker's perspective.

Checking to make sure the door was locked Otis grabbed a prescription bottle filled with weed along with a pipe from his duffel bag. He pulled a book from the shelf and tucked them both inside a hidden compartment. The only way Otis could survive a full workday without sleep was to periodically sneak out and smoke sativa in his car. He leaned against the edge of his desk and ripped open the envelope. He skimmed through half of the letter and stopped:

> It's been cited. The kitchen staff supervisor failed to execute routine protocol. *Please refer to citation 634 in the handbook.* Consider this your first warning. Please note that this report may or may not result in a further investigation within your department. You can contest this document by filling out *form 143* found on the department website. For further questions, please contact us.

Otis snatched his phone from his pocket. "Call Dad," he commanded as he rolled his eyes at the document. The phone rang once and stopped.

"Dad?"

"Hang on a second, son."

"Fine, I'll hold—check your text messages," Otis said. He tapped his phone onto speaker mode and snapped a picture of the document.

The back-door buzzer roared through a mounted speaker system above his head. The loud noise made Otis jump and slide off the edge of his desk, nearly dropping his phone. The shrill sound bounced off the walls of his tiny room just like blowing a foghorn inside a doghouse.

"Was the man here before me deaf or something?" Otis yelled out loud as he marched out of his office, stomping hard on his feet. He punched down at the door handle of the employee entrance, leaned back, and kicked the door open with his foot. The door wailed open and clocked a woman in the shoulder.

"Ahw," the woman yelled, holding her arm as she slipped backward.

Two colleagues standing behind the woman caught her fall and lifted her back on her feet.

"Why would you stand so close to a door?" Otis asked. "Hurry up inside and I'll get everyone checked in." He stared at the woman who was struck by the door and watched her as she rubbed her arm. "You can blame the wind on that one."

"Otis?" a man's voice echoed over the speaker of his phone.

"Sorry, just a minute—checking staff in." Otis tapped his phone off speaker mode and slid it in his pocked.

An employee walked out from the locker room and greeted his coworkers as they walked through security. The man stood across from Otis and waited for the rest of the staff to finish the check in process.

"What are you looking at?" Otis asked the man.

"I believe yer wearing my uniform sir," the man said.

"Nope. I'm wearing my uniform." Otis turned away and reached for his phone.

"See that stain—in the front? I left it in the locker room overnight and soaked the mark with stain remover. Think it was ketchup," the man said.

Otis stopped walking. He covered the phone speaker with his hand and looked over his shoulder at the man. "What?"

"Check the tag. My wife wrote my initials—should say MT on it."

"Someone must've mixed up our uniforms, then. I'll change in my office and lay it outside my door. Give me five minutes to wrap up this call."

The man nods and walks away.

"Sorry about that. See the picture I just sent?" Otis walked in his office and closed the door.

"Hasn't even been two weeks this time, how the hell did you get written up already?" his Dad asked.

Otis tapped the phone off speaker mode and held it to his ear. "I told you, people are out to get me because of our family name—believe me now? I do everything perfectly. Plus, they don't like a younger guy coming in the place and telling them what to do."

Otis's dad paused and let out a gasp of air. "I'll have a meeting next week. This has got to stop."

"I know. It's not fair to me—to be a target. And you, of course."

"Yer mum and I are leaving a meeting and heading to a charity breakfast, we can discuss this later."

"Fine. But I'd like to know who reported me. I'm uncomfortable starting out my day this way—bet it was Pete."

"Don't accuse anyone yet. Pete's been at that kitchen a long time."

"I know, but I got the job he always wanted." Otis walked to the corner of the room and plunked his duffel bag on top of a box sitting on a chair. He pulled clothes out from the bag and stopped to stare at the box.

The box contained the chicken for the lunchtime meal. In order to make it on time to the party, Otis sent everyone home fifteen minutes early and insisted on finishing up the last of the tasks. He was supposed to pull the box of chicken from the back freezer and move it to the main kitchen fridge before he left work. He lugged the box of frozen poultry into his office incidentally after hearing his phone ringing mid route.

"I gotta go dad, call you later." Otis hung up the phone and stared at the box. He looked up and saw it was sitting underneath a blasting heat vent.

A knock at the door startled Otis. "Hang on. I'm getting yer stupid uniform now. Next time don't leave it laying out in the middle of the locker room."

"It's Pete."

"Oh, hang on Pete, I'm changing." Otis removed the uniform and stretched it across his desk. He grabbed a marker from one of his drawers and pressed it against the stain. "Be right there."

"Just had a question about today's meal prep," Pete said.

"One. Second." Otis said as he slipped on his old clothes. He grabbed the envelope from the top of his desk and tucked it inside his back pocket. "What's up?" he asked as he opened the door.

"Cleaned up yer little kitchen display." Pete scratched his face.

"Not sure what you mean by that—but continue."

"Was going over the prep list. There were three boxes of chicken for today. Where's the third box of chicken?" Pete asked.

"Chicken's right here." Otis pointed at the box. "Was gonna prep the second meal, but the phone rang, and the buzzer went off."

"What'd I just say about meal prepping?" Pete asked.

"I started this morning, before you got here and before yer little lecture. I'll put the chicken back in the fridge." Otis laid the uniform on top of the box. "Excuse me for a few. Uniform mix up."

Otis waited for Pete to step out of his doorway before he lifted the box. The bottom of the cardboard was soggy from the chicken thawing underneath the heater. He walked to his shelf and ripped one of the pot pens free he had taped underneath one of the lower shelving units.

"Be right back. Need to check my car for a spare uniform—someone took mine. Here, take yer uniform back. Yer right about that stain—not sure that one's coming out." Otis tossed the uniform to the man and kicked open the back door.

Otis hit his pot pen and strolled to the dumpster. "That'll do," he muttered under his breath. Pulling up his sleeves he leaned over the front of the garbage, grabbed an empty box with his fingers, and plucked it over the top. He swiped the pot pen from his pocket and stopped as a woman turned the corner pushing a baby in a stroller as she fought against the wind. Otis fiddled with his pen behind his back as he waited in the cold for the woman to load her baby in the car. His phone vibrated.

Mark: *Found it.*
Otis: *My uniform?*
Mark: {*picture of a girl dancing in Otis's uniform*}

A navy blue rusted four door sedan pulled into the kitchen parking lot. The vehicle circled the parked cars and backed into a parking spot next to a cab. The driver rolled his window down a crack and signaled for Otis to come to the car.

Otis shook his head at the driver.

The driver cracked the window lower and held a wad of money out the window.

Otis stormed to the vehicle and yanked the money from the driver's hand. "I'll do it later you idiots. Just bought you a bunch for you little shits last night."

CHAPTER 26

Present: 5:00 p.m.

"Norwick?"

I open my eyes. "Aye."

Peeling my body from the hard surface is like digging a tick out of my skin. My head's stuck looking to one direction from sleeping on my side. I sit up and use an arm to turn my head straight. It reminds me of being a little boy and cutting the arms and legs off my Mr. Potato Head toy, twisting its head to a larger body frame. The head was jammed to one side until my older cousin forced it straight. I'm the older inmate potato head—packaged with a jumpsuit and angry facial expressions.

I lean over and add another piece of bean to my homemade clock. It's five in the evening.

"Norwick?" I hear a woman's voice.

"Aye."

"Any food allergies or dietary restrictions?"

"No. And I'd like to pass on the meal," I say.

"Please take the tray. It's important you eat." She hands me the tray.

Preventing any conflict, I grab the tray and set it in front of the door.

A man screams from his custody suite down the hallway. I lean toward my door and look out the slit.

"Yer trying to poison us in here. Is this what you do to clean up yer streets, huh?" The man's coughs and gags echo down the hallway.

"I feel it too. I need a real bathroom," another man shouts.

I look down at the tray of food.

* * * *

Four Hours Earlier

1:00 p.m.

Kitchen Crew

Otis peeked through his office blinds. Dishes clattered as the kitchen staff finished their lunch break and began the second wave of lunch cleanup. Rock and roll music played in the background while they worked through stacks of trays filled with uneaten food. Garbage bags piled up along the back door. One of the guys unloading dishes attempted the Bon Jovi chorus midsong.

> *"Shot through my heart,*
> *and yer the blame,*
> *and you made love the bad way.*
> *I gave you my heart while you played mind games,*

you give love a bad name …" he sang, using a spoon as a microphone in one hand while punching the air with his other hand.

"You got some of the chorus right," a coworker said, handing him another stack of dishes.

"Don't worry, man. You did everything for that woman. Yer better off, Mikie," Pete chimed in.

Otis stepped out from his office. "I'll take the garbage out today, guys—"

"And ladies—not all guys in this kitchen," the woman from the early morning door incident interrupted Otis.

"Guys and *woman*. Feel better now?" Otis snarled.

The woman turned her back to Otis and dried the next dish.

"Good talk." Otis grabbed two of the garbage bags and shoved the door open. The door sideswiped a construction worker. "Sorry, gentlemen— I meant man and, uh, woman? My bad." He stood in the doorway and nodded at the two construction workers walking by.

Fighting through the wind, Otis jogged to the dumpster and hoisted the bags with full force. He took a long hit from his pipe and stood out in the cold.

* * * *

Present

10:00 p.m.

"Norwick?"

"Aye." I lean over and add another bean to my time line. It's time. Ten o'clock—twenty-two hours. I stand up and stretch, ready for the piece of paper.

* * * *

Four Hours Earlier

6:00 p.m.

Kitchen Crew

Kitchen Staff Dinner Cleanup

Otis stepped out from his office.

"Made sandwiches for dinner," Pete said.

"I'm starving. Thanks." Otis grabbed a sandwich and ate it on his walk back to his office.

* * * *

Present

11:00 p.m.

"Norwick?"

"Aye." I look down and recount my markings. It's just after eleven at night. I turn and stare at the slit in the door.

Officers crisscross in front of my door as they tend to their duties. They look like shadowy blobs in hats as they spring across the slender rectangle I now identify as my window. I close my eyes and rub my lids with the back of my knuckles. A flick to my forehead feels like a large insect or a sticky dart, interrupting my thought process. I rub my forehead.

"The hell?" I gasp.

I notice a crumpled piece of paper rolling across the floor. I reach for the wad of paper and open it.

"Wait for Victoria.:

Really? "Wait for Victoria" it says? Is this a joke? I sit down and rub my jaw. *Who the hell's Victoria?*

* * * *

Four Hours Earlier

7:00 p.m.

Kitchen Crew

Otis stretched his arms above his head. "Sandwich was good," he said as he strolled by Pete.

"Leftover chicken always makes for good sandwiches," Pete said.

"Leftover chicken?"

"Aye."

"From today?"

"Aye. I'm clocking out. See you tomorrow."

Otis stopped walking and held his stomach. He burped.

* * * *

Present

Lights cut out at 11:14 p.m. I look around and jump to my feet. "Victoria?" I whisper.

CHAPTER 27

The Life Force Preserve

10:00 a.m.

Arthur strolled down the hallway, passing the newest swarm of wrongdoers as he made his way toward the exit of the police station. He ignored the checkout signage as wandered past a large glass window. A large man with a burly beard squatted on the ground and forced his leg between the metal divider separating the entrance from the exit lines. Arthur stopped and watched the man's leg pop out from underneath the barrier as he attempted to trip him on his way out.

"Really?" Arthur rolled his eyes at the man.

"I'll get yeeeww," the burly man barked.

"Get up, ye drunkard," the burly man's arresting officer said as he yanked at the man's handcuffs.

Arthur slid forward and stepped on the edge of the burly man's shoe, forcing it off the man's foot. The man stumbled back and tried to fight free from the officer's grip. When he didn't get his way, he leaned back and spat at the officer. The wad of spit missed the officer and flipped over his bottom lip, smearing into the man's burly beard.

Arthur balled his hands into fists and glared at the man. "Disrespectful piece of shit," he muttered. He lowered himself to reach for the man's shoe and stopped.

"Hey! Hey, you—sir—*must stop, sir,*" a voice called out from behind Arthur. "Must check out before you leave." The voice was firm.

Arthur swiveled around to acknowledge the man calling after him.

"Ye gotta check out here—back here, *hey*." An employee popped his head out from the checkout window. His bowl cut bounced like a jellyfish as his skinny arms dangled over the window frame. He was a young officer and looked like a teenager in a Halloween costume hanging from the passenger window of a friend's car.

"Sorry—didn't see you," Arthur said as he turned and walked toward the checkout window.

"Ye must sign out." The young officer waited for Arthur to reach the counter before he tucked himself inside the window and jumped to the ground.

"I would've walked out without my things—thanks." Arthur leaned forward, sloped his head to one side, and squinted at the young employee's mouth.

"Why're you looking at me like that?" the kid asked.

"Oh, was looking at yer shiny teeth."

"Shiny teeth?" the kid chuckled. "No, it's a clear retainer."

"I should start wearing a mouth guard to work too," Arthur said, stepping underneath a brightly lit ceiling light.

"It's not a mouthgu—never mind. I need to scan and keep yer visitor badge," the kid said, staring at Arthur's eye wound under the light.

"What? My eye?" Arthur rubbed his face.

"Need some ice? Yer eye looks bad."

"Nah, I'm fine."

"It looks like it hurts, like yer bleeding inside the white part of yer eyeball. We've got ice."

"I'm fine," Arthur said as he handed over his visitor badge.

The young officer shot the scanner at Arthur's badge as though he was offing a bad guy in an easy level of *Call of Duty*. The childish action revealed a low probability of his role being more than part time or internship. His basic uniform suggested early stages of law enforcement training. "Yer scan's showing a coat and one bag?" he asked.

"Aye, thanks." Arthur handed the clipboard to the young intern and watched him fumble around the room, knocking over other visitors' valuables. Arthur lowered his hand and brushed his fingers across the front waistline of his pants. He wedged his thumbnail underneath one of the buttons, popped it off his pants, and cupped it into his hand. Using his thumb, he slid the button between his pointer and middle fingers.

"Found 'em," the kid said, bumping Arthur's bag to the ground. He jerked the bag from the floor and stomped across the edges of the coat as he dragged it to the window. He packed the two items in a ball and handed them to Arthur.

"You must be busy back there—two police stations under one roof." Arthur leaned over the opening in the window and planted the bug underneath the window ledge a he used his other arm to reach for his things. "Hopefully they're paying you enough. Seems like a lot for one person."

"No, they're at lunch. Typically, there are three of us."

"I was going to say, you deserve more pay with the new law going into effect, but there's three of you, so unless they have you working longer hours—"

"What's considered longer hours?" the kid interrupted.

"If yer working day through evening shifts. It's dependent on age group. It's not something employers want to promote right now, but as a lawyer, I'll be handling cases once the new labor law goes into effect."

"Got a business card?" he asked.

"Just ran out, but I'll be back to see my clients in a few hours. What time you here until?"

"Stuck here till midnight."

"Perfect. I owe you a card. I should tell you now …" Arthur bowed further into the checkout window. "Yer station's currently trying to combat the new law, so I wouldn't discuss our conversation with anyone right now—not even yer friends."

"Would be nice to save money and pay off my school debt."

"No one wants debt, especially when they're trying to start a career." Arthur grabbed his jacket and bag and stepped away from the counter. "I'll check back with you later, Kevin." Arthur pointed at the kid's name tag.

"I'd appreciate it."

Arthur walked down the hallway and slowed next to the burly drunk man. The arresting officer yanked at the man's handcuffs while he conversed with an officer standing behind him in line. The line hadn't moved since Arthur turned back for his belongings.

The burly man stretched upright and glared at Arthur. His shoe remained partially wedged under the line divider. Arthur rolled his eyes at the man, bent forward, and scooped up the man's shoe.

"Give me my shoe," the man demanded. "Give me my damn shoe—"

"You like fetch?" Arthur waited for the officer to turn his head and drop-kicked the shoe toward the exit. "Hope they spit back at you in prison—disrespectful piece of shit," Arthur muttered at the man as he walked away.

The hallway opened to the station's waiting room. Cheap foldout chairs were lined in rows positioned in front of a hanging television. Additional chairs circled the border of the room, all occupied with guests of all ages. Arthur walked behind the last row facing the floating television and stopped.

In world news, like a wildfire overnight in Bangkok, what doctors are saying started as cold virus symptoms has hospitals overflowing with sick patients this morning.

"This just happen?" Arthur asked the waiting room. He searched around the room, looking for a response. "Never mind," he announced as he hauled his bag around a woman in a chair.

"Ow, watch it, dummy. Ye hit me in the head with yer stupid bag," the woman scoffed.

"I'm sorry—was an accident." Arthur darted past the television and pushed open the men's bathroom door. The bathroom was small and looked like it hadn't been cleaned in a while. The trash can overflowed with garbage, and someone left the faucet running. Arthur walked up to the sink and washed his hands. He glanced in the finger-smeared mirror and saw two men standing over urinals. A toilet flushed from a single stall next to the sink. Arthur opened his bag, grabbing a pair of sunglasses from one pocket and a hat from another. He unfolded the hat and gripped the price tag.

One man zipped his pants and walked around Arthur to rinse his hands before exiting the bathroom. The other man stepped away from the urinal, rubbed his hands on his jeans, and walked out. Arthur pivoted and lodged his foot against the door. He bent forward to check on the status of the man hanging out in the bathroom stall. The only thing Arthur could see was a pair of white running shoes planted in front of the toilet. He held the hat in one hand, squeezed the price tag between his thumb and middle finger of the other hand, and snapped the two. The finger snap shed a layer from the top of the label, revealing an oval-shaped clear plastic puff that resembled a miniature version of a dog toy squeaker.

Arthur skimmed the stall. It was decorated with paint-chipped dents, permanent marker, and threats carved into the pastel-blue paint. The deepest knife gash ripped through multiple layers of paint colors, ongoing attempts to blanket the profanities caused by impatient guests. He watched the shadows from a stranger's foot shuffle through the open space separating the stall from the floor. Arthur squeezed at the plastic tag twice, causing two high-pitched snaps.

Three clicks echoed from inside the bathroom stall. The stall door busted open, smacking the wall. "You're late." A large muscular man stormed out from the bathroom stall.

Arthur jumped backward, dropping his hat. "Shit, Julian, calm down. Almost gave me a heart attack." Arthur held his chest. "Don't do that—been intense in there."

"Sorry, man," Julian said.

"Where's—"

"Hang on." Julian stretched upright to his six-foot-six stance and held his finger over his mouth. He grabbed a pen from his pocket and slid his finger against the jagged volume control dial. "Had to turn the reception blocker back up. We're good now—lowered it to preserve battery."

"Where the hell's Finn?" Arthur stepped backward and propped his foot against the bathroom door.

"Last minute change."

"Clearly I see that. Figured something changed when I looked under the stall and saw bigfoot sitting on the toilet taking a shit." Arthur lunged forward and scooped his hat from the ground. He shuffled backward and guarded the door.

Julian removed his hat and rubbed his buzz cut. "Didn't think I'd be waiting here this long. Looks like I've been on the crapper over forty-five minutes. Had crazies threatening me for the toilet."

"The crappers?" Arthur asked.

"Crapper—no, s—never mind. American slang that you've used and have been for years now."

"Maybe, but when you say it with yer accent and really loud voice, it sounds different."

"Nice to see you too, dick." Julian smiled and rubbed the top of Arthur's head. "The older you get, the crankier—"

"Yer older than me."

"But I'm aging better than you."

"Yer bald," Arthur blurted.

"I shave my head. You're just too short to see. Need your notes on the floor plan."

Arthur reached inside his sleeve, grabbed his notes, and held them out in front of him.

"Try standing on your toes. Can't reach you that low."

"A cane or a walker would do the trick. Helped my grandma with bending."

"Just give me your damn notes. Piece of work, you are." Julian laughed and yanked the paper from Arthur's hand. "Go look in the mirror and look at your eye—there's red all over the white—"

"Eye's fine," Arthur interrupted. "Why're you even in here? What happened with Finn?"

"We're improvising," Julian said as he scrolled through the notes.

"I saw a news release on Bangkok a few minutes ago. What do you know about this?"

"Finn'll explain. He's out front waiting for you. I just need another minute or so. The computer's downloading your last bug to the second live-feed chip." Julian looked at his watch. "You want to explain why you planted that last bug at the checkout counter? It's adding time. You knew I tapped the phones and hacked their cameras."

"I'd like to listen in on the front-desk conversations. Those guys working checkout are our weak links. It's so simple." Arthur flung his arm in the air.

"What? No. Horrible idea. There'll be people checking in on the other side of the divider, and there'll be more arrests in the evening, meaning more eyes watching from the check-in line. You hit your head in there?"

"No one would expect it if it's done right."

"If you're suggesting a plan where we'd be walking two of their captives in front of the checkout counter and out the front door—"

"Aye." Arthur shrugged. "They'd never expect it. They're easily distracted interns. Just listen to my idea—"

"You're not thinking clearly, and the fact you feel comfortable with your idea alarms me. They've got security watching cameras closely from a room behind your so-called interns."

"Aye, so shock the camera and surge it back a couple minutes. They won't notice."

"We can't be reckless. You're being reckless."

"I made up a realistic story and said I'd be back later. He bought it. I'd distract the—"

"The more you say, the worse your idea gets. You've already compromised yourself by stepping in the spotlight, so why make it worse?"

"Exactly my point. Might as well use me once more before I'm forced into hiding."

"It's obvious you've hit the first stage beyond exhaustion. Decision-making and rational thinking—poof, out the window." Julian folded his hand into a ball and popped it open like an exploding firework.

Arthur gritted his teeth at Julian and stopped.

"Come on, man. You know what I'm saying, right?"

Arthur yawned.

"You're kidding me, right? It's like your frontal lobe separated from the rest of your brain and decided to jump ship. Glad you got your chance to mingle around the station in a lawyer costume, but the last thing we'd ever do is send you back inside. Was a one-time deal."

"Yer not giving me the chance to elaborate," Arthur growled.

"We've found our weak link: a pretentious idiot running the back kitchen."

"Fine, then. If you need me to improvise, I've got an idea."

"You should hear yourself right now. Maybe the punch to your eye was worse than we thought."

"Just forget it."

"Yeah, I'll make a note. You're juggling a lot of weight, and now we need you to relax a bit. Is there anything else in your notes I need to know?"

"I made some modifications to the original blueprint of the station. The place is a zoo. You've seen it on the cameras. The overcrowding is what we must play in our favor."

"Yeah, it's a mess in there. Finn needs this chip to be flawless so he can walk us though obstacles."

"Was it the Stags?" Arthur stopped Julian.

"Stags?" Julian glanced up from the sheet of paper.

"Did they infect a host in Bangkok?"

"We'll know soon. Finn's been on a call with main headquarters, which is why I'm playing computer hacker on a toilet, using a beach towel as butt padding in the middle of the Glasgow Police Departmen—"

"Main headquarters?"

Julian nodded.

"You said Finn's been on the phone with main headquarters. In yer country?"

"No, the one on Mars."

"Just tell me what's happened. Too tired for yer crap right now."

"My only concern right now is getting you out that door with the chip. Finn'll give you instructions." Julian leaned in the stall and poked the computer screen. "Our bugs are coinciding nicely with internal activity. There'll be no delays. Two more minutes, and I'll have you out of here."

"You hear us in the interrogation room?"

"Yeah, your bugs were clear—heard everything."

"And?"

"You were told to deliver Will the news, check in with Jose, and not piss off the officers on duty."

Arthur rolled his eyes. "I think I did fine in there."

"Ah, imagine hiring a mime but getting a clapping monkey instead. It's fine, though. You were fine. We're under a great deal of stress. You were very confident."

"Yer holding back something. Say it."

"You belittled that Larkin guy so much in front of the interrogation glass he stepped out and ran a background check on your made-up name." Julian scratched his face. "I'm biased in the situation, but I think he overreacted. I've got the report. Want to see it?"

"No."

"After they brought Will out of the room, Larkin asked an officer to crank up the heat, which they did. They also ate a snack, drank coffee, and had a cigarette before they grabbed Jose. And once Jose was in the room, the heat was all you could talk about."

"I liked Larkin."

"Hate to throw a pie at your face, but Larkin doesn't like you. Plus, you added thirty minutes of unnecessary time."

"Why don't you sit back down on yer little desk chair with the door closed and finish yer work."

"My back's hurting, so I'd prefer to stand up another minute and poke at you." Julian twisted around and cracked his back. "You're right about one thing: even though you made my blood pressure rise, you did better than I'd ever do in there."

"Yer bald with high blood pressure—clear signs of aging."

"Banter aside, shorty, you honestly did a good job with Will. You did exactly what you were supposed to do, little things aside, and

I'm proud of you. You released some heavy shit on the guy, and I'm only pressing you." Julian leaned over and patted Arthur on the back.

"Thanks. Now quit with the mush. Will was close to sober and didn't want to go to jail, so he listened. It felt weird in there, though, walking around talking to Will—talking to people. Felt like I was performing on a stage, and I'm not used to being outspoken like that."

"Going to stop you there. You're very outspoken."

"Aye, with you guys."

"Not sure I understand how it's any different."

"It's hard to explain, but since we don't have social lives, I feel conversing's a bit—"

"What? A little what? Socially stupid?" Julian laughed.

"No."

"Agoraphobic? Stir-crazy? Psychotic? Pathetic? Hack it up already."

"Strenuous."

"Strenuous?"

"Aye. It's hard to explain."

The door clunked against Arthur's foot. Arthur nodded at Julian and pointed at the stall. He dragged his bag in front of the sink, released his foot from the door, and hovered over his gear.

A man entered the bathroom and walked to a urinal, ignoring Arthur on the ground. He held his phone in one hand and attempted to send a text as he stood over the urinal. He tapped his foot against the floor as he fidgeted with his phone.

Arthur rummaged through his bag as he waited for the man to leave the bathroom.

"I'm going to throw this stupid phone," the man muttered.

"Service is shit," Arthur announced.

The man zipped up his pants and stormed out.

"Yer good," Arthur shouted over the stall.

Julian kicked the door open. "What was that? You sounded like you were over a mic."

Arthur shrugged.

"Chip's done. I'm just testing it."

"Hear from Jose? He dropped both bug chips in his lap while he was signing the papers."

"I've heard from Jose, and I'm okay leaving him in his little custody suite. That high-pitched lunatic's been driving me up the wall, gabbing through his damn bug chip. If it didn't track Jose's cell location, I would've destroyed his bug chip by the press of a button. He's on mute."

"He's living in his worst germophobic hell."

"Depending on the custody suite locations, the food dumpster shoot may be Jose's only way out." Julian laughed.

"Just leave him in there, then. He'll find his way out."

"Desensitization. It'll be good for him. I'll be going down with 'em. Once we cut the power, we'll have the entire police station searching for answers to the problem with guns drawn. I'm not taking chances today."

The door tapped against Arthur's foot. He waved at Julian. "Ah, sorry. Standing too close to the door." Arthur dropped his bag on the floor and rummaged through it. He looked up and watched the door brush open from the corner of his eye. "Sorry about that."

"Excuse us." A man and a boy walked into the bathroom.

Arthur grabbed his bag and walked to the sink. He avoided himself in the mirror as he washed his hands.

"Dad, it hurts. I gotta go bad," the boy cried to his father.

"Someone's been locked in the stall over an hour," the man declared.

"You sure?" Arthur turned and asked the man. "Because—"

"I'm grabbing security," the dad interrupted.

"You sure? I just used the stall minutes ago, and it was empty when I walked in," Arthur said.

The toilet flushed, and Julian stepped out from the stall. He moved to the side, holding the door open for the kid. "Awl yewers," Julian said.

"What?" the man asked.

Julian nodded and pointed at the empty stall.

"Sorry for the mix up. Yer wearing the same shoes as the man in the stall from earlier," the dad apologized to Julian as he waited outside the stall with his arms crossed.

Arthur turned away from the bathroom chatter and grabbed his peacoat. He reversed the coat from black to light gray as he pulled the sleeves inside out before sliding his arms inside. Avoiding eye contact with Julian, he put his hat on and tugged it over his eyes.

Julian crouched to the ground. "Sir, yu dropped tis on the ground—yewer button," Julian said as he stood up and handed Arthur a button.

"What?" Arthur pulled his head back and looked at Julian.

"Yewer butto—"

"I heard you," Arthur interrupted Julian.

"Someone pure gave you a doin', eye?" Julian nodded at Arthur.

"Hawd yir wheesit." Arthur looked at the man waiting for his son and pointed at Julian. "He is pure wired tae the moon."

"Aye, stoater." The man laughed.

"Eye," Julian agreed.

"Awright, efters." Arthur grabbed his bag and yanked the door open.

"Your truckie bottoms are budgie deed. Tanks," Julian called out behind him.

The door clunked shut, hitting the back of Arthur's shoes. "Trousers are too short? Now he's socially stupid." Arthur gritted his teeth and shook his head. "What the hell's wrong with that man?" he grumbled to himself as he buttoned up his coat and stormed toward the exit. "I'm gonna kill 'em. No, I'm gonna smack 'em as hard as I can in the back of the head and force him on a plane back to the States." He slipped on the pair of sunglasses and kicked open the front door of the police station.

CHAPTER 28

The Life Force Preserve

10:30 a.m.

Arthur watched his breath as it swirled into the sky. It was brisk outside. Charcoal-colored clouds clumped together in the sky like mounds of dirty mashed potatoes. The windchill danced alongside Glasgow's coldest day of the year while depriving its residents from experiencing the vitamin D effect from the sun. A debadged four-door taxi resembling an older body-style Ford SUV sat at the end of the crowded police station parking lot. Arthur walked to the edge of the sidewalk and watched the brake lights flare red. The taxi sped around the parked cars and stopped in front of him.

Arthur skimmed the lot and took a deep breath as he ripped opened the back door of the cab. He exhaled as he glided across the back row of the vehicle.

"Where to?" the driver asked, adjusting his black-framed sunglasses while tilting his head toward the mirror.

"Nearest liquor store." Arthur slammed the door.

The driver bopped his head down, knocking his sunglasses to the tip of his nose. Denim-blue eyes peered over the frames of his sunglasses. "Yer late."

"It's messy in there, Finn. You—"

"You know that station's been a mess." Finn interrupted. He tightened his grip around the steering wheel. Patches of light brown stubble covered his chin, adding distraction to his rosy cheeks. He adjusted his posture and skimmed the police station parking lot.

"What's the story with Bangkok?" Arthur asked.

"I'll brief you on the Bangkok after we discuss yer day as defense attorney." Finn shifted the car into drive and pulled away from the police station.

"Everything was fine until I ran into some American meathead in the men's bathroom."

Finn forced his foot on the gas, whipping Arthur's head and shoulders against the seat. "Buckle up."

"Back in America, I'm sure he improvised all he wanted and got away with it, but he's in Scotland now—"

"Drop it." Finn forced his foot on the brake, thrusting Arthur's face into the back of the seat.

"He does whatever he wants."

"Unbelievable. Yer tolerance for physical pain is like watching a robot plowing through a brick wall, but yer so damn sensitive." Finn glared at Arthur through the rearview mirror. "Julian's been on our squad for thirteen years now—longer than his squad back home."

"He's ignorant and only does what he wants."

"And yer not? You know what, go ahead and get it out. Whatever it is yer mad about," Finn merged into traffic, "you got less than three minutes to whine like a spoiled child before I drop you off at day care. Then yer partner Maggie can change yer diaper and coddle you."

Arthur scooted to the middle seat.

Finn glanced over his shoulder. "I don't get it. You love him like a brother, but get so angry. What happened?"

"He tried to patter."

"What?"

"He thought he'd patter to a random in the station, but sounded like he was chewing a pack of gum—the entire pack—with a nose plug on with chewing tobacco wedged inside his bottom lip."

"He wasn't supposed to say anything. We gave him hearing aids and told him to sign if he finds himself trapped in any personal encounters."

"Well, he wasn't wearing them." Arthur stared out the window. "We've got a giant American who patters like a Muppet on crack prepping to go through the Glasgow Police Department's plumbing system. Why is it that Americans like to slap their pits?"

"What?" Finn looked over his shoulder.

"Wait. That was wrong. I'm overtired. They clap their mitts? I can't remember the stupid phrase."

"Flap their lips?"

"Aye, that's the one. Julian gives me secondhand embarrassment."

"The two of you haven't slept in forty-eight hours, and yer starting to drive me crazy. I don't know if I should give you a shot of adrenaline or a horse tranquilizer."

"A combo of both could make for a good time." Arthur laughed.

"Nope. No, that would be reckless—cost us money." Finn looked out the window. "Sad face."

"What?" Arthur spit out air and coughed. "Sad face?" He laughed. "Can't believe I'm the only one witnessing this night now. It's not a verbal expression."

"Sad face cartoon thing."

"Emoji?" Arthur interrupted.

"The. Sad. Face. Cartoon. Thing," Finn said, raising his voice.

"You serious right now? What the hell's wrong with you?"

"You said to talk slowly."

"I said the word *emoji*."

"Whatever. We've got different phone technology than the rest of the world, and we don't get to use those bitmojis." Finn gripped the wheel.

"And bitmoji is a different thing."

The car was silent.

"So it's not that I dislike children. Love everyone else's—just didn't want any of my own." Finn rolled through a stop sign. "But had I known I'd end up with five adult children of my own—one of them large enough to equal a sixth child—I would've chosen a different division."

"Stop. I get it." Arthur removed his sunglasses and stretched his arms in the air.

Finn peered at Arthur through his mirror and lowered his sunglasses. "You should take a look at yer face in mirror here." Finn lowered the rearview mirror. "Yer eye's getting worse. There's more red than white."

"I know."

"Looks like you popped a blood vessel."

"I know." Arthur put his sunglasses on and leaned his head against the window. He rubbed his finger across a scratch in one of the frames.

Snow flurries dropped from the sky. Blotches of chalk-white snow draped across the windshield as Finn steered around traffic. He turned on the windshield wipers and gazed through the smeary glass. Brake lights flickered from the cars controlled by overly cautious drivers.

"You think Jose's mopping his suite with his uniform?" Finn asked, passing around the car in front of him.

"I'm sure he did that hours ago."

"Bet he's having a stare down with the urinal, then."

"Julian can't take him through the food-waste line. You know that. Jose's only getting worse."

"We should leave him in there, then. He'll find his way out."

"That's what I said. Why insult a man who specializes in solitary escape technique?"

"We're on a time crunch, and I'm not taking risks. Jose's going down the waste line."

"Then Jose goes down the waste slide. Guess it could help him—being in there. Maybe peel back a few layers—dirt, spit, urine."

"Lately he's been better." Finn cleared his throat. "Hasn't affected his ability to complete tasks."

"Sure. Whatever, I guess. Here's yer chip. Julian said there'd be no delays." Arthur popped the chip from the button and waved it in the air.

Finn swerved the car down a side street and pulled into a grocery store parking lot. He coasted between two cars coated with a fresh layer of snow and shifted the car to park.

"Been waiting for this." Finn reached for the chip and grabbed a device the size of a business card from the passenger seat. He inserted the chip and plugged the device into a USB cord connected to the navigation screen. "Take a look. A student in one of our tech programs designed this little device. Location's untraceable, and it'll convert any vehicle navigation screen into a live bug feed and will also mirror everything on Julian's laptop screen." Finn tapped at the navigation screen to activate the chip. "Each section will light up in red according to activity strength, and you'll be able to set up streaming according to sound strength or filter through them manually like a station on a police radio."

"Impressive." Arthur watched the screen load.

"I'll be able to walk Julian and Victoria through the police station as they snag Jose and Will."

"Victoria's going in? For Will? I thought I'd be with Will."

"I need you for something else."

"Victoria's aggressive. She'll scare the shit out of Will. You'd be sending in Luke Skywalker, only with the mouth of a dirty pirate and worse manners. She's got the worst manners. You sure?" Will leaned forward.

"Aye."

"Fine, then." Arthur pointed at the screen. "There's a lot of red on the lower right corner. Click on it."

Finn tapped the frame and turned up the volume.

"Intentional? Get. Me. The. Hell. Outta. Here. What's taking you guys so long?" Jose's voice grumbled through the speakers of the vehicle.

"Where's the mute button?" Finn fumbled around with the screen.

"Too loud. Lower the damn thing. He must've planted one of the bugs and is holding the other one up to his mouth." Arthur jolted between the front seats and cranked the volume down.

Finn tapped a button on the screen. "There we go—muted. Jesus, yer right. Jose's unstable."

"He's driving Julian nuts in there. Never heard him like this."

"He's lost it. Sounds like a reckless amateur. Furloughed the moment he steps foot from the building. This isn't good." Finn shifted the car into reverse.

Snow speckles dusted the windshield as Finn stepped on the gas, fishtailing the sedan as he countersteered across four lanes of traffic. He swerved down a back road and turned into a back lot of a large retail space. The wipers swiped rapidly across the windshield as Finn pulled up to the entrance of an indoor parking garage.

"What's the plan for me now?"

"Maggie'll be grabbing you from here. I need the two of you at the police department—back lot access to the kitchen door. Need prints and further intel on the kitchen manager. Maggie has the report, and she'll brief you. Once yer done, I'll brief you on Shelly's evacuation."

"Shelly? Evacuation?"

"Aye."

"Is this tied to Bangkok? Stags?"

Finn nodded.

"Yer talking evacuations? What the hell, Finn? Yer being so damn causal!"

"Calm down. I told Julian to keep his mouth shut because I thought I'd tell you one on one instead of dropping a bomb on you." Finn pulled inside the parking garage entrance and veered onto an upward ramp.

"Yer still dropping a bomb on me."

"Wanted you to have a moment to catch yer breath—some normalcy before I took it away from you."

"Normalcy? What's normalcy to us, Finn? Huh?" Arthur ripped his glasses off his face. "I've lived incognito for eighteen years. What's normal?"

"You stepped inside that police station, and seconds later code red was initiated. Felt it was the right thing to do—give you a moment before I added another layer of stress. You haven't slept, and it's showing. The six of us are dwindling."

"It's what we're trained for."

"Correct, trained for a catastrophe, and it'd be less of one if you and Julian did yer job right now without bitching like teenage girls. We've got Jose with a full-blown, onset, and raging case of PTSD. And Maggie—Maggie and Victoria—actually, they've been angels."

"Angels?"

"Did I say angels?" Finn shook his head.

"If you cut their horns off, maybe."

"Maybe. No, I retract that. They'd need some—"

"Manners?" Arthur interrupted. "Angels with loaded guns and foul mouths—truck driver mouths, as Julian calls it."

"Either way, the girls are pulling their weight right now."

"I hear what yer saying, and I'll step it up." Arthur reached over the seat and patted Finn on the shoulder.

"I'd like you to nap twenty minutes before you take a shot of adrenaline."

"Aye, will do. Just so you know, Julian's doing fine in there. I'm the idiot."

"Noted."

"Please brief me. What happened?" Arthur asked as he adjusted himself in his seat.

Finn turned off the engine. "The situation in Bangkok was a virus launch more potent than anything our scientists have sampled in the past. The cells are unique, which we predicted, but far more complicated than projected. We had a unit from one of our labs visit one of the nearby hospitals. Of the reported cases, seventy-seven percent were already deceased."

"That fast?"

"Aye, media was swarming the hospitals, so we had agents disguised as camera crew, reporters, and journalists positioned around the entrance. The agents were instructed to block shots and talk over the live news reports. They said even though the 'fake global news teams' were set up with equipment, they were still filming everything live to one of our media departments in order to assess the grade of media damage control. We staged an accident, creating a divergence as our team staggered through the front door and other building access points dressed as doctors and nurses. The accident allowed us to initiate a partial power outage with a full reception blocker, which helped scale down the media coverage. During the brief blackout, we gained entry through ground-level employee access points throughout the circumference of the hospital. Aerial view of movement would resemble something like a deflating octagon as our agents trickled into the circular building."

"Creative."

"Agents targeted the hospital worker they were assigned to—doctors, nurses, lab specialist—you get the point. Each employee chosen was based off their history with the hospital, personality, and most likely to comply during a covert operation. Employees were given their rights: participate or be removed for thorough questioning and briefing."

"The reaction?"

"Every staff member acknowledged the CIA-Division1-LFP Code Red and signed without asking questions. The hospital reached an overnight record of patients checking in and reporting related symptoms, with most cases resulting in death. They were relieved by our presence, willing to follow order, vowing they'd do whatever it took to help on the forefront and fight the pandemic."

"Knowing nothing of the virus strand?"

"They were insistent, acknowledging the deadly magnitude of a monster virus. Our scientists sampled blood from each body and are currently conducting research on virus components while special forces safeguard the staff to prevent further news leaks on the situation. Preventing further news coverage will calm chaos, giving us a narrow of enough window to evacuate Interhybrids. Once this thing reaches pandemic mode, the world will enter panic mode." Finn exited on the third floor of the parking garage and coasted to the middle of the lot.

"Is the virus gastrointestinal or respiratory?"

"Respiratory, but our scientists think there'll be several stages. First stage will infect the elderly and high risk. Second stage will amplify the infection. Just when we see a peak, there'll be a third stage. Third stage will wreak havoc through the weakened economy, maybe inflict deadly remission on those showing improvement, especially if antibodies are used from a survivor toward a vaccination."

"Dormant components?"

"Exactly. Stags know humans will use the antibodies toward a cure. Anyone receiving a vaccination will be infected with dormant cells waiting for activation. This is to guarantee virus effectiveness through a second, third, and fourth wave. Our labs are examining the dormant cells, but they're, well, alien."

"It's happening fast. Thought we'd have another year," Arthur said.

"That's why it's happening now. This is the virus. Three of the doctors grew ill during the briefing. That's how fast this virus works through the body."

"Was there a sense of panic from the other doctors?"

"No, not from the discussion earlier. They remained calm and were moved to quarantine, where our agents will train them until their release. Immediate family are being briefed, then moved to one of the bunkers. Future first responders will all receive the same deal for immediate family members."

"When was the projected time of the virus launch?"

"Launch happened at approximately oh three hundred hours Bangkok time. LFP arrived at oh six hundred hours due to the alarming number of hospital check-ins in our database. Military officials were ordered to report to their designated locations with their assigned doctors and teams. They were assigned to one of the custom-built Jeep tankers you love."

"Wish those things were street legal."

"Apparently, the Jeeps have some new crazy trailer component Chrysler built. They're packed to the brim with hazmat suits and safety equipment for the hospital, and the thing even serves as a panic room."

"Panic room for what? Stags?"

"No, lunatic humans. It's also a protective hub in the event we end up reviving sick humans above ground level. Military officials were assigned coordinates to plant their vehicle attachment. When activated, the vehicle will release the trailer hitch, and the attachment will burrow itself into the ground. The bottom of the trailer will lock over one of the underground bunkers. Obviously, bunker access won't be initiated until phase three." Finn twisted around in his seat. "Phase two is hospital lock down and border control, but let's focus on our situation right now. You okay?"

"I'm okay." Arthur scratched his head. "Overwhelmed by the tactful planning and quick response—proud, actually."

"Due to the severity of the situation, do I have yer consent to brief you—"

"Come on, Finn."

"Do I have yer consent to brief you, apart from our current operation, registered with the Glasgow Police Depart—"

"Aye, Finn. Stop talking. Just stop talking. Quit with the formal CIA big-time banter. It's me."

"Legally, I—"

"Legally? Yer serious with that shit? Just give me orders. Yer like blood—I trust you. Talking like a programmed robot right now is not what I want to hear. We're all in this together."

"I'm ordered to—"

"Finn, I get it, and you've got my consent for anything. We're all married to one another through our lifelong work, so forget the formal chat."

"Fine, then. Any questions?"

"My sister and parents—what's their evacuation process?"

"They'll be informed at the same time of our evacuations. Depending on our departures, they'll likely be joining the same underground location. Given the severity of the situation, evacuations will be grouped in waves."

"Evacuation waves?"

"Aye. Panic will cause chaos. It's a matter of time. Days or weeks—who the hell knows. People act barbaric when in fear, so main headquarters initiated Interhybridal evacuation waves. Because of you, Arthur, our squad made the first wave."

"When do we have to be out of here?"

"We're out of here at nightfall." Finn backed between two cars and shifted the car to park. "Yer driving me crazy, but you did a nice job with Will today, and I'm proud of you."

"I was doing my job."

"We're going to aim for Shelly's departure on the same flight. I'll be staying behind with Maggie, Victoria, and Jose."

"Maggie? Why Maggie?"

"I don't want to divide you and Maggie."

"Switch me with Jose. Maggie and I work best as a team. I should stay back with you guys, not Jose. Jose will freeze. He needs to get out of here."

"I need you and Julian to keep Will safe. Maggie's a sniper, and I'm going to need her through our evacuation in case something goes wrong with the division backing us."

"Shit, Jose knows nothing."

"Thought it'd be best for him to leave with me, as he's not going to take being furloughed very well, but we can't have him freezing up on the frontline at the first drop of a body."

"I think yer overreacting there. He's got a contamination OCD from the blood, not from a gunshot."

"If we were under attack, would you trust Jose to cover you as you reloaded ammunition while bodies dropped around you?"

"Aye, I trust Jose. Jason's blood splattered on him when his body hit the concrete in front of him. Sounds are not the issue—wait, let me retract that. You said dropping bodies. A dropping body will most definitely trigger something. Yer doing the right thing."

"I know I am." Finn tossed Arthur a set of keys. "I need to get over to the hospital and have a little discussion with Shelly. Wait in the vehicle until Maggie arrives and take a nap. She'll brief you on yer next assignment."

"Nope, Maggie'll scare the shit out of me."

"Nah, she's knows you need rest right now and doesn't want to be partnered with a whiny teenage girl."

"Boy would be more appropriate, but point taken." Arthur slid out the back of the car and nodded at Finn. "See you soon."

"Take a nap," Finn yelled and drove off.

CHAPTER 29

The Life Force Preserve

12:00 p.m.

Arthur hopped in the driver's seat and shut the door. The clunk echoed through the desolate, dimly lit garage. He adjusted the driver's seat and glanced around the drab site filled with dust-coated vehicles and overflowing garbage cans. The parking spaces in the garage were tight. If one car parked over the parking space line, it would throw off the entire row, exposing the end cars to potential sideswiping from the vehicles entering and exiting the ramp. Ceiling ventilation systems exuded high-pitched putters throughout the garage.

"Where you at, Magoo?" Arthur mumbled to himself as he rubbed his hands together. He watched patches of his breath swirl into air before jamming the key into the ignition. His hand shook as he tapped the heat dial to the highest temperature level. Arthur waved his hands in front of the vents and waited for the car to warm up before powering it down. He cranked the driver's seat back, crossed his arms, and closed his eyes.

A blaring siren rumbled from outside the vehicle. Arthur jumped up in the driver's seat, cracking his head on the ceiling of the car. He rubbed his eyes and looked out the window. The garage was dark and filled with smoke. A blue light flashed outside his window like a strobe light under a fog machine on the dance floor of a nightclub. Arthur cranked the seat back upright and grabbed the gun from his ankle bolster. He opened the door. The door popped midswing like metal whacking a pole.

"Ow!" A women tumbled to the floor. The siren stopped, and the light cracked as it smacked the ground. Batteries rolled under the vehicle.

"Maggie, what the hell? Scared the shit out of me. Yer the worst partner, I swear it."

"Think you just broke my nose." Maggie peeled herself from the ground.

"Good—you deserved that. What the hell you thinking, pulling that crap in public? And right now of all times."

"Calm down, grumpy. I cleared the premise. Cameras have been streaming yesterday's footage since early this morning. We're good. I was bored waiting around for you."

"What? Bored? I just fell asleep. Yer going to give me a heart attack one of these days. We're not that young anymore, Maggie. People can have heart attacks in their upper thirties."

"You've been sleeping for an hour." Maggie reached for Arthur's hand and pulled herself up.

"An hour?"

"Aye. Feel yer hands; they're frozen."

Arthur pulled Maggie to her feet and looked at the back of his hands. "Yer right."

Maggie adjusted her glasses and wig.

"You look scary like that—very unnatural. You look like Betty Rubble with a man bun and eighties sunglasses."

"Well, you look like shit."

"Whatever, Magoo. Where's Finn?"

"Finnley should be just getting to Gartnavel Hospital for Shelly. He said to let you rest an hour before we drove back to the jail."

"What's everyone else's ETA?"

"Julian's crawling around in the ceiling of the station."

"Crawling slowly, I hope. He's a big man—old ceiling structure." Arthur chuckled. "Go ahead, continue."

"Victoria's back at headquarters and working the control room. She's monitoring the live bug feed, station cameras, and walking Julian through hiccups."

"No more food dumpster shoot?"

"No, Jose's definitely going down the shoot. Victoria and Julian are locating his custody suite through the tracker in his bug so Julian knows where to cut the hole and install the ladder rope. He said he'd lie to Jose and push him down the food shoot once they get close to the site. Told them to let Jose find his own way out."

"Finn doesn't want to take chances."

"And I don't blame him," Maggie said, jogging in place. Her wig bobbled side to side as she bounced off the ground. "Holster yer gun and get in the van. It's time to have some fun."

"Yer wired. Shot of adrenaline?"

"Two shots of adrenaline."

"Jesus, Magoo." Arthur locked the car and walked over to a construction van parked over the line, taking up two parking spots.

* * * *

Finn turned off his windshield wipers and stared at the cross-like structure of the Gartnavel Hospital. Snow tapped the windshield and melted upon contact, allowing a clear view of the hospital from the back of the parking lot. The lot was filled with cars and people walking briskly toward the entrance. Finn looked at the empty passenger seat. He bent forward and pulled a duffel bag from the ground, plopping it onto the seat.

Finn's phone vibrated.

Victoria: *Call me.*

Finn tapped a button next to his emergency flashers and waited for the window film to darken. He grabbed a burner phone from the glove box and dialed Victoria. "I'm here."

"Like what I packed for lunch?" Victoria asked.

"Yer good, Vick. I'm shielded."

"Good, we're on schedule. You've got twelve minutes to spare," she said. "You open the bag?"

"Doing that now." Finn unzipped the duffel bag and pulled out a bouquet of flowers. Petals fell from one of the egg-yolk-yellow roses. "Flowers? Awe, you shouldn't have, Vick."

"Awful dad-joke-type phrase? I'm going to stop you right there." Victoria spoke over Finn.

"Great, yer grouchy too."

"Nope, stop." Victoria cleared her throat.

"Was speaking in more general terms, as everyone's acting grouchy."

"Grouchy? Me? Maggie and I shoot guns with you boys—eat, sleep, and share bathrooms filled with nose hairs and toenail clippings from you boys. Please don't call me grouchy."

"Fine." Finn sat in the driver's seat and cracked his knuckles. He straightened himself upright in his seat. "Then let me tell dad jokes." He cocked his head to one side and smirked at the Bluetooth speaker.

"Anyways, the flowers. Bring the bouquet to Shelly, but lift them high enough to cover one side of yer face. I've hacked into the hospital's security camera systems but left Shelly's floor running live until you make it up to her room."

"Anything else?"

"Hang on, Finn. Jesus, Julian, you're an impatient American meatball—*meathead*." Victoria's raspy voice trailed off. "Stop right where you are and turn to yer other left—forty-five degrees. Now crawl straight—*straight*—and slightly to the left—er, right. You know what, just lay flat and play dead a minute. Let me finish up with Finn."

"Vic?" Finn raised his voice.

"What the hell's that?" Victoria asked. "You ripped through yer glove. Reach in yer bag and change yer gloves because I can see yer thumb poking through a hole in yer thumbs-up." Victoria laughed. "Finnley?"

"I'm here."

"Julian stuck his thumb through a nail. Saw it happening through the night-vision system too, but it was too late. You should see the screenshot I took of his face. He looked like one of those zombie raccoons we've watched on YouTube."

Finn ignored Victoria and pulled out a coffee thermos from under his seat. "Did he grab the nail?"

"Aye." Victoria blew air into the speaker as she laughed. "I told him to seal the nail and put it in his bag, and he rolled his eyes at me. Zipped the nail in his back pocket and sat on it when he was leaning to one side."

"Geez, he's slipping up. He's going to do something stupid from sleep deprivation."

"He can hear you loud and clear." Victoria stopped talking. "Julian says to make a pit stop at the men's bathroom once you enter the hospital. Stick yer head in the nearest stall and flush the toilet."

"Okay, whatever. The nail—did he bleed?" Finn ignored her comment.

"Nope, no blood. Hang on, Finn." Victoria's voice trailed off. "I'm gonna mute the damn camera, dummy, if you don't sit still. Yer like the miming version of Jose right now."

"Victoria?" Finn raised his voice.

"I'm back—sorry."

"Don't mute the camera. That goes to main headquarters."

"Relax, I know. Trying to keep 'em on his toes—er, forearms, I guess. He's crawling."

Finn exhaled.

"What? Finn?" Victoria growled.

"It's not the time for bullshit."

"Bullshit? Come on, we're following orders. I'm trying to keep my partner alert."

"Yer too comfortable." Finn cleared his throat. "All of you are too damn comfortable during a crisis. People around the world will be hoarding food and taking shelter, and my squad will be performing a circus act in front of the other squads on the frontline—dancing monkeys."

"You being serious right now?" Victoria's voice muffled through the phone. "Julian, lay flat for a few more." Victoria took a deep breath. "Go ahead, Finn. What were you insinuating?"

"Last thing headquarters wants on the frontline during a crisis is a bunch of show-offs."

"Excuse me? Show-offs?"

"Stop interrupting me." Finn exhaled. "One thing that needs to stop immediately is the cockiness."

"Cockiness? What the hell are you talking abou—"

"Please stop interrupting me. I don't wanna deal with backlash, because my squad's shooting at the enemy with one hand while annihilating their partner in the face with a squirt gun with the other."

"Yer kidding me, right? We'd do something much more productive than shooting a squirt gun."

"My point: yer egos."

"Confidence. We're confident."

"Just take yer job seriously—all of you."

Victoria sucked in air.

"I don't want attitude either."

"Attitude? You take my silence as attitude?" Victoria snapped. "I take my job very seriously. So does the rest of the squad. The hell's wrong with you?"

"Sometimes you forget I know you all more than my siblings. Just please, please, tone it down." Finn rubbed his chin. "You guys don't get that most of the other agents around the world have worked hard to perfect their skills. Yer confidence could annoy the other squads. No one wants to work with show-offs."

"Okay. Wait. Let me get this straight: you think we'd be show-offs around other squads?"

"Unknowingly."

"When the hell have any of us ever been a bunch of egotistical show-offs? Who are you right now?"

"It's mind-blowing that you've never once listened to me mention the rumors from headquarters aloud."

"We just don't care."

"Good, then. Just please do what I say and stop acting like you don't know your stats."

"Stats? Who gives a shit about stats? You ever hear any of us talking about our stats?"

"You know what—forget it, not worth an argument right now between two overtired individuals in the beginning stages of a global crisis. Go ahead. Do what you want. You'll do it anyways, so why waste the energy?" Finn paused. "Guess I'd rather be having this type of conversation over the opposite. Jose, as an example."

"Going back to yer little circus analogy. When you said the hand that's firing the pistol—so what if I was shooting Julian in the face with a squirt gun from my other hand? Would I hit my target?"

"Yes, Victoria, you all would. But that's not my point. Remove yer ego now and think about how you'd be distracting the other agents who need to focus directly on their targets. That's simply not normal."

"Well, when you say it that way …"

"Just do what I say and quit with the pranks," Finn interrupted. "Headquarters asked me earlier. Basically, they wanted to know how the hell we pulled this one off. Wanted some further intel on our evacuation system for the other squads."

"What system? And we've got a normal sized squad."

"Twins, Victoria. We had twins with less than half a normal squad. How the hell'd you forget about Jason?"

"I'm not forgetting about Jason. What did you tell them?"

"Only answer I had was quick out-of-box thinking."

"I think we just have strong chemistry. But Jose's sitting in a jail cell about to go through a dumpster shoot with Julian. Maybe it's a combination of both."

"I think about it some more." Finn stopped the conversation. "What's my time?"

"Five minutes to game time. I'll tap into the rest of the camera systems in exactly two minutes from when we hang up."

"What do I need?"

"Yer ID is in an envelope in the bag. Shelly's uncle's on life support in Inverness, and the family hasn't spoken to him in over a decade. He went by Charlie, but sign in as Chuck."

"Anything else?" Finn asked, pouring himself a cup of coffee from the thermos.

"Ethan and Sarah are inside right now visiting Shelly and talking to the officers. Their neighbor friends who live in Shelly's neighborhood called them and gave them their story of the incident. They're stepping out from the room now."

"That's all I need. Keep a watch on everyone until I'm out of here."

"Always do. Talk soon. Bye. Wait, what's yer plan? I need to supply yer evacuation plan in case yer able to get Shelly on board."

"She'll be coming with us. I'll convince her."

"She's fresh out of surgery, but go ahead and try. Plant the seed for us to go in tomorrow. Realistic, following William's evacuation."

"She's coming with tonight. Just make sure Maggie and Arthur are here to scoop us up."

"Humbleness versus cockiness, or are you just a confident individual?" Victoria stopped and waited for Finn to say something.

"Just unlock one of the snowmobiles and lay a doctor's uniform over the seat. Less cars on the lot the better once visiting hours are over."

"You've negated yer show-off speech."

Finn hung up. He adjusted the mirror and pulled his sunglasses off his face. Ambulance blares sounded in the distance. The siren rings rumbled as the emergency vehicle approached the entrance of the hospital. Finn tapped the navigation screen and loaded the live bug chip feed.

His phone vibrated in the cupholder.

Victoria: *Get off the feed and get in there.*

Finn exited the screen and watched the ambulance speed through the parking lot. He tapped the radio button, flipped the dial to a rock station, and cranked up the volume. Nine Inch Nails' "The Day the World Went Away" draped across the navigation screen. Light sounds of guitar strings slowly faded out until the car was silent.

Finn looked at himself in the mirror. His blue eyes looked gray under the overcast skies. The whites of his eyes were striped with streaks of red.

The bags below his eyes swelled outward enough to look like they were holding his eyeballs in their sockets. He closed his eyes and inhaled through his nose. Jaggy echoes from an electric guitar intensified as the rhythm from the song's sound bridge vibrated through the speakers of the vehicle. Finn ground his teeth and exhaled as he popped his eyes open. He turned the music up louder.

Finn straightened upright in his seat and cracked his knuckles. He flipped open the center console and grabbed a small case. The case had the words "colored lenses" smeared across the top in black sharpie scribble. Finn unzipped the case and pulled a pair of dark brown contacts from the batch. He leaned toward the mirror and pressed the first contact lens to his eye. Blinking away tears, he tapped the second contact to his other eye.

Finn blinked and stared at himself in the mirror. He cracked open the glove box and reached for a comb and sunglasses. Another ambulance emerged into the parking lot of the hospital and parked behind the line at the entranceway. The driver jumped out of the ambulance and ran to the back of the vehicle to assist the other EMTs with the patient. Finn sipped his coffee and laid it in the holder. He ripped his shirt over his head and looked down at his bare chest. Sliding his seat back, he leaned over his shoulder and grabbed a shirt from the back seat.

Goose bumps swarmed his arms as he twisted forward in his seat. Finn rubbed his arms and stared at his shoulder tattoo. A python wrapped around the back of his arm with its mouth opened wide. The mouth of the python was stretched wide over a bull's-eye. The snake's fangs lodged into the circumference of the bull's-eye inches above a bullet wound. Finn rubbed his finger over the raised lump at the center of the target and pulled the black shirt over his head. He reached behind him and grabbed his leather jacket. Glancing at his dark brown eyes in the mirror, he combed his hair together and swiped it back creating a long pompadour style. He reached in the glove box and grabbed a small bottle of hairspray and sprayed the top of his hair. He rubbed at the buzzed-cut sides of his head and slid on his sunglasses.

He grabbed the bouquet of flowers and brushed open the door. He stretched his legs as he stood up tall and put on his leather jacket. A woman and child hopped out from a vehicle fifty feet ahead of him and scurried toward the hospital entrance. Finn locked the car and strolled behind the family. The words Gartnavel General Hospital spread across a large white sign in gunmetal blue, matching the blue metal beams that formed a flat canopy over the entranceway of the hospital. Blood-red signs lined the automatic doors with images of patients on respirators with lung damage from cigarette smoking. Finn held up the flowers to his face for the plastic wrap to shield part of his face. He spotted the camera above the glass door, bowed his head at the bouquet, and winked at Victoria as he maintained his low stare.

Plum-purple hand railings ran along the eggshell-colored walls. The gloss of the white floors shined through the entranceway leading up to the camel-colored wooden desk and matching trim throughout the rest of the first floor. Finn stood behind the woman and child at the hospital check-in. The little boy tugged at his mother's hand and teetered his body toward Finn. The boy looked up and stuck his tongue out at Finn.

Finn slid his sunglasses from his face and tucked them in his pocket. He looked away from the boy and tilted his head in the direction of the check-in camera. The little boy released his mother's hand and collapsed forward, whipping his arms around like a fan until he dropped on his butt. He looked up at Finn and stuck his tongue out a second time. Finn looked at the boy and stuck out his tongue. The boy stood up and took his mother's hand before walking down the hallway. He turned around a few steps in and flipped off Finn.

"Baby Artie," Finn mouthed to himself.

"How can I help you?" the woman asked behind the desk.

Finn bit his lip and steered his attention to the woman at the front desk. "Afternoon. Here to visit Shelly Norwick."

"We're allowing immediate family only right now," the woman said, typing at the computer.

"I'm her uncle. Closest relative to the hospital, until my brother arrives— her dad. Her mum and dad will take a while to get here. Here's my ID."

"We have to confirm relatives—policy."

"I appreciate policy." Finn handed the woman his ID.

"One moment." The woman grabbed the ID, stood up, and walked to a separate phone on a desk behind her. "Got Shelly's uncle here." She lowered her voice and turned her shoulder to Finn.

Finn looked down the hallway and saw an officer walking Ethan and Sarah toward the exit of the station. Ethan had one arm crossed over his chest and the other arm bent upward. His hand was folded under his chin as he listened to the officer speak. Sarah blew her nose into a tissue and wiped her eyes. She was wearing her dress from the event with a long peacoat and house slippers. Ethan released his arm from his face and wrapped his arm around Sarah's shoulder, causing her to cry harder. They stopped in front of the restrooms, and Sarah ran inside the women's bathroom.

Finn stretched an arm in the air and turned to the desk.

"Sorry about the delay, Charlie. They had to verify yer a blood relative, given the circumstances." She handed the ID back to Finn. "Please sign in."

"Chuck Anderso"

"Thank you." Finn nodded.

"She's in room fifty-one—"

"Five fourteen—family already told me. Thank you," Finn said as he walked down the hallway.

Ethan and the police officer stood in front of the bathroom as Finn strolled by. He squinted at the officer's name tag as he followed the curvature of the hallway toward the elevators. Finn passed an open elevator and side-checked his body against a door next to the elevator marked "Stairwell."

The bright white walls of the hospital's first floor transformed to a dreary gray as Finn entered the stairwell. The light flickered over a concrete staircase filled with scuff marks and paint splatter. He ran his hand through his hair and jogged up the staircase with the bouquet of flowers. One of the flower buds burst open as he climbed to the top of the fourth floor. Finn looked down the stairwell and watched the petals flutter like confetti to the ground. He jabbed his arm out and grabbed one of the dwindling petals as the rest of the petals vanished under the patches of light flashes.

Finn flicked the flower petal as he reached the fifth floor. He brushed the door open.

"Ahh." The little boy from check-in jumped backward and dropped his toy on the ground.

Finn scooped up the boy's action figure as he entered the fifth floor.

The boy looked at his mom, who was busy texting.

"Here you go, kid." Finn handed him the toy and patted him on the head. He squeezed around the preoccupied mother blocking the stairway entrance and strutted toward Shelly's room.

The hallway leading to Shelly's room was calm. Nurses entered an exited patient's rooms while a group of doctors huddled together as they read through charts. Finn stopped in front of Shelly's room. He adjusted the bouquet, exhaled, and entered the room.

A faint air muffle vibrated from the bathroom fan of Shelly's hospital room. Lily-white linen curtains were drawn closed and rippled underneath an air-conditioning unit. A streak of daylight from the overcast skies glowed through a slit in the curtains, highlighting a bouquet of burnt-orange and marigold-yellow roses placed in the middle of the window ledge. Shelly was turned onto her side, facing the window in the fetal position.

"Sarah?" she asked with a scratchy throat.

Will searched for Shelly's purse. "No," Finn answered.

"Dr. Pratt?" she whispered, adjusting her head on her pillow.

"Try not to strain yer vocal cords. My name's Finn. I'm here to discuss your accident."

"I already told the other officers—William didn't do this to me. Please come back another time. I'm tired."

"Yer family's been calling your cell phone."

"Didn't exactly have time to pack a bag for this."

Finn grabbed a burner phone from his pocket. "So yer phone is at home?" He dialed a number and looked around the room.

"What are you doing fumbling around my room? I can hear you, and I've not nothing here for you to take."

"I'm not with the Glasgow Police, and I'm not a thief, Shelly. I'm here to discuss the red eyes you saw."

Shelly straightened her legs in her bed and rolled onto her back.

"Can I come in and sit down?"

"You a shrink or something? I'm not crazy."

"No, I'm not—"

"Then what do you want?"

"I'd like to sit down with you and talk to you about what happened."

"Please come back another time. I'm exhausted." Shelly rolled toward the window.

"Astargarians, they're called. They look mostly human and can blend in society if keeping their hands and eyes covered. William's been noticing them now, well, since Jason's death."

Shelly reached for a hand control attached to the side of her bed. She fumbled with the controller, pulling the gadget to one side of her face to read the buttons. She held down on one of the buttons and adjusted herself forward as the back of the hospital bed slowly moved at an incline. She waited until the bed brought her to a sitting position and directed her attention to Finn.

Shelly's eye was patched with medical tape and gauze that covered a fourth of her entire face. A narrow tube that matched the size of her IV was connected to the side of her face. Her blond curls were pulled back tight into a ponytail on the top of her head.

"Thought Will was losing his mind from the alcohol. He's been drinking himself to obliteration since—"

"Jason's death?"

"Aye. If yer not with the police, then who are you?"

"May I grab a seat?"

"Sure." Shelly nodded.

Finn grabbed a chair from the corner of the room and dragged it next to Shelly's bed. He leaned next the bed and yanked the chord from the phone. "These are for you." He laid the bouquet next to the vase of roses and sat down in the chair.

Shelly tilted her head at the bouquet.

"Before I talk, if and when that officer comes back up here, I'm yer Uncle Charlie."

"Uncle Charlie wouldn't come here."

"Doesn't matter. This is a matter of life and death—what I'm about to tell you—so do you agree to follow my lead?" Finn reached in his gun holster and unhooked his creds.

"CIA?" Shelly pulled Finn's credentials to her eye.

"As this is an emergency, I thought it'd be appropriate to dig this from the safe. First time I've ever had to use it. I'm with the LFP, a special division within the CIA."

"I'm confused. Did Will do something to get him into trouble?"

"No." Finn snapped his credentials back into his bolster. "Before I discuss the magnitude of the situation, will you comply with my story? I'm visiting as yer uncle Charlie."

"If that's not a fake badge, then aye."

"People with fake badges wouldn't have stopped the red eyes from strangling you to death from the top window of your house while yer ex-husband was passed out on the couch."

"You could've watched the news for all I know."

Finn scooted his chair closer to Shelly. "You know what you saw, and I know what you saw. And I can tell you all about what you saw, because what you saw won't stop until Will's gone, and yer being used as bait."

"Will's honestly not a bad guy. Whatever he's been mixed up with, I can help make it right."

"Will's done nothing wrong."

"Oh."

"I didn't want this conversation to start so intensely." Finn rubbed his hand across his chin.

"We're in a hospital setting. What did you expect?"

"How you holding up?"

"Please just cut the bullshit and get to what it is you came here to discuss."

"Wow, drugs make you—you don't normally swear like that."

"How would you know?"

"I'll get to that. Just so you know, you'll regain over fifty percent of yer vision. They're telling you two more surgeries, though there may be a better way."

"How do you know all that? You discuss this with my doctor?"

"No, we watched the surgery. Not me, but some of our doctors did at our Scotland main headquarters. We tapped into all the electrical devices and video technology used in the room during your surgery. They told you two surgeries, but our team believes three less invasive procedures will have better results."

"So did you sneak in pretending to be my uncle to discuss my eye?" Shelly's voice was coarse.

"No, we need you to get strong again as soon as possible. Can I get you anything?"

"No. Please just tell me what's going on—yer freaking me out. Is this some drug working through my system?"

"Would make one hell of a drug." Finn leaned back in his chair and scratched his chin. "What if I told you that my squad and I've spent our life's work safeguarding William and Jason—and you, technically."

"Jason's dead."

"His death was staged by the Astargarians, or the Stags—slang term. You know now. You've seen them—the red-eyed, devilish, scary-looking thing in yer window who put that hand mark around your throat and nearly choked you to death. We stopped them, but they'll only grow more violent and public from this point forward."

"Not sure what yer talking about."

"We heard you telling Sarah and Ethan through their cell phones."

"How can I trust you and know what yer feeding me is honest?"

"You ran into us after the event. We told you to go back up to the main road."

"I wanted to call the police on you."

"Well, both of you would be dead had you walked down to the bottom of the stairs, but they tried again hours later." Will pointed to her eye and throat.

"What do they want from us?"

"They want Will dead, and harming Will's loved one's will lead to weakening an already mentally weak man, drawing him out into the open for the kill."

"Why would someone want to kill Will?"

"They want to deplete Will's bloodline before activating a virus that'll decimate the human race. Will has what scientists say is the most precious blood on earth—a walking antidote, if you will. And this afternoon the virus was launched in Bangkok. So you see now why this is urgent, and I'm trying the best I can do to deliver the information in a courteous manner. We wouldn't get this moment if we weren't evacuating during phase one of this thing."

"You realize what yer telling me sounds like something right out of a sci-fi movie?"

"Aye."

"And I'm doped up from surgery?"

"Aye, I can make this very simple. You just have to trust me."

A knock at the door interrupted Finn.

"You know what you saw. They've been stalking William, and he drinks himself stupid every night to avoid seeing them."

"Shelly, I'm stopping in really quick to check yer temperature," a nurse said, walking in the room.

"Aye, fine," Shelly forced out in a curt tone.

"Another visitor." The nurse walked around the bed.

"My uncle Charlie."

Finn nodded at the nurse.

"Nice to meet you. I'll only be a moment, and then the doctor would like to get some further imaging." The nurse stood over Shelly and scanned her temperature. "She's been quite the trooper."

"She gets it from her father," Finn said.

"Temperature is normal. I'll back in a moment with Dr. Pratt," the nurse said as she walked out of the room.

"I'm going to cut to the point here and tell you that we are evacuating Will before midnight tonight, and I'd like to get you on that plane. If not tonight, early morning. We will work on getting immediate family and friends out the following day. I'm not messing around when I say this is life or death. I know Will would want you with him." Finn turned and looked toward the door. "We can explain everything as thorough as you'd like when we get out. Will's already agreed. One of my agents posed as his lawyer. Jason's death was not an accident, and Will knows it. You heard him announce it, remember?"

"Please understand that it's hard to listen to some stranger who showed up in my room with a badge, releasing an overwhelming amount of information before proceeding to tell me that I have to leave immediately. I've got no proof William's even agreed. After all, this could be some sick joke. It sounds like a sick joke."

"Yeah, but what you saw attack you was real, Shelly. We knew the hardest part of protecting someone like Will was this moment right now, interrupting yer normal lives with something this complicated. But guess we did our jobs well enough that you were able to live normal lives until this past year. We never wanted for things to get to this place, because we know how this can change people."

"I need to know I can trust you. How can I trust you?"

The nurse walked in the room, grabbed Shelly's charts, and stepped outside the room.

"Give me three things," Shelly demanded.

"Three things?"

"Aye, three things. The stuff yer saying to me sounds absurd. Give me three things that would make me trust you even though I'm on drugs and can only see out of one eye."

"Three things?"

"Aye." Shelly coughed and cleared her throat.

Finn grabbed a cup of water and a straw sitting next to Shelly. He popped the straw against the table and removed the wrapper. "Here, drink some water." Finn held the cup for Shelly to drink. "Jesus, its hand fit around yer neck—one hand, all the way around. Would take a human two hands. But I know this print."

"Yer right. Whatever yer talking about was like a marine on steroids," Shelly whispered and took a sip."

"For starters, the red ruby earring you found—that was one of our agent's earrings. Her name's Victoria, and she had to help carry him in from a night of drinking himself stupid."

"I guess that's somewhat personal."

"Recent example."

"William went out with Ethan before the ceremony and opened up about what happened the day of Jason's death. Told him it wasn't an accident—that Jason was pushed, and Ethan believed it was the alcohol clouding his mind. Ethan was discussing this with you earlier that day."

"Is my room bugged?"

"No, there was an officer in the room when Ethan was telling you the story, and we've got the entire Glasgow Police Department tapped for security purposes."

"Sorry for the delay." Dr. Pratt opened the door and turned to sign paperwork from a nurse who approached him from behind.

"Losing the baby with a incoherent partner—you did the right thing. I think he hit his rock bottom now."

"I see you've got another visitor. I'm Dr. Pratt," he said, extending his hand.

"I'm Shelly's uncle, Charlie, but call me Chuck." Finn reached out and shook the doctor's hand.

"What time will you be coming back?" Shelly choked out the words as she raised the pitch of her voice.

"Before you go to bed. Get some rest." Finn stood up and leaned over for a hug. He cupped his hand into hers and slid a crumpled-up piece of paper between her fingers. "Hang in there."

* * * *

Arthur jerked open the rear sliding door of the van and climbed inside. "Gonna change in back."

"One of the hospitals in China reached maximum capacity." Maggie dug through the center console and grabbed a pair of sunglasses.

"What?" Arthur shouted to the front of the van.

"I said first hospital reached maximum capacity."

"Yer mumbling, Magoo."

"Yer gonna fail next physical," Maggie grumbled to herself as she switched sunglasses. "I said I'm so grateful to have you as my partner, and you haven't aged a bit."

"Cut the shit."

"Yer the worst today, like someone beat you with the angry stick, er, paddle. I was trying to tell you the virus is spreading rapidly in China, and one hospital already reached their limit."

"No shit?"

"They've got high-volume air travel entering and exiting the country today, which is a recipe for disaster. Hope we're able to get the hell out of here before border lockdown." Maggie peered at Arthur through the rearview mirror. Large square-framed sunglasses covered half her face.

"Please put the other glasses back on. You look like a robot." Arthur searched around the van.

A high-pitched ring blared through the vehicle.

Arthur knocked into the side of a tool chest. "Turn down the volume. Yer going to make me go deaf."

"You already are."

"What?"

Maggie turned down the volume and connected a burner phone to a chord dangling from a screen in the dash. Maggie coughed into the speaker.

"V," a woman's voice said.

"We're good, Vic. Equipment's activated."

Arthur crawled toward the front of the van and leaned over an electronic device the size of a shoebox. "I confirm—we can talk."

"Get some rest, Artie?" Victoria asked.

"I'm good," Arthur shouted from the back of the van as he unzipped his pants and yanked off both shoes.

"Hang on, Vic." Maggie ripped off her sunglasses and glanced over her shoulder. "Yer uniform's in the red toolbox."

"The red one—thanks." Arthur leaned his back against the driver's seat and squinted at the five elongated red toolboxes lining half of the utility van. He plunged on all fours and crawled to the closest red toolbox.

"How we looking?" Maggie tipped her head to the speaker.

"We're sitting pretty. You've got a little more time, so sit tight. I'm activating a bug Finn placed in Shelly's room. Shelly may be on the first flight after all."

"Impressive," Maggie said.

Arthur ripped open one of the shelves and slammed it shut. He slid to the next toolbox and ripped open the door.

"It's the red toolbox—behind my seat," Maggie growled.

"Great, you've eliminated fifteen percent of my options."

"Hang on, Vic." Maggie wrapped her arm around the passenger seat and glared at Arthur in his underwear. "Right there—the bright red one.

Oh shit, my bad. It's a new van—sorry." She bowed her head, knocking her oversized glasses to the tip of her nose as she reversed the vehicle. Black hair fell down from her wig and brushed across her cheek.

Arthur looked at Maggie and shut his eyes. "Please put yer robot glasses back on."

"What? Why?"

"You look like this guy from training—"

"Guy?"

"Aye." Arthur turned to the toolbox. "Steve was his name. He had black hair and no eyebrows."

"Are you hearing this, Vic?"

"Oh yeah, this is great. I'm recording it too." Victoria laughed. "Hold please. Julian needs my help with navigating."

Maggie waited for Arthur to unbutton his shirt and pull an undershirt over his head. She lunged between the front seats and shoved Arthur onto his side. "Yer lucky I'm not back there with you."

"Really, Maggie? Come on, you chose a jet-black wig pulled into a man bun, but you have platinum blond hair, eyelashes, and eyebrows. It's bloody hysterical." Arthur opened the toolbox and grabbed his uniform.

"Yer being a jerk."

"Yer never this sensitive, and I've said way worse. Yer like my little sister, and you know I don't mean it. I can tell yer scared."

"I'm not scared. I've trained my entire life for this."

"All of us have. Not knowing how bad this will get is a scary thing. We've made it to the first round of evacuations, and we're a strong squad."

"Okay, enough with emotions. I'll turn it down a notch."

"Awe, that was all being recorded." Victoria laughed.

"Fine with us," Arthur said.

"You should see the shit we've got on film of you and yer partner," Maggie said and turned to look at Arthur.

"Not sure what you mean by that," Victoria said.

"You and Julian both know what we mean."

"I'll need you at the back of the kitchen in twenty minutes. Yer under ten minutes away with weather and traffic right now. Leave in ten. Julian's working on my access point through the kitchen locker room. Once you get the kitchen manager's fingerprints over to me, I'll be in just after dark. Finn will evacuate Shelly at twenty-one hundred hours. We will be out at twenty-three fifty. You two are set to cover the motherboard while the two operations are in effect."

"Got it," Arthur said.

"Sending you the full assignment now. That was my only open window of time today, and I gotta get back to working the motherboard." Victoria hung up the phone.

CHAPTER 30

The Life Force Preserve

1:00 p.m.

Maggie drove out of the parking garage. Tiny snow particles swirled across the windshield as the wind shook through the trees alongside the exit ramp. The van fishtailed as she accelerated through a fresh layer of snow down the exit ramp.

"So we need a fingerprint from this kid, Otis. His file's on yer seat. I'll hand it back to you."

"Otis?"

"Aye, young kitchen manager who can't hold a job. He has family embedded in politics."

"What do I need to know to get his fingerprint? I'll read it while we're waiting for Finn if I have to."

"His fingerprint unlocks the back door to the kitchen, where employees walk through a security checkpoint during a morning check-in and anytime the kitchen staff exits or reenters the building."

"There's no way we'll get an imprint on the keypad from earlier. Our technology requires an hour or less for usable prints on these new security systems. I know you already know their systems are updated."

"They're certainly up and running on the latest system." Maggie swerved around a pothole and pulled up to a stop sign.

"Then what? Prints from his car?"

"Easier than that. Won't even have to waste time searching for prints. Camera tapes showed him exiting and reentering the building almost twice an hour since early this morning."

"Perfect. Prints'll be easy."

"There's more. Finn posted up while you were in the police station and saw Otis ripping shots from a flask and smoking from a pipe next to the dumpster."

"And here I thought those front-desk interns were the weakest link of the station."

"You were close. Those interns gave Otis money to purchase weed during their lunch break."

"Those little shits pawned all the work on their coworker while they manipulated another."

"Nope, yer wrong," Maggie interrupted Arthur. "If yer slightly suggesting they manipulate Otis, Otis likes having power over others."

"Let me get my own read on this Otis guy."

"Sure enough." Maggie turned on the windshield wipers. The snow streaked across the glass. "The department's dabbling with some student internship program. I read up on it earlier. It's some experimental internship program—"

"Doesn't matter."

"Guess yer right." Maggie pulled up to a four-way stop and tapped the turn signal. The blinker ticked as she waited her turn at the stop sign. Maggie inhaled and turned down a street. She increased her speed.

"Watch out, copilot, incoming." Arthur dumped two helmets onto the passenger seat before swatting them to the ground. He kneeled on the center console and reached for the handgrip above the passenger window.

"Wait, wait." Maggie sped across four lanes of traffic and slammed the brakes to avoid a vehicle backing out from a business. The construction van swerved around the vehicle.

Arthur kicked his feet into the air and toppled over the passenger seat onto his chest. He missed the handgrip, punching the window instead.

"That's my face—my face. Get yer foot off my face, Arthur."

"Sorry."

"Look at you. Yer stuck now. Can't see if you move, so stay right where you are. We only had a minute left in the drive. Why the hell couldn't you just hop out the back once we parked?"

"Realized this may be the last time we ride together for a while. Wanted to make it memorable." Arthur planked his arms on the floor.

"Don't you dare block the window." Maggie leaned over the center console and pulled one of his arms out from under him.

"Geez, woman, you take shots of adrenaline or steroids?"

"Yer window's fogged up, so stay there a minute."

Arthur picked himself up on his forearms.

"And this won't be the last time," Maggie said.

"What?"

"You said this might be the last time we get to ride together as partners."

"Aye." Arthur lifted his head from the ground. "Because I know yer staying back with Finn."

"Speed bump—brace yerself." Maggie pumped the brakes and decreased speed as she approached the obstacle in the road.

Arthur's head lodged between two hard hats on the floor. "I know you, and you did that on purpose."

"Can't wait to watch you exit the vehicle." Maggie laughed.

"Yer acting like a reckless child."

"Yer acting all emotional. Stop." Maggie held a hand on the wheel and grabbed the back of Arthur's shirt with her other arm. "Get up—one, two, three—"

Arthur pushed himself up to the passenger seat, grabbed the handle above the window, and swung his legs over the center console. "Thenk ye."

"Uncoly."

"It's okay to show some emotion for once." Arthur adjusted his construction uniform and looked at Maggie. He looked away and gritted his teeth. "Where's yer bag? You gotta change that disguise."

"I'm not."

Arthur leaned over and yanked Maggie's glasses from her face. "So you wait till evacuation day to wear something that'll make you stand out, not blend in?"

"Fine." Maggie ripped out the hair tie and tucked the short waves behind her ears. "Better?"

"Aye. Maybe some dark eyelash paint will make the hair on yer head match yer eyelashes and eyebrow color. Put the eyelash paint on yer eyebrows too."

"Mascara," Maggie interrupted.

"What?"

"The 'eyelash paint.' It's called mascara." Maggie laughed. "Is the hair any better?" She combed through the chunks of hair with her fingers.

"It's messy now, like you've been camping in the woods for a week—three weeks. Actually, you may be able to get away with telling people yer Bilbo Baggins's older sister."

"Cute."

"Just slap on a basic pair of sunglasses, and yer fine."

"Going to miss yer nonsense every day."

"*Finally*, some emotion."

"Shhh." Maggie steered inside the back parking lot of the police station. "Come on, Vic."

"You just shush me?"

"Aye, shhh. Victoria said she'd trigger one of the light posts, so look up. I tried handing you our assignment so you'd know what's going on."

"Now why would I do that when I've got you?"

"Watch for a flicker in one of the light posts." Maggie searched the parking lot. "Never mind, there she goes. We're driving right up to it see." Maggie backed the van under the spotty light post and unbuckled her seat belt. "Victoria's fudging with their security cams, so hang tight a couple of minutes."

"Wait." Arthur turned to Maggie. "I'd like to chat with you about the evacuation. Give me thirty seconds."

"We've got three minutes to gear up and get out of the vehicle."

"I'd like to talk for a moment," Arthur said, slipping his sunglasses from his eyes.

Maggie glanced at Arthur, bit her lip, and squinted her eyes shut. She opened an eye, avoiding eye contact.

"Why're you making that face?"

"What do you mean?"

"You look like yer about to projectile vomit."

"Yer eye—eye stuff. I can handle blood all day long, but eye stuff makes me cringe some."

"I feel fine. Yer lucky yer not flying back with us tonight. I'd save you a special seat between me and Shelly."

"Please put yer glasses on if you want me to look at you."

"Fine."

"Time's ticking. Say whatever it is you wanted to say."

"See, I know what yer doing now, stalling for time. I've got to talk as you switch to yer robot-mode passive-aggressive act I've watched you pull with the others. Yer shutting me out." Arthur stared at Maggie. "Look at me, Maggie McNevins."

Maggie dropped her seat belt and turned toward Arthur.

Arthur leaned backward. "While we're at it, you might want to put yer sunglasses back on too, Miss Baggins."

Maggie ripped her sunglasses back from Arthur.

"You know I'd prefer for us to not be divided during the evacuation process. Never thought we'd be divided—you and I. We work well as a team." Arthur sat up and adjusted himself in his seat. "Yer loud and obnoxious a lot of the time, but yer a hell of a sniper, so I understand why Finn needs you here to watch his back."

"Thanks." Maggie opened the center console and reached for a stick of gum. She wadded the gum into a ball and popped it in her mouth.

"I'm not done talking, and I'm not the best with talking emotions myself. You've got Finn, Victoria, and Jose. Finn and Victoria are the strongest two of the squad." Arthur put on his hard hat and handed Maggie the other.

"You done talking? Was that it?"

"Aye, that's what I got."

"Good chat. Not sure what on earth that was all about."

Arthur looked out the window.

"Two minutes—just follow my lead. Look around and notice the backdoor emergency exits around the L-shape building, including both entrance and exit doors of the kitchen. There are electrical boxes alongside each of the doors. They position us perfectly for prints."

"It's just … I love you like a sister, Magoo, and I want you to make it back safe."

"Um, hello?"

"No, I heard you. Electrical boxes will position us for prints. Just want you to know I care, is all."

"Got it. Feel better now? Done venting?"

"That's not venting. Yer people skills need some serious work. I'd love to witness you on a first date just one time. I'd slap one of our microcams across yer forehead and watch yer date's facial expressions any time you answered a question." Arthur laughed. "Such a beautiful woman to look at, but once you open yer mouth—"

"Good thing Finn sent you to play solicitor, not me." Maggie leaned over an empty coffee cup and spit out her gum.

"See that? Right there—just hacked yer gum in a cup. Now that right there is an example of why you wouldn't score that second date."

"The light fizzled underneath the light pole. It's showtime." Maggie slipped the hard hat over her wig, reached over the back of the passenger seat, and grabbed a construction belt. "I've got the fingerprint scanner. Grab something from the back to carry as a prop. We're going to walk around the back lot and check power lines and electrical boxes until our target comes out for his next fix. Just follow my lead. You ready?"

"Ready. But before we step out from our safety shield, keep code to a minimum right now, in case they're watching too."

"You on drugs, crazy man? We get to clock out after this last job, and I've gotta pick up my kids from their lessons. Let's get to work."

"You make this character up while I was napping?" Arthur opened the door and hopped out from the vehicle. He slid open the side door of the van and grabbed a measuring wheel.

"Don't think we'll need a measuring wheel. Snow's covering the ground," Maggie mumbled, walking around the van.

"It's fine. We may need it," Arthur replied as he gripped the measuring wheel and followed Maggie to the edge of the building. He looked around the lot as he walked with Maggie down a narrow sidewalk strip running along the perimeter of the building.

Maggie grabbed a device from her belt. "I'll scan the electrical boxes around the back of the building. They said they've been having problems on the north side of the building, even with their backup generators."

"Light post shouldn't be flickering like that during the day. Something wasn't installed correctly. We might have to run in and get a list of recent lot work."

Arthur jumped over a patch of snow as he followed Maggie to an electrical unit next to the kitchen door exit. He searched the lot as Maggie leaned over the box. "Light's on again, flickering." Arthur pointed to the light pole above the construction van.

"Huh? It powered on again?" Maggie stood up and turned to look at the light.

A gust of wind funneled around the back of the building. The door lashed open, clipping Maggie as she sidestepped toward the sidewalk.

"Sorry, gentlemen. I meant man and, uh, woman? My bad." Otis stood in the doorway and nodded at Maggie and Arthur, waiting for them to pass by.

Maggie turned her head away from Arthur and walked ahead of him. She signaled for Arthur's help. She grabbed at his arm and lunged over a mound of snow to reach the next electrical box. "We'll come back to that one. There's an entranceway system that could've been installed incorrectly."

"If yer sure about that, Bilbo. We should start with the kitchen."

"I'd like to look at this electrical box first. The others should match this one. We'll have something to compare."

Arthur glanced at Otis and watched him hoist two large garbage bags over the top of the dumpster. He watched Otis stop and take a hit from a pipe before he reentered the building. "The light went out again. It's definitely linked to a poor installation job around the kitchen region. We should start there if you want to pick up yer kids from school on time. We can always finish the job in the morning."

"Aye, fine." Maggie pulled herself up and reached out for Arthur's arm.

"Scan the label on the system to see who could've installed it locally." Arthur walked with Maggie to the entrance of the kitchen.

Maggie slipped her hand inside the tool belt, grabbed the fingerprint scanner, and attached it to device in her hand. She walked up to the door and zapped the finger pad. "I'll email this to our office and see what type of unit we're messing with. How 'bout we wait for an answer and come back in the morning?"

"Fine with me." Arthur followed Maggie to the van.

They jumped inside and slammed the doors.

Maggie held a finger in the air. She turned on the vehicle and pressed a button. "We're good."

"That was easier than I thought. You can tell that kid's nothing but problems." Arthur buckled his seat belt. "Where to?"

"Back to headquarters. We're running the motherboard with two operations at once. I'll need yer help with Julian and Victoria, then yer walking Finn through the hospital."

"We picking them up?"

"Yer picking up Finn and Shelly, then snagging Jose, Victoria, Julian, and Will. I'll be waiting in another vehicle close to the halfway point to the plane. I'll then transport those going out tonight."

"Sounds like a plan, Baggins—"

"*That* stops now."

CHAPTER 31

The Life Force Preserve

8:00 p.m.

Victoria grabbed a burner from the glove box and ripped it out from a plastic wrapper. She peered over the smudge mark on the lens of her brow line–framed eyeglasses as she powered on the phone. Arching her back in the driver's seat of an unmarked car, she reached for a piece of paper tucked in her back pocket. "Remember, yer not shielded in that vehicle" was written inside the slip with a phone number scribbled below.

She cracked her knuckles and opened and closed her hands, which wrapped tightly inside a pair of black leather gloves. Nightfall surrounded her as she skimmed the back of the police station from the parking lot across the street. She leaned up in her seat and tapped the side of her glasses, initiating night-vision mode. Snow sweeping off the hoods of surrounding parked cars looked like sand spraying out from the sides of a strainer. Victoria tapped the side of her glasses, dimmed the phone, and dialed the number on the paper.

"You almost home?" Finn answered.

"Hey, just wanted to call and let you know I'll be home soon." Victoria held the phone to her ear. "Did Sonny leave work yet? He said something about going to his friend's house …"

"Sonny hasn't left work yet and wasn't answering my calls. He said he worked a long day, so I wouldn't be surprised if he put his phone down and took a late nap." Finn cleared his throat.

"I'd really like to know soon if he's coming home tonight. Don't want to waste money on dinner if he's going to a friend's later."

"I'm sure he'll call me soon. He may've left his phone in his office, as he's not read my messages."

"Then I'll be home shortly."

"There shouldn't be much traffic with the snow. Take yer normal route, but drive slowly. Some parts may not have been cleared just yet."

"Will do." Victoria hung up the phone and snapped it in half. She put it back inside the plastic, pulled open her coat, and slid it inside one of the pockets in her bulletproof vest.

Victoria tapped the side of her glasses and adjusted the lenses to binocular mode. She stared at Otis's vehicle in the parking lot and cleared the rest of the perimeter. Light blares glittered across the bare-branched trees that surrounded the front of the police station as police cars entered and exited the premise. Grunts of vehicle engines echoed through the cold winter night, with the occasional blare of a horn.

She shimmied onto the center console and leaned backward until her shoulders touched the seat bottom of the second row. Balancing her weight onto her forearms, she forced the rest of her body over the bump in the center console and onto the second row of the vehicle. Victoria let out a light groan as she stretched her body across the cloth of the back row and bent her knees up. She dropped her hand to the ground and patted around for the strap to a contraption slightly smaller than a golf bag. Grasping ahold of the handle, Victoria slid the object behind her head and angled it upright against the door.

Subtle grinding of rubber and rock chips trailed off in the distance. Victoria released the handle, dropped her legs, and rolled onto her knees behind the driver's seat. She leaned forward, pressing her forehead against the tilted contraption. Crackled ice and pings from rocks popping out of tire treads grew louder. Victoria twisted her neck and strained her eyes over her shoulder. Through the smudge in her glasses she watched a light bounce through the car windows as the vehicle drove over the speed bump closest to her vehicle. The sounds stopped, and the inside of the vehicle went black.

Victoria forced her arm down her leg and unsnapped her ankle holster. She cupped at the base of the gun and pulled it out of the leather. Whirling wind interrupted the silence from outside the vehicle. Ice sprinkled against the window and stopped. Victoria stretched her fingers inside the leather gloves and locked her grip on the gun. She straightened her arm behind her body, aligning it with her kneel, and dipped her body below the base of the front-seat headrest. She slowly cocked the pistol.

Headlights flashed through the windshield, and an engine turned over. Mangled shadows crisscrossed against the headliner and swirled around like string toys dangling from a baby mobile underneath a starry night-light. Victoria held her breath and tightly gripped her pistol. The gray obscurities divided and vanished as the vehicle reversed over the speed bump and away from the parking lot. She gasped for air, flipped her glasses to night vision mode, and lifted her eyes to the gap between the headrest and seat.

There were zero traces lingering behind the unknown vehicle. Victoria held her stare for ten minutes rarely blinking until the bottom of her eyelids filled with water. She uncocked the gun, wedged it inside her ankle holster, and snapped it shut. Stretching her legs, Victoria crawled back on top of the seat and headed toward the window. She grabbed ahold of the manual window crank and slowly lowered the window until the glass disappeared inside the frame of the window.

Victoria crouched next to the door and grabbed the handle above the open window. She hoisted her body up with one hand and lifted a leg over the window, centered her weight, and hooked her arm over the top of the vehicle. Snow blew off the top of the car, sticking to her glasses as her feet touched the frozen ground of the parking lot. She leaned inside the open window and lifted the contraption through the window.

Snow smeared to the sides of both lens as Victoria rubbed the glass with her leather glove. She activated night vision and walked to the outskirts of the dark lot and stopped at the street separating the desolate lot from back of the police station. Cowering alongside a row of frosted bushes, she watched for movement. Snow crunched as Victoria stepped inside boot prints leading to the corner of the block. She powered down her glasses, set the contraption on the ground, and pressed a button. Wheels appeared through the bottom of the bag. She tapped a lever unlocking the handle like a suitcase. She cracked her back and crossed the street, rolling the accessory behind her.

One of the lampposts flickered as Victoria walked along Otis's vehicle and up to the kitchen entrance. She waited for the light to strengthen before slipping off one of her gloves. Another glove made up of a thin-coated, skin-matching rubber fit snug over Victoria's hand and wrist.

She lifted her finger to the security pad and wheeled the contraption behind her.

The kitchen was dark except for a dull light left on from an oven tucked in the far corner of the kitchen. The room was one sound away from utter silence. A light whizzing sound from an oven fan left running was not strong enough to serve as a sound shield. Victoria looked at a light glow from underneath Otis's office. She glued her eyes to the crack in the door as the pulled the door until it clicked shut.

Victoria crawled underneath the side of the security scanning and gently knelt. She adjusted the handle and size of the accessory before pulling a thin fabric sheet from a side zipper. Placing the piece of fabric on the ground, Victoria lifted the contraption onto the sheet and gently dragged it underneath the side of the scanner.

Lowering her body on all fours, she pressed her cheek against the tile and watched for movement. Victoria reached in one of her pockets and grabbed a black container the size of a roll of lip gloss. She unrolled a long narrow strip and bent the pieces together until they formed a firm line like a tape measurer. The strip was black on one side and off-white on the other. Victoria flipped the strip to match the light-colored floors and grabbed an attachment piece and a tiny cord from her pocket. She connected the tiny microcamera gadget to the end of the strip and powered it on. The cord was clear and connected the microcamera to the side of Victoria's watch.

Plugging the other end of the clear cord to the side of her watch, Victoria tapped on her watch screen and slid the strip under Otis's door. She looked at her watch as she skimmed his office, tapping the side of her watch to adjust the angle of the camera lens. Sliding the strip to the center off his office, she tapped her watch, and raised the camera angle to the top of Otis's desk.

"There you are," Victoria whispered to herself.

Otis was passed out at his desk. His legs were crossed on the top of his desk, partially blocking his face. Everything was cleared from the top of his desk except for his flask and vape pen. His neck was bent over the back of his chair, and his mouth was hanging open like a fish with a hook caught on the side of its jaw. He closed his mouth, and it lodged back open.

Victoria pulled the strip out from under the door and unplugged the equipment. She rolled up the strip, camera, and cord, zipping them back in their places. Unlatching the top of the contraption, she stretched out the handle and stood up. Victoria looked down her watch and turned around.

"Who the hell are you?" Otis demanded as he rubbed his eyes. The front of his hair looked like the tail of a bird. He smacked his mouth.

"I'm getting ready to leave—just finished sanitizing the kitchen. Who are you? Yer not supposed to be here. Employees aren't supposed to be here this late."

"I'm not an employee—I'm the manager."

"How does that not make you an employee?" Victoria clenched the handle of the contraption.

"I get security clearance."

"As do I. I'm calling the front, and they'll figure this out." Victoria walked toward the nearest phone.

"Wait." Otis stopped Victoria.

Victoria turned around and walked up to Otis.

"I'm sorry. I'm new still." Otis cleared his throat. "Did you turn up the heat or something?"

"No. Why?"

"It's a little war—m." Otis burped and held his stomach. "It's wa—rm—" Otis jerked his head back and projectile vomited on Victoria.

"What the—you serious right now?" Victoria gagged and ducked out of his line of fire.

"I'm so—" Otis pushed past Victoria and slid across his mess on the floor. He punched both hands against the bathroom door and gagged. He moaned as he coughed.

"You little jerk." Victoria gagged and held her breath as she ripped open the zipper of the contraption and grabbed for the small fabric sheet. She yanked off her glasses and used the sheet to wipe her face.

Victoria took off with the contraption, wheeling it behind her through the locker room. She kicked open the women's bathroom door and fumbled with the faucet. "You drunk, cheating piece of shit who can't hold a job." She filled the sink with water and dipped the front of her glasses. Setting the glasses next to the sink, Victoria dunked her face in the water. She ran her leather glove under the faucet and wiped the front of her shirt, patting patches of water over the larger spots on her clothes. Reaching for the towel dispenser, she waved her hand in front of the sensor. The word "Refill" flashed in red. Victoria swiveled around and saw an empty toilet paper roll.

Racing out from the bathroom, Victoria ran to the side of the locker room and closed the handle on the contraption. She searched around the ceiling until she saw a red string. Sliding the contraption underneath the string, she locked the latch and kneeled to the ground. Victoria cupped her hand underneath one of the wheels and pressed a button twice. The wheels folded in, and the contraption suctioned to the ground.

Victoria tapped a side switch and opened the top as though she was ripping open a jack-in-the-box. She unlatched two compartments in the middle of the contraption and swung them open. The sides swung open like two wings.

"Shit. I can smell his puke all over me," Victoria grumbled under her breath as she flipped open two prongs and stuck them to the ground.

Victoria jumped to her feet and applied force to the top, wobbling her body weight side to side. The contraption stuck tight. She opened the top and pulled a narrow ladder from the center. Choking sounds echoed from inside the men's bathroom, causing her to gag once more. She cranked it up five feet and locked in each of the sides along the single steps.

Looking around the room, Victoria found a uniform slopped over a partially closed locker. She walked up to the uniform sopped in water and food stains. The other lockers were closed and sealed with locks. She reached inside her vest, pulled out a pair of lock snippers, and stopped.

"Forget it," she snarled and put the tool away.

Victoria tore the uniform from over the locker and sprinted to the women's bathroom. She doused the uniform under running water and smeared hand soap into the fibers. Rubbing two ends of the material together, she created a foamy rag and scrubbed it against her neck, the front of her jacket, and down her pants. Victoria wadded the uniform into a ball and shoved it in the garbage. She slid her glasses on and closed the women's bathroom.

The toilet lid clanked shut from the men's bathroom. "What the hell?" Otis moaned from inside the men's bathroom as he flushed the toilet.

Victoria dashed over to the ladder, hopped on a bench, and climbed onto the second step. She adjusted her stance and climbed to the stop. Feeling around the ceiling she, ripped out the red string and pushed open a circular hole in the ceiling.

"Boo," Julian whispered.

"Quit dicking around and help me up," Victoria uttered.

"What the hell happened down there? You're a hot mess." Julian grabbed a loop in the back of Victoria's jacket and pulled her in the ceiling.

"Hurry—Otis is coming out of the bathroom." Victoria crawled inside.

"Is that what I was listening to?" Julian leaned over the hole in the ceiling, dropped a line, and connected it to the device. Using his other hand, he dropped a rod and pressed the release for the ladder. He pulled the ladder up like he was pulling a bucket from a well.

The bathroom door opened as the ladder dangled halfway between the floor and the ceiling.

"Hello? Cleaning lady? You here?" Otis gagged and ran back inside the bathroom and slammed the door shut.

Julian pulled the contraption through the ceiling hole and slid the cover back on. "Like a glove." He snapped open a glow stick and laid it over the top. "You need more than one? Don't want you falling through the ceiling."

"One's fine."

"What's that smell? You step in something in the parking lot?"

Victoria cleared her throat.

"Please stop talking. I need a second to breathe."

"Me too."

"Why you? You've had an hour of downtime."

"Come on, Vic. I've been crawling around the roof since early afternoon."

"I know. I walked you through it."

"Very different than sitting in a desk chair playing director. Imagine a giant wheeling around on a three-year-old's tricycle."

"I—"

"Backward—and in the dark. I was pedaling backward on that tricycle." Julian grabbed the glow stick and held it in front of his face.

"I apologized. We haven't slept much." Victoria reached inside her jacket and handed Julian three rolls of mini guidance-light cubes. "Here."

"Well, I know my way around now. Hardest part was cutting ceiling holes with a half a pack of light cubes."

"Could've gotten them to you—said you didn't need them."

"I'm sweating my ass off is all." Julian wiped sweat from his forehead. "The last few hours have been a little rough."

"Open the bottom of the ladder." Victoria yanked the glow stick from his hand and held it over the contraption.

"Well, well, well … what do we got here? Let me backpedal on my tricycle for a second."

"Wouldn't you need to pedal forward, then? Said you were pedaling backward to begin with—never mind. Forget it."

Julian grabbed a portable air-conditioning pod, a package of limb coolers, and hydrating mouth squares. He ripped open the packet and gobbled one down.

"There's water in there too."

"Thanks. Just leave this thing up here." Julian pointed to the contraption. "Lock it and press the acid trigger."

"Okay."

"There's an inflatable catcher next to the hole. Since you're going out the same way you came in, make sure you drop it through the hole first. Hold on to the cord in case you need to move it over some before you initiate inflation."

"I know. You think I was born this morning?"

"Moving on, the attachment to the hole cover is weak. It's the ceiling material, so drop the inflatable catcher and then drop the line for the ceiling cover. Make sure you tell Will not to pull at it when he jumps, or there'll be a huge hole in ceiling."

"Aye, okay."

"We won't be able to patch that hole in the ceiling, and it'll be left open."

"Okay."

"This is important—pull the ceiling attachment toward the kitchen entrance. Point to the direction so I know I installed it correctly."

Victoria grabbed the glow stick and pointed behind her.

"Good, perfect. If you yank it, it may snap. So slide it over gently before you snap off the attachment." Julian cleared his throat. "You sure you didn't step in something in the parking lot?"

"Otis puked on me."

"He saw you?"

"What do you think? He didn't catapult vomit over his shoulder. Believed I was the cleaning service—you heard him."

"That won't be pleasant after you've been up here an hour—it gets hot."

"Great, thanks."

Julian grabbed a light cube and attached it to the band on his forehead. He grabbed a headband from his bag and attached a light cube before handing it to Victoria. "Here's half the pack." Julian snapped the light cube package in half and handed it to Victoria.

"Let's get these things planted."

"Follow me." Julian opened the pack and stuck one of the lights along the crawl space. "See how much easier this is with lights?"

"Drink some water, cranky man."

"No sound once we cross over this marker." Julian pointed and stuck three light cubes along the path. "Once you cross over to this side of the marker, you can speak softly. No talking until you reach this point."

"Got it."

"Follow me to Will's location—precisely a ten-minute crawl. Mine's on the other end of the building—forty-five minutes in crawling time."

"You'll be sore tomorrow. Anything else I'll need to know?"

"I've marked the spot you'll open to drop your little note."

"What should I write?"

"Something simple, like 'Look up.' He'll know. He's going to be in the ceiling."

"Look up? Yer shitting me, right? The guys had an epic bomb dropped on him today." Victoria scooted toward Julian.

"Just hint that he'll be going upward with you."

"The guy's going through major detox too. Keep that in mind. I'm sure crawling around in a ceiling's the last thing he's hoping for."

"Maybe elaborate on that a bit more—short and sweet. Unless he's a zombie, Interhybrid adrenaline'll kick in, and he'll react. He just doesn't know it yet. He's not activated it."

"In five words or less? I'm horrible at words."

"Five words or less, woman. You've got plenty of time to think of something."

"I'll think of something."

"I've got the hole ready above Jose's cell, but I have some more work to do above the hole in the dumpster shoot." Julian stuck the glow stick in his mouth and grabbed at his bags. "Come on, lil lady. Let's make a move," he grunted between his teeth.

"Following you."

* * * *

Life Force Preserve

9:00 p.m.

Finn walked around an old wooden barn and knelt. Sinking his knees through a fresh mound of snow, he lifted one of the vanilla-stained panels and felt around for the security access panel. Snow speckles swayed across his face as he looked up into the night's sky. Trees rattled from the distance. Finn paused and glanced over his shoulder until the sound stopped.

He rubbed two fingers together and leaned toward the panel, forcing his thumb against the security pad. A neon-green light flared between the wooden boards. Finned lunged to the corner of the barn and pulled at the trapdoor. He rubbed at the snow pressed against the bottom of the door and found an empty water bottle. Tucking the water bottle inside his jacket, Finn cracked open the door and crawled inside the barn.

The water bottle dropped to the ground as Finn tugged at the door and locked it behind him. Scooting across the cement ground of the pitch-black space, he forced himself into a squatting position and stretched upright. He reached an arm out to the wall and grazed the surface until he latched his finger against a light switch.

A dull light bulb flickered on from the opposite side of the hidden space. Finn stretched his arms above his head and watched his breath streak across the air, fogging his view of the giant wooden beams that spread across the width of the roof. He walked around the narrow room and knocked into the empty water bottle, sending it rolling toward the middle of the floor, where it nestled against a matte-black snowmobile. A Post-it note was tapped across the vinyl seat cover:

DON'T get on that snowmobile without your gas card.

It's in your secret spot.

—Vic

Finn walked around the back of the snowmobile and stomped his foot against a crack at the edge of the cement wall, where the barnwood panels met the floor. The crack in the floor split into two halves. He scooped the two false tile slabs from the ground and broke them over his knee. Stacking the pieces together into a pile, Finn lowered himself over the hole in the ground and looked inside. He slid a second cover over to one side and dropped the broken tiles into the hole. Feeling around the sidewall of the secret space, he slid his thumb into a clay-colored keypad blending into the cement floor of the barn. He opened the safe and pulled out two sets of hospital scrubs, two gadgets the size of a soda-pop tab, a headband, and a hospital employee identification key-swipe card. At the very bottom of the pile, Finn recognized the black leather credential holder that was given to him as a gift before taking his oath. He stopped and stared at his initials embroidered across the slender leather flip-fold before pulling out a replacement faux floor tile and closing the safe.

Finn popped the in the replacement tile and pressed himself up to his feet. He opened the black leather flap and pulled out a folded-up note sticking out from the side.

Finn,

I was ordered to initiate evac mode at our home base. The board passed an agreement allowing us to use our creds in last-case scenarios with air traffic control only at this point and time. They'll add more to the list when deemed appropriate for crowd controlling, ordering military personal/other essential workers.

Haven't seen these things since arriving in Glasgow!

Heading to the ceiling now. Maggie and Arthur are working the motherboard from the van. They'll have the hospital cameras under control.

19:00

Stay confident,

Victoria

He rubbed his fingers across the leather grains and flipped open the fold. Grasping the leather billfold in the palm of his hand, he snapped it shut like the mouth of a Venus flytrap. He lunged over his foot and unclipped his gun holster, sliding his creds and the two gadgets inside a hidden compartment before removing an encryption eye lens from one of his holster clips. Finn swiped open the sliding case lid and stuck the contact lens on the tip of his finger. He pressed the lens to his eye, blinking it into position. Once the contact was centered, he rolled up his sleeve and glanced over the printed floor plans draped across his forearm in invisible ink.

"Should be good to go." Finn nodded to himself.

He slipped off his shoes and ripped off his jacket. He jogged in place on the frozen concrete and rubbed out goose bumps as they appeared on his skin. Clatter rustled once more from the trees. Finn yanked his shirt over his head, stepped out of both pant legs, and stopped.

The rattling of rustling branches dissolved in the distance as wind whistled through the old cracks in the wood panels of the barn. Finn grabbed the scrubs from the snowmobile seat and searched for the front of the pants. A faint tapping, mimicking the inconsistency of a leaky faucet drip, appeared between wind gusts. Finn leaned over and flipped off the light. He slid the scrubs on and tiptoed to the wall dividing the inside of the barn and the hidden room.

Finn pressed the side of his face to the wall and cupped his hand around his ear. He sucked in air and held his breath while he listened. The taps grew louder, overthrowing the whooshes of the wind, and stopped. The wind gusts slowed before vanishing completely. He patted his frozen sock foot against the ground and slowly slipped one of his shoes over his foot.

Without making a sound, Finn grabbed ahold of the back of the snowmobile seat and used it for balance while he wiggled his foot into the other shoe.

Shifting his balance from two hands to one, he slid his free hand over the frozen vinyl seat until one of his fingers hooked around the neckband of the hospital identification tag. He slid the accessory around his neck and clamped it to the front pocket of his uniform. Finn collected his clothes from the frozen floor and slid them over the scrubs. He leaned his head against the wall and cupped his ear as he lowered himself to snatch his jacket from the ground.

The wall vibrated against the flesh of his ear, echoing through his ear canal as the tapping initiated from the other side of the wall. Finn dropped his jacket on the ground and whipped his head away from the wall. Holding his breath, he unsnapped his gun from his ankle holster. He listened as the taps shifted across the wall in front of him, timing his gun cock with one of the taps. Finn tiptoed backward and lowered himself behind the snowmobile. He gripped the gun in both hands as he nestled his forearms into the vinyl padding.

The tapping evolved into a rapid scratching from the other side of the wall. Finn followed the sound with the tip of his gun. The wall shook as the scratching intensified. A person would have stopped clawing from the copious amounts of wood chips and splinters lodged underneath their nail beds and fingertips. The scratchy racket migrated to the ceiling of the barn and duplicated to two separate sounds above Finn's head. The sound divided apart on opposing sides of the roof. A high-pitched squeal caused the sounds to stop. Finn exhaled and clenched his fingers around his jacket, pulling it off the ground. Rapid stomps shifted from one side of the roof to the other, followed by a vibrating wail as the two animals quarreled.

"Damn raccoon nest," Finn grumbled to himself as he swiped for the light.

He slid his jacket over the top layer of clothing and grabbed the helmet from center of the machine. Pulling open a flap in the side of the wall, Finn pressed his thumb inside the security pad. The wooden wall barrier lifted halfway from the ground like a garage door.

Finn pushed the snowmobile underneath the barrier and powered on the machine. He walked over to a wood panel on the main side of the barn and held his thumb against the pad. A red light flashed before it activated the door barrier to close. He squinted at the empty water bottle on the ground had a white sheet of paper rolled up inside it—a message in a bottle. Finn jogged to the edge of the wooden door as it lowered and swung his leg under, kicking the plastic bottle on his side of the barrier seconds before it hit the ground and locked.

"The hell is this?" Finn uttered as he unscrewed the top of the water bottle. He slid the rolled-up note out from the bottle and unrolled the note:

There's a big raccoon nest on the main side of the barn. Just an FYI.

—Victoria

"Thanks for the heads-up." Finn crumpled up the piece of paper and stuck it in his jacket pocket. He zipped his jacket, snapped his helmet, and pushed the snowmobile to the edge of the main entranceway of the barn. Hopping onto the snowmobile, Finn flipped open an aftermarket control pad installed next to the speedometer and powered off the barn lights before opening the garage door. He blinked off the headlights and watched the snow from against the outside of the door pour inside and onto the concrete floor of the barn.

Finn gave the machine some gas by holding down on the throttle and sped out from the garage. He tapped a button on the control pad to shut the garage door and another one to activate silent driving mode. Gaining speed through an open patch of fresh white snow, Finn flipped down the face-shield attachment on his helmet and powered it on to night-vision mode. He tapped a separate button, adding infrared thermal tech to the night vision.

Finn looked over his shoulder and squinted back at the barn. Three small blobs mixed with ruby-red and coral-orange surface temperatures staggered across the rooftop of the barn.

"One, two, three …" He counted the raccoons as he slowed his speed. "Four …" Finn watched another raccoon appear as it crawled over the far side of the building, joining the others.

Another figure lurked out from the back of the barn and scampered around the side toward the main garage entrance. Finn squeezed at the brake handle, causing the snowmobile to swerve before propelling heaps of snow out from underneath the skis. He hit at the zoom feature on the side of the helmet.

The figure had a tangerine-colored shell mottled with a smidgen of marigold in various regions. Finn held down on a helmet attachment and snapped a photo. He tapped at the infrared settings, changing the image portrayal, and stopped. "Stag." The silhouette was tall and narrow and filled with marbled colors of navy blue and smoky charcoal. Finn zoomed in on the target and focused the camera. The figured stepped out of the frame and vanished behind the barn.

"Where'd you go, you piece of shit?" Finn whispered under his breath as he fumbled with the helmet's reset settings. He flipped up the face shield and lowered it back down, securing it back in position. The camera lens locked in on the figure's face and froze on the helmet setting.

Devious red eyes glared back at Finn. The helmet settings unfroze as he stared back at the demonic figure's eyes. It blinked and tipped its head to one side as it watched Finn from the front of the property. Slowly, he raised a hand to his helmet and snapped a picture before resetting the helmet's screen settings. Finn held down on the throttle and sped the color-contrasting machine away from its snow-white open land of an eyesore. He steered the machine to the edge of the woods, coasting slowly along the shadowy tree line as he waited for the helmet to reset.

Finn strained his eyes to one side of the helmet as he watched for a light to appear on the inside lining. A dim gray light blinked on. Finn activated night vision mode and looked behind him once more. He added the infrared thermal tech to night vision and swiveled his to face forward. Tangerine outlines of tall, superhuman-like bodies watched Finn from open patches in between the groupings of bare trees lining the outskirts of the woods. He rubbed at the goose bumps protruding from the skin on the back of his neck as he held down the throttle.

Steering the snowmobile into the wind at full speed, Finn maneuvered the machine around a bend, making a wide circle instead of a sharp turn. He zipped across a main road and drove the snowmobile down a bumpy hill toward a ditch running parallel to the main road. He stood up and positioned himself into in a half-squat stance as he hit full throttle in the bitter night.

Flashes from the headlights of the passing vehicles driving along the main road casted light on the fresh snow in front of him as he searched through the dark spots for orange-and-yellow body outlines. He slowed his speed and forced the steering back toward the main road. Finn waited for a car to pass and darted back to the other side of the road. The bottom of the snowmobile scraped against the frozen pavement as he forced the machine into a vehicle lane filled with tire tracks. He turned on to a side street at the first sign of headlights approaching from behind. Finn drove down the street, around a circle drive, looping around in various directions before turning back on to the main road. He followed behind the tracks of a turning car, then turned again and coasted through a school parking lot a quarter of a mile from the hospital.

Finn parked the snowmobile under a broken light along the side of an overflowing dumpster. He hopped off the seat and jogged backward through his tracks until he reached a sidewalk filled of paw prints and shoe marks ranging in all sizes. Sliding the helmet over his head, Finn popped out the chip and set the helmet to self-destruct mode before tossing it inside a garbage can. He wiped sweat from his forehead and jogged down the slick sidewalk until he came close enough to another random nightwalker.

Finn walked inside the shadows surrounding the outskirts of the back hospital employee parking lot. He yanked his sleeves from his jacket and dropped it to the ground. He ripped his shirt over his head, rolled it into a ball, and whipped it underneath a parked car. He waited until he was between to large vans before shedding his pants. Finn dipped his hands in the snow, wet his hands, and combed his fingers through his hair.

He tucked in is shirt and adjusted his hangtag before stepping underneath the high-beamed lights circling the employee parking lot.

Voices from the employees huddled outside for their evening cigarette break ricocheted off the parked cars and echoed through the circular structure of the back lot. Finn strolled between parked vehicles as he angled his path to the door along the taller vehicles. One of the employees shouted good night to the group before walking underneath the light post closest to Finn's position. Key jingles rattled louder as the employee picked up their pace. Finn took a few steps through the untouched snow surrounding the back of the vehicle. He rolled his foot over a ball of ice that was frozen to the top of someone's murky man-made coffee puddle. The ice ball crinkled against the surface of the fragile pond and stopped as Finn jerked his body weight in the opposite direction. He swayed and clamped his hand to the bumper of an older van. He leaned into the vehicle, unable to detach his foot from the source as though he stepped on a land mine. The key jingles intensified as he watched the nurse find her vehicle through the back window of the van.

Finn waited for the woman to start her car before releasing the back of the van. He approached the back door of the employee entrance behind the single file line of smokers. Swiping his tag, he lingered behind the snail-paced group as they dispersed to their individual departments.

The conversations fizzled down to silence as the group divided like a ruptured firework. Finn glanced at his forearm and linked behind two others taking a right from their reentry. He grabbed a clipboard and pen from an open door of an empty hospital room and intently scribbled notes across the paper as he made his way to the elevators.

The elevator doors opened, and two doctors stepped out. Finn exchanged nods and stepped inside the elevator. He strolled the hallway, stopping periodically to write notes and wait for the hallway to clear. A man stepped out from the bedroom next to Shelly's room and walked briskly toward the men's bathroom. Finn clipped his pen to the clipboard and slipped inside Shelly's room.

Shelly looked at Finn and slid upright in her bed.

Finn opened his eyes wide at Shelly and pressed his pointer finger over his lips. He turned to the door and reached inside his holster. He handed Shelly his credentials and grabbed the two small devices. Pin-sized legs folded open from one of the gadgets. Finn walked to the window and planted the device. He held his hand in the air and signaled a five-second countdown. The device blinked green.

"You ready?" Finn turned to Shelly.

"What does that thing do?" Shelly's voice screeched.

"That guy?" Finn pointed to the tiny contraption.

Shelly nodded.

"It blocks all reception, location trackers, internet, phones recording key words, and people from listening in—hackers. Shields us like we're in a private bubble, but only for fifteen minutes."

Shelly held Finn's credentials toward him.

"You hold them for now—that's my entire life's work in yer hands. It's important we trust each other right now, so just safeguard that for me."

Shelly nodded.

"Before I disable everything in yer room, you understand there's no going back, right?"

"I understand." Shelly cleared her throat.

Finn watched the door. "I had to dump my snowmobile on the way here because the Stags—red-eyed demons we spoke of earlier—were on our property, and I'm fairly certain they'll be staring at us through the window here soon if we don't move. You think you can follow my lead?"

"I'll follow you."

"We've got a narrow window to pull this off." Finn knelt next to the hospital bed and swiped open a copper pin-like attachment from the bottom of the second of the soda tab–sized gadgets and clamped it into the cord streaming Shelly's vitals. "One, two, three, four, five—we're good to go." He slipped the ivy out from her hand and unhooked the rest the rest of the equipment.

"What did that do?" Shelly asked.

"That put the everything reading your vitals to sleep without alarming the staff. Just so you know, a doctor will be aboard the plane, and you'll get the best care once you land in Boulder."

"Boulder? Where's that?"

"United States—Colorado. You'll be combining with another squad, then heading to Utah from there. Utah's where our main headquarters reside, and that's where I'll be landing with yer immediate family members a day or two behind you." Finn unlatched the side rail of the hospital bed. "Try to stand up for me."

Shelly grabbed ahold of Finn's arm, teetering to one side as she applied weight to the ground.

"Doing okay?"

"Aye, just groggy."

"Yer going to feel off. I'd concerned if you weren't. I'd also be forced to run a test on you in case you carried an even more rare recessive version of the gene."

A shadow brushed across the window of the hospital room door.

"Walk with me to the corner of the room so I can get you changed. Yer going to have to pull off being my nurse." Finn pulled a set of scrubs and the headband from his waistband. He walked Shelly to the corner of the room and lowered her into a chair. "Wait right here." Finn tucked Shelly's pillows under her covers, fluffing them together like a sleeping patient.

"We're going to do a little practice run—walk, I meant—around the room after we get you changed into yer scrubs." Finn sat on the ground next to Shelly and unfolded her clothes.

"Okay."

Finn rolled up his sleeve and stared at the floor plan draped across his forearm.

"What're you doing?" Shelly looked over Finn's shoulder from her chair.

"Reading something really quick."

"Yer lying. I can see you."

Finn slowly turned around and looked up at Shelly. "You feeling okay?"

"I fine." Shelly shrugged. "Yer freckles talk to you or something?"

"I'm just reviewing the floor plan in case I need to get creative for—oh, I'm wearing a lens—invisible ink. I'll explain it later, but I see how this looks funny."

"I remember when I used to play with Barbies too—"

"Shell?"

Shelly nodded off.

"Shelly?"

"Sorry, they just gave me a night dose right before you walked."

"Shelly?"

"Huh?"

"We'll get the blood flowing and circle the room a few times. We'll be out of this room in the next three minutes and out the back exit in ten minutes flat. We've got a car waiting." Finn lunged to the ground and unfolded the pair of pants and top.

"Good job today, Mr. Penguin."

"I'd like to say the same for you." Finn grabbed the uniform top and slid it gently over her head. He grabbed one of her lifeless arms and slid it through one of the armholes and repeated with the other arm.

"Huh?" Shelly nodded off.

"How are you not feeling this right now?" Finn grabbed the silk scarf and wrapped it around the circumference of her head twice before tying it into a bow. He pulled the bow over her patched-up eye. "That doesn't look right."

Shelly had a wide grin on her face.

Finn shuffled back and stopped. "Damn it—shirt's backward."

"Please don't yell at me," Shelly pleaded.

"What? No, I'm not yelling." Finn searched around the room. "Shit, shit, shit." He grabbed the key card from the pants pocket, slid it around her neck, and clipped the key card to the front of her shirt.

"We doing this or what?" Shelly opened her eyes.

"Yer awake now?"

"I've got my dancing shoes on."

"Nope—you've got no shoes on." Finn found Shelly's shoes in the corner of the room and scooped them up. He opened the pants and slid her legs into each side.

"Whoa."

"Try to stand up." He stared at Shelly slumped over the chair. "Yer getting outta here tonight if it's the last thing I do." Finn walked behind the chair and hooked his arms underneath Shelly's, standing on her feet. "Stand up."

Shelly opened her eyes.

"Never seen you like this—ever. Not even when you've been really drunk." Finn reached around the back of her pants and pulled the scrubs over her butt. He wrapped her arm around his neck. "This isn't working." He lowered Shelly back onto the chair and slid her shoes over her feet. Running to the bathroom, Finn yanked a towel from the bathroom countertop and doused it under cold water. He cupped the towel in his hands and ran it over to Shelly.

"Shelly?"

"Wha?"

"Sorry to do this to you." Finn pulled open the back of Shelly's shirt and rang the cold water down the inside of her shirt.

Shelly jumped to her feet. "Okay, you win."

"Thatta girl. Stay awake for five minutes is all—this'll be simple. Just walk with me to the elevator. We go down the elevator. We walk out the back door. Nod if you got it."

Shelly nodded.

"It was easier talking to you earlier. This was supposed to be one of the most challenging moments of my career. But nah, not with you." Finn walked to the door and searched out the window. "Walk to the left side of me and grab on to my arm. I'll walk us past the person sitting at the desk."

Shelly yawned.

"Less than five minutes, Shell, and you get to see Will and sleep."

"Less than five."

Finn ran to the window ledge, swiped up the gadget, and dunked it in the garbage. He grabbed the door handle and bent it down. He slid out from the room and yanked Shelly to his side. Peering over his shoulder, he noticed a group of nurses walking together at a brisk pace from behind them. Stretching his hand below her shoulder, he pinched at Shelly's waist.

Shelly straightened up and increased her speed.

"Now look at these results." Finn tapped the elevator and turned the clipboard to block Shelly's face. He tugged Shelly by her shirt and moved her into the elevator. Finn stepped in front of the elevator buttons, rapidly tapping the door close.

The group of nurses approached the elevator. "Hold the—"

"One minute," Finn said as he pulled Shelly out from the elevator door. "Taxi should be pulling up." An extended van drove up to the awning marked Employee Exit. Finn slid open the back door and pointed. "Ladies first."

CHAPTER 32

The Life Force Preserve

10:00 p.m.

Maggie waited for the rear sliding door to click shut and sped off. "You cut this one close. I was getting a little anxious." She glanced up and looked through the mirror. "Nice to meet you, Shelly. I'm Maggie."

"Arthur." Arthur waved his hand in the air. "Real proud of you. This isn't an easy situation for anyone to come to terms with. We've got you and Will. Impressive."

"How you holding up?" Maggie interrupted.

"Now that's a stupid question. She just had a surgery," Arthur snarled.

"It's rude to not ask how someone is doing, especially after a surgery," Maggie snapped back.

The front row grew silent as she pulled up to a stop sign. Maggie turned around in her seat and opened her mouth. "I—oh."

Arthur flipped around.

Finn smirked. "Keep going. I want to watch one more conversation spiral out of control for old time's sake. Don't mind me."

"She okay?" Maggie swiveled her body so that she was facing forward in the driver's seat and turned on to a dimly lit street running parallel to the river Clyde.

"Perfectly fine—all doped up."

"Glad I didn't give it a second thought, dividing you two up for evac."

* * * *

10:30 p.m.

Victoria waved her hand in front of a lighter as she laid across the ceiling above William's cell. She shined the flame up and down her limbs, skimming her vomit-stained clothes as she searched for missed spots. Beads of sweat dripped out from her pores while Victoria patiently waited to drop the note to William. She raised her arm and leaned over to smell the shirt. "Gawk." Victoria dry heaved and rolled onto her back. She stared up at the sooty black ceiling and closed her eyes.

A quick clunk, like a drumstick tapping a bucket, echoed from the other side of the ceiling. Faint rustles followed the unexpected plunk. Victoria sat up and rolled over on all fours, facing the direction of the noise. She patted around for her glasses and froze.

Lunging to a knee, Victoria ran her fingers down her leg and gently unsnapped her gun from her holster. She stretched forward.

A glowing light ball rolled across the floor from behind her. Victoria released the grip of her gun and snapped it back into the holster. She grabbed the light and held it toward the sound.

"What the hell are you doing?" Julian whispered.

"Nothing. What the hell are you doing?" Victoria rolled the ball across the ceiling to Julian.

"Deciding how I'm going to break both of Jose's legs. You draw your gun?" he asked.

"Practicing in case that little shit from down below follows me up here."

"Smell you from here."

"Please stop talking about it. Jose causing a scene over the bugs again?"

"Hang on." Julian scrawled across the floor and laid in front of Victoria. "I'm a lot louder than you when I crawl."

"Because you look a giant crawling around in Papa Smurf's attic," Victoria whispered. "What's going on?"

"I went to cut into the dumpster shoot, and the little shit was gone."

"Larkin could've asked him to step out for further questioning."

"Doubtful. But since this is evac, I need to be sure."

"Remember, Jose's been left in the blind."

"They're going to put this damn place on lockdown once they see he's not in his room," Julian interrupted. "I'll hold my position all the way through until you see me at the end of the dumpster shoot.

* * * *

Finn leaned up between the driver and passenger seat. "You want me to drive the evacs to the flight base?"

"And miss the final hour of bickering with my squad partner?" Maggie looked at Arthur. "Nah, I'm driving."

"That's fine. Just wipe this vehicle before you come back to the E-home. It's the only one linked to the motherboard," Finn said.

"I'll have this puppy soaking in acid in no time." Maggie smiled.

"Thanks." Finn patted Maggie on the head.

"Did you just pat me on the head?" Maggie rolled her eyes.

"Get back in yer seat, weirdo." Arthur shook his head.

The streetlights beamed off.

"Thirty minutes till showtime," Maggie said.

"Damn streetlights will give me flashbacks, after Maggie's getup today. Should've taken pictures. *Woof* is an understatement."

"He's just pissed because I scared the shit of him today in the garage."

"How's yer face, Magoo?" Arthur asked.

"It's fine."

"She got popped hard in the nose."

"What the hell happened to yer face?" Finn intervened.

"Uh, nothing actually. My face ended up fine." Maggie turned around in the driver's seat and glared. "Why? What's wrong with my face, Finley?"

"It's her time of the month. She gets all insecure and shit the week before." Arthur shrugged his shoulders at Maggie.

"Please stop talking."

"Stop talking please," Finn interrupted Maggie. He turned to the back row and looked at Shelly curled up in a ball. "How can she sleep through this crap?"

"Drugs." Arthur and Maggie said at the same time.

"Please tell me how the hell Maggie ended up with a face injury."

"We're clear, right?" Arthur looked out the window and searched around the lot.

"Aye, it's clear," Finn confirmed.

"What're you going to do? Pull out the damn foghorn?" Maggie snarled.

"Foghorn? What foghorn?"

"No foghorn. She scared the shit out of me, is all." Arthur grabbed ahold of the door handle. "In reaction to her little prank, I popped open the door and pop."

The wind added extra force as Arthur opened the door. The door plowed into a hollow object creating a low-pitched crack mimicking metal whacking a tree stump and slammed shut.

"What the hell was that?" Finn looked out his window.

"Thanks for the flashbacks, dick," Maggie scoffed.

A light moan dissolved in the wind. Finn cracked open the sliding door of the van. "You just knocked out Jose!"

"Two in one day. How's that even possible?" Arthur opened his door.

"Nope. Stop. You may whack him again." Finn stuck his hand out from the sliding door and clasped the door shut. "Child locks, Maggie." Finn adjusted his hat and leaned out from the vehicle. He turned to Maggie and Arthur and pressed his finger over his mouth. Finn locked his arms underneath Jose's, lifted him inside the van, and slammed the door shut. He tapped the shield button.

"Good God, ye knocked him out cold," Maggie scorned.

"Hell was he doing lurking around the van in the first place?

"I'd ask him, but—"

"Everybody stop." Finn felt around Jose's throat and stopped. His watch timer activated. "Shit timing." Finn scratched his cheek, smearing blood across his face.

"It that Jose's blood?"

"What's going on?" Maggie squinted her eyes at Finn. "Finn, what's happened?"

Finn ripped his shirt over his head. He clamped his teeth along the stitching of the armpit and ripped the sleeve from the rest of the shirt. He wrapped it around Jose's neck and tucked the rest of the shirt underneath his head for support. "Just give me a minute to think, guys. Arthur, switch seats with me."

Arthur touched the handle of his door.

"Stop! River Clyde in the summer."

Arthur widened his eyes at Finn, released the door handle, and sat still.

Finn reached for a bag behind the driver's seat. He opened a device the size of a sunglasses case and pulled out a pen. The edge of the pen glowed a fuchsia pink as he used his mouth to pull the top off and spit it on the ground of the vehicle. Finn held the device around Jose's neck. He moved the laser up and down Jose's arms and legs.

"Gear up. Need you to snipe," Finn demanded.

"Snipe? And why'd you pull that thing out?" Arthur pressed himself up in his seat and lunged over the center console.

"What the hell's going on right now?" Maggie asked.

"Don't touch Jose, Artie. Just gear up." Finn pushed Arthur away from Jose as he gripped the backs of the driver's and passenger seat.

"Victoria and Julian will be off the grid through the blackout. Need you to post up near the kitchen exit." Finn crawled to the front of the vehicle. "Maggie."

"What?"

"Move. I'm driving."

"I'm driving fine."

"No, it's not because yer a woman. I've just had more experience."

"When you say it that way now," Maggie interrupted Finn.

"Just get up and get back there with Jose," Finn ordered. "Stop him from bleeding out."

"What?" Maggie ripped off her seat belt.

"Stay calm." Finn stopped her from diving over the seats. "Take a deep breath. Look at me. *Look* at me. Stabilize him—that's all you can do for now. They'll be able to cauterize him on the plane."

"Cauterize? How hard you whack 'em with that door?" Maggie asked.

"I hit him with the door like I hit you," Arthur shouted from the back of the vehicle. "And yer acting worse than ever."

"Maggie, shut up and listen," Finn raised his voice. "Jose couldn't have crawled this far in his condition if he saw us from afar—doesn't make any sense. Jose doesn't even know the evac plan or the fact we're in midst of evacuation. He may've crawled between the cars an hour ago for all we know and saw us drive up." Finn scratched his head. "They've not chipped him, which is a good sign. The laser would've caught it."

"No, yer lying." Maggie shoved Finn out of her way and dove over the seats.

"How bad?" Arthur asked.

"They got 'em good enough to keep him alive and have possibly tailed him to us," Finn said.

"It's bad, Arthur," Maggie said.

"Omit yer emotions right now. You know the drill. Do whatever it takes to keep him going until we get him to our people. I don't give a shit if yer blowing lines up his ass to keep him alert. Keep him alive."

"What? I made the final blow when I whacked him with the door? I may've jammed the door through the side of his neck."

"Now yer just talking like an idiot. He'll bleed out no matter what if we don't get him to that plane in the hour," Finn growled. "You must be on the same cycle as Maggie."

"No, wait—he's breathing. He's just in shock," Maggie said, calmly lifting the wrapping. She flipped open a side panel and pulled out a first aid kit. "We've got some time once I slow the bleeding."

"I'm impressed, Mags. Keep calm—you got this," Finn said.

"Now she's calm—wow," Arthur grumbled.

"Zip it."

"No, it's fine. His bickering's actually easing me," Maggie interrupted.

"Now that's messed up."

"No, she knows I love her. Right, Magoo?"

"Love you too, shithead."

"William will be on board the plane. It'd be a good first lesson to him on what his blood's capable of. Jose will be fine. Just get him to the plane, and Will's blood will heal the wound." Finn watched Arthur through the rear-view mirror. "We've either been pegged, or he was targeted from the moment he walked in that jail cell as a pop-up friend."

"Julian was done cutting the hole over Jose's cell hours ago," Maggie said.

"Heard about Jose all day though his bug chip. Bet he got antsy, found the ceiling hole, and his own way out. They got him before he got to us." Arthur popped the magazine into one of his guns.

"We won't know and can't assume. We gotta react as though our operation has been compromised." Finn slipped on a pair of night-vision glasses and handed the others out. "Lock them in at infrared mode."

"We can't stay in here," Arthur said.

"Don't we have some sort of signal for the sniper squad?" Maggie asked.

"Come on, Magoo. You really think our squad has a sniper squad surrounding us? We would've found them. That was a game we stopped playing ten years ago."

"Quiet, I'm trying to improvise," Finn interrupted. "We need a new vehicle." Arthur flipped on his glasses and searched around the exterior of the vehicle. "Maggie, stabilize Jose and administer Shelly another sleep aid so she doesn't wake up. I want you two to take Shelly and Jose out through the emergency release from underneath our vehicle. Once you've dropped, I'll drive off and park over one of our emergency hubs and drop down."

"You'll have to wipe the vehicle," Arthur said.

"No shit. I'll wipe the vehicle." Finn shook his head. "I'll grab an emergency vehicle from one of Scotland's E-spots. It'll activate an emergency alert, which will help our situation."

"Think you'll have Stag's stalking you?" Arthur asked.

"First time they've been on property was today. They easily could've killed Jose. Maybe they're studying us now. I want you two to get Shelly and Jose loaded up in the chase car Victoria parked in the lot. The spare keys—"

"At the edge of the rear tire under the left-side passenger door. We know," Maggie said as she cleaned Jose's wound.

"Maggie, you'll be taking Shelly and Jose to a hotel parking garage and use a burner. Call main headquarters and wait for them to send a vehicle. 'Tiger Clyde' is our squad code for our departure squad. Thirty seconds—"

"Or less. Aye, got it."

"When yer with our departure squad, let them know we had Stags on our property this evening."

Maggie nodded as she flicked at one of Joe's veins.

"Artie, once you get them out, post up. Drop an ink bomb in the snow six feet from your location."

"Aye."

"Only shoot the damn alien if it affects William directly. Anything you shoot not only affects our departure but the chances of getting other Interhybrids out of our country safely."

"Got it."

"Give me another minute to get him good enough to drop. We need to get him to evac squad immediately," Maggie said.

"I'm good to go. Toss me the sleep aid, Magoo. I'll get Shell." Arthur held his hand in the air and caught a plastic wrapped kit.

"Spray it once inside each nostril," Maggie said.

Finn ripped open a red envelope. "Take these burners and use them as last resort. These calls go right to main headquarters. I'm giving you each two." Finn held four phones over his shoulder.

Maggie grabbed the phones and tucked them in her vest. "Got 'em. I'm ready to drop."

"We're—I'm ready. Not sure why I'm speaking like Shelly's agreeing to this," Arthur said, tossing the spray to one side.

"Move Jose over to the center panel slit, and I'll lower it; then lay on the panel alongside his," Finn said.

Maggie wriggled Jose onto the center panel. "Lower him."

"You realize how awful this situation could play out," Arthur said.

"With the Stags?" Finn turned to Arthur.

"No, no." Arthur held his forehead. "A man carrying a doped-up woman hospital escapee and woman dragging a bleeding prison runaway were caught in an abandoned vehicle parked on the outskirts of the Glasgow Police Department belonging to a woman found hiding in the ceiling of the police station with a giant American man."

"Wow." Maggie adjusted herself on the panel aligning next to Jose's. "My mind was going more toward the whole *Weekend at Bernie's* kinda thing, you freak. Go ahead, lower me." Maggie dipped below the vehicle.

Finn waited a couple minutes and raised the panels back up.

"Just lower Shelly's and my panels at the same time. I want to make sure Maggie's okay." Arthur laid Shelly next to him and bent his knees up.

"Fine." Finn turned toward Arthur. "I'll be back with the vehicle." Finn handed Arthur a pouch of hand, head, feet, and core heaters. "Yer the man I assigned to take my place if something happened to me."

"Not having this conversation right now."

"Hang on." Finn cleared his throat. "I've been pressing you hard lately because you're a lot like me in many ways."

"Come on, stop talking like yer never coming back from this drive. Stop expressing emotions—period. Yer bad at it, and I don't like it hearing it."

"Fine. Just know we're getting out of here tonight because of you— made me proud today."

"Wow, thanks, Dad. Lower us before Shelly sobers up from this conversation."

"I'll snag you guys by Julian's exit." Finn shook his head and lowered Shelly and Arthur out from the bottom of the trapdoor. He searched around the lot and gripped the wheel. "Five. Four. Three. Two. One."

CHAPTER 33

Present

The lights cut out.
When darkness falls,
they will hunt.
They'll creep and crawl;
they will hunt.
In vulnerable states,
they will hunt.
Try and E. Vacuate,
Oh—
How they will . . .
Hunt.
You.
Down.

The lights flutter on and off like a malfunctioning strobe light in a night club. The flimsy light inside my custody suite flickers on for several seconds, then powers off. I stand up in my cell and look around—nothing. It's pitch black. I squint at the slit in my door. Nothing. Howls echo from the surrounding suites. Pops, taps, and clunks filter through the raging voices of my angry neighbors as they adjust to the darkness. What the hell's going on? I shuffle to the corner of my cell, press my back against the wall, and lower myself to the ground. Chills ripple up my spine, driving the hairs on the back of my neck upright. I cup the back of my neck and squint around the radius of my shitty room.

Flashlights bounce up and down as officers dash across my door. One of the light flashes casts a shadow on the ceiling from outside my door. I look up and see a tar-black bubble that looks like paint oozing from the ceiling. The voices amplify from outside my door. I tilt my head at the blob and wait for another flash of light to beam through one of the door crevasses and cast a light on the ceiling once more. Muffled voices blare through walkie-talkies as I wait in the dark.

My head pounds, and I feel as though I swallowed a tablespoon of salt. "I'm never drinking again." I nod at myself in the dark.

"Promise?" a woman's voice whispers from the ceiling.

"Whaw—" I drop onto my stomach and crawl toward the bench. This is it. I finally did it—drank myself stupid. I ram my head into the edge of the bench. "Oh shit."

"Will?" the voice whispers again between siren blares.

Just freeze. Don't move. It's all in yer head. A yellow glow appears from the ceiling of my suite. The dim light reveals a woman's face.

"Whoa—"

She swats her palm out and waves it around inside the ceiling.

"Victoria? Is this the Victoria thing?" I call up.

She flickers her light off and on. I hear officers shouting through their radios as they cross in front of my room.

"Are you Victoria?" I ask.

The woman pulls the light to her face and presses her finger against lips. I nod at her.

She holds up her finger, raises an electronic device, and turns off the light. White font glows in the middle of the gadget.

This device is adjusted for your vision … the words stream across.

Cough if you can read this …

I cough.

I'm dropping a ladder. Put both feet inside the two bottom loops and grip your hands around the knot. It will automatically pull you—just hold tight. We'll be exiting through the ceiling. Are you okay to hold on? If so, cough.

I cough.

There's a small attachment above the rope. If you feel weak once this ladder drops, cough twice, and I'll walk you through administering the adrenaline shot. Cough once if you follow …

I cough.

A high-pitch alarm blares through the building.

"You do that?" I ask.

She flickers the light on and presses her finger to her lips.

The light flickers off.

You've got thirty seconds to step into the loops and grip the knot. If you need the adrenaline shot or can't make it up within two minutes, I'll come down to help. Tug at the rope twice if you need me to come down and help. Cough if ready …

I cough.

The rope slaps me on my shoulder. I lower it to my feet and feel around in the dark for the two footholes. My hand slips through one of the footholes as I fumble around with the rope. I stand up and feel around for the knot. Gripping the knot tight with both hands, I tap my foot around for the first foothole and miss. I switch feet—nothing. I pull twice on the road.

The woman in the ceiling flickers the light on and holds up the gadget once more.

One of your red-eyed friends is approaching the door …

"No, no, no," I choke out. I grip the knot and wrap my legs around the rope. "Go! Hurry, lady. Let's go!"

My body jolts down. Both legs shake and wobble around the rope as I feel the force of the rope gliding upright. One of my legs slide down the rope, and I leave it dragging behind me. The death-grip rope burn feels like I grabbed a scorching casserole dish from an oven with my bare hands as I balance my body weight between my forearms.

My legs dangle in the air as I grasp the knot in the rope. I squeeze my eyes shut and see Jason. He's walking out of our house after the last dinner we had with Ethan and Sarah, nodding at me before he walked out the door for his date. I slide one of my hands up on the rope, above the knot, and hold on.

The ends of my shoulders rub against the edges of the ceiling as I wedge through the top of my custody suite. I open my eyes.

"What are—"

"Quiet," she whispers in my ear.

There's pinching from underneath my arms as she lodges her hands around the bottom of my armpits.

"Hold still," she whispers.

My arms tremble as I face-plant over a wood beam.

"Watch out," she whispers. She pulls both of my legs through the hole. "Stay right where you are—gotta patch the ceiling back up."

"Don't worry." I blow a cobweb from my mouth. "Can't go anywhere—can't move," I whisper.

I hear the woman rustling around from over my shoulder in the dark. Two snaps, and a light appears. I lift my head from the beam and look around the dust-filled space.

"I've gotta sneeze," I whisper.

"Choke it down."

"Allergies don't work that way."

"Choke it down."

I pull my other hand to my face.

"What part of don't move did you not hear?"

"Sorry. Thought holding my nose would help."

"Yer hands in dust—horrible idea," she says, pulling out a tool from a belt. The woman flips on a laser and seals the patch, unclamping the temporary brackets.

I wiggle my nose and look over my shoulder. "Never seen a tool like that before, and I know them all."

"Oh?" she whispers as she tucks the clips in her pocket and unzips a compartment in her bag.

"What's it called?"

"A thingamabob." She crawls over and slides me upright. "Here, we gotta change yer clothes."

"Okay."

"Hold still. Don't move, or I'll cut you."

"You here to help me or kill me?" I whisper.

"I'm cutting yer uniform off, dummy. Hold still." She taps her glasses and blares a light in my face.

"Geez, woman."

"Name's Victoria."

"Could've been a little more descriptive with yer note earlier—scared the shit out of me."

"Great."

I see red and orange from the bright light from under my eyelids. "Yer not the best with yer words." I squint one eye open and peek through the stinging light.

"I'm fine with my words. Was able to activate yer adrenaline and get you up here in record time."

"Those things weren't outside my door?" I feel the uniform linen ripping open, exposing my bare skin.

"Nah, put yer arms up." Victoria forces my arms through two long sleeves.

"What's this?"

"Yer a Glasgow police officer for the next ten minutes." She pops a hat on my head.

"And you?"

"Cleaning crew. You'll be escorting me out from the current situation happening down below. Give me her legs." She stuffs my feet into the base of two pant legs and pulls. "Lift up yer ass please."

"Aye." I lift my bottom from the ground.

"Now yer going to crawl behind me and mimic my every move."

"I can't see."

Victoria unzips her vest and grabs at my hat. "Now you can." She clips a light to the front of my hat and clicks it on. "Ready?"

"Aye," I whisper.

I watch Victoria pack up her vest.

"It smells like someone puked up here."

"Let's go. Follow me."

Victoria folds from her crouched position onto all fours.

I bob my head up and down and adjust the light toward Victoria. Her swift crawl looks like a combination of a scouting tiger and a soldier moving in for an attack. To imitate her nimble crawl as a hungover and out-of-shape man in his thirties feels the same if I were to put on a ballet costume and shoes for the very first time and twirl across a stage— unnatural looking and stiff.

"Shit," I whisper and stop.

"What?" She freezes.

"Can't hold it in any longer. Gonna have a sneeze attack."

"That bad, eh? Hang on." Victoria kneels upright and unzips a pouch.

I force my head in the armpit of my police uniform and bite at my lip. I push out air. "Choo."

"Stop doing that. We're right on top of their main security room."

"I can't—choo—it's not that easy—choo."

"Here, hold still." Victoria wads up two pieces of tissue and lodges them inside each of my nostrils. She grabs a rag and wraps it around my face from my nose to my mouth. "Hang on." She slides her hair tie from her head and grabs the two ends of the rag behind my head before tying them together.

I squint my eyes shut to fight back the next sneeze.

"Still there?"

I nod.

Victoria unzips a pouch and grabs out a black baseball cap and another light clip. She slides the baseball cap on and clips the light to the front before twisting the hat bill backward. "Hold yer breath and look up at this when you feel like sneezing." She turns over on all fours and clicks on the light so it's on my face.

"Whoa—stop. What're you doing? That makes it worse."

"Thought lights stop a sneeze."

"Other way around. People always mess that up."

"Shit, sorry." Victoria rips the light from her hat. "All of us are treated with allergy vaccines. I wouldn't know. Just hold yer breath. We're almost there."

"Keep moving—it's getting harder to breathe." I follow her across a narrow bridge-like crawl space made up of two-by-fours connecting the older building structure to the newer building add-on. "It's right here. Scoot back."

Victoria leans over a ceiling tile and positions it next to a chalky marker. She rubs off the mark and turns toward me.

Victoria slid the ceiling tile and dipped her head through the hole. "Finally." She exhaled. "Mr. McPukepants finally partied his way home."

"Who?" I ask.

"Sorry—not talking about you and yer drinking," Victoria whispers.

"Yer not only choosy with yer words. Yer sympathetic and nonchalant."

"Messy roadblock earlier is what I meant to say." Victoria adjusts her vest and grabs at a bag.

"I'm not sure how to respond to that." I choke back a sneeze.

"The road closures ended, and we're moving at full speed."

"From the minute we've known each other, I'd say you'd make a messy traffic reporter."

"I'm talking code for babies. Yer gonna hate learning real code, then." Victoria pauses. "Ready to jump?"

"Jump? Me? Through a dark hole?"

"I'm dropping an inflatable catcher and a line for the ceiling closure. I'll jump first and shine a light up for you." Victoria drops a square object through the hole and presses a button. "It'll feel like landing on a padded trampoline. When you drop, cross yer arms over yer chest and let it catch you. Don't reach out for the rope. You'll pull the ceiling tile to the ground. Got it?"

"Aye."

Victoria drops the line and flips on her glasses. "Almost forgot. Here, put these on." She grabs a pair from one of her crazy compartments and hands me a pair of glasses. "Night vision."

"Thanks." I slide them on my face and look down at a balloon ball the size of two beanbag chairs put together.

"We need to move faster—the alarms stopped. You ready?" Victoria turns to me.

"Aye."

"Just do what I do." Victoria crosses her arms and drops in the center of the bag. She stands up and waves at me to jump.

I hold up my hand. "One minute," I mouth.

She shakes her head and points at the bag. One. Two. Three. She holds her fingers up.

I hold out my hand and glare at her.

She holds out her fingers once again to count. One. Two.

I drop through the ceiling. My stomach flips upside down as I hit the beanbag. "Tell me that's the only one," I whisper.

Victoria nods and points at the door.

I tuck in my uniform and adjust my hat.

She bends over and pops the catcher, rolls it up in a ball, and stuffs it in the very top of her bag.

"Victoria," I whisper.

Victoria grabs the rope and looks at the flashlight shining from the front of the kitchen. She pulls the rope gently toward the exit.

"Hey, I hear you. Freeze!" a man yells from the kitchen.

Victoria pulls the tile once more and snaps the line loose. "Escort me to him, William. Tell him you found me hiding in the locker room." She yanks off her glasses and slides them on my face. Walk close behind me and hide yer feet. I'll distract him. Okay?"

"Okay."

"The moment I say I'm only the cleaning woman, you turn and run out that door. Tilt yer hat over yer face and walk out of this building slowly as though yer searching the premise of the building for a criminal. Got it? I'm going to draw my gun at you." Victoria points to the exit less than ten feet away.

Shadows from the kitchen grow larger as the officer storms toward the locker room.

"The power went on, which means my squad's watching us live again. Turn right when you walk out the door. I'll be five minutes behind after I put this man down for a short nap," Victoria whispers.

I nod.

"'Get down now!' Yell that at me." Victoria pushes me away from her and kicks a pile of dirty towels over my feet.

"Get down—now!" I yell.

Victoria draws her gun and points it at my face.

My heart drops, and I shuffle backward, dragging the towels with me.

"No, you freeze, or I'll blow off yer head." Victoria cocks the gun as an officer turns the corner.

I hold my hands in the air as she points her gun at my forehead. My legs tremble. I realize I don't know this woman holding the gun.

"Found her hiding. She knocked me down." I say, holding my hands in the air.

"Drop yer weapon," the officer orders.

"I'm the cleaning woman," Victoria says. She turns and fires the gun at the officer's leg.

"You shot him!" I yell.

"That's not my real gun. This one's built to shoot someone to sleep. This one's my real gun." Victoria draws a gun from her holster. "Run! Now!"

I stop and stare at the officer on the ground. I look at his leg. No blood. He fumbles around as Victoria steps on his wrist and disarms him."

"See? He's going to sleep. Get the hell out of here while I hide 'em. He's going to sleep for an hour."

I stare at the man.

Victoria grabs my arm and drags me to the exit. My heart's thumping through my chest like an out-of-tune drunk beating on a snare drum—irregular heartbeat. I can't make it stop. She kicks open the door and shoves me outside.

The wind coils at my face, and we both stop.

"Freeze!" a man yells out.

I know that voice—a familiar voice. "It's Larkin," I whisper to Victoria.

"Take this." Victoria hands me her gun. "Don't use it unless they've got red eyes." She backs inside the kitchen entrance and slams the door.

CHAPTER 34

I see lights flickering from over the other side of the building's roof and turn right. The brutal air feels like it's triggering a frost infestation inside my lungs. The sting is like inhaling paint thinner and bleach at the same time. If I don't move, my feet will freeze to the pavement. Maybe stepping out that door was my entrance to hell—guess I deserve it. I walk to the edge of the building and slip around the corner, stepping inside the building shadows. I'm face-to-face with a man in a hooded jacket.

"Please spare me tonight—just tonight," I beg and hold up my gun.

"Who gave you that gun?" the man in the hooded sweatshirt says as he disarms me. "It's me, Arthur. That's Victoria's. Where's Victoria?" he whispers.

"Think she's having some issues in there—with Larkin."

"Stay close to the building. We had a situation."

"Is Shelly okay?"

"She's with my partner, Maggie. She's resting."

"So she's okay."

"She'll be fine," Arthur says. "Shit, where's yer shoes, man?"

A laser flashes across the top of my foot and stops. I read the letters "LFPS."

"Don't move," Arthur says.

"Who's doing that?" I whisper through gritted teeth.

"One of our snipers." Arthur smirks. "Wish Maggie could see this right now."

"What?" I ask, watching the light blink off.

"It's backup. They're with another division. I'm going to get you to Julian and go back in for Vic. Follow close behind me." Arthur stops and removes his gloves. "Not sure what the hell she was doing, sending you out the door without shoes. Slip these over yer feet."

"Yer gloves?"

"Aye. Hurry."

I slide Arthur's gloves over the front of my feet.

"Tiptoe."

"Okay."

I look down at the snow. Between Arthur's and my prints, it looks like someone's skulking around the circumference of the police station on all fours backward. I grab ahold of the back of Arthur's jacket as we track through higher mounds of frozen snow. A surge of wind whacks the front of my face as we edge around the corner of the building. Arthur bends forward and pats his hands over a large shoot protruding from the side of the building.

"Here," Arthur backs me into the wall. "Crouch down next to the shoot. We wait here." Arthur looks at his watch.

"For what?"

Clonks and thumps rattle from nearby.

"Don't move." Arthur cowers to the ground. He taps a setting on his glasses and searches the perimeter. "

The vibrations increase like thunder echoing off a lake from afar. Arthur leans over and grabs ahold of the giant tube. He folds his body over the giant hose, slowing down the vibrations, as he looks off into the distance. "Finley," he says to himself.

A large blob plummets to the ground and squirms in the snow.

"Get me the hell out of here," a man grumbles under his breath.

"Julian—"

The man swipes his gun from his holster.

"Julian?"

"Artie?"

"Aye."

"Can't hear anything—so much shit in my ears. Literal shit. What the hell you doing here?" Julian murmurs.

Arthur reaches inside his vest and grabs a towel. He steps over Julian and wipes muck from his eyes. Arthur presses his fingers to his lips. "Change of plans—get up."

Julian peels an eye open and looks at me. "Oh, hi."

"Hello," I whisper.

"I've gotta go back for—pew." Arthur steps backward.

"Huh? Help me up."

"Yer big and strong. Just stand up."

"Really?" Julian interrupts Arthur.

I force my frozen body up and reach out my hand.

"Thanks, man." Julian grabs at my wrist and pulls himself up. "I'm gonna ring Jose's neck."

Arthur stops in his tracks. "Very poor choice of words." He pulls a pair of gloves out from his vest. "Finn's eight sheets to the wind."

Julian squats to the ground.

The wind spirals at my face. Traces of rotting meat and expired milk taint the air. I bend down and rub my hand and wrist around in the snow. I hear officers yelling from the front of the building.

"Going back in for Vic."

"Why? She still in there?" Julian yanks the towel from Arthur and wipes down the rest of his face and ears.

"Had a problem. SVH vehicle override with a high risk. Coach likes what he sees."

"You take 'em while I grab my partner."

"You? No. Yer not going in there smelling like a rotting garbage disposal. I'll grab her. I can talk to Larkin." Arthur backs away.

"No. What're you doing?" Julian whispers after Arthur.

Arthur lunges over a mound of snow and grips the side of the building as he backtracks toward the corner of the building. He halts at the corner and looks around before vanishing.

I look down at my feet and march in place.

"Where the hell are your shoes?" Julian asks.

I point at the building, wiggle my legs, and step on my toes.

"You wearing gloves on your feet?"

I nod.

"From waist down, you look like a pigeon-toed ostrich that's been kicked in the shins."

"My feet are going numb," I mumble.

"Need a piggyback ride or something?" he asks.

The wind blows, wafting Julian's odor toward my face. I shake my head.

"Stay behind me. Got it?"

"I'll follow you, Arnlad."

"You're stuck in the past." Julian pulls a gadget from his pocket resembling a miniature golf ball. "If I say *floor*, you collapse to the ground. Okay?"

"Aye."

Julian taps the top of the ball and wails it in front of him like a professional baseball pitcher.

A debadged black SUV accelerates at high speed in our direction. The vehicle slows a few feet in front of us, skimming along the pavement with its lights off. Julian draws his gun, swiveling his head around as he leads me to the SUV.

"Door—get the—" He whips around.

I inhale the snowy surface as though I'm attempting to eat the top of a tricolored snow cone in a single bite. I cup my hands over the top of my head.

"Trip over your bird feet? Forget it. How 'bout you clear, then and I'll get the door."

"Thought you said floor. Yer accent—"

"Get inside." Julian backs into the SUV, rips open the door, and searches the surroundings.

I push through the snow and dash toward the car, losing a glove from my foot. My heart wallops inside my chest as I see freedom before my eyes. I dive inside the vehicle and hear the door clunk shut behind me.

"Stay on the ground," the driver demands. "I'm Finn, by the way."

"Hello," I choke out.

My nose stings from the frigid air pouring in from underneath the seat as Julian cracks open the passenger door of the vehicle.

"We're clear." The passenger door clunks shut. "Here's your shoe." Julian tosses the glove at me.

"Get out the masks. Smells like you've been collecting dog poop and using it as soap," Finn says. He coasts through the parking lot. "I'm moving us away from the lot—easy exit, in case something else goes wrong, and we've gotta flee."

Julian leans over and slides a compartment out from under his seat. He unlatches one of the sides and rips open a packet of masks.

"Here, Will," Julian says, holding a bag of masks over the seat.

"Where's Shelly?" I ask, grabbing a mask.

"Shelly's boarded on the plane waiting for you with one of our wounded agents."

"Wounded agent? Who?" Julian stops Finn.

"Stags attacked Jose. But he's gonna live," Finn says.

"What happened?" Julian asks.

"I'll tell you later." Finn adjusts himself in his seat. "I found Arthur's ink trace—saw 'em with you two, then watched him take off. And where's Vic?"

"Art said he's grabbing Vic."

"It's critical we leave now—while we're cleared." Finn stops Julian. "Officers will be all over this end of the building at any moment." Finn releases his grip on the steering wheel and grabs his binoculars. He presses the binoculars to his eyes and scans the premise.

I clear my throat. "Victoria's still inside."

"So they're both insid—"

A violent blast reverberates as the building explodes into flames. A second burst erupts into the sky like an air balloon packed to the brim with dynamite. Interwoven blotches of calypso orange and aluminum gray bleed into patches of ebony and dandelion as they braid together in the night's sky. One of the larger gray cloud puffs replicate an image of the human brain rolling up into the sky. The lingering clouds below are messy, like spewing brain matter. The flames mimic a triple-headed pitchfork.

I cover my hands over my face. "What's happened?" I shout. "I'm not responsible for that, right? I don't want to be a part of this. I never asked to be a part of this."

Julian rips open the door.

"Stop! Close the door and sit down," Finn orders. He fumbles with his binoculars. Tears run below the eyecups and down his cheeks as he forces them over his eyes.

Julian raises his hands to the back of his head and stops. He inhales and exhales, grips the door handle, and pops it open.

"Get in the fucking car and close the door," Finn growls. "That's an order." Finn lowers his binoculars and forces them into Julian's hands. "Take a look. You tell me what you'd want me to do, and I'll do it. I swear I'll do it."

Julian yanks the binoculars from Finn and thrusts them against his face. He plants his body weight over the dash of the vehicle, juggling the binoculars between his hands. Both hands shake as he pulls them toward his eyes.

"Arthur just went in to get Vic. They can't be in there," Julian pleads as he searches the premise.

"Do you see anybody?" I ask.

"No." Julian adjusts himself in his seat. "Come on, guys, where are you?"

Fire truck and ambulance sirens blare from afar. A mushroom cloud of smoke rises into the air as building debris flutters around the block like confetti.

Finn taps. "Here they come."

"Where?" Julian interrupts.

"The ambulance, not Art and Vic."

"Damn it."

"I'm trying to catch some movement from the infrared setting—got nothing but a ball of heat."

"Was it for me?" I ask.

"What?" Finn asks.

"The explosion." I squeeze my eyes shut.

"Most likely. They were trying to get you and anyone involved," Julian says.

"I feel sick—think I'm gonna puke." I hold my mouth and search around the vehicle for a bag.

Without ungluing his eyes from the scene, Finn reaches inside his vest and hands something over the seat to me.

"A poncho?" I ask.

"Just puke in it ..." Finn's voice trails off.

"All those people—gone." I rip open the poncho and dry heave inside. My stomach is twirling. I'd rather eat heavy Italian food during a hot summer day and spin as fast as I could in a circle for five minutes straight. If I was given the chance to turn back time, that would be a blessing. "I'd rather they just take me and kill me off."

"No, think of all the people in this world yer about to save," Finn says and stops. He bows his head down and cups his hand over his forehead.

"I'd like to go down there and see for myself—I need to be sure." Julian hasn't moved the binoculars from his face since the explosion.

"I've gotta get you two on that plane. I want you to keep Will safe. Maggie and I will go back after takeoff."

"Come on, Vic. I know you got out." Julian drops the binoculars and bobs his head down. "Arthur's like my little brother."

"And like a son to me." Finn shifts the car into drive. "I'm coming right back here. I'll be thorough."

"How the hell we telling Maggie the news? Can't bare to break her heart." Julian wiped his eyes. "I'm hopeful, though."

"Maggie will be a mess."

"Think I may've been in love with Victoria." Julian leans forward and holds his head between his hands.

"You two?" Finn turned away from the crime scene. "No shit?"

"How you holding up?" Julian asked.

"Who? Me?" I ask.

"Yes. You okay? Your feet thawing out back there?" Julian asked.

"I'm okay."

I lean against the door and hold the poncho like a popcorn bowl cupped in my hands on my lap. My stomach turns as Finn steers onto the bridge that crosses River Clyde. I look out the window. Multicolored lights from the buildings surrounding the river reflect off the frozen bits of the water. The tangerine and fuchsia glows on one side of the river, enhancing the deeper shades of lime-and-violet glimmerings from the opposite side. Patches of slow slither across the frozen bits of ice. I press my head to the window and stare into the eyes of the tiger mural as we cross to the other side of the river.

The staggered streetlamps lining the sidewalk highlight several colorful murals as Finn passes the city center. I fold up the homemade puke bag and lean into my seat back and look at the rows of restaurants and bars—memories of the good times. Can't remember the bad.

"So you guys have been following me around a long time, huh?" I look at Finn and Julian.

"Oh yeah—and you can be one crazy son of a bitch." Julian adjusts himself in his seat and turns toward me. "Had to knock you out and shove you in a car with Victoria before the owner of the bar rallied up his buddies. You remember that?"

"Vaguely."

"It happened so often this past year—felt like we were saving you from yourself," Finn says.

"Well put." Julian nods. "Don't worry. We've got years of stories to share from our end."

"We've seen it all." Finn drives the car into a parking garage. "Switching cars. Ready?"

I lock eyes with Finn in his rearview mirror and nod at him.

"Next car's ready to go—main headquarters dropped this for us." Finn drives the car next to a smaller SUV, thrusts the vehicle in park, and hops out. "We're only a mile from the plane."

"Where the heck can you guys hide a plane?" I ask.

"That's simple," Julian says.

We turn down a private road and swerve between two trees. Finn drives the front tire over a small speed bump that's hidden underneath frozen shrub and activates the machine. The platform separates from the ground and lowers below the ground.

"This is crazy. You guys build all this?" I lean between the driver and passenger front seats.

"No, UK headquarters," Finn says.

"You haven't seen nothing yet. Just wait until we introduce you to the bunkers," Julian says.

"An underground community." Finn waits for the car to reach the ground level and turns the vehicle off.

"They'll be restaurants and shopping."

"It's only temporary. Otherwise, we'll be adapting to a new way of life below the Astargarian's new world," Finn interrupts Julian.

Lights blare on. The garage space replicates a tiny shop-like atmosphere similar to a local oil change garage.

"Ready?" Finn looks at Julian.

"No, not at all, man." Julian shakes his head. "But that's how we do things around here. You sure you don't need my help here? May be best for Maggie to get out."

"No, Maggie's going to be upset, and she'll want revenge. I'll watch her. We don't want reckless behavior from bottled-up anger." Finn cracks open his door and stops.

"She's a spitfire as is—probably a smart idea to have some one-on-one time with her before bringing her to main headquarters."

"Aye—makes sense," Julian says. "You think they got out before the explosion?"

"I'm going to be optimistic and prepared for the worst at the same time. You should do the same," Julian says.

"So, you ready?" Finn asks.

"Eye," Julian says.

"One would think that an American man living in Glasgow for more than half his life would be able to pronounce *aye* by now."

"Eye, right." Julian chuckled.

Finn sits up in the driver's seat and lifts his arms.

"You want a hug? I smell like shit," Julian says.

"Don't care."

Julian leans in and hugs Finn. "Going to have separation anxiety from you people."

"Couldn't be prouder to have you on my squad. Get them there safe." Finn pats Julian on the back, then releases him.

"I'll see you in a few days."

"You ready, Will?" Finn asks.

"Aye."

"They should have something for your feet." Julian turns and looks at me. "I'm gonna need some wet wipes and new clothes if we want a comfortable flight."

We open the doors and walk down a narrow hallway made entirely of some stainless steel and metal combination. Dim lights stream down the hallway, positioned every six steps I take. We stop at the end of the hallway in front of a steel door. Finn holds his hand against a keypad. The door opens like an elevator. We step inside and watch the door close. Finn holds his palm against a second security pad. The door slides open to a bright white room with about a dozen people having a discussion. A young woman cries with her head down. The talking stops, and the group turns toward us.

"Evening," Finn says.

The crying woman stands up and looks at Finn.

"Looks like she already knows," Julian uttered under his breath to Finn.

Finn and Julian storm over to the woman. "Come here, Maggie." Finn tucks her under his arm.

I walk toward the group.

"Evening, William. You prefer Will—I know." An older man with white hair and glasses reaches out his hand. "I'm Han."

I shake his hand.

"Han's head of operations for the United Kingdom," Julian says. He leans over and shakes his hand.

"Hey, buddy, been a while." Finn turns his head from Maggie and nods at Han and the men standing around him.

"Wanted to personally see off the UK's first Interhybrid and say good job to my sharpshooter unit. But I'm afraid I've become the bearer of bad news."

"Jose?" Finn asks.

"Jose will be fine," Han says.

"Stags got 'em off premise. His escape was solid," one of the men standing next to Han says.

"The doctor treating him on the plane specializes in head, neck, and spinal trauma," Han says.

"Where's Shelly?" I ask.

"Shelly's in the bed next to him, resting peacefully. They're ready for takeoff. Just waiting on you guys."

"Victoria?" Julian asks.

Han nods. "She—"

"And Arthur?" Julian interrupts.

Han nods. "I'm really sorry for your losses."

Maggie gasps for air between sobs.

"Was going to take Maggie back there with me. Show me yer proof." Finn releases Maggie and turns to Han.

Julian wraps his arms around Maggie.

"Meet Marcin and Leon, two of our most talented snipers."

Finn and Julian nod at the two men.

"Nice to meet you," I say.

"Leon and Marcin have been trailing you for the past year," Han says.

"Full year—no shit." Julian nods at Finn. "You guys are good."

"No, you guys are good—your entire squad, Finn. You should be proud. Never seen anything like it." Leon walks over and shakes Finn's hand, then turns to Julian and shakes his hand. Marcin follows.

"LFPS—that light on my foot—Arthur said it was a sniper," I say.

"That was Leon," Marcin says.

"Leon's scope camera caught it all. Would you like to see the footage?" Han asks.

"No, just tell me."

"Marcin was posted up in the front of the building, and I was posted up in the back. The explosion triggered within a minute of Arthur entering the building," Leon says.

"Victoria? She could've gone out another way."

"No, man, she was still inside. I'm sorry."

Julian pinched his forehead and looked down.

"I'm sorry too," I say.

"Finn and Maggie, you'll be going with Marcin to aid another squad in Inverness once you're through with your work here. Will and Julian, yer set to leave here and will be joining a squad from Chicago, Illinois—the first evac squad, a female in her early twenties."

"I'll be joining," Leon says.

"Yes, Leon will be an active squad member—sniper when needed. Here are yer detailed assignments." Han lays microchips on the table. "I'm going to give you guys a moment. We'll be waiting on the plane."

"Thank you." Finn nods.

"I'll be waiting in the vehicle," Marcin says.

"I'm going to get on board and see Shelly." I walk over to the three grieving agents. "Thanks, guys, for saving my life—lots of times."

Finn gives me a hug. "See you soon."

"Maggie? Right?" I look at Maggie.

"Nice to meet you." Maggie gives me a hug.

"A little story for you: When Arthur and I were walking around the building, and he pointed out the LFPS signal on my foot, the first thing he said was that he couldn't wait to tell you. He had a big smirk on his face. There's not much more I can say but thank you, and I'm sorry for your losses."

Maggie opens her eyes wide. "I like you so much better sober." She hugs me once more.

"See you on the plane," Julian says.

I follow Leon and Han through another door and see a plane with people scrambling back and forth inside the windows.

"Watch your step," Han says.

As I approach the plane, I close my eyes. *Please protect us, Jase.* I grip the handle and pull myself up a small flight of stairs. I search around and see two beds in the back of the plane. I nod at people as I storm down the aisle and drop next to Shelly. I grab her hand tightly, sliding my fingers into hers.

"They'd given her a sleep aid so they could move her in the dark. She'll be up in a few hours," a nurse says.

"Aye, thanks." I lean over to Shelly's side and whisper in her ear. "I love you, Shell, and I'll never hurt you like that again."

CHAPTER 35

Boulder, Colorado

"Can't wait to shower." Julian scratches the back of his neck.

"I can't wait for you to shower," Leon says, trailing behind us.

"Is this where yer from?" I speed walk to keep up with Julian's massive strides as we walk down a gravel road.

"No, further south," he says.

"What about you? Where're you from?" I look over my shoulder at Leon.

"Milwaukee," Leon says.

"Canada, right?" I ask.

"Milwaukee, Wisconsin," he says.

"That's by the beach boys—California?" I follow Julian down a flight of stairs.

"California's on the other—"

"You're wasting your breath," Julian interrupts Leon. "Geometry's not one of Will's strengths." Julian laughs.

"They're here from Chicago. Know anything about Chicago?" Leon asks.

"Al Capone?"

"That's a start." Julian laughs.

"How about—"

"Can you point to any of those places on a map?" Leon asks.

"Nope."

"You'll need to learn." Julian stops over a large tree stump and kneels. He slides his hands around the base of the stump and pulls up.

"Whoa! What're you trying to do? You'll break yer back."

The stump flips open to a sewer-like steel door.

"That looks so real," I say.

Julian sticks his palm over a security pad and unlocks the steel door.

"I'm posting up. Tell them tanker's ten minutes out." Leon holds open the door.

"You got it." Julian nods at Leon. "Will, watch your step." Julian sits over the edge and climbs onto a ladder.

I wait for Julian to reach the ground before I climb down the ladder. We stand snug at the bottom of a dark pit.

"What now?" I ask.

"We wait. I triggered their security alert system when I opened the door. Wave at the cameras and smile."

"Can really smell you now through yer change of clothes."

"I'll just tell them it's you—hey." The door opens, and Julian looks at a younger guy with dark hair. "Julian Kimball, Glasgow, Scotland."

"You made it," he says.

"This is William."

"Call me Will."

"I'm Jack, nice to meet you guys." He holds the door open. "Heard a lot of stories about your squad in training. Sharpshooters—you guys are tough."

Julian looks at the ground.

"Sorry for your losses. We heard what happened."

"Thanks, man." Julian follows behind Jack.

I see a woman sleeping next to a man pouring coffee out of a thermos from underneath a lantern. He pours two cups and walks them to us.

"Sorry for your losses. It was hard to hear. We followed and studied your squad dynamic very closely through the years. You guys were my example squad at main headquarters. Name's Donavan." Donavan hands Julian a cup of coffee and shakes his hand. "And William." He hands me a cup of coffee and shakes his hand. "I'm sorry about your twin, Jason. You've had a rough year, but we'll get you strong again. Glad Shelly made the flight."

"Nice to meet you."

"This is Cindy. Went into shock after seeing Stags attack and capture two of their own."

Jack looks at the ground.

"I'm sorry for your losses," Julian says.

"They may be alive—don't know for certain," Jack says.

"I understand how you feel, kid." Julian pats Jack on his shoulder.

A door swings open from the corner of the room, and a young lady with long auburn hair walks in carrying a lantern.

"You find the bathroom okay?" Jack walks over to the young lady, takes the lantern from her hand, and holds it for her. "Julian and Will, meet Anna."

Anna walks toward us. "Julian, right?" She shakes his hand. "Nice to meet you."

"Likewise," Julian says.

Anna turns and smiles at me. Her smile is warm and comforting. "Nice to meet you, Will." She wraps her arms around me and hugs me tight, like a little kid hugging a parent after something terrified them. "I'm so glad you're here."

An alarm blares. Anna and I jump.

"I need to get to a public place and make a call. I think we've got another squad en route," Donavan says.

www.ingramcontent.com/pod-product-compliance
Lightning Source LLC
Chambersburg PA
CBHW020412110726
47899CB00006B/1955